CHRISTMAS AT HOLLY TREE COTTAGE

ELIZA J SCOTT

Storm
PUBLISHING

This is a work of fiction. Names, characters, businesses, places, events and incidents are either the products of the author's imagination or used in a fictitious manner. Any resemblance to actual persons, living or dead, or actual events is purely coincidental.

Copyright © Eliza J Scott, 2024, 2025

The moral right of the author has been asserted.

Previously published in 2024.

All rights reserved. No part of this book may be reproduced or used in any manner without the prior written permission of the copyright owner. This prohibition includes, but is not limited to, any reproduction or use for the purpose of training artificial intelligence technologies or systems.

To request permissions, contact the publisher at rights@stormpublishing.co

Ebook ISBN: 978-1-83700-368-6
Paperback ISBN: 978-1-83700-369-3

Cover design: Rose Cooper
Cover images: Shutterstock

Published by Storm Publishing.
For further information, visit:
www.stormpublishing.co

ALSO BY ELIZA J SCOTT

Welcome to Micklewick Bay Series

The Little Bookshop by the Sea

Summer Days at Clifftop Cottage

Finding Love in Micklewick Bay

Christmas at the Little Bookshop by the Sea

Cupcakes and Kisses in Micklewick Bay

A Snowy Seaside Christmas

A Wedding at the Little Bookshop by the Sea

Life on the Moors Series

The Letter – Kitty's Story

The Talisman – Molly's Story

The Secret – Violet's Story

A Christmas Kiss

A Christmas Wedding at the Castle

A Cosy Countryside Christmas

Sunny Skies and Summer Kisses

A Cosy Christmas with the Village Vet

Heartshaped Series

Tell That to My Heart

To my family, as ever, for their love, support and endless cups of tea xxx

ONE

JUNE – SIX MONTHS EARLIER

Romy

The cottage had been the furthest thing from Romy Stainthorpe's mind that sunny June morning. Indeed, it had been a while since it had last ventured into her thoughts.

She'd been ensconced in her chair at O'Connor & Dunn Hair Design in Rickelthorpe for the last forty-five minutes, waiting for the caramel highlights to "take" in her long, chestnut hair. She'd been absently skimming through the pages of a local magazine, trying hard to ignore the thoughts of her ex that had insisted upon taking up every inch of headspace since she'd run into him and his elegant girlfriend a couple of days earlier. But the moment her sea-green eyes alighted on the photograph, her heart jolted, sending all thoughts of Russ and the glamourpuss scurrying away. The conversation around her faded into the background, taking with it the salon's pulsing playlist.

It can't be! Convinced she must be seeing things, Romy blinked several times in quick succession, but the image was still there, gazing up at her from the glossy advert of The Rickelthorpe Holiday Cottage Company. *Holly Tree Cottage!* She was shocked and thrilled in equal measure. She glanced around her, making sure no one was watching, and surreptitiously took a photo of the page, being sure to capture the holiday cottage company's details. She was particularly keen not to arouse the interest of Ciaran, her hairdresser, who was snipping away at the locks of a young woman sitting in the chair next to her. As lovely as he was, he had a voice like a foghorn and Romy doubted he'd even know the meaning of the word "discreet" if it bit him on the bum. His warm, inclusive personality meant he favoured a salon-wide conversation, ensuring no one was left out. His wife and business partner, Roberta, was equally effusive and friendly. But right now, Romy didn't want to go into the details of why the cottage had piqued her interest and risk setting off a whole host of fresh gossip about her family. That thought sent a shiver rushing through her. They'd been the topic of enough of that over the years.

The events that had made such a dramatic impact on her life may have happened a long time ago – though, at times, it felt more recent – but she knew it wouldn't take much for the gossipmongers to leap into action and set the rumour mill turning again. And Romy really didn't want that. She cringed at the thought. Her mother, in particular, would find it difficult to cope with despite the fact she now lived miles away. Still, given the circumstances, it was entirely understandable. The so-called "scandal" would be dredged up and given another airing, and be thoroughly pulled apart until the next piece of juicier, fresher gossip took their attention.

Unable to get the cottage out of her mind, Romy was barely able to concentrate on the latest news Ciaran was imparting about some Z-list celebrity who'd been spotted in town, as he continued snipping away.

'What the bloomin' heck's got into you today, Romes? You're away with the fairies,' he said, when his question after her plans for the weekend hung unanswered in the air.

She gradually became aware that he'd stopped talking, sensing the weight of his gaze upon her. Glancing up, she caught sight of his reflection in the mirror at the station next to her, noting the amused look in his eyes. 'Oh... um... Sorry, Ciaran, I was just lost in thought; I've been commissioned to make a picture of a cottage garden and my mind had started to wander. The customer wants it quickly and it's got me panicking a bit 'cos I'm not sure I can get it finished in the time she's allowed me.'

Romy ran her own business making items from the felt she'd made herself, ranging from pictures to bags, pieces of jewellery and a whole host of other bits and bobs in between. Adding an extra level of detail, she trimmed her work with hand stitching, as well as pieces of fabric and beads. She also occasionally ran felt-making classes. Thanks to her work recently being displayed in a local art gallery, she'd been inundated with commissions and orders, which had made her wonder if she even had time to complete the latest request, especially since the customer had set a tight deadline.

'Ughh! There's nowt worse than a tricky customer.' Ciaran rolled his eyes. 'Tell 'em your work's worth waiting for, and if they don't like it, they can sling their hook.'

'I doubt that'll do her business much good, Ci,' the client in the chair next to her said, chuckling.

'I'm not so sure it will.' Romy giggled too, an image of Mrs Wilkinson who'd commissioned the picture appearing in her mind. The woman had a haughty, superior air about her and had made Romy feel small, that her work didn't quite come up to standard. 'Mind, I don't want to rush the piece and risk it not being at a quality I'm happy with.' She didn't doubt for a second Mrs Wilkinson would relish the opportunity to complain.

'You'll get it done and it'll be gorgeous, flower,' Roberta said, chipping in. 'I use that tote bag you made me all the time and it gets loads of compliments.' She flashed Romy a warm smile.

'Thanks, Roberta, that's lovely to hear.' Romy beamed back at her as the conversation in the salon switched back to the Z-list celebrity and their latest Instagram and TikTok posts.

Despite the momentary distraction, and as desperate as she was to seek out Holly Tree Cottage's details on her phone, her fingers twitching impatiently, Romy decided to wait until she got home to investigate further. There, she'd be able to take advantage of the bigger screen on her laptop – not to mention privacy and peace and quiet.

By the time she left the salon, Romy's curiosity had built to a crescendo and was at serious risk of bubbling over. With her pulse thrumming through her, she hurried to the car park. All she could think about was getting home and firing up her laptop so she could start her search, and find out all she could about Holly Tree Cottage.

Had it really been almost twenty-one years since she'd last visited Lytell Stangdale? Almost twenty-one years since she'd last set foot in Holly Tree Cottage? The place that held so many happy memories for her? Where had that time gone? Was it her imagination, or had the summers there always been blissfully warm and balmy, with weeks of uninterrupted sunshine stretching out? Halcyon days was how her mother used to refer to them at the start. And she'd been right.

Reaching the car, Romy zapped the door with the key fob and slid into the driver's seat. Taking a moment, she brushed her newly-styled hair off her face, sat back and closed her eyes. She drew in a deep breath, letting it out slowly. So much had happened in the intervening years since they'd left the cottage and Lytell Stangdale in such haste. So many life-changing things. She'd never been able to recapture nor replicate the happiness she'd felt during her time there; no matter how hard she'd tried, it had proved elusive. Though she'd kept it to herself, Romy always had the notion that the place was somehow connected to her on a higher level, that she *belonged* there. Inevitably, she found her thoughts travelling back to memories she had of the owner of a pair of bright blue eyes, whose warm, soft kisses had made her heart beat faster. She wondered what the man in question was doing now. And if he'd still be there.

TWO

JUNE

Finn

Finn Tindall bumped along the track to Castlegate Farm in his old
Land Rover, his bright-blue eyes sweeping over the surrounding
view that was peppered with farmsteads, the thatched rooftops of
Lytell Stangdale visible in the distance to the right. His gaze
snagged on Danskelfe Castle further along, a flag fluttering briskly
above one of the turrets. It was the ancient seat of the titled
Hammondely family who owned the Danskelfe Estate that encompassed most of the surrounding moorland. Its grey, battle-scarred
walls always made for an imposing sight. Though he was
Danskelfe born and bred and it had always been his home, Finn
never tired of the dramatic landscape, from the vertiginous riggs
that ran around the edges of the deep valleys – or dales as they
were known locally – that had been carved out of the land by the
last ice age, to the rugged crags upon which Danskelfe Castle was
perched, to the soft undulating swathes of heather that bloomed
later in the summer, filling the air with its heady scent. He regularly marvelled at how the North Yorkshire Moors managed to be
both bleak yet beautiful at the same time. And he had no yearning
to live anywhere else; he never had. The moors were part of him,

ingrained in his very soul, just like the generations of his forebears. Here was where he felt he belonged.

Which had been the crux of the problem, or so Britt, his ex-wife, had told him.

In the passenger seat beside him, his loyal Labrador, Ted, was peering out of the windscreen, ears cocked in interest as he observed a flock of sheep grazing in a nearby field, their bleating filtering in through the open window. Finn reached across and gave Ted's ears a ruffle. 'All right, lad?' he said. The Labrador pushed his head further into Finn's hand, his tail swishing against the seat, sending a smile spreading over his owner's face. He'd been glad of the Labrador's companionship over the last year.

Finn slowed the Land Rover, turning the heavy steering wheel as he headed towards the cluster of stone buildings that included the rangy, sandstone farmhouse he'd called home for the thirty-eight years he'd been alive. It had been in the Tindall family for the last five generations, his parents only moving out and into Castlegate Cottage – the barn they'd converted further down the track – when Finn and Brittany had married, allowing the young couple to take up residence in the larger property.

The brood of hens that had been scratting about the age-worn flagstones of the yard scattered, clucking noisily, as Finn pulled up in front of the old, redundant stables. 'Come on, fella,' he said, as he climbed out, clicking his tongue at Ted. The Labrador didn't need telling twice. He jumped down, his tail wagging as he trotted around, nose glued to the ground, inhaling myriad interesting scents. He was so engrossed in his sniffing, Ted was blissfully unaware of how close he'd ventured to Queenie, the stately-looking matriarch of the flock, until he found himself on the receiving end of an angry squawk and a reprimanding flap of the hen's wing. He gave a yelp and scuttled backwards.

'Push your luck there, did you, lad?' Finn asked with a chuckle, his eyes creasing as the Labrador rushed over to him, shooting the bird a wary look. He wagged his tail when Finn reached down and gave him a reassuring tickle behind the ear, soon distracted.

The sun that had blazed down on the moors earlier that morning had gradually been smothered by a swathe of thick, dense clouds and the once blue sky now resembled an angry, purple bruise. A stifling mugginess hung heavy in the air creating a sense of foreboding. Feeling a cold splash on the end of his nose, Finn swiped it away, glancing upwards as he closed the door of the Land Rover. It wouldn't be long before the clouds released their displeasure in a deluge of rain. He blinked as another drop landed near his eye just as a low rumble of thunder travelled ominously down Danskelfe Dale. A gust of wind rushed in between the buildings, setting Queenie and her feathered friends complaining noisily and scurrying off to their coop in the small enclosure on the other side of the stables.

Relief that they'd got the silaging done swept over Finn. That particular job was always a race against the weather. The local farming community had been aware the long, dry spell their part of the North Yorkshire Moors had enjoyed for the last couple of weeks was about to break, and they'd been rushing to get the baling done in the farms and smallholdings that studded not only Danskelfe Dale, but nearby Lytell Stangdale, Arkleby and Beckinthwaite. Ant Ford, who was a member of the local family of farm contractors, had stayed 'til gone eleven o'clock the previous evening, along with his father, the strong beams of light from their tractors moving determinedly back and forth in the field as the balers had spat out great cylinders of compressed hay. Thanks to their endeavours, the sweet scent of freshly-cut grass now lingered in the air.

With Ted at his heel, Finn was making his way to the farmhouse, when the heavens opened, a torrent of rain bouncing off the flagstones, sending the scent of earth into the air. Head bowed, he quickened his pace, Ted trotting alongside him. As he reached the heavy oak door that gave access to the kitchen porch, Finn became aware of his mobile phone ringing from the back pocket of his jeans. He pressed down on the latch and rushed inside, Ted scooting past him. Shaking the rain from his hands, Finn reached for his phone, his heart sinking when he saw the name of the caller glaring back at him. It was Britt. He felt his mood slump all the way down to his wellies. They'd been divorced for six months; their Decree Absolute had arrived the week before Christmas of last year. Any communication with her was never good news, not these days at least. He paused a moment, debating whether to accept the call or return it later, after the tea break with his dad. If there was one person Tommy Tindall didn't like, it was his former daughter-in-law, and Finn didn't want to sour his father's mood, or for Britt to dominate the conversation over their break. He glanced at the time displayed on the screen; his father would be joining him any minute, if he wasn't already in the kitchen. The decision was taken out of his hands when the phone fell silent. Telling himself it would be best to deal with it later, Finn went to slide it back into his pocket, only for the ringing to start up again. He groaned wearily as he heeled off his wellies.

Since the house was quiet, and there was nothing to suggest his dad was already there, Finn decided it would be best to accept Britt's call; she was clearly keen to speak to him. He knew from experience that she wouldn't ease up until she'd said what she needed to say, and was in no doubt that he'd understood. Plus, he didn't want to run the risk of being accused of ignoring her in case there was a problem with one of their sons. It had happened once before when he'd been busy with lambing and hadn't heard his phone ringing from the pocket of his waxed jacket. He'd found out later – during a particularly savage tongue-lashing from Britt – that their eldest son, who'd been eight at the time, had ended up in A&E over at Middleton-le-Moors hospital after an accident in a PE lesson at school. Kyle had received a nasty bump to his head which had left him with a mild concussion and had warranted a couple of steri-strips. Finn had felt like the worst father in the world at missing the call, the feeling exacerbated by Britt's accusations that he cared more about the farm and its animals than he did his own sons. He made a promise that day that he'd never find himself in that situation again.

He braced himself and pressed "accept".

'Britt, what's up?'

'Why is it you never answer your phone straight away?' she answered snappily. Finn had come to learn that being irritated was his ex's default mode whenever she spoke to him these days.

'I was just—'

'Oh, never mind, I've no time for listening to your excuses, I've got something important to tell you.'

His face fell as his brain registered his ex-wife's determined tone. It was the one she used when she wanted something but wasn't prepared to brook any resistance or get involved in any negotiating with him. She'd already made up her mind. Nothing would change it. Nothing was open for discussion. They'd been here many times over the last eighteen or so months since she'd gone to live with Felix Andrews, her boss at the estate agents where she worked. But now Finn was growing weary of it. Usually, he'd back down for the sake of their young sons, Kyle who'd be ten in a couple of months and Toby who'd just gone seven, in an endeavour to make the split between their parents as smooth and hassle-free as possible. But this time, as Britt's words gushed out in a forceful torrent, he could barely believe what he was hearing.

'That's what we're doing, Finn, so don't try to talk me out of it. I've put a lot of thought into it – *we've* put a lot of thought into it – considered every aspect. It'd be incredibly selfish of you to try to stop it, though knowing you as I do, I don't doubt you'll give it a damn good try.'

It felt as if the air had been sucked out of his lungs. She'd been talking so fast, surely he'd heard wrong?

'Britt, hang on, can you... Will you just give me a minute, please? This is... I mean, I need to process this.' Finn's grip tightened on his phone, his knuckles blanching as he paced around the kitchen, the fingers of his free hand raking through his mop of unruly dark hair, droplets of rain glistening amongst the waves.

How could the tone of the day change so quickly? He paused beside the old scrubbed-pine table, swallowing in an attempt to quell the nausea that was churning wildly in his stomach, but it wasn't easy now his throat had been rendered so tight and dry after the bombshell she'd just lobbed at him. It had literally stopped him in his tracks.

Britt huffed out a sigh, her impatience travelling down the phone line. 'I can't see why you're being so dramatic about it, Finn. I've explained everything clearly, been totally upfront, haven't said anything complicated. The world's not a big place anymore, it's never been easier to get flights anywhere.' The cold edge to her voice didn't escape him. 'Let's not pretend you didn't already know Felix had been considering it. I mentioned it months ago, so it can hardly have come as a shock to you.'

How could she possibly think that? It was a complete and utter shock! She'd totally blindsided him; there was no other word for it. Surely she must know that. And what did she mean, the world wasn't a big place? As far as he was concerned, it was massive! 'But that's the thing, Britt, you said it was *Felix* who was considering it. You never mentioned anyone else, which is why I didn't think—'

'What? You mean you thought he'd be going out to the States on his own? Leaving me and the boys here?' She gave a scornful laugh, making him feel like an even bigger idiot than he usually did whenever he spoke to her. 'You still don't get it, do you?'

His heart sank further.

'Well... I... um... I thought you might be consid—'

'Oh, come off it, Finn!' she said, barging through his words again. 'Surely even you can see beyond that tiny world you inhabit, and appreciate what an amazing opportunity this is for Kyle and Toby. They're literally bouncing with excitement at the prospect, it's all they can talk about – not that they *dare* mention any of it to you, they're too conscious of upsetting you.' She waited a moment for that to sink in. 'They're the main reason I've agreed to it. And on top of that, it's a big deal for Felix. He's been headhunted, and the real estate company that's interested in him is getting a really big name for itself. The lifestyle is on a totally different level to over here. I mean, they actually have *sunshine* in Orange County, unlike the North Yorkshire Moors.' She practically spat the last words out. 'And the house is totally *amazing*. It has an infinity pool, four bathrooms, and it's even got its own cinema.'

In that moment Finn felt grateful she'd cut him off before he'd made an even bigger fool of himself. When she'd first mentioned that Felix Andrews – the cocky hot-shot estate agent from the USA she'd left him for last year – was considering relocating back to Newport Beach in California to work for a real estate company there, Finn had nursed a tiny hope that it would mean Britt and their sons would come back home to the farm and make a fresh start. But her harshly-delivered words had unequivocally quashed even the tiniest hope of that. There was no way he could compete with an infinity pool; the closest thing to one of those at the farm was the murky pond at the bottom of one of the fields. He very much doubted that would count. And as for a home cinema... there was no chance he could match that. He felt his legs go weak beneath him as her words started to take on greater meaning. Britt obviously had a very different kind of fresh start in mind, and it was one that didn't include him. It was a reminder how easily she had her head turned by material things. Fifteen years ago, she'd raved about the farmhouse, the cluster of outbuildings and sprawling fields that went with it.

The sound of wood scraping across the York flagstone floor filled the room as Finn pulled out a chair at the table, her words tumbling into his mind. *Even I should be able to appreciate what a great opportunity it is for the lads?* He dropped heavily onto the seat, his heart pounding hard in his chest, his pulse whooshing in his ears. Was he too blinkered to see that it really was a great opportunity for their sons? Was Britt right? Was he pushing his own feelings onto them without realising? But his head was spinning, making it impossible to get his thoughts straight.

He swallowed again, feeling suddenly foolish; he really hadn't seen this one coming. 'It's just... I mean... it's a heck of a shock, Britt... I need to get my head around it. It's—' But his ex-wife was apparently in no mood to listen as she continued to run roughshod over his feelings, listing the ways he needed to see why her plans were so fabulous, and why it would be selfish of him to make it difficult for her and the boys to go. Her question, asking if he really wanted to upset his sons by putting his own needs before theirs, only added to the chaos unfurling in his mind.

He slumped back in his chair, scrunching up his eyes and dragging his hand down his face. Why was she doing this? he wondered. Didn't she think taking the lads to live almost sixty miles away in a vast rambling house on the outskirts of York with Felix flaming Andrews had been unsettling enough for them? Granted, they still lived in the same county, but the fact that it wasn't exactly on the doorstep meant Finn hadn't been able to see his sons as much as he'd like. It tore at his insides and hadn't got any easier since they'd first left. Kyle and Toby were his world, and he'd always prided himself on being a hands-on dad, just like his own had been. But now, there were no more impromptu games of footie in the farmyard, no taking them to and from the village school in the Land Rover, and no more enjoying lively mealtimes, filled with chatter, in this very room, the boys brimming with enthusiasm as they told him about their day. All were the things he'd taken for granted, until the day Britt had announced she was leaving him and, worse, taking their sons with her. And despite what they'd agreed, Britt had somehow orchestrated it such that Finn only managed to have access to the lads once a fortnight – unless she and Felix were having a weekend away. *Then* it was different. Then he could have them from Friday right through to Sunday night, or even Monday morning if he was lucky and it was the school holidays. Any other time she claimed it was disruptive to their routine, that it was easier for them to stay with her so they could get to all the clubs they attended at the weekends, rather than "uproot" them. 'I don't mean to sound unkind, Finn, but seeing you actually upsets them,' Britt had said when she'd dropped them off one Friday evening. Those words had cut through him; the last thing he wanted was to upset Kyle and Toby, or for them to ever get the sense that they were caught up in some sort of power struggle between their parents, so he'd agreed to her terms for their sake. But it had broken his heart.

And now she was throwing this at him. Moving to a different country, in a different time zone, expecting him to comply without a whimper? The gaps between their visits would stretch out into months not weeks. Surely he must have misunderstood. Was he dreaming? Having a nightmare, more like. He rubbed his hand over the stubble of his chin, his shoulders heaving with a sigh. 'So, let me just get this straight, Britt. You're telling me you and...' He could barely utter the man's name without a snarl in his voice.

'Felix,' Britt said impatiently. Finn could almost hear her rolling her eyes.

'Yes, him.' He took a moment, marshalling his thoughts as he pushed away the image of Felix Andrews' face, with its smarmy smile, that had barged its way uninvited into his mind. 'You're telling me you're planning on moving halfway around the world and you want to take the lads with you?' Even saying it out loud sounded ludicrous.

'There's no *want* about it, Finn, I'm taking them. They're desperate to go, it's all they can talk about. Like I said, the house is *amazing*, as well as the infinity pool and home cinema it's even got a gym and loads of land for them to run around *safely*.' Her emphasis on the word didn't go unnoticed. When she'd lived at the farm she'd always been vocal about it not being a safe environment for the lads to play, fussing about them being out with him. And it rankled that she didn't even have the sensitivity to keep the excitement for her new plans from her voice. 'I'm just being fair by giving you plenty of notice. I thought you'd appreciate it, bigger fool me.'

Fair? Being ambushed like this felt anything but fair, though he bit down on the thought. 'Surely I have to agree to you taking them to live in a different country?'

'Well... yes, you do, but let's be honest, to refuse would be totally selfish of you.'

'*Selfish?*' Was she for real?

'Yes! Selfish.' He could sense her anger bubbling, the threat of it spilling over increasing by the second. 'I'd never forgive you. And the boys would never forgive you for that matter. Are you honestly telling me you'd be happy to hurt them?'

Wow! Dragging their sons into it was a low blow. Finn's stomach twisted and he felt the unexpected burn of tears. Blinking quickly, he attempted to process the prospect of his sons being desperate to move thousands of miles away from him, of being okay with not seeing him for months on end, but the agony of it was tearing at his insides, rendering him unable to think straight. How had it come to this?

'Oh, and I thought you should know,' Britt's voice pulled him back into the moment, 'Felix has proposed; we're getting married, but I don't want any drama about it so I'll say goodbye now.' With that, the line went dead.

THREE

Romy

Romy drove home from the salon on autopilot, her mind whirring, her memory parading images like a cine camera. Seeing the cottage in the magazine, so completely out of the blue, had to be a sign, she repeatedly told herself throughout the twenty-minute drive back. Fate had drawn her to that particular publication rather than the inspirational home periodicals she usually plumped for. The universe was trying to tell her something. There was no other explanation for it.

And Romy was more than keen to listen.

Holly Tree Cottage, set in a quaint village in the North Yorkshire Moors, had been in her mother's family for decades when Dulcie Fairfax – to use her maiden name – had inherited it from a childless, elderly Aunt Maud. Dulcie, who had fond memories of visits to the moorland village, and her husband Vernon, decided to use the cottage as a holiday home rather than advertise for a full-time tenant or put it on the market. That Dulcie had Fairfax relatives in the village was further reason to keep the property. It became a place they ventured to at every opportunity. As soon as school broke up for Romy and her siblings, the car would be packed to the hilt, the three children crammed into the back, and they'd set off for Lytell Stangdale, the journey one of great excitement. Romy loved the summer in particular, since the whole of the school holidays would be spent there. Only her father would head back home, work beckoning after his usual fortnight off. Even then, he'd return to his wife and children on Friday evenings and travel back to the successful accountancy company he owned and ran in Rickelthorpe late the following Sunday afternoon. Romy, who'd been close to her father, had loved seeing the relaxed version of her dad at Holly Tree Cottage, despite bringing work home with him or taking work-related calls.

It had been idyllic and she had nothing but happy memories of her time there. Until that last day when her world had fallen apart...

But, as she turned into the side street that led to the small row of houses on Myrtle Row where her tiny two-up two-down rented home was located in the less than salubrious part of town – a stopgap after her divorce, and until she got herself back on her feet – she pushed that memory from her mind; nothing could eclipse the excitement that was now coursing through her veins.

Once inside number six, Romy didn't waste a moment. She dumped her felted bag in the hallway, raced to the living room and retrieved her laptop from the drawer in the sideboard then hurried into the kitchen that wasn't big enough to swing the proverbial cat, settling herself at the little table for two. Her heart was pounding as she lifted the lid on her laptop and typed in her password.

Moments later, her eyes were roving over the image that filled the screen before her. 'Hello there, Holly Tree Cottage,' she said softly, a smile spreading across her face. *Oh my days!* A warm feeling of nostalgia stirred inside her. It was as if she'd bumped into a dear, old friend she hadn't seen for years. She drank in the details greedily, her heart rate upping its speed. The quaint moorland property looked just as she remembered.

Eager to see more, Romy ignored the little niggle that warned her she was delving into something that had the potential to garner disapproval or irritation from her family. That she was venturing into territory that would put her out of favour with them if they found out crossed her mind, particularly her mother and older brother, Tristan. They'd no doubt accuse her of stirring up unhappy memories. She was less sure how her little sister, Tally, would take it since she'd been so much younger on that dreadful day. 'You're only *looking*,' she told herself. 'No one needs to know, and since when did only looking cause any harm?'

Romy was used to dealing with her mother's disapproval and looks of despair; she'd had years' worth of practice. The traits in their daughter Vernon had described fondly at the time as being "free spirited", having a "zest for life and a "sense of adventure", had, at times, driven her mother to distraction. It was fair to say, mother and daughter were polar opposites, and despite her best efforts, Dulcie regularly found having a daughter so very different from herself somewhat challenging, unlike her relationship with Tristan. It had been no secret in the Stainthorpe family that he was their mother's favourite which Romy had always put down to the pair of them being more alike. Apart from her chestnut hair, the only characteristic Romy shared with her mum was their artistic streak. Dulcie was as quiet and introverted as her daughter was outgoing and bubbly. Her mother favoured sitting quietly at home, reading a book, doing a spot of embroidery or painting, the thought of which Romy found stifling. And while she loved to sketch and paint, and enjoyed lively family times around the table playing board games and sharing news over hearty dinners, Romy got her biggest thrill from being outdoors, exploring the moors, feeling the wind in her hair. And she'd thrown herself into village life in a way her mother never had, having fun and laughing with her moorland friends, attending clubs and accepting as many party invitations as was possible. She'd slotted into the local community with such ease, it was as if she'd been Lytell Stangdale born and bred. It was there she'd made her best friends, and it was there that she'd first fallen in love. Which was what had made it so agonisingly painful to leave.

Romy couldn't argue that the reason they'd left in such haste, with the property being immediately put on the market and sold to the highest bidder, was anything other than heartbreaking, but it was hardly the cottage's fault. Just because her mother and her siblings had chosen to turn their back on it, didn't mean she should continue to do so too. It was circumstances that had been the problem, not their cosy moorland home. And, if Romy was being honest with herself, Dulcie had hardly been blameless in it all, not that she would ever suggest this to her mother – that would trigger a whole load of trouble and was best left alone.

But right now in this moment, Romy felt she'd quashed her happy memories for far too long.

Clicking on the photos in the gallery, she pushed thoughts of her family away and gave free rein to the happiness that now flooded in. Set in the middle of a sprawling well-tended garden and surrounded by a neatly-clipped holly tree hedge, from which the property had taken its name, the vernacular moorland cottage was located in a peaceful spot on the edge of Lytell Stangdale, boasting spectacular views of Great Stangdale and Danskelfe at the rear. Its heavily thatched roof had always put Romy in mind of a thick, overgrown fringe desperately in need of a trim. Its chunky stone walls were finished with a chalk-white limewash, the windows a quirky mix of sturdy sandstone mullions and wooden horizontal sliding sashes, so typical of the villages that peppered the North Yorkshire Moors. The squat front door, once painted a vibrant blue her mother had been so fond of, was now a fashionable sage-green, while a hanging basket, filled to busting and positively groaning under the weight of so many plants, was suspended from a hook to the right of it. The lean-to that housed the utility room still looked as characterfully wonky as Romy remembered, its cat-slide pantile roof glowing warm in the sun. From what she could make out, other than the apple tree growing in stature, a new wrought iron gate at the foot of the path and the addition of an oak-framed conservatory at the rear, very little appeared to have changed.

'The perfect rural idyll,' Romy read the caption beneath the wide-screen photo of the cottage aloud. Releasing a wistful sigh, she felt a tug of longing in her chest. She'd give anything to go back there, breathe in the familiar smell of the place which was predominantly of the logs that crackled in the grate of the fire. It would, without doubt, upset the applecart if her mother caught even the slightest whiff of Romy's thoughts.

As she sat gazing at the screen, thoughts of her father filled her mind. She wondered what he'd have to say about her yearning to see Holly Tree Cottage again. When he was alive, he'd always been the first person she'd go to whenever she needed guidance or advice when something was troubling her. And even now, long after he'd passed away, whenever Romy was faced with a challenging time or difficult decision, she often tried to imagine what words of advice he'd offer. It had not only helped her deal with the grief that had swamped her after she'd lost him, but she'd also brought him to mind when Russ had announced he wanted a divorce. Romy had pictured her dad telling her to stay strong, not to let it quash her spirit and, though it might not seem it at the time, that things would get better. It made her somehow feel he was watching over her.

'What would you say about this, then, Dad?' she said softly, but she didn't have to think too hard. He'd always described Holly Tree Cottage as a wonderful place, filled with happy days, which was exactly how Romy felt about it. Before she knew it, she could hear her dad's voice in her mind, growing louder by the second and making her heart pump faster.

'Follow your heart, Romy.' It was something he'd regularly told her.

'Oh, Dad,' she said, a tear spilling from her eye and rolling down her cheek.

It was time to go back.

FOUR

Romy

Romy dried her eyes, her gaze drinking in the wide-shoot photo of Holly Tree Cottage with the gardens either side, the idea that had sneaked its way into her mind suddenly gaining pace. Before she knew it, she'd clicked on the website's calendar, checking the cottage's availability. Her pulse took off at a gallop but there was no doubt in her mind that she was doing the right thing. She scrolled through the weeks, then months until she arrived at December. Her heart leapt and a gasp escaped her lips when she saw the two weeks encompassing Christmas and the New Year were available. The timing couldn't have been more perfect. 'The universe is definitely talking to you, Romy,' she said aloud. After the year she'd had, that included a divorce, albeit as amicable as divorces ever could be, and losing Judith, her beloved friend, Romy had promised herself she'd spend Christmas and New Year away from home, alone – and away from everyone and everything that would remind her of what an utterly pants year she'd had.

She knew it wouldn't be received well by those close to her. She'd only been divorced from Russ for just over five months and it drove her potty that people assumed she'd feel better by being in a relationship, that her existence was somehow sad or inferior if she wasn't part of a couple. Indeed, her mother seemed to take every opportunity to remind her of how loud her biological clock was ticking. 'At your age, you can't afford to be too fussy. There aren't that many single men out there, particularly those that come without a whole load of baggage. Before you know it, time will have run out for you, darling, and you'll have missed the boat,' she repeatedly told Romy. She was only thirty-seven for goodness' sake! But no one seemed to get that the last thing she wanted was to be in a relationship right now – or any time soon, for that matter. Her divorce from Russ may have been "clean" and straightforward, and they were still on speaking terms of sorts, but Romy was still a little raw from the whole experience. She needed time to herself, *by* herself. She needed to contemplate her future. The notion of making a fresh start had been calling to her, its voice growing increasingly urgent.

It wasn't just that she craved the opportunity for some headspace, she was also keen to get as far away as possible from the pitying glances of her family and friends over the festive period, in particular those who seemed intent on fixing her up with any single male on their radar. She had a feeling Christmas would intensify their campaigns, but telling everyone she had plans would put a stop to that. Her experience with "Mr Slimeball" as she now referred to Sheridon Templeton, had sealed her decision to escape. Romy had only agreed to the double date with Kayleigh and her fiancé, Dom, as long as her friend agreed to stop banging on about getting her back into the dating scene.

'You know what they say, use it or lose it, Romes,' Kayleigh had said, shooting her a hopeful grin. The two friends had been sitting in the White Horse pub on Rickelthorpe high street, sipping glasses of chilled white wine.

'I don't even want to know what the heck you mean by that, Kay.' Romy had quirked an eyebrow at her.

'Hmm, neither do I actually.' Kayleigh had pulled a puzzled

face. 'Now I think about it, I'm not sure that's the expression I'm looking for.' They'd both collapsed into a fit of the giggles at that.

'I'm not so sure it is, either,' Romy had said, spluttering through her laughter. 'I have no intention of *using* anything on this supposed double date. I'm just going to sit there, make polite conversation and smile in all the right places.' She'd fixed a fake smile to her face by way of demonstration.

'Well, that's by-the-by,' Kayleigh had said, waving her hand dismissively. 'And while we're on, I'm not so sure about that grin, it looks more like a grimace and is more likely to send your date rushing off in the opposite direction.'

'Perfect.' Romy had pulled the smile again.

But Kayleigh had continued undeterred. 'Dom says Sheridon is very keen to see you since he showed him your profile pic on your website. He thinks you're really *hot*.'

Romy had groaned inwardly, refraining from saying he sounded shallow. 'But what does Dom say he's like – as a person, I mean?'

'Um, well, he says he's *okay*.'

'Ah, high praise indeed. Let no one accuse Dom of not selling him well.' Though Romy had laughed, it hadn't escaped her attention that her friend suddenly seemed reluctant to make eye contact with her. She'd got the awful feeling there was something Kayleigh wasn't telling her. Her heart had sunk.

Romy's fears had been confirmed when Mr Slimeball had attempted to play footsie with her under the table all night. She'd almost jumped out of her skin when she'd felt his foot travelling slowly up her leg. *Eeew!* It had been accompanied by him sending her meaningful glances that had made her stomach churn. Annoyingly, she'd ended up with cramp in her calf muscles from having to keep herself out of his reach, tucking her legs firmly under her chair like some sort of contortionist. As if that wasn't bad enough, he'd taken every opportunity to place his hands on her, pressing his sweaty palm into the small of her back as he'd guided her out of the restaurant, brushing his fingers down the side of her face, and worse, he'd attempted to kiss her. *Bleurgh!* He'd made her skin crawl. She'd dived into the shower as soon as she'd got home in a bid to get rid of the scent of his cloying aftershave that had somehow managed to cling to her. Kayleigh had been mortified when Romy had told her about it later, crossing her heart and promising with all her might that she wouldn't try to fix her up again. It was a promise she'd kept until Dom had suggested double-dating with another of his colleagues.

'No way,' Romy had said, a fierce look in her eyes.

'Okay, you win!' Kayleigh had said. 'No more trying to set you up on dates. But I should probably warn you that Shannon's thinking of fixing you up with one of her brother's friends, which has absolutely nothing to do with me.'

This news had been enough to send Romy running for the hills and vowing to spend Christmas and the New Year well away from Rickelthorpe.

Putting her dating horrors out of her mind, Romy spent several minutes weighing up the pros and cons of spending the festive break at Holly Tree Cottage, giving the greatest consideration to her work commitments. She had a tendency towards impetuosity which had landed her in a bit of a fix on several occasions and she'd regretted some of her hastily-made decisions – the deep-pink faux fur maxi coat she'd bought online sprang to mind. What had she been thinking? Her wardrobe being made up of an array of brightly-coloured clothing, Romy had been swayed by how striking the garment looked on the model. But then again, she realised later, it was bound to look good on a six-feet tall willowy blonde with a funky haircut and makeup to match. When it arrived and she'd tried it on, Romy had soon realised it had a very different effect on anyone with a curvy five-feet-three frame. With the hem of the coat pooling on the floor around her, she'd pulled up the generous proportions of the hood and stepped in front of the mirror. 'What the—?' She'd been unable to control her giggles. The ridiculous reflection gazing back at her had put her in mind of a fluffy character from a children's television programme. Russ had howled with laughter when he walked into the bedroom. 'Please tell me you're wearing that for a laugh, Romes,' he'd said between his guffaws. It had taken some time for their hilarity to subside. And she didn't even want to think about the time she'd arranged a bungee jumping session for them and she'd had to send Russ off to buy her some new knickers and pair of yoga pants. She'd completely disregarded her fear of heights when she'd booked it, telling herself it would be fine, that it would help her overcome her fears. It hadn't, something which her bladder had very kindly reminded her.

Such examples meant Romy wanted to give the break some careful consideration before she took the plunge and booked a stay at the cottage. She opened up her personal calendar on the laptop, swiping through to December, happy to see that the last craft fair she'd booked a stall for was on Saturday the fourteenth. The fact that she'd always kept a date in mid-December as the final date for posting off any commissions, not wanting to risk delays since the orders were invariably Christmas gifts, fitted in perfectly with that timescale too. She just needed to ensure she wouldn't be hit with any last-minute orders. She toyed with the idea of placing a "closed for the holidays" sign on her website, social media pages and Etsy shop over the festive period. It was something she'd never done before, being happy to send out her pre-made items over the Christmas break. But then again, Romy mused, she could take some of the items she'd already got plenty of with her and post them out from Lytell Stangdale, maybe even reduce the variety of items that were available. And there was always the option for her to take enough equipment away with her, that way she could replenish some of the stock that was less time-consuming to make. It wasn't as if her work was a hardship. It was something she found incredibly soothing and had been grateful of over the last six months. And what better place to be inspired to create new needle-felt images than the North Yorkshire Moors? That thought sent a wide smile spreading across her face and it was enough to help settle her decision.

Not wanting to waste another moment, or risk someone jumping in and making a booking before she got the chance, Romy rushed to the hallway and grabbed her bag, reaching inside for her purse. With her bank card at the ready, she checked over the dates she'd selected and clicked "confirm", her heart thumping with nervous excitement.

Never one for wishing her time away, Romy found herself willing the days and months from now to December to rush by. Determined as she was not to venture over to the moors until the time of her break – she didn't want to spoil the magic and anticipation of first arriving in the village and opening the door of Holly Tree Cottage that was already brewing inside her – she was desperate to set eyes on her beloved Lytell Stangdale once more.

FIVE

Romy

Romy and her brother Tristan were already familiar with Holly
Tree Cottage when their mother inherited the property getting on
for thirty years ago. With their mother being close to her Aunt
Maud, they'd been regular visitors and had enjoyed the freedom
the moorland village had afforded them as well as the more laid-
back pace of life.

Romy had been eight at the time, Tristan twelve, and one of the
things she'd loved most about her time there – apart from the old
Land Rover her dad had bought from Titch Ventress over at
Ellerby Farm in nearby Arkleby which had made her feel like a
proper rural local lass – was the friends she'd made in the village.
Lytell Stangdale was where she felt she could be her true self,
where she felt happiest. She'd grown particularly close to Ella
Welford who lived at Tinkel Bottom Farm which sat in a
picturesque spot just out of the village. Romy and Ella were a
similar age and had clicked straight away, their love of animals and
tearing about in the fresh air, roaming the moors whatever the
weather, cementing their friendship. It was Ella who'd suggested
Romy might like to join the Danskelfe Dale Young Farmers' Club,

which was the local branch not only for Danskelfe, but also the surrounding villages, including Lytell Stangdale. Both girls had signed up for the club as soon as they'd celebrated their tenth birthday, having reached the minimum age required. Along with Ella, Romy had eagerly attended the meetings whenever her family stayed at Holly Tree Cottage, learning all she could about farming, delighting in visiting local farms. It was there she'd got to know fellow Young Farmers, Joss and Richard Campion whose family farmed at nearby Camplin Hall Farm, Joss being Ella's best friend. Of course, she already knew Jimby and Kitty Fairfax, them being her cousins, not to mention Ollie Cartwright, Jimby's best friend and partner in mischief, as he was known locally.

And, of course, there was Finn Tindall.

It was Finn, with his kind eyes, gentle nature and ability to make her laugh to whom Romy had grown the closest, regarding him as a brother. Not only did she look forward to seeing him at their Young Farmers' meetings which were held at Danskelfe Village Hall or local farmhouses – the parents would take it in turns to drop the Young Farmers off and pick them up – but, as she'd got older, she'd enjoyed an open invitation to Castlegate Farm where she'd revelled in being able to help out as if she were a young farmhand. Romy had particularly loved the hens, entertained by their quirky little mannerisms, delighting in their friendliness. They'd rush towards her as soon as she arrived in the yard which had thrilled her no end. Dressed in her scruffy jeans, sweatshirts and wellies, she'd scatter their feed, chatting away as the birds clucked and scratted around her feet. And she'd collect their eggs, gingerly scooping them from the nesting boxes, marvelling at their warmth as she cradled them in her hands. And she'd been beyond excited when Finn's mum Jill had invited her to feed the orphaned lambs, their little bodies solid in her arms as they guzzled noisily from feeding bottles. Indeed, Jill and Tommy Tindall grew fond of Romy and soon came to regard her as a member of the family, with Jill in particular enjoying her visits. 'It's nice to have another lass around the place, I don't feel so outnumbered by the lads when you're here. You're like the daughter I never had, lovey,' she'd regularly said.

Finn had an older brother. There was five years between the lads, and though they both shared their father's height, broad-shouldered build and dark hair, it was only Finn who saw farming in his future. Dougie had his sights set firmly on escaping the farm as soon as he left college and had secured himself a job at a small computer technology firm in Middleton-le-Moors.

Romy had savoured her time at the farmhouse where the approach to life had been relaxed. Much as she loved her parents dearly, and was particularly close to her dad, Castlegate Farm had been so different from her own home. There, Dulcie had liked everything spick and span and in its place, and the Stainthorpe family had been required to adhere to her strict list of house rules and chores, a new copy of which was stuck to the back of the kitchen door every week – no coming downstairs on a morning until your bed was made, no going out until your bedroom had been tidied, clothes put away, shoes polished, the washing up done, the fire emptied and re-set, coal brought in from the bunker out in the back garden... the list had sometimes felt endless. Under Dulcie's regime there was no fun time until you'd ticked everything off your daily list of chores. The only person, as far as Romy could see, who had skilfully wriggled his way out of doing much at all was golden boy, Tristan, who was never a stranger to taking full advantage of his position as their mother's favourite – he'd even somehow managed to pass some of his own jobs on to Romy which had enraged her with such a passion she could have throttled him at times! Even little Tally hadn't escaped their mother's dreaded list, despite being eight years younger than Romy. 'You're never too young to pull your weight,' Dulcie had regularly espoused, along with, 'It's character building; doesn't do any harm; makes children feel valued if we put our trust in them to do small jobs.' The only rules at Finn's home had been shoes or wellies off at the door after traipsing through the farmyard, and wash your hands before you eat. Romy had been happy to abide by those!

But despite her mother's rules which, in fairness, the whole family were used to and were no different to the ones in place at their home in Rickelthorpe, the Stainthorpes had simply cherished their time in Lytell Stangdale and Holly Tree Cottage.

Romy, in particular had thrived there. She'd loved nothing better than running around the moors with Finn, Ella and Joss. But at the age of sixteen something happened that changed her friendship with Finn and meant she could never look at him in the same light again.

SIX

DECEMBER – THE WEDNESDAY
BEFORE CHRISTMAS

Finn

'Ey up, me 'aud mucker. Need a hand there?' Finn turned to see Jimby Fairfax leaning out of the window of his Land Rover, a woolly hat pulled down over his closely-cropped dark hair. Fumes from the vehicle's exhaust curled out into the frosty air. The local blacksmith was wearing his trademark wide grin, his friendly brown eyes crinkling at the corners.

Finn returned his smile. 'Now then, Jimby. Aye, I could do with an extra pair of hands, thanks. I'm having a bit of a job getting this one untangled.' Finn had been travelling down the road to Lytell Stangdale when he'd spotted a sheep apparently in difficulties. Further investigation revealed the ewe had got one of its horns lodged in a tangle of wire fencing and he'd spent the last twenty-five minutes struggling to free it. That there was part of a hawthorn hedge involved hadn't helped, the plant's vicious thorns piercing his thick gloves. On top of that, the solid animal had insisted on wriggling frantically.

'No bother.' Jimby, who like Finn, was wearing a waxed jacket and a sturdy pair of wellies, was beside him in a moment, rubbing his hands together. 'Right, let's have a shuftie.'

Ted, who'd been standing beside his owner, observing patiently, trotted over to Jimby, wagging his tail enthusiastically. 'Hello there, fella.' Jimby gave the Labrador's glossy broad head a pat. Ted's tail wagging upped its pace.

Just then, the ewe made another frantic bid for freedom, kicking her legs out every which way. 'Woah, settle, lass.' Finn spoke soothingly, tightening his grip on the sheep.

'I think we'd best get this 'un fettled before she gets herself any more distressed,' said Jimby, stepping closer to investigate.

Between them, the two men had the creature free in a matter of moments, Jimby tackling the wire while Finn held the sheep steady, his muscles pulling taut over his broad shoulders.

'Looks like it's one of the Campions' hefted ewes,' said Jimby, as they gave it a quick once-over, checking for signs of potential injury sustained from its ordeal. Like Finn, Jimby was used to handling sheep. He'd grown up on a smallholding and still kept a flock of his own, albeit on a smaller scale.

'Aye, it is.' The green daub of paint – also known as a smit mark – on the ewe's back gave away the ownership, while the Tindall's hefted flock wore blue. Satisfied the ewe hadn't come to any harm, Finn released it and it trotted off down the road towards a cluster of other sheep that roamed freely over the moors, bleating noisily as it went and sending a couple of rabbits scampering off.

'Try to keep yourself out of mischief in future, madam,' Jimby called after her, chuckling.

'Thanks for helping out, I owe you a pint.' Finn pulled himself upright, checking his gloves for stray thorns.

'I'll hold you to that, mate,' Jimby said. 'It'd be good to see you in the Sunne, haven't spotted you there for ages. Jonty's got a guest ale on at the minute and it's like nectar. Old Micklewick Magic it's called; it's from that trendy little microbrewery over in Micklewick Bay, and is seriously not to be missed.'

'Sounds good.' Finn did his best to force a smile, hoping it belied his true feelings, all the while aware of the hollow sensation in his chest. He hadn't had the heart to socialise since Britt and the lads had left. In fact, he hadn't had the heart to do anything but throw himself into his work on the farm. Keeping busy helped stop his mind from wandering, stopped him from stewing. Well... at least it did most of the time. He knew the gut-wrenching ache inside him would never disappear; it had almost become a part of him now; the norm. The pain of Britt taking the boys to live in the States had cut deep and he couldn't imagine it ever healing. He intended to simply plod on with his life and keep his distance from everyone, especially if they happened to be female. He'd sworn to himself he was never going to be fool enough to get into another relationship. He was never going to let his guard down and run the risk of being hurt again.

'Tell you what, Bea and Jonty are having a bit of a do at the pub this Saturday, Bea's putting on one of her awesome festive spreads and there's going to be a bit of music. I know of a couple of tickets going spare, if you fancy it? I don't know about you, but I can't think of a more tempting combo than Bea's grub and a pint or two of beer, especially if it's Old Micklewick Magic.' Landlady Bea Latimer was famous locally for her delicious, hearty food, and tickets for the pub's foodie events always sold out quickly.

Finn's heart sank. Jimby was a great bloke, was always upbeat. He did a lot for the community and was well liked. And he was difficult to say no to. But, much as he didn't want to offend Jimby by refusing his offer, Finn was conscious of his brain scrambling for an excuse as his friend smiled at him, awaiting his answer. He sucked his breath over his teeth as he scratched his head. 'This Saturday you say?' In the background, the rumble of a tractor struck up in the direction of Tinkel Top Farm, joining the cackle of a pheasant as it skimmed over a nearby five-bar gate.

'Aye, Vi and me are going to be there around seven o'clock. The usual crowd are joining us: Kitty and Ollie, Camm and Moll. Zander and Livvie were forced to drop out on account of the new little 'un; it's their tickets Vi and me said we'd try and get rid of on their behalf.'

The fact that Jimby was listing couples made Finn's heart

slump even further. Standing out as being the only single person of the group couldn't sound less tempting if it tried. 'Er... I'll have a think—'

'Ey up, that's a big fella. Looks and sounds like a goshawk to me,' said Jimby, cutting him off mid-sentence and casting his gaze skywards.

Finn was grateful for the timely distraction created by the call of a bird of prey that was hovering over the field to the left of them.

'Aye, I reckon it is.' He followed Jimby's line of sight, squinting up at the clear expanse of blue sky, taking in the bird's vast wing-span. He drew in a lungful of the crisp, moorland air as he watched it circle overhead, its cries echoing around the dale.

'Right then, I'd best be getting back to the forge. I'll keep them tickets for you.' Jimby gave Finn a hearty clap on the back before heading over to his Land Rover. 'Oh, and I daresay you'll have heard about the recent spate of break-ins we've had locally, have you?' For once the blacksmith's smile had fallen.

'Aye, my dad was telling me about them. Last I heard a Landie and two quad bikes were taken from over Arkleby way a couple of nights back.'

'Yeah, that's right.' Jimby tutted and shook his head gravely. 'It's a disgrace that some people think nowt of stealing from other folk rather than do a day's work.' It was a grievance that regularly came up on the local social media pages. 'I'd keep an eye on that, if I were you, make sure you keep it locked away.' Jimby nodded in the direction of the Polaris all-terrain vehicle Finn had recently bought and had been handy for getting around the fields, affording the driver a decent amount of cover, unlike the quad bikes which had them exposed to all the elements.

Finn nodded. 'Aye, we're looking into getting an alarm fitted up at the farm.'

'Shame it's come to that. I've just had one installed over at the forge.' Jimby shrugged resignedly before opening the door of his Land Rover. 'Anyroad, I'll see you on Saturday. Should be a laugh,' he said, his smile making a reappearance

Before Finn had a chance to reply, the vehicle's door was pulled shut and Jimby drove off down the lane. Finn huffed out a sigh, his breath hanging in a plume of condensation. He was going to have to come up with a decent excuse before then.

Back at Castlegate Farm, Finn poured himself a large mug of tea and took it out into the south-facing garden at the front of the farmhouse. He made his way carefully down the path, steam rising from his mug, Ted trotting along at his heel. From here the views out over Danskelfe Dale and across to Lytell Stangdale were breathtaking, and today it was looking extra stunning thanks to the flurry of snow that had fallen overnight and was now sparkling in the hoar frost that had lingered that morning. Overhead, the sky was a vivid blue with barely a cloud in sight, the winter sun hanging low, drenching the fields and moorland in its pale-golden glow. Though it was four fields away, he could hear the river as it gushed its way along the base of the valley, a dense line of trees hugging its route. The recent snow meant the springs had been well fed, adding to the beck's might. His gaze swept over the farmsteads that punctuated the landscape, their patchwork of fields marked out by dry stone walls and hedges, a sight that had barely changed for hundreds of years. Only sheep remained in the fields, other livestock having been taken in to over-winter in the barns. Clusters of trees, their skeletal branches decorated with frost, huddled together in groups before thickening into Danskelfe Wood. Finn's eyes alighted on Danskelfe Castle, emerging from the great crag upon which it had been built. The local landmark, with its angular battlements, made for a formidable sight.

His gaze was caught by a hare as it raced across the snow-covered field directly in front of the farm, the goshawk of earlier following its path from the sky above. He watched as the hare darted across the exposed stretch of land, seeking safety in the dense branches of a hawthorn hedge. The bird of prey gave a disgruntled cry before flying off to hunt elsewhere.

Finn heaved a sigh and took a sip of his tea, the baying of the Danks's dairy herd in the barns over at Tinkel Top Farm echoing around the dale. He couldn't think of anywhere more beautiful to live than here, up on this hill, with this view. He still couldn't get his head around how Britt had grown tired of living there, found it dull and boring. She hadn't felt like that when they'd been first married. It had been quite the opposite; she'd been so impatient to move in she'd pretty much chased his parents out of the farmhouse and into the barn before the conversion was properly finished. Finn felt the familiar pang of guilt when he recalled how his parents practically had to camp out in the newly-created living space while the plastering was finished in the bedrooms. 'Aye, well, what Britt wants, Britt gets,' his mother had said at the time. His father had agreed. 'Owt for a quiet life, lad,' Tommy Tindall had said as they'd unloaded furniture from the Land Rover and deposited it at the end of what would be the living room in the barn. Finn could have kicked himself many times over for not standing up to his ex, but, as he regularly told himself, hindsight is a wonderful thing. He'd been so besotted with her, and she'd had a way such that it had made it difficult not to back down or give her what she wanted. 'Mind, just watch yourself with that one, lad,' his dad had said in a warning tone when Finn had first introduced her. 'I reckon she could be a bit of a handful if you're not careful. Strikes me she's a bit wilful.'

'She's not that bad, Dad,' Finn had said defensively. But he'd always known at the back of his mind Britt been quite forward, and forthright with her views, not always delivering them kindly. And despite her telling him before they'd got engaged that she'd always wanted to marry a farmer, that he was her "dream man", how she couldn't wait to start working on the farm, the reality was very different. It hadn't taken long for her to change her mind, announcing she wasn't cut to be one of the "farm yakkers", as she'd put it, who lived in and around Danskelfe. She felt she didn't fit in, hadn't been made to feel welcome. It was why she'd ended up getting a job in Middleton-le-Moors, first serving behind the bar in

The Golden Fleece before securing a job as a PA at the estate agents a couple of years ago when Toby had started full-time at school. Finn hadn't known it at the time, but it had signalled the end of their marriage.

As he went to head back inside, he took one last sweeping glance of Danskelfe Dale, his gaze settling on the cottage next to Oak Tree Farm. His heart gave an unexpected leap. It had been years since he'd last visited Holly Tree Cottage; he'd been a regular visitor at one time. The thought set his mind heading in a very different direction.

SEVEN

DECEMBER – THE SATURDAY
BEFORE CHRISTMAS

Romy

Squashing her tote bag into the tiny space available in the footwell of her little Mini, Romy fired up the engine and fastened her seatbelt, waiting until the demisters had kicked in and cleared the windscreen. There'd been a frost the previous evening and she'd had to scrape ice from the car's windows, but Romy didn't mind. The morning had dawned with a clear blue sky, and the sun was shining, making it the perfect day for a journey to the moors. Resting her hands on the steering wheel, she gave a little squeal of delight. 'The adventure starts now!' she said. There was nothing she could do to stop the enormous smile that tugged at her mouth, nor the excited laugh that escaped it. She could hardly believe the day she could actually head back to Lytell Stangdale and Holly Tree Cottage had finally arrived. And though she'd been tempted to sneak a quick trip there before today, she'd somehow managed to resist, which she now found herself being glad of. It meant she'd still be able to enjoy the undiluted thrill of seeing both the village and the cottage together for the first time in over two decades. She had, however, Googled it – who wouldn't? – telling herself seeing somewhere on a laptop was nothing like physically visiting the place, that the images wouldn't give her a feel of the village, a proper sense of the moors. You had to be there to appreciate the full effect of its charm. Rather than take the edge of her excitement, her jaunt on the internet had only served to add fuel to it.

Flicking the indicator, she eased her car out of its parking place and tootled down Myrtle Row, the Mini bursting at the seams with everything she needed for the two weeks she'd be away. She'd even packed her sewing machine and overlocker, with the intention of filling any spare moments with replenishing some of her stock, which had been pretty much depleted over the last few weeks. It was only when she'd joined the motorway that reality kicked in and a hint of nervousness joined the excitement that was bubbling inside her.

According to the information she'd been sent by Maisie at The Rickelthorpe Holiday Cottage Company, she wouldn't have access to the cottage until four o'clock that afternoon. But that hadn't deterred Romy from wanting to set off from Rickelthorpe bright and early. She'd already decided she'd make the most of the day once she got closer to Lytell Stangdale. She'd planned to stop off in Middleton-le-Moors en route and pick up some supplies. If her memory served her right, it was the nearest town to Lytell Stangdale and the surrounding villages, and where the villagers travelled to do their supermarket shopping. Not that she'd be able to get too much with there being barely any room left in the car, but she'd been taken with the idea and quite fancied a quick browse around what she remembered as being a rather pretty market square. Like Lytell Stangdale, Romy hadn't visited the town since she'd left. Following that, she'd have a steady drive around the moors, taking the chance to admire the scenery, seeing what she could remember. She'd wondered many times since she'd made the decision to return, if the area would match the images she'd kept tucked away in her memory. She hadn't been able to dig out any old photos since her mother had destroyed every one of them in the aftermath of events that had forced them to sell their moorland home, not wanting any reminders of why they'd had to leave; the shame that had engulfed her. 'You need to forget about it and move on, Romy! Pining after something you've lost where there's absolutely no chance of you ever having it again, will do you no good at all,' her mother had said sharply when, a couple of years later, Romy had enquired after the albums brimming with photos of their time in Lytell Stangdale they'd once had. The photographs of Romy with her friends from the village had suffered the same fate as all the others, which had made her sob hot angry tears, especially when she'd discovered the destroyed photos included those of the person who'd stolen her heart.

As she drove on, Romy found her mind wandering, wondering if she'd bump into *him*, wondering if he still lived there. How would it feel if they saw one another again? Would he speak to her, or would he still bear a grudge that she'd left without saying goodbye? It had been more than half her lifetime since they'd last set eyes on each other. Would she recognise him? An image of his face flooded her mind, making her heart flutter. Her first love. Yes, without a doubt, she knew she'd recognise him; she'd never forget those bright-blue eyes and how they'd reached deep into her soul. After all, they say you never forget your first love.

Romy was thrilled to see the traditional black and white road sign directing her to Danskelfe and Lytell Stangdale was still in situ – albeit at a slightly wonky angle – and hadn't been replaced by some incongruous modern metal monstrosity. She took the junction with caution, mindful of the conditions. The frost that had danced over Rickelthorpe had taken a firmer grip here on the moors, and evidence of a recent snowfall, albeit light, was lurking on the roadside and in the hedgerows, which was what she'd expected.

Heading along the twisty-turny narrow road, Romy gasped at the view stretched out before her. 'Oh my days!' It was even more beautiful than she remembered. Her eyes roved over the vertiginous riggs of Great Stangdale and Danskelfe Dale that stood proud, as if running a powerful arm around the valleys they each encompassed, offering them protection from the worst the moorland weather could throw at them. Dusk was already starting to settle and the fields and surrounding moorland sparkled in the fading afternoon sunshine, affording them a magical quality. The squeeze of emotion in her chest and the burn of tears caught Romy off guard. She was only on the edge of the moors and her feelings had already been stirred. What the heck was she going to be like when she arrived in Lytell Stangdale? A blubbering wreck if this was anything to go by.

She drove on, blinking back her tears, her heart surging as she took in the names of farms, smallholdings and cottages that hadn't crossed her mind in years. Before she knew it, she was passing the village sign for Lytell Stangdale, her eyes darting all around her, eager to take everything in as she negotiated a couple of cars and a tractor heading in the opposite direction. She continued along the broad road that split the village in two, the thatched cottages that lined it looking achingly beautiful, fairy lights twinkling on the Christmas trees displayed in windows and front gardens. She spotted a huge Christmas tree bedecked with shiny baubles and more fairy lights that took pride of place on the village green by the duck pond, its branches swaying gently. That was something new, there'd never been a village Christmas tree in her day. Further along was the local pub. 'The Sunne Inne,' she said, reading a tastefully hand-painted sign that was swinging from a sturdy post by the path that led to the hostelry's door. 'Wow!' It had certainly undergone a transformation since she'd last set eyes on it, as had the village shop by all accounts. She looked forward to venturing to both.

Her pulse rate increased as she drew closer to Holly Tree Cottage, following the gentle curve of the road as she passed Oak Tree Farm, fleetingly wondering if her Fairfax relations still lived there.

Pulling up outside the holiday cottage, Romy stilled the engine and checked her watch. There was still an hour to go before she was officially allowed access. Her heart was beating a lively tattoo and now she was here, she hardly dare look at the property, which felt bizarre, especially since she couldn't wait to get inside. Noting there was no other car parked nearby, she waited a few moments, wondering if whoever it was that cleaned the cottage had been and gone. It didn't take long before curiosity got the better of her and she unbuckled her seat belt and climbed out of the car. Moments later, she was pushing open the gate and taking her first step on the flagstone path to Holly Tree Cottage.

She paused, closing her eyes and taking a moment to steady the emotions that were hurling themselves around inside her. Inhaling a lungful of crisp air, Romy released it slowly and opened her eyes, absorbing the quirky details of the cottage that stood before her, a large festive wreath fixed to its stout front door.

Admiring the neatly-kept garden, she followed the path that led around the cottage and to the shed at the rear where, according to The Rickelthorpe Holiday Cottage Company's information, the key safe would be located – apparently the homeowner hadn't wanted to spoil the look of the doorway with an unsightly lump of metal so had fitted the safe out of sight instead. After a brief but unsuccessful search, she fished around in her bag and pulled out the booking details she'd printed off, making sure she hadn't imagined the information about a key safe, but there it was, including the combination she'd need to unlock it. Despite retracing her steps and a further hunt around, she was disappointingly still unable to locate the keys. The cold was now nipping at her cheeks, seeping through her boots and making her fingers tingle. Romy didn't fancy the prospect of having to hang around outside for much longer. Checking the information from the holiday cottage company one more time, and satisfying herself she'd followed the instructions properly, Romy decided there was no other option but to call Maisie at the holiday cottage company.

From her phone Romy could see a slew of missed calls and text message notifications from the company in question, all asking her to contact the office urgently. She guessed they must've arrived while she was driving, which would explain why she hadn't heard her phone ringing or pinging. A sinking feeling crept over her as she tapped the number on the screen and waited for her call to be picked up.

'Oh, Romy, I'm so glad you called back.' Maisie sounded more than a little relieved to hear from her. 'The homeowner contacted us to say they're putting the cottage on the market and have given the keys that were in the key safe to the estate agent.'

Helpful! 'Oh, right. So how am I supposed to unlock the door?' She was struck by a worrying thought. 'Please don't tell me my holiday's been cancelled.'

'Oh, goodness no, nothing like that.' Maisie gave a little laugh. 'The family next door at Oak Tree Farm – a Mr and Mrs Cartwright; lovely couple – have always kept a spare set, just in case of emergencies. Unfortunately, they were out when the homeowner called round to get the keys for the estate agent, which is why he took the ones in the key safe.'

'Oh, okay.' Despite her relief, Romy wondered why the lovely Mr or Mrs Cartwright couldn't have simply placed their keys in the key safe rather than be troubled by having a stranger call round. But then again, Romy reminded herself she hadn't actually found the said key safe anyway, so maybe it was good thinking on their part.

'If you'd just like to pop round there, they're expecting you. Oh, and if you wouldn't mind dropping the keys off with them when your stay's over that would be great; just post them through the letter box if they're out. The homeowner said there'd been a problem with the key safe, it wasn't locking properly or something, so he removed it,' Maisie said in her jolly tone. 'I realise it would've been more helpful if he'd let us know before now, and I do hope it hasn't inconvenienced you.'

'Not at all,' Romy said cheerily. She was just relieved it had been resolved so quickly and that her holiday was still very much on.

'And if you need anything else, just get in touch, we're happy to help, but in the meantime, have a lovely holiday.'

Ending the call, Romy slid her phone back into her bag. 'Mr and Mrs Cartwright,' she said to herself as she headed towards the gate, thinking that her Fairfax relations who used to live there must've moved on. She felt a pang of disappointment at that, wondering if they'd settled in the village or one nearby. Her next thought was to wonder if this Mr and Mrs Cartwright were related to the Cartwright family who used to live in Lytell Stangdale.

She walked cautiously along the worn sandstone trod that ran between Holly Tree Cottage and Oak Tree Farm, the thick hoar frost that covered it making it slippery despite the chunky grips on the soles of her boots. A chorus of bleating caught her attention and she looked up to see half a dozen or so sheep ambling along the middle of the road, clumps of snow clinging to their dense fleeces. The sight brought a smile to her face, resurrecting fond memories of her earlier times there. In the distance, the crowing of a cockerel echoed around the village. It was joined by the rumble of a Land Rover that drew up behind the sheep, waiting patiently as the ewes sauntered along at their own pace. She stole a look at the driver's face to see a woman looking back at her, a woolly hat with a large pompom pulled over her chin-length dark waves. A stab of recognition set Romy's mind racing but before she could place her she'd reached the gate to the thatched vernacular longhouse of Oak Tree Farm – which looked just as she remembered – and the Land Rover had driven off. She knocked at the door, admiring the luxurious festive wreath that hung there. A chorus of barking instantly struck up followed by the soft tones of a woman telling the dogs to hush, and the skittering of claws along the floor. In the next moment, the door was flung open and a petite, dark-haired woman wearing an oversized turtle neck jumper in a rich shade of raspberry-red and baggy jeans appeared. She had a pixie crop and large brown eyes. 'Hello there,' she said, giving a friendly smile as she bent to grab the collar of a black Labrador who'd pushed its grey-flecked head around her. It was joined by a lemon working cocker spaniel with a jaunty expression. 'Settle down, you two rascals.'

Romy was rendered momentarily speechless. There was something strikingly familiar about the gentle eyes looking back at her.

Puzzlement flickered in the said gentle brown eyes.

'Mrs Cartwright?' Recognition struck like a bolt of lightning. 'I mean, Kitty? Kitty Fairfax?'

'Er, yes to both; I was Kitty Fairfax but I'm now Kitty Cartwright.' Though she was still smiling, the woman's voice faltered slightly as she searched Romy's face. 'Are you... are you here for the key?'

'I am.' Romy nodded, smiling. 'It's been a while since I was last here; over twenty years, but the place has barely changed.' She watched, her smile growing wider as realisation dawned on Kitty's face. 'I'm Romy Stainthorpe, I don't know if you remember but my family used to own Holly Tree Cottage. And I do believe we're cousins of some sort, however many times removed.' She gave an embarrassed laugh.

'Oh my days! *Romy!*' Letting go of the Labrador's collar, Kitty clapped her hands to her face. 'Of course I remember! Gosh! Oh wow!' In the next moment, she'd wrapped her arms around Romy and was squeezing her tight, enveloping her in a cloud of light floral perfume mixed with the aroma of baking which Romy found rather comforting. 'How have you been? How is everyone?' The two dogs were dancing around them, tails wagging. Kitty released Romy and took a step back, her smile faltering. 'We were so sorry to hear about your dad. Uncle Vern was a lovely man,' she said, her tone soft as she rubbed a hand down her cousin's arm. 'But it's so wonderful to see you back in Lytell Stangdale.'

'Thank you.' Romy's heart squeezed at the mention of her dad, but she pushed her smile back up. 'It's good to be here again.'

Just then, a tall man with ruffled dark-blond hair appeared behind Kitty, resting his hands on her shoulders. 'Thought I'd come and see what all the excitement's about.' He had a warm, friendly smile that Romy felt sure she'd seen before. 'Hello there.' He nodded in her direction.

'Hi.' She smiled, her memory scurrying to place him.

'You remember Romy Stainthorpe, don't you, Ollie? Her parents used to have Holly Tree Cottage.' She turned back to Romy. 'And I dare say you remember my husband Ollie Cartwright, he's been my brother Jimby's best friend since forever.'

Ollie Cartwright! Of course! Romy recalled there'd been a thing with Kitty and Ollie when they were in their teens. Though she was sure it had fizzled out and Kitty had started dating a rather pompous man who'd moved to the village with his parents. Something told her he was a barrister or a solicitor and she could remember thinking at the time how ill-suited they were.

'No way! Romy? It's great to see you.' Ollie's greeting was as warm and friendly as his wife's. 'And you must be freezing, us keeping you here on the doorstep. Come on in, you're very welcome to join us for a cup of tea, I've just made a pot and Kitts has just made some of her legendary shortbread.'

'Oh, yes, sorry, how rude of me. Come on in, you must be absolutely nithered out there.' Kitty stood back, opening the door wide, the dogs shooting by and racing down the hallway.

'Actually, much as that sounds very tempting, I wouldn't mind getting settled in at the cottage. I've got loads of stuff to unpack, but I'd love a catch up later, if you've got time, that is?' She hoped she didn't come across as rude or unfriendly.

'Of course, I totally understand. I'd be just the same.' Kitty's smile told Romy she hadn't taken offence. 'But let us know if you need anything; we're happy to help if we can.'

'Thanks, Kitty, that's really kind.'

'In that case, I'll just grab the key,' said Ollie. 'Two ticks.'

'Tell you what – and please feel free to say no – there's a do on over at the Sunne this evening. With it being the run-up to Christmas, the landlords, Jonty and Bea Latimer, have organised some food and a bit of music, the proceeds are going to charity. My son Lucas works there, he's studying at catering college over in Scarborough and doing an apprenticeship with Bea. From the hints he's dropped about what they've prepared for the buffet, it sounds as though it's going to be amazing. Anyroad, there's a couple of tickets going spare – our friends had to drop out last minute – and you'd be very welcome to join us, if you fancy? It's always a good night and you wouldn't recognise the place now. The Latimers have totally transformed it and Bea's cooking is legendary round here. Oh, and Gabe Dublin, who lives in the village with Ollie's daughter, Anoushka, has said he'll do a few songs.'

Gabe Dublin was an internationally famous indie/folk singer from Southern Ireland. He'd bought The Manor House in Lytell Stangdale and retired from performing a couple of years ago, focusing instead on writing songs for other artists.

'Oh, right. Wow! I love Gabe Dublin's music.' Though Romy recalled how friendly everyone was here, she hadn't expected to be welcomed into the embrace of village life quite so quickly. It was as if she'd never been away, the decades shrinking to nothing. And, being of a sociable nature, she had to admit, what Kitty had described sounded rather appealing, especially if Gabe Dublin was going to make an appearance. It was evidently an evening not to be missed.

'You don't have to decide now. Ollie and me are heading there at around seven o'clock. If you like, we could give you a knock and you could walk over with us.'

'Sounds fun,' she said, just as Ollie appeared.

'Here you go, one set of keys.' He smiled warmly. 'And I overheard Kitts mentioning the do at the Sunne; I can guarantee if you join us, you'll be in for a good night.'

'In that case, how can I refuse?'

EIGHT

Romy

The key turned with a satisfying "clunk". Romy paused and took a fortifying breath before she pressed down on the metal latch and pushed at the heavy oak door, being careful not to disturb the Christmas wreath that hung there. A wave of warmth rushed at her. It was accompanied by a fragrance that was distinctly festive if its spicy cinnamon notes were anything to go by. Sensing a frisson of anticipation, Romy loitered a moment in the doorway.

Her stomach flipped as she picked up her suitcase and stepped into the low-beamed hallway. She'd forgotten how dark these old houses could be and flicked on the Bakelite switch by the door which set a warm glow emanating from the wrought iron wall lights. Glancing around, Romy's first thought was that the space was bigger than she remembered, broader somehow, but that probably had something to do with the clutter of furniture the hallway had been filled with in her parents' day. Her gaze landed on the sisal rugs strewn over the old Yorkshire flagstones, the eighteenth-century door facing her at the opposite end with its small, square window fitted with wobbly glass. A heavy linen curtain was fastened back on the hinge side of it, no doubt to pull across in a bid to keep out the winter winds that blasted along the dale. The floor to ceiling dark oak panelling on either side of the hall that divided the rooms looked just as she remembered, each run punctuated by wide, low doors that gave access to the kitchen and living room respectively. An oak coffer stood against the wall to the left, upon which sat a rustic stone vase filled with winter foliage, the vibrant red of the holly berries, glossy and bright. Beside the vase was a large bowl filled with fir cones and winter-themed potpourri which Romy assumed was responsible for the fragrance that filled the air. An antique ladder back bench was set against the panelling to the right, a row of plumped cushions in a mix of contrasting contemporary prints snuggled up side-by-side on its seat. Beside that was a chunky cast iron radiator.

Setting her suitcase down, Romy kicked off her boots and took the door to the right, heading into what used to be the kitchen. A thrill rushed through her as her eyes alighted on the cream, four oven Aga that was radiating a gentle heat from its place tucked in the embrace of an old inglenook fireplace. Taking a closer look, Romy could swear it was the very model that had been there when her parents had owned the cottage. She used to love warming herself against it as a child after a day spent playing outside in the fresh moorland air. She turned, her gaze sweeping the room. 'Oh, wow!' she said, taking in the Shaker-style kitchen painted a tasteful shade of dove grey and finished with pale quartz worktops – a new addition since her family's era of hotch-potch, mismatched cupboards – and the broad proportions of the dining table with spindle-back chairs set around it. A built-in dresser, painted to match the rest of the units, sat at the opposite end of the kitchen, its shelves lined with an eclectic mix of recipe books, jars filled with spices, and artfully placed bits of pottery. A chunky vase, filled with a display of winter faux flowers and foliage sat in one of the mullioned windows. Completing this new kitchen arrangement was a centrally placed island with four barstools in a style that matched the dining chairs. At the far end of the island, a large jar filled with what she assumed were faux lemons sat beside a wicker picnic hamper bulging with goodies. Romy decided she'd examine that more closely later. Whoever had designed and fitted this room had exquisite taste – not to mention deep pockets – the room oozed style and quality. It could easily have come straight from a country homes magazine. From the corner of her eye, she spotted an all-singing, all-dancing coffee machine, closer inspection triggering a happy smile; in amongst the tray of coffee pods were a selection containing hot chocolate powder. 'Happy days, I'll be sampling one or two of those.'

A quick peek into the utility room told her that the homeowner had even managed to make the space that housed the laundry equipment look tasteful, not to mention neat and tidy. The curtain beneath the sink matched those at the low, horizontal sliding-sash window as well as the peg bag that hung on the hook above the washing machine. A chunky radiator sat below a line of coat pegs. It was a far cry from the chaotic room filled with muddy boots, dog bowls and pawprints she remembered.

Heading through the half-glazed door on the back wall Romy found herself in the single-storey, oak-framed extension she'd spotted on the holiday cottage company website. The paleness of the wood suggested it was a fairly recent addition. She was thrilled to find the space had a cosy feel to it, despite the large proportion of windows and the polished terracotta tiled floor. The heat currently seeping through her socks and warming her chilled feet suggested the room benefited from under floor heating. She wiggled her toes happily as she quickly scanned the room. It was furnished with a sofa and chairs in calming, neutral shades that were set around a television that sat on a reclaimed chest of drawers. A large table and chairs was situated at the other end of the room, which she visualised being used for lively boardgames – the thought that her family would have loved it crossing her mind. It would also be the perfect place for her to do a spot of crafting.

Eager to check out the rest of the cottage, Romy padded back through the kitchen and across the hallway. Her heart started to gallop as she pushed open the door to the living room, her mind's eye rushing back to her family sitting there, her older brother Tristan sprawled out over his usual chair, his lanky legs hanging over the arms – it was the only thing her mum ever used to check him about – dogs roasting themselves in front of the fire. She flicked the switch and in an instant a gentle glow spilled from the wall lights. 'Oh, wow!' she said with a gasp. What had once been a room filled with the clutter of mismatched furniture and the threadbare carpet her mother had inherited with the property, was now a vision of effortless style and comfort. Romy couldn't help but gaze around her in awe.

She'd thought it had looked tasteful from the holiday cottage website but now she was here, seeing it for real, she realised it was on a whole different level. A rash of goosebumps erupted over her skin; it felt distinctly strange seeing the room like this, familiar and yet somehow so very different. The large inglenook fireplace, with the initials WF and HF together with the date 1664 commemorating the wedding of William and Hannah Fairfax (according to her father's research into the cottage's history) carved into the stone mantel, looked just as she remembered – though now a large wood-burning stove occupied the space below – as did the squat mullioned windows and the built-in settle by the fire. It was the same with the spice cupboards, the beams and the chunky cruck frame. But it was incredible how a change of décor and new furniture could completely alter the look and feel of a place. The garish wall paper and busy soft furnishings from her memories had been replaced with a neutral colour scheme that was offset by accessories made from natural materials including a wicker log basket, and a selection of rustic table lamps interspersed with pots of foliage, while watercolours in muted shades adorned the walls.

A squishy-looking sofa dominated the room from its place in front of the fire. It was piled with an array of plump cushions, while soft-wool throws were draped over its arms. Flanking it were two equally comfortable-looking armchairs, and sitting before them was a coffee table made of reclaimed oak, upon which a handful of books were arranged alongside one of the biggest scented candles

Romy had ever seen. The mullioned windows had been dressed with heavily-lined linen curtains that pooled at the floor, while a grandfather clock ticked metronomically from its place on the far wall. It was all the perfect foil to the soft finish of the uneven newly limewashed walls. There was so much to take in!

Romy rushed over to where a Christmas tree stood in the window that looked out onto the front garden – it was in the very spot her family had placed their own Christmas tree. She plugged in the fairy lights, setting the tree aglow, noting that the colour scheme of the baubles echoed that of the room. *So tasteful!*

She heaved a happy sigh before heading over the coir carpet to the dog-leg staircase, eager to see what awaited her upstairs. Reaching the bathroom, she clapped her hands to her face. It was barely recognisable! In fact, the only thing that didn't appear to have changed were the exposed beams and the little dormer window that now had a stone sculpture in the shape of a shell sitting on the sill. In place of the shabby avocado suite was an immaculate white replacement fitted with gleaming chrome taps. Against the wall by the door was a Victorian-style towel rail, layered with fluffy white towels, quietly heating the room. Though the space was small, every inch had been ingeniously utilised, with pride of place being occupied by the deep, tub-style bath. Luxurious complimentary toiletries caught her eye on the shelf. 'I'll look forward to giving those a try!'

Of the cottage's three bedrooms, the one Romy ventured to first was the one she'd shared with Tally. She felt a flutter of nerves in her stomach as she pressed her thumb down on the latch and slowly opened the door. Turning on the light, the first thing that struck her was how toasty warm it was where previously it had been chilly thanks to the draughty windows and ancient, inefficient central heating. She gave a laugh of delight as her eyes searched the room. It came as no surprise that the rickety nineteen–forties bedroom suite that had been way too big for the space had been banished along with the matching twin beds. In their place was a queen size bed made with crisp, white bedding and set between the cruck frame that rose up through the floorboards and reached up to the roof where it was held in place by oak pegs. The bed boasted a studded tweed headboard and luxurious velvet throw at the foot, its billowing pillows plump with the promise of restful sleep. White-painted wardrobes had been built into the space either side of the chimney breast, and a neatly-proportioned dressing table in limed wood was positioned opposite, a padded chair tucked beneath. And, just like the living room, an eclectic mix of old and new accessories in accent colours had been dotted about, adding interest and texture to the room: a faux plant in a wicker pot and draped with fairy lights on the dressing table, cushions on the bed, a plush rug in the centre of the floor, and lamps on the bedside tables.

Romy made her way over to the small dormer window, the deep pile of the cream wool carpet soft underfoot. Peering out, her heart gave a leap. She was thrilled to see that there was still nothing to obscure the view of the dale, nor the cottages and farmsteads over in Danskelfe. One building in particular caught her eye: Castlegate Farm, its lights twinkling in the encroaching dusk. She watched as what looked to be a Land Rover bumped up the track to the farmhouse, disappearing from view as it drove between the barns. Her heart gave another leap. Did he still live there? she wondered. Did he still have a connection to the place? As she pulled herself away from the window, she found herself rather hoping he did.

It came as no surprise to find the other two bedrooms were decorated in the same style as the rest of the property. And though she usually favoured vibrant colours, Romy found herself falling for the new, relaxed version of the cottage, and the soothing atmosphere it generated.

One thing was for certain, she thought as she headed back downstairs, the photos on the website certainly didn't do the place justice. And though she knew the rooms must have been carefully curated by someone with a keen eye for style – she wouldn't have been surprised if the owner had employed the skills of an interior designer – the redesign hadn't snuffed out any of the happy vibes she'd loved so much during her earlier visits, nor detracted from its rustic appeal. That a selection of old items had been used added a layer of charm to the contemporary design and meant it still felt like the Holly Tree Cottage of her youth.

Reaching the foot of the stairs, she rested her hand on the banister as a thought eased its way into her mind. Hadn't Maisie from the holiday cottage company mentioned something about the homeowner putting the property on the market? *Hmm...* She stood a moment, surveying the exquisite living room and contemplating why on earth they'd want to do that. A smile crept over her lips and before she knew it, her mind was carrying her off on a whole new train of thought, ignoring the warnings she'd previously given herself about reining in her impetuous nature. But, she told herself, she'd been looking for somewhere to make her fresh start, and there was the small matter of a rather sizeable nest egg burning a hole in her pocket. And besides, it wouldn't hurt to make a few enquiries; it wasn't as if she was going to make a decision now, that would be foolish! She'd see how she felt at the end of her stay, and in the meantime, she could always pick Kitty's brains about it, find out why the owner was selling such a beautiful cottage. And it wouldn't hurt to give Maisie at the holiday cottage company a call, see what she knew.

It hadn't taken long for Holly Tree Cottage to start working its magic of old.

NINE

Finn

With his insides in turmoil, Finn opened the passenger door of the Land Rover. 'Come on, lad,' he said to Ted. The Labrador leapt in, sitting himself down on the passenger seat, watching keenly as his dad walked around to the driver's side. He wagged his tail as Finn climbed in beside him, his eyes full of expectation for the adventures that lay ahead.

'You're looking a heck of a lot more enthusiastic about going out than I am,' Finn said as he pushed the keys into the ignition, the low rumble of the vehicle filling the farmyard. Ted gave an excited whimper and wagged his tail some more. Finn had never known a time when his canine companion had been anything less than enthusiastic about anything. He'd go as far as to say Ted had been a great source of comfort to him over the last couple of years, particularly the last six months after his divorce had been finalised, signalling there was no hope that Britt was going to change her mind and realise that it was Finn she wanted to be with. The Labrador's upbeat presence always managed to raise a smile when Finn was feeling low.

He headed down the farm track, frost glittering in the Land

Rover's headlights, his shoulders slumped with dread at the thought of what lay ahead of him. It was twenty past seven in the evening and he'd been hoping for a quiet night in front of the television, tucking into the pot of stew and dumplings his mum had placed in the Aga's simmering oven. But he hadn't factored Jimby bloomin' Fairfax into his plans when he'd answered his phone an hour ago. In fact, Jimby had called several times during the course of the afternoon but, anticipating the reason behind it, Finn had ignored him, telling himself he'd reply tomorrow and claim the do at the Sunne had completely slipped his mind. Which was true – Finn had been busy with his work on the farm, not to mention the several lengthy phone conversations he'd had with Britt while they negotiated access to Kyle and Toby over the festive period. She and Felix had returned to the UK for the Christmas holidays, hoping to catch up with family over here, and from what he'd experienced so far, it would seem his ex-wife hadn't softened since she'd been enjoying sunnier climes. If anything, she'd seemed pricklier with him than before she'd left and it had taken a while for them to work out what days she was happy for their lads to spend with him; every suggestion he'd made had been met with an impatient huff and reason why it really wouldn't do. And, much as he'd been tempted, he'd held back from saying that as far as he was concerned they'd already agreed this by email before Britt and their sons had left the States, that *she* was the one changing their plans, not him. He'd been gutted that he was no longer going to have their sons at the farm on Christmas Day – despite how his parents now thought of her, the invitation had been extended to Britt, too, thinking the two lads would enjoy having their parents together on such a special day. But Britt had coolly declined, citing that to do so would only confuse them or give them false hope about them getting back together. But Finn told himself it didn't matter when the lads came to the farm; they could have two Christmas Days. As long as he had the opportunity to spend some quality time with them, and they had fun together, that was all that mattered. The prospect of seeing their smiling faces, of hearing them chattering away nineteen to the dozen, was what had kept him going these last few months. The thought of them moving to the States had been bad enough, but the reality had just about shattered his heart into millions of tiny pieces. He'd been looking forward to their return more than he could put into words, even though it was only a fleeting visit. So too had his parents, particularly his mum who used to look after them during the holidays and pick them up from school when Britt was working and he was busy on the farm. Them leaving had made a big hole in her life too.

Which was why he'd answered Jimby's call without thinking, assuming it was Britt ringing with yet more rearrangements. He could've kicked himself when he heard Jimby's jovial tones booming down the line.

'Finn, lad, I've been trying to get hold of you to remind you about the ticket going spare for tonight's do at the Sunne. I've spoken to Bea, so she knows not to turn you away when you line up for some grub.' Jimby had chuckled at that and Finn had found himself mustering up a small laugh.

'Er, Jimby, I... er... I'm not sure.' He'd pushed the event at the Sunne to the back of his mind since Jimby had first mentioned it the other day, but now when he thought about it, he didn't find it any more appealing than he had then. He'd got used to not going out since Britt had taken the boys and moved out. And he couldn't face all those well-meaning folk with their sympathetic smiles. He'd seen enough to last him a lifetime. Not to mention those that were bound to ask him about how the lads were enjoying the States. It still felt surreal just thinking about it, never mind talking about it.

While he'd been racking his brains for a suitable excuse, Jimby had broken into his thoughts. 'Our Moll and Camm are going, and Moll said to tell you they're happy to take a detour on the way from Withrin Hill and scoop you up, if you fancy a couple of beers, that is. Everyone's looking forward to seeing you.' His voice had softened. 'And you might not think it now, but it'll do you good to get out, mate. The pub'll be heaving, so it's not as if you'll be under a spotlight with folk queueing up to interrogate you. Everyone'll just be intent on having a good time. And don't forget the music'll make it hard to have a conversation.' Jimby had chuckled again. 'Oh, and did I tell you, Bea managed to talk Gabe into treating us to a few of his belters.'

Finn had released a heavy sigh, mulling over Jimby's words. He was bloomin' persistent, Jimby Fairfax, that was for sure, but Finn couldn't be too annoyed, the blacksmith had a good heart. Chairman of the Lytell Stangdale Village Committee, Jimby was a cheerleader for the local community and was regularly banging his fundraising drum – in the nicest possible way. The events he'd organised meant the village now benefited from a defibrillator, a minibus that was used for trips out which the older members of the community in particular enjoyed, along with a whole host of other amenities. His affable nature ensured his suggestions were always well supported.

It had suddenly struck Finn that the lads might want to meet up with some of their friends from the village, so it wasn't as if he was going to be able to hide away and keep himself to himself as he'd been doing. He couldn't keep them cooped up at the farm, that wouldn't be fair. Kyle and Toby used to love heading into Lytell Stangdale, joining the kids in the village, building snowmen on the green and having snowball fights, or going sledging in Danskelfe where there were some pretty impressive hills to sledge down. He'd done just that when he was a child. Would it really hurt to show his face in the Sunne? he'd wondered. Much as it was kind of Molly and Camm to offer him a lift, he'd mused, if he went in the Landie, it meant he'd be able to slope off early if it all got too much. Surely that wouldn't be too bad?

Which was why he now found himself parking up on the road-side near the Sunne Inne, anticipation and doubt swirling around his insides as he stilled the engine, watching locals heading towards the pub, chatting away happily. *Why am I doing this?* The last time he'd ventured inside he'd been with Britt. They'd been celebrating their wedding anniversary with one of Bea's delicious meals. The memory of that particular evening had probably contributed to his reluctance to venture back. But, he supposed, now was as good a time as any to push it out of the way and create a new one. *That's right, think positive!*

Finn sucked in a deep breath, releasing it steadily. *Let's get this over and done with.* He turned to the Labrador who was looking at him expectantly from the passenger seat. 'Right then, Tedster, I was going to say, I hope you're going to be on your best behaviour in the pub, but since it's that long since I've mixed with folk, my social skills have got a little rusty, I reckon I should take heed of those words myself.' With his tail swishing, Ted leant across and delivered a quick lick to his dad's cheek, making Finn chuckle. He gave Ted a tickle between the ears. 'Come on then, fella.'

TEN

Romy

Romy couldn't help but marvel at how achingly pretty Lytell Stangdale appeared that evening as she walked along the trod to the Sunne with Kitty and Ollie.

'By 'eck, it's a bit nippy,' said Ollie, rubbing his hands briskly together.

'You're not wrong,' said Romy; the chilly air was already nipping at her cheeks and nose, and she was glad she'd opted for a thick knitted dress and contrasting chunky-knit tights. She glanced up at the clear, inky-blue sky that stretched out above, scattered with millions of glittering stars, the low level of light pollution in the middle of the moors showing the Milky Way off to its full advantage. Frost had crept over everything in its path, sparkling in the pale, luminescent glow of the moon and that of the vintage streetlights. Recalling how cold the winters could get on the moors, she'd wrapped up in a boiled-wool coat she'd made herself in a rich shade of green, dotted with handsewn flowers. A raspberry-red cloche covered her head and matching scarf snuggled around her neck.

'At least there isn't far to walk,' said Kitty, her breath misting in the air along with her husband's.

'So, have you managed to get unpacked and settled in at the cottage, Romy?' Ollie asked.

She nodded. 'I have, yes, thanks. And, I know it's going to sound weird given how much the interior's changed and how long it's been since I was last there, but it almost feels like I've never been away.' She hoped it didn't sound daft, but it was true, it was as if the cottage had welcomed her back with open arms. Nothing about it felt like she was staying in a holiday let, or that it was now someone else's property. It still felt very much as it did when it had belonged to her family, albeit a much warmer version thanks to the efficient central heating.

'It doesn't sound daft at all.' Kitty smiled, linking her arm through Romy's. 'It'd been in your branch of the family for generations, it's to be expected; the cottage will have soaked up so much of the Fairfax's energy into its walls. Pretty much like our place.'

'I suppose you're right.' Romy nodded. She knew Oak Tree Farm had been in Kitty's father's branch of the Fairfax family for numerous generations too. She recalled her dad saying how the farm, and the other properties Kitty's parents had owned in the village, had been put in a trust, which she assumed was why Kitty still lived there.

As they walked on, her eyes were drawn to the thatched cottages that lined the wide road. They made for a heartwarming sight with wreaths on their doors and Christmas trees at their windows, fairy lights winking out into the dark. Many had Christmas trees in their gardens too, or suitably proportioned shrubs that had been draped with festive lights. A warm glow filled Romy's chest; she felt inexorably happy she'd decided to come back to the village.

'I don't suppose you've seen many familiar faces yet – other than our lot,' said Ollie, 'but I daresay you'll more than make up for it tonight; the pub's set to be heaving with locals.'

'Oh, too right it will,' said Kitty. 'I reckon you'll have caught up with pretty much everyone by the end of the night.'

A ripple of nerves ran through Romy.

Much as she was desperate to ask if a certain person still lived locally and was likely to be there, she held back just in case the answer wasn't one she'd hoped for. She knew she had no right to have any expectations, but still, now that she was back, it hadn't stopped her from wondering about him. In fact, he'd started to dominate her thoughts. But she needed to keep them under control for tonight.

'So does Ella Welford still live round here?' she asked.

'Aye, she does,' said Ollie.

'She lives up at Camplin Farm with Joss Campion – remember him?' asked Kitty.

'Of course.' Recalling how fond they'd been of one another when they were younger, this news didn't come as a surprise to Romy. She was looking forward to having a catch-up with her old friends and hearing how they'd finally become an item. She tried not to dwell on the thought that they might not be as thrilled to see her as she them, bearing in mind the way she'd left the village and seemingly turned her back on their friendship.

'I reckon they'll both be chuffed to bits to see you,' said Kitty.

The nerves squeezed tighter in Romy's stomach. She hoped her cousin would be proved right.

Before she knew it, they'd arrived at the characterful thatched property that was The Sunne Inne, its broad oak door flanked by two Christmas trees in pots and decorated with more fairy lights. Ollie held the door open while Romy and Kitty stepped inside.

'Oh *wow*!' They were greeted by a wall of warmth and the mouthwatering aroma of what could only be Christmas dinner which made her stomach rumble loudly. Christmas carols played softly in the background accompanied by the burble of chatter. Romy could hardly believe the difference in the place. She felt her mouth fall open but was too shocked to do anything about it. '*Wow!*' she said again, when the ability to speak returned.

Kitty and Ollie exchanged glances, laughing at Romy's reaction. 'It's a bit different since Hacky Harold had it, isn't it?' Kitty said, referring to the quirky character who'd been the landlord when Romy's family still owned Holly Tree Cottage. By the time Harold had put it on the market, the thatch had slumped and was leaking badly and the place was filthy. The carpet in the bar and restaurant – not that anyone in their right mind ever ate there! – was sticky and dancing with fleas and other undesirable creatures. And the grimy, smeared glasses he'd served his drinks in had become the stuff of local legend.

'Er, I reckon that could be the understatement of the year.' Romy's eyes swept around the bar which was already humming with people. It was completely unrecognisable. The once stained, shabby curtains and soft furnishings had been replaced by tweed fabrics in rich, moorland colours; the thick, black-painted beams had been stripped and restored to their natural aged-oak and the grubby walls had been replaced with a soft limewash. The infamous carpet had been lifted, revealing an original York flagstone floor which had been scrubbed and sealed. Lighting was courtesy of iron wall lights, wrought by Kitty's older brother, Jimby, which cast a cosy glow around the room. And, sitting proudly against the back wall was a solid oak bar, crafted by Kitty's husband and local joiner, Ollie. It was offset by a row of highly polished beer pumps by which stood a tall, slender man with combed back hair and a pair of glasses perched on the end of his generous nose. Romy had a feeling he was the current landlord Kitty had told her about earlier. The bushy boughs of a Christmas tree standing in the corner caught her eye and she noted the way it had been decorated looked remarkably similar to the one in Holly Tree Cottage.

'Ooh, look, our Jimby and Vi are already here. Moll and Camm, too,' Kitty said, standing on her tiptoes and peering over at a table by a large inglenook fireplace where a fire was blazing brightly.

Romy followed her gaze to see a cluster of smiling faces looking their way, a woman with purple hair waving at them, triggering a memory. Before she had a chance to catch hold of it, the three of them were standing in front of the table.

'Everyone, you remember, Romy Stainthorpe, don't you?' Kitty asked, unwinding her stripy scarf. 'Her family used to have Holly Tree Cottage.'

'Bloomin' 'eck, talk about a welcome blast from the past,' said Jimby, his already cheerful smile spreading further across his face. 'Course we remember. It's grand to see you, Romy.' Jimby was instantly recognisable as Kitty's older brother thanks to the large brown eyes and dark, cropped curls they both shared.

'Yeah, welcome back to the village, flower,' said the woman whose purple hair was sculpted into elegant nineteen-fifties style waves.

'Thank you.' Romy smiled as it dawned on her that the woman she was talking to was Violet Smith whose parents used to have Rowan Garth Farm just outside the village. Trying not to stare – which wasn't easy when Violet's outfit stood out as looking about as far removed from Romy's idea of a farmers' daughter as was possible – Romy took in her stylish olive green fitted turtle-neck sweater, a silk scarf in contrasting shades of purple, green and a dash of white tied at her neck. Her make-up was equally immaculate complete with cat-flick eyeliner and perfectly sculpted eyebrows, not to mention her glossy rosebud mouth with its slick of plum-coloured lipstick. If it wasn't for her friendly smile, Romy felt Vi could almost come across as more than a little intimidating.

'Hiya, Romy.' A woman with a brunette chin-length, wavy bob and dark eyes that picked her out as being related to Kitty and Jimby – and, therefore, her, too – flashed her a friendly smile. It suddenly struck Romy that it was the same woman she'd seen in the Land Rover outside Kitty's house when she'd first arrived.

'Hi. It's Molly, isn't it?'

'Aye, bang on the nose there, flower. Well remembered, and it isn't half good to know the years haven't been so cruel that they've left me haggard and beyond recognition.' Molly gave a throaty chuckle.

Before Romy had a chance to reply, Vi said, 'Right, shuffle your bum up, Moll. Let's make some room for Romy to park herself.' She gave Molly a nudge.

'Bloomin' 'eck, Vi, go steady. Those elbows of yours should come with a warning.' Molly inched herself along the banquette, rubbing her ribs dramatically.

'Honestly, what a drama queen! Since when did you become a delicate little flower, Moll?' Though Vi rolled her eyes, her smile suggested she was joking.

'Since you sharpened your flippin' elbows, that's when.'

'Take no notice of those two, they love each other really,' said Jimby, chuckling as Romy eased herself onto the banquette, while Kitty took the seat next to her brother on the other side of the table. 'And this fella here is Camm.' Jimby pointed his thumb in the direction of a raven-haired man with shining, dark eyes sitting in the seat beside him. 'He's our Moll's long-suffering other half, moved to the area quite a while after your family had left, so I doubt you'll have met him before.'

Camm leant forward, and gave a warm smile. 'Hi there, Romy, it's good to meet you.'

She'd definitely never met Camm before. 'Hi, Camm, you too.' Her mind hurtled back to when her family owned Holly Tree Cottage; she was sure Molly had been with someone called Pip then. It crossed Romy's mind that she had an awful lot of catching up to do.

Just as she was wondering what had happened with Pip, Ollie said, 'Right then, anyone need a top-up?' He hung his jacket over the back of the chair next to Kitty and glanced around the table.

'I'll give you a hand, mate,' Jimby said, getting to his feet and clapping Ollie on the back as requests for drinks were made. Romy opted for a glass of Pinot Grigio, her offer to pay refused. She watched as the two men headed over to the bar, laughing at something Jimby had said, their camaraderie reminding her that the two men were lifelong best friends.

By the time she was halfway through her glass of wine, Romy

was feeling thoroughly welcomed into the group. She was listening with interest as Kitty and Vi explained about their fledgeling plans to expand Romantique Designs – their business designing and making wedding dresses. Vi took out her mobile phone and pulled up their newly created website, scrolling through the gallery of their exquisite gowns.

'Oh, they're absolutely gorgeous,' said Romy.

'Thanks,' said Vi.

'We're thinking about opening a shop in Middleton-le-Moors,' said Kitty. 'But it's early days; there's still lots to think about.'

'Yeah, we can't make up our minds between there or one of the units on the Danskelfe Estate,' said Vi. 'But the way business is booming, we're going to have to reach a decision soon, we're outgrowing our little workshop.'

Before Romy had a chance to reply, a black Labrador appeared out of nowhere on the banquette beside her, two friendly amber eyes gazing at her hopefully, and if she didn't know better, Romy could swear the said Labrador was actually smiling. 'Hello there, aren't you just adorable?' She had a soft spot for Labradors; they'd always had at least one when she was growing up. Her experience of the breed told her the large, square head belonged to a male Lab. She held out a hand to her new friend and a wet nose sniffed at her fingers, tickly whiskers making her giggle.

'Ey up, who's this fella, then?' Jimby smiled before taking a sip of his pint.

'Looks like you've made a friend there, Romy,' said Camm, smiling.

'I wonder where his owner is,' said Molly, looking around the room. 'There are that many black Labs round here, I can't always tell them apart.'

'Aye, I know what you mean,' said Ollie.

'So what's your name, handsome lad?' Romy gave him a quick rub under his chin before taking a look at the identity disc attached to his black leather collar. 'He's called Ted,' she said, laughing fondly. 'Oh, I love that name for a Labrador. I reckon you look like a Ted.' Ted inched closer, resting his paw on Romy's thigh, nudging her hand. Romy took the hint and gave him a thorough ear ruffling. 'I could take you home with me.'

'Ah, Ted, eh? He belongs to—' Jimby's words were cut off by a tall figure who appeared by their table, the smell of frosty air clinging to his heavy winter jacket.

The tall figure clamped a hand to his forehead. 'I'm so sorry, I hope he hasn't been making a nuisance of himself, he's normally well-behaved.' He turned to the Labrador. 'Ted, what did I tell you about being on your best behaviour tonight?'

Ted's ears flattened momentarily, lifting as soon as Romy spoke. 'It's honestly not a problem.' She smoothed her hand over Ted's silky head. The Labrador's tail gave a quick wag. He glanced between Romy and his owner. 'He's absolutely gorgeous and no bother at all. He's just being a friendly lad, aren't you, Ted? He's come to say hello.' Romy switched her gaze from the Labrador to the man standing in front of her, her heart almost leaping out of her chest. 'Oh, I... er... oh!' Butterflies started fluttering around her stomach in a frenzy. She'd know those bright blue eyes, the colour of forget-me-nots, anywhere.

A flicker of recognition crossed the bright blue eyes. 'Romy?' the owner said softly.

With her heart stampeding, she nodded, conscious of the weight of several pairs of eyes watching the interaction with interest. 'Finn?' she said, the atmosphere around the table suddenly changing. She tried to make sense of the situation, conscious of her mind hurtling back to twenty-one years ago and the last time she'd seen him, the last time he'd held her in his arms, the last time she'd felt the soft brush of his lips on hers. The already frenetic butterflies in her stomach upped their game, rendering her unable to utter another word.

ELEVEN

Finn

Finn swallowed, hardly able to believe the message his eyes were sending to his brain. Romy Stainthorpe was sitting here in The Sunne Inne and had apparently been befriended by his wayward Labrador. Surely not. This wasn't making any kind of sense. He scratched his head. Was he dreaming? Was he hallucinating? It wasn't as if he could blame it on being on the wrong side of too many beers since he hadn't had a chance to take so much as a sniff of his shandy – which was hardly potent stuff anyway – thanks to charmer Ted slipping his lead and ingratiating himself with... well, the last person he'd expected to see sitting with Jimby and his pals. Granted, she looked a little older, but she was bound to, she was only sixteen the last time he'd seen her. But those eyes, the way they sparkled with mischief, he'd know them anywhere, they were indisputably Romy; *his* Romy, or at least, that's how he used to think of her. His heart flipped over at the reminder. What reason could she have for being here after all this time? he wondered. And was it really her and not some pathetic wishful thinking on his part? After all, she had popped into his mind the other day, completely out of the blue. Or was it another woman sitting there who was also called Romy and who simply bore a strong resemblance to her, which wouldn't be that odd when he thought about it considering she had relatives in the village. And, if he was being completely honest with himself, it wouldn't be the first time he'd been convinced he'd spotted her in Lytell Stangdale or Danskelfe, only to find he'd been mistaken, though, granted, it had been a long time since that had happened.

Conscious that his mouth was hanging open as his brain did all it could to process the latest unexpected scenario to have knocked him off-kilter, all Finn could do was blink, as thoughts continued to fly wildly around his mind. After his earlier phone call with Britt there was no wonder he was feeling bamboozled and struggling to think straight. *Get a grip of yourself, man! It's glaringly obvious it's Romy Stainthorpe! Your Romy Stainthorpe, and not some doppelganger! And you need to wipe that gormless expression you're no doubt wearing right off your face before you terrify her and she runs off before you even get to say hello.* Finn clamped his mouth shut, blinked some more and inhaled a steadying breath as he attempted to push his way through his muddle of thoughts.

It took a couple of seconds for him to realise that Romy appeared to be as shocked as he was.

Romy

She always knew there was a strong chance she'd run into Finn Tindall, but Romy hadn't expected it to be on the first day she arrived in Lytell Stangdale. She'd anticipated putting out little feelers, making subtle enquiries, being able to prepare herself for what to say to him. But seeing him there in the pub, standing before her, had made her heart leap and all but whipped her breath away. There was definitely no doubting it was Finn Tindall; like she'd already told herself, she'd know those bright-blue eyes anywhere. And though they still shone with the gentleness that used to turn her insides into a mushy mess, she noted it had been joined by an air of weariness.

Her eyes roved over him; he seemed taller than she remembered and he'd been over six-feet back then. His shoulders had filled out too, though his face was less full, his strong jaw now more angular and defined which suited him. His dark, once-tousled, hair, which she used to love to run her fingers through, was cut more closely. It was fair to say, the seventeen-year-old boy who had made her heart race with youthful passion had grown into an out-of-the-way handsome man. And Romy found her heart had started racing all over again.

TWELVE
TWENTY-ONE YEARS EARLIER

It was a Friday evening in June that Romy first noticed Finn in a different light.

She'd been wishing the week away, counting down the days until she was back in Lytell Stangdale for the weekend, glad when it finally arrived. She, Finn and his older brother Dougie, along with Ella and the Campion brothers, had been invited to Becky Ventress's birthday party. Becky was one of their Young Farmer friends and the party was being held in a specially done out barn over at Ellerby Farm in nearby Arkleby. The friends had all been looking forward to it. With time being tight on account of having to wait until her father had finished work before her family could travel over to the cottage, Romy had got ready for the party at their home in Rickelthorpe. Arriving on the moors, her dad had taken a detour en route to Lytell Stangdale and dropped her off at Castlegate Farm, which was where she'd been waiting for the last fifteen minutes, sitting at the kitchen table, chatting to Finn's mum. It was a room she loved, always warm and cosy and bouncing with easygoing family banter. The delicious aroma of the many meals imbued into the walls courtesy of the huge Aga that dominated the kitchen only added to the welcoming atmosphere. It was impossible not to feel at home there.

'Typical lad, taking so bloomin' long to get ready, isn't it?' Jill said.

Romy giggled, returning Jill's affectionate eye roll. 'It was a quick turnaround for me. I landed in from school, wolfed down my tea, quick shower, then threw my clothes on by which time my dad had arrived home and we all jumped in the car and set off for here.' It was always a mad rush to get to Lytell Stangdale on a Friday evening, the Stainthorpe family eager to spend as much time there as possible.

'And in the time you were doing all that, our Finn's been hogging the bathroom and tarting himself up, which is typical of him these days,' said Dougie, who'd wandered into the room and joined in the conversation. Romy noted he'd swapped his usual jeans and hoody for a smart shirt and chinos. 'The landing stinks like one of them perfume counter places with all the stuff he's been spraying and splashing over himself. It's just as well I had a shower before he took up residence in there or I'd run the risk of that pong lingering on me when we get to Ellerby Farm.'

Romy and Jill exchanged amused glances. 'To be fair, he has been in there a long time. I hope it's going to be worth it,' Jill said.

'I reckon he'll be that clean, he'll squeak when he walks.' Dougie leant against the worktop, arms folded, looking on as Romy and his mother burst out laughing.

'Now there's a thought,' said Jill. 'He'll have to watch out in case someone tries to oil him.'

'By 'eck, it's nippy out there.' Tommy burst into the room, clattering the kitchen door and making them all turn in his direction. 'Now then, Romy flower, it's grand to see you.'

'Hiya, Tommy, s'good to see you too.'

'Wellies off, Tommy!' Jill looked at Romy again, shaking her head good-naturedly. 'It's chucking it down out there, and I've not long since cleaned this floor, the last thing I need is you paddling mucky footprints all over it.'

'Sorry, love.' He pulled an "oops" face and stepped backwards into the small porch where he removed the offending footwear along with his dripping jacket and flat cap.

After he'd washed his hands, Tommy pulled out a chair at the table as Jill poured him a mug of tea from the pot. He was in the middle of updating them on some news he'd heard about the new tenants at Rigg End Farm in Great Stangdale when Finn sauntered into the room, towel-drying his hair.

Dougie snorted. 'Ey up, look what the cat dragged in.'

'Hiya, Romes,' Finn said, ignoring his brother and flashing her a smile, his gaze lingering on her a moment before turning to Jill. 'Don't suppose you've seen my blue shirt, have you, Mum? The one with the button-down collar.'

'Hiya.' Romy's heart stilled at the sight of him; she barely heard Jill's reply. As if that wasn't enough to contend with, her stomach started looping the loop as an inexplicable heat simultaneously crept over her body, burning particularly hot in her cheeks. And, as much as she struggled against it, she found nothing could make her tear her eyes away from Finn. He was standing barefoot by the Aga, a towel tied low around his waist, his shoulders still glowing from the shower. A pulse of attraction fired through her, making her feel slightly dazed. *Oh my days! What was happening?* There was no way on this earth she should be having feelings like this about her best friend, but something about him seemed so... so different; something she couldn't put her finger on. Her nostrils twitched as the unmistakable scent of masculine bath products wafted under her nose while butterflies joined the drama playing out in her stomach, adding to her distraction as they fluttered around frantically. Her eyes went to the tan lines on his arms defining where the sleeves of his T-shirt ended and the sun had kissed his skin. She found herself longing to touch him there, feel it beneath her fingertips. Droplets of water glistened in his hair, and there was a smattering of dark curls across his chest she hadn't noticed before. And where the heck had those muscles that were rippling across his shoulders and down his arms come from? The last time she'd looked he was all skinny limbs and pointy elbows. The word she'd have used to describe him then was gangly or scrawny. But there was no way she could associate those words with this new version of Finn standing before her now. "Hot" more like. She scrunched her eyes tight shut. *Warghh! Stop! Don't go there! He's your best friend and he is very definitely not hot!* She opened her eyes again, hoping no one had noticed, then swallowed, which wasn't easy since her mouth had inexplicably become as dry as the desert. She felt utterly discombobulated by this bizarre set of circumstances.

As her brain attempted to make sense of the reason her body was reacting in such an unexpected way, Romy gradually became aware of Finn looking at her. In an instant, her mind began scrabbling to find the question for which he was clearly awaiting an answer. Somehow, thankfully, she managed to dredge it from her subconscious. She heaved an internal sigh of relief.

'Oh, yeah, my week hasn't been too bad. How 'bout you?' *You need to get a grip of yourself, Romy Stainthorpe!*

'Aye, not bad. Busy.' He rubbed his hair with the towel some more, making it stand up on end and giving Romy the urge to run her fingers through it. *For goodness sake, will you calm your jets, woman!*

'Tell you what, after the hours you've spent in that flippin' bathroom we were expecting something a bit more spectacular to emerge than the pathetic specimen standing before us, little bro',' Dougie said with a smirk. It was a display of brotherly banter Romy was familiar with and knew it wasn't meant unkindly. She'd witnessed it plenty of times over the years to know that Finn was more than capable of giving Dougie as good as he got.

'Haha. Very funny, Dougster. You're just jealous 'cos sitting at a desk all day, tapping away at a computer, doesn't give you muscles like these.' Finn struck a comedic pose, flexing his impressive biceps at his brother. Everyone burst out laughing, including Romy as she battled the new feelings that had taken up residence inside her and seemed intent on causing as much chaos as possible if her galloping pulse was anything to go by.

'Trust me, you've got nowt I'd be jealous of.' Dougie clipped the back of his brother's head with the tips of his fingers as he passed on his way across the kitchen.

'Ow! Watch it!' Finn shot him a faux warning look.

'Yeah, yeah. When you're big enough, squirt.'

'Hey, don't forget I'm taller than you now which means I'm plenty big enough, *squirt!*'

Come to think of it, since when had Finn got so tall? Romy wondered, her eyes roving over him. He was now easily a couple of inches taller than Dougie. She hadn't noticed that before, he must've shot up over the last month or so.

Jill caught Romy's eye and shook her head, smiling. 'What are they like, the pair of them?' she said. Romy smiled back, hoping Jill hadn't caught her staring.

'And you might want to cover yourself up a bit, you don't want to ruin poor Romes's night. She's at serious risk of chucking up at the sight of your pathetic pasty body,' Dougie said, throwing the comment over his shoulder as he disappeared through the door and into the hallway.

Finn pulled a face at his brother's retreating back while Romy felt her blushes deepen. This was *agony*.

'Aye, and on that happy note, have you seen the time, lad?' Tommy nodded to the clock on the dresser. 'Our Dougie has a point about you shaping yourself and getting dressed, it's not long before you'll need dropping off, and in case you forgot, we're scooping up Ella and the Campion lads on the way. I dare say it'd turn a few heads if you landed at Ellerby Farm looking like that.'

'Turn a few stomachs more like.' Dougie's disembodied voice floated down the stairs.

'Funny man.' Finn laughed, his eyes flicking to the clock as he draped the hand towel over his shoulder. Heading towards the door, he turned to Romy. 'Won't be long.' He flashed her a smile and she felt her insides melt.

. . .

It was still stair-rodding it down when Tommy dropped the six of them off at Ellerby Farm. Knowing they were heading to a notoriously messy place, they'd all set off in their wellies, with their shoes stashed in bags. They piled out of the Land Rover and made a dash across the farmyard, rain splashing up at them, changing into their smart footwear once they were on the other side of the barn door where music was pulsing.

As far as Romy was concerned, the party would have been perfect if it hadn't been for the presence of Colette, Becky's twenty-year-old cousin, who was staying with the Ventress family for a couple of days. Colette was looking stylish and sophisticated in a teal silk slip dress that clung to her curves. On her feet were a pair of heels so high Romy wondered how she didn't topple over, especially considering the uneven surface of the ancient flagstones underfoot. The young woman had an impossibly glossy curtain of long, blonde hair that she kept flicking over her shoulder. And, much to Romy's chagrin, she'd been talking to Finn for the last half hour and she seemed very taken with him, if her body language was anything to go by.

'Who's that new lass?' asked Ella, tilting her can of Coke in the direction of Colette who was twirling a lock of golden hair around her finger and laughing at something Finn was saying. 'I haven't seen her round here before. D'you reckon she's from the new family who've moved in at Rigg End Farm over in Great Stangdale?'

The two friends were sitting beside one another on one of the oblong bales of hay that lined the barn. The incongruous glow of the fairy lights looped from the exposed beams somehow worked against the whitewashed walls of the agricultural building, adding a celebratory, party feel to the room. The chill was taken off the space by two large fan heaters, though it did little to stop the cold from seeping up through the floor.

Romy shook her head. 'No, I was told she's Becky's cousin and is here for the weekend apparently.' She felt her heart sink as she followed Ella's gaze.

'Oh, right. She keeps touching Finn's arm. I wonder if he minds? Seems a bit over-familiar if you ask me.' Ella took a swig from her can, almost choking. 'Oh my God! And why's she touching his hair like that?'

'I've no idea.' Romy felt an unfamiliar twist of jealousy. She didn't like herself for it. She could understand perfectly well why Colette would touch Finn's hair, there was something about the way he wore it, the way it stood up, that made it so tempting. After all, she'd ruffled it plenty of times herself. She stifled a sigh. 'She's all right, actually, quite bubbly and friendly, no edge to her. Got the impression she's a girls' girl.' It would have made her feel so much better if Colette had been a cowbag – as Romy, Ella and their friends referred to girls they considered frosty and aloof. It would've gone some way to justifying these weird, new feelings that had taken hold – she couldn't bring herself to label them, but the word "envy" circled around the periphery of her mind. She'd already had a conversation with Colette and, despite herself, Romy had found she liked her. The only problem was, Colette seemed pretty keen on Finn and, if the looks he was giving her were anything to go by, not to mention the way he'd been laughing with her, the feeling was mutual. Romy felt suddenly very dowdy and childish in her navy blue cotton slip dress with the short sleeved T-shirt beneath.

Before Ella had a chance to say anything further, the two friends were joined by Dougie. 'Ey up, lasses, looks like our Finn's pulled at long last. The jammy git's only gone and hooked himself a gorgeous older woman and it looks like she's single.' He gave a snigger that grated on Romy. 'Seems his lengthy bathroom tarting-up session's paid off; there's been loads of lasses sniffing around him tonight. No accounting for taste, I s'pose. But if my suspicions are right, I reckon you won't be seeing much of lover boy this week-end, Romes. Mind, I dare say you'll welcome a break from him and his annoying habits.' He flashed her a grin, oblivious to the turmoil raging inside her.

As difficult as it was, she managed to force a laugh and joined in with Dougie and Ella's joking, hoping her efforts didn't sound as half-hearted as they felt. Looking over at Finn, it was glaringly obvious why girls would be attracted to him. He was tall, good-looking and easy going, always ready to laugh and smile. Why had it taken her so long to realise? He glanced over at her, his bright-blue eyes twinkling as his smile broadened. Her heart responded with a flutter. Despite what Dougie had said, the last thing Romy would welcome was a break from Finn. In fact, right now she'd quite happily spend every waking moment with him.

'Ey up, Romes, how're you diddlin'?' Romy turned as Finn plonked himself beside her on the bale, a bottle of beer in his hand. She'd been sitting by herself for the last five or so minutes, lost in her thoughts, while Ella and Joss had a dance.

'Not bad, how about you? Where's your friend?' She mustered up a smile, hoping she didn't sound like she was being snarky.

'My friend?' He looked genuinely puzzled.

'Yeah, Colette; she seems nice.' He looked a different kind of handsome in his smart clothes compared to his usual farming garb. And his eyes looked extra twinkly in the half-light of the barn. Romy felt a flutter in her stomach which being in close proximity to Finn suddenly seemed to generate. It was taking some getting used to.

'Ahh, Colette. Last I spotted she was talking to the Dougster, I introduced them; he's got the hots for her apparently.' He turned to her, his eyes glinting with mischief.

'Yeah, I kind of got the impression he liked her,' she said, as a tsunami of happiness surged through her, her smile spreading further across her face. Finn can't have fancied Colette if he'd tried to fix her up with Dougie. Oh, happy days! This was the *best* news!

'Aye, I s'pose the drooling was a bit of a giveaway. Our Dougie's a bit obvious like that. I've tried telling him to have a bit of class, but the daft lad won't listen.' He grinned at her before taking a slug of his beer.

Romy was trying to think of a witty reply but all she could focus on was the feeling of Finn's leg pressed against hers, the heat burning through the fabric of her dress.

She was given the perfect excuse not to have to come up with an answer when the intro of *The Ketchup Song* filled the room and a roar went up. Finn looked at Romy, his eyebrows raised in question; the song was a huge favourite of theirs and their friends, and they always danced to it whenever it was played at a party. Ella and Joss rushed over, excitement radiating from them.

'Come on, you two!' Ella grabbed Romy by the hand and pulled her to her feet as the volume of the music was cranked up.

'Aye, come on, Finn lad, put that beer down and let's hit the floor. It's time to bust some moves,' Joss said, his voice raised as he clapped his friend soundly on the back.

Romy couldn't remember the last time she'd had so much fun as they recreated the much-loved routine the song had become famous for, the four of them laughing and singing at the top of their voices. Finn grabbed Romy's hand and twirled her around, making her dizzy and almost sending her flying. He threw his arms around her to steady her and her heart fluttered as she felt his breath on her neck, the scent of his cologne dancing under her nose. Oh, how she wished she could stay in that moment forever.

THIRTEEN

Clad in an old T-shirt and a pair of scruffy jeans, with her hair scraped back into a ponytail, Romy had perched herself on the five-bar gate that opened out into the field where Finn and his dad were training Moss, their new sheepdog. Calls of 'come by', 'away' and the shrill squeal of Tommy's sheepdog whistle filled the air along with the bleating of sheep. It was three weeks after Becky Ventress's birthday party and Romy was enjoying the summer holidays, looking forward to starting at art college in September. As usual, her family had decamped to Lytell Stangdale and were glad to find the moors were enjoying a stretch of fine weather. With a clear blue sky above and the sun beating down, Romy looked on, her sketchbook on her lap, pencil in hand, as Moss and Fly raced around the sheep, Fly in particular responding swiftly to Tommy's commands, Moss copying his mother. It wasn't the first time she'd observed father and son round up the sheep, and marvelled at the skills and intelligence of the sheepdogs as she'd sketched them, but it was the first time since she'd noticed her feelings for Finn had changed. And it was more than a little unsettling.

Finn was wearing his favourite Foo Fighters T-shirt which he'd had forever and Romy found her eyes drawn to his newly broadened shoulders, the fabric of the T-shirt pulled taut, accentuating the muscles that rippled across his back. Her gaze dropped to his biceps which seemed to have appeared out of nowhere. And how was it that his jeans looked so different, hugging his thighs that had gone from puny to muscular almost overnight? What the heck was going on? It set a heady mix of feelings stirring inside her. Feelings she was struggling to marshal as he ambled over to her, wearing an easy smile, his blue eyes looking even brighter against his sun-kissed skin. He stopped before her, resting his hand on the gate. Her stomach responded by performing a hattrick of somersaults setting her pulse off at a gallop. Try as she might, there was nothing she could do to steady it. Her eyes went from his full lips that looked soft and warm, to the graze of stubble that peppered his jaw. Despite the fact it had been weeks since she'd first become all too aware of her changing feelings for Finn, she was still unsure how to act in front of him. It wasn't exactly easy when her skinny, gangly best friend with a mischievous smile and shock of messy hair had transformed into a heart-stoppingly, drop-dead gorgeous hunk with sexily-tousled locks she longed to run her fingers through.

'Dad reckons Moss is going to make just as good a sheepdog as his mother, if not better; he's a quick learner,' he said, sounding pleased.

'Oh... um... yeah.' Finding herself uncharacteristically tongue-tied, Romy struggled to meet his gaze. Mortification rushed through her as she felt her face glow crimson. She hoped Finn hadn't noticed.

'You okay?' he asked, squinting at her and giving her leg a nudge with his elbow. 'Your face has gone bright red; it's like a beetroot.' He gave an amused laugh.

His touch sent an unfamiliar jolt shooting through her. *Not helping, Finn!* 'Mm-hm. I'm fine.' She nodded, struggling to ignore these alien feelings as embarrassment flooded through her like a raging tidal wave. 'I'm mafted; that sun's roasting.' She hoped with all her might her voice didn't sound as weirdly strangled to him as it did to her. She wafted the neck of her T-shirt as if to demonstrate just how hot the sun was making her, hoping it would stop him from looking at her so weirdly. The last thing she wanted was for him to read her mind; she hadn't got her head around what was going on in there herself.

'Aye, you're right, it's a hot 'un today.' His gaze lingered on her for a few moments as he studied her expression which only added to her discomfort. Giving a light shrug, he pushed his fingers through his already ruffled hair then turned to look at the sheep, hooking his thumbs through the belt loops of his jeans.

Romy's eyes were drawn to the back of his neck, burnished golden where the sun had kissed it, before slipping to the strong shoulders she'd been admiring moments earlier. Before she knew it, she was overcome with a sensation that felt like every nerve ending in her body was on fire and she found herself wishing he would turn around, take her in his arms and kiss her. *Oh my days! What's happening to me? I'm losing control! I seriously, seriously need to calm my jets!*

Finn turned back to her and she hurriedly flicked her gaze to the sheep, fearful her eyes would betray her feelings.

'The forecast says it's supposed to be grand weather for the Young Farmers' barbecue this weekend which Mum and Dad are chuffed about,' Finn said. The Tindall's had volunteered to hold the summer barbecue at Castlegate Farm that year and it had caused great excitement in the family, all except for Dougie who hadn't been looking forward to the disruption or having a load of rowdy Young Farmers wandering around the farm.

'Hmm.'

'Mind, with this heatwave, they're going to have the barbecue in the yard, keep it well away from the fields; don't want to risk causing a fire.'

'Yeah.' *And what was it with his voice?* How come had it gone all husky and... well, made her go all of a dither and feel things she really shouldn't be feeling about her best friend? Everything about him seemed so very... *un-Finn*, so *different*, so... *fanciable*.

She gradually became aware that Finn had stopped speaking, a weird silence hanging in the air. She glanced his way to find him looking at her intently. 'Honestly, Romes, what the flippin' 'eck's up with you? I reckon you haven't heard owt I've just said.'

His words pulled her up straight. She needed to stop this foolishness, needed to get her mind back to where it had been before, well... back to when everything was just as it had always been, before she ruined things with the best friend she'd ever had. 'Nowts up,' she said. Her Yorkshire accent always became broader when she was in Lytell Stangdale, with more dialect slipping in. 'Like I said, I'm mafted, that's all.'

'Right,' he said, his tone telling her he wasn't entirely convinced. After a moment, he said, 'So let's see what you've been drawing, then.' He went to reach for the sketchbook in her lap and looked shocked when she angled herself away from him.

'No!' Panic gripped her and she covered her drawing with her hands. 'It's rubbish. I didn't get much done, there's nowt to show.'

'Oh, come on, there must be. I saw you sketching away, and I can clearly see you've drawn summat there.' Laughing, he reached for the sketchbook. 'Come on, Romes, nothing you draw is ever rubbish, you're brilliant at art.'

'Finn! I said no, okay!' Increasing her grip, Romy pulled back just as Finn let go. She gave a squeal as she found herself falling backwards off the gate, landing unceremoniously in a heap on a mound of prickly grass. She lay still a moment, winded. *You idiot! You've only got yourself to blame for this!*

'Romy! Flippin' 'eck. Are you okay?' Finn quickly lifted the latch on the gate, which luckily opened into the field, and rushed to her. Bending to help her up, his eyes went to the sketchbook, lingering there before glancing back to her, a baffled expression on his face.

Refusing his offer of help, she scrambled to her feet and grabbed her stuff together, her cheeks blazing. 'Loser,' she said, roughly pushing past him before stomping off towards the track that led to the village, her ponytail swishing from side to side. A cocktail of anger, embarrassment and regret simmered inside her as she strode on, ignoring Finn's cries telling her to wait. She'd never felt so embarrassed in her life. How could she face him again without feeling like the biggest fool ever? And, much as she desperately wanted to get the friendship that she'd cherished for so many years back on track, her mind was too muddled to see how that would be remotely possible now. There was only one thing for it: she'd have to avoid him, and if they happened to bump into one another, she'd act as if she was indifferent to him. Her heart sank like a stone. How could she even contemplate treating her best friend in such a way? She kicked a pebble in frustration, watching as it bounced down the track. Why did she have to go and give into temptation and let loose with her pencil and sketch him, today of all days? She could just as easily draw him from memory; she already had. Several times, as the sketchbook under her bed at Holly Tree Cottage was testament.

FOURTEEN

Finn

Finn watched Romy disappear down the track, his mind turning over what had just happened, wondering what could have caused such a dramatic switch in her mood. In all the time they'd been friends, they'd hardly ever fallen out, and when they had, he'd been in no doubt as to the cause. But this...? He scratched his head in confusion, barely noticing the cackle of a pheasant as it flew by. It was totally unlike her, she was usually so even-tempered. His mum regularly said they were alike that way, going on to explain it was why they rarely fell out or exchanged cross words, but Finn had never given it that much thought. He just knew that he enjoyed her company; she was easy to be around and good fun. That she was more impetuous than him only encouraged him to be more adventurous, which he secretly enjoyed.

But something had bothered her that morning, which could probably explain why she'd seemed so distracted when he was talking to her, not that he had a clue what it could be. He rubbed his hand over his chin, half-aware of the intensity of the sun's rays as they beat down on his back. And then he'd gone and annoyed her by trying to grab her sketchbook, which was something he bitterly regretted now. He hadn't meant to upset her, her reaction had come as a total shock. She never usually minded him seeing a drawing or watercolour she was working on and was yet to finish, in fact, she often asked his opinion, gave the impression she valued it, or at least that's what he'd always thought. But then again, he'd never been the subject of her drawings, well, not unless you counted the jokey one she'd done that was more of a caricature. It was of him on the quadbike and she'd given him long, cow-like lashes and emphasised his eyes. As for his hair, she'd made it look like a massive birds' nest, complete with a pheasant perched on it at a jaunty angle. He'd hooted with laughter when she'd shown him, as had the rest of his family. 'By, Finn lad, I'd say young Romy's captured your spirit pretty well there,' his dad had said, chuckling. Finn had thought the drawing was fantastic. He'd had it framed and hung in his bedroom, laughing whenever it caught his eye. He'd always been proud of his friend's artistic streak and thought she was seriously talented as well as versatile, as the water-colour of the farmhouse and garden she'd done for his mum's birthday showed. Jill had been overjoyed with it. His dad had been the same when Romy had given him a pencil drawing of Moss recently.

His mind went back to the sketch she'd been working on of him that morning, a frown creasing his brow. It was odd that she hadn't focussed on Moss or Fly with the moors and fields in the back-ground, like she usually did. Maybe she'd grown tired of drawing them. After all, she'd got a whole load of them and the other farm animals, some of which she'd used in her portfolio when she'd gone for her interview for a place at art college.

He breathed out a noisy sigh as his mind segued to the feel-ings that had crept up on him over the last few weeks and had caught him unawares. Instead of thinking of Romy as his best friend, the rough and tumble tomboy he'd climbed trees and scrambled over becks with, he'd started seeing her through very different eyes. He'd first noticed these feelings when they were sitting side by side on a bale of hay in the barn, seeking shade from the blisteringly hot sunshine. They'd been laughing together as he relayed how one of the farm's geese had taken exception to him earlier that morning and chased him, honking noisily and flapping its wings in warning. 'Looked bloomin' terrifying it did, has a massive wingspan. I haven't a clue why the daft bird doesn't like me, it's not as if I've done owt to her,' he'd said, feigning hurt feelings.

'Ah, poor old Finny, don't take it to heart, lad. I'm sure she didn't mean it. And anyway, at least you know *I* like you.' Romy had giggled as she'd nudged him with her elbow.

The warm touch of her skin against his, combined with the floral scent of her shampoo that lingered in her hair, had sent his encounter with the goose whooshing from his mind. All he'd been able to think about was the new, unfamiliar feelings that had surged without warning through his body and sent his hormones into overdrive. He'd been overwhelmed by the urge to take her in his arms and kiss her but, difficult as it had been, he'd held back, telling himself she was his best friend and kissing her would risk losing her friendship which was something he desperately didn't want. The thought that it would very probably earn him a wallop from her had crossed his mind too, and he didn't fancy being on the receiving end of one of those.

He'd thought of little else since. And now those feelings were out of the box, he'd been struggling to push them back in every time he set eyes on her.

A thought struck him, sending panic careering around his insides. What if she knew? What if she'd sensed what he was thinking? Maybe that's why she'd gone funny with him. Had she noticed the way he'd been looking at her that morning? He'd done his best to hide it, but she'd looked so beautiful, sitting there on the gate, the sun behind her making her chestnut hair glow. He'd always thought she had a sunny smile, but now it made his insides dance. He clapped his hand to his forehead. 'You bloomin' idiot!' he said to himself. 'You've stuffed things up for good now, you plonker!'

'You all right, lad?' his dad asked as he made his way across the field, Moss and Fly at his heel.

'Yeah, I'm okay.' He tried but failed to sound convincing.

'Where's Romy?' Reaching his son, Tommy cast his gaze around the surrounding farmland. He slid his flat cap from his head and smoothed a hand over his hair, so like his son's, then signalled for Moss and Fly to sit beside him. The pair obeyed in an instant.

'She's gone home. Said she was mafted. I reckon the sun got a bit much for her.' Struggling to meet his dad's eye, Finn feigned nonchalance, willing his father not to pursue the matter.

'That's not like her.' Tommy fixed his son with a knowing look. 'Are you sure you didn't say owt daft to upset her?'

Finn felt the colour rise in his cheeks. 'I just asked to see what she'd been drawing.'

Tommy pulled a disbelieving face. 'And that's what sent her off home? Are you sure there's not summat else?'

Finn squirmed, focusing his attention on the toe of his welly as he kicked at a clump of grass. 'I tried to grab her sketchbook and she fell backwards off the gate.'

Tommy still looked doubtful. 'Right. And was she hurt?'

Would you please stop with the flippin' inquisition? 'Winded... seemed okay though.'

His dad nodded, a knowing look in his eye. 'I reckon you two need to sit down and have a chat, lad.'

'What d'you mean? Chat about what?' His father's response startled him and Finn felt his blushes deepen.

Tommy gave a throaty laugh. 'Well, it's pretty obvious summat's shifted between the pair of you, your mother and me noticed it a few weeks ago. It's not just on your part either, lad, Romy's as sweet on you as you are on her. And just like you, she hasn't come to terms with her feelings yet. I dare say the pair of you'll get there in your own time if you don't fancy talking to each other about it just yet.' He patted his son's arm and winked at him. 'Come on, Romeo, don't know about you, but I'm gagging for a cuppa.' With that, he whistled for the sheepdogs and ambled back in the direction of the farmhouse.

Finn stood rooted to the spot as his mind worked through what his dad had just imparted. Pushing aside his embarrassment at being rumbled by his parents, he wondered if they could he be right. Did Romy feel the same way about him as he felt about her? Wow! He couldn't even begin to think about how that might change things between them. Was that the reason she was sketching him and didn't want him to see? He felt the despair that had descended upon him lift as a little glimmer of hope crept in, a smile pulling up the corners of his mouth.

There was only one problem. How the heck was he going to find out for sure?

FIFTEEN

Finn

Saturday arrived in a blaze of sunshine, perfect for the Young Farmers' barbecue. Finn and his family had been up early, making sure everything was set up to welcome the Danskelfe Young Farmers, along with those belonging to the Middleton-le-Moors branch whom they'd invited to join them for the end of year event – the YF took a break over the summer with it being such a busy time of year in the farming calendar. Romy, who usually helped out whenever the Tindalls played host to a Young Farmers event, had been conspicuous by her absence; she hadn't returned to Castlegate Farm since she'd stomped off the previous Wednesday. In fact, Finn had seen neither hide nor hair of her in Lytell Stangdale when he'd driven through in the Land Rover, which he'd used any excuse to do, and not just because he loved driving the Landie. He'd parked up and thought about knocking on the door of Holly Tree Cottage but had talked himself out of it. Her mum could be a little on the stern side and he was reluctant to cause any unnecessary hassle for Romy if Dulcie Stainthorpe sensed that something was wrong. From what he could gather, she wouldn't let things drop until she'd got to the bottom of whatever it was that had aroused her interest. It had driven Romy to distraction at times, and now wasn't the time to increase her irritation levels towards him.

Since then, he'd hung onto the hope that Romy would put what had happened with the sketchbook behind her, realise that her reaction had been over the top, and come back to the farm, just like she always had. He'd be happy to continue as if nothing had happened, if that was what she wanted. He'd mulled over his dad's suggestion that they should sit down together and have a chat but Finn couldn't imagine how to even start a conversation about *that* without it being toe-curlingly embarrassing. And there was always the risk that his dad had got it wrong, that Romy's feelings didn't match his. He cringed at the thought of declaring his love for her only to be met with her looking back at him, utterly mortified before running off again. But one thing he knew for certain was that he didn't want to lose her from his life, even if it meant it wouldn't be the kind of relationship he now hoped for. She'd been his best friend for years, been the person in whom he'd confided all his secrets and worries and insecurities. Her friendship meant too much to throw it away, to no longer have her in his life. *Romy* meant too much to him. The mere thought of losing what they had caused a squeeze in his chest. He needed to speak to her, to put things right, and whatever had happened between them the other day, he hoped she'd be able to push it to one side and come to the Young Farmers' barbecue; she'd been looking forward to it and she had every right to be there.

By early afternoon, Castlegate Farm was teeming with Young Farmers, a thrum of excitement and jovial voices filling the air along with the smoke from the barbecue that Tommy was watching like a hawk. With the weather still being hot and dry, he and Finn had lined up buckets of water alongside the hosepipe, just to be on the safe side.

'Can I have your attention, please?' said a tinny voice through a megaphone, echoing around the dale. 'The lasses' tug of war is due to start in ten minutes. Could those taking part make their way over to the top right of the field. Thank you very much.' The tug of war competitions were always popular amongst the Young Farmers and today, the Danskelfe and Middleton-le-Moors male and female teams were going head-to-head.

Finn's heart jumped at hearing the announcement. Romy was supposed to be on the Danskelfe team. It would be most unlike her to let anyone down but he hadn't spotted her yet. He searched around the sea of people, hoping to catch a glimpse of her, but was to be disappointed. There was only one way to find out if she was there.

As he was making his way over to the field, his heart lifted as he heard a familiar laugh. He turned to see Romy walking along, chatting happily with Ella Welford, Kitty Fairfax – who, he noted, was making a rare appearance since she'd started dating that pompous barrister – and Molly Harrison. The four of them were dressed in their tug of war gear of the sky-blue Danskelfe Young Farmers' polo shirts, cycling shorts and stout walking boots – perfect for digging a heel in and pushing against the ground – and heading in the direction of the field where the tug of war was being held. There they were joined by Becky Ventress and the three other girls that made up their team.

Before long the girls were lined up, with the rope stretched out on the ground to the right of them. Despite the laughter of the spectators, the team wore determined expressions and a sense of tension was palpable in the air. Any competition between the YF branches was to be taken seriously; there was no such thing as "just" a tug of war. The adjudicator, Dave Marsay, a farmer from Beckinthwaite, stood where the central point had been chalked onto the ground. He called for them to take their positions and, in unison, they kicked the rope up to hand-height. They stood poised, rope in hand, waiting for his signal. Once the start was counted in, cries of encouragement rang out. 'Lean into it, Becky!' shouted Tim, her brother. 'Tiny steps, Danskelfe!' cried

John Danks from Tinkel Top Farm, as the two opposing teams heaved with all their might, leaning back and digging their heels into the ground, pulling and tugging, faces distorted with exertion. Finn's eyes were fixed on Romy who was putting her all into it.

Just then, Jimby Fairfax appeared beside him. 'Ey up, me aud mucker. I hope you've got your muscles flexed for when it's the lads' turn.' Jimby flashed his trademark smile, his eyes twinkling.

'Aye, summat like that.' Reluctantly tearing his eyes away from Romy, Finn threw Jimby a quick smile, spotting Ollie Cartwright and Molly's husband Pip beside him. Jimby and Ollie were on the Danskelfe tug of war team like Finn. However, Pip, who originally hailed from Wychwood Farm just outside of Middleton-le-Moors, and up until his recent move to Lytell Stangdale had been a member of the Middleton branch of Young Farmers, had decided to abstain from today's competitive events, citing split loyalties as his reason. His "deflection", as it had become jokingly referred to, had meant he'd endured endless ribbing from his fellow Young Farmers and he'd decided to wait until he'd lived in Lytell Stangdale for a few more years before joining in with any of the competitions.

'How're the Danskelfe lasses doing?' asked Ollie, peering over to where the battle was playing out. It was the perfect excuse for Finn to turn back to the tug-of-war – and to Romy.

'They're putting up a good scrap, but it looks like the Middleton lasses have the upper hand at the minute,' said Pip. 'And to be honest, being Middleton born and bred, I'm not sure where I should pitch my loyalties.'

Jimby and Ollie exchanged mock horrified expressions. 'Don't let our Moll hear you saying that, she'll have your nuts off before you've even noticed,' said Jimby – his cousin Molly was known for her feisty temperament.

'I reckon Pip might notice losing his nuts pretty quickly,' Ollie said dryly.

Finn couldn't help but chuckle at that.

'Hmm, point taken,' said Pip, wincing. 'In that case, it's definitely Danskelfe.'

'Aye, quite right an' all.' Jimby grinned at him. 'On those words, I reckon we need to give our lasses a bit of moral support.' He didn't waste a moment. Cupping his hands around his mouth, he shouted at the top of his lungs, 'Come on Danskelfe, give it some bloomin' welly!'

A loud cheer rang out followed by a chorus of, 'Danskelfe! Danskelfe! Danskelfe! Danskelfe!'

It seemed to work like a charm, and before they knew it, the Danskelfe team had hauled the Middleton lasses across the centre mark. A great roar of victory rang out and the Danskelfe girls leapt around, clapping, hugging one another and whooping with joy.

Not long after, the men's teams were being called for. 'Come on then, fellas, let's go and show Middleton Young Farmers how it's done.' Jimby winked at Pip then threw an arm around Finn and Ollie as the three of them headed over to where the rope was laid out.

Standing between Jimby and Ollie, Finn quickly swept his eyes over the crowd of spectators, desperate to catch a glimpse of Romy nearby. He'd been hoping she'd stick around long enough for him to get a chance to speak to her, but was disappointed when he couldn't spot her. The adjudicator's voice cut through his thoughts and before he knew it, the tug of war was underway. In amongst all the cheering and calling, he became aware of Romy's voice; he could pick it out anywhere. Feeling a surge of strength, Finn pulled back with all his might, Romy's voice running round his mind, sending happiness pulsing through him, overriding the burn in his muscles.

It must have been Danskelfe Young Farmers' lucky day since, just as the Middleton-le-Moors lads looked as though they were inches away from pulling their opponents over the centre mark, the Danskelfe team gave one final heave, taking Middleton by surprise. Their fortunes had changed in the blink of an eye.

As soon as they were done, Finn spotted Romy standing next to

Ella – it had always struck him how similar the two young women looked which he'd attributed to them sharing a relative in the same family tree, but today, with them dressed in matching T-shirts, their hair tied back in matching plaits, the similarity was even more striking. He'd hoped to join them, thinking that Romy might be a little less frosty towards him if Ella was around, but by the time he'd managed to extricate himself from the victors' celebratory conversation, Romy and Ella had gone. 'You've got to be kidding me!' Finn said under his breath. He wiped the sweat from his brow and blew out a sigh, conscious of the intense heat of the sun beating down.

Despite his attempts at trying to find her, Romy had remained elusive and he was beginning to think she must still be avoiding him. His heart lifted when he finally set eyes on her in the middle of a game of rounders with the Danskelfe team competing against the visitors. He stood, watching and sipping on a can of Coke, as Romy walloped the rounders ball with a hefty whack, sending it flying to the far end of the field. Giving a squawk of delight, she raced around all four bases amid rapturous cheers from her team-mates. By the time the ball was returned, she'd completed the full "rounder" and was leaping around with her friends who'd been lined up, waiting to bat. Finn couldn't help but smile. Whatever Romy did, she did with great enthusiasm, her upbeat temperament and friendly nature drawing people to her, just as it had him when he'd first got talking to her all those years ago. Watching her like this, Finn felt a rush of emotion encompass him. Is this what it felt like to be in love with someone? This was definitely more than just a teenage crush; the feeling was overpowering, it sent a tingle running over his skin, had his heart racing and his insides performing somersaults. He'd been talking himself in and out of telling her how he felt but now he realised that if he didn't tell her today his mind was in serious danger of exploding with it all.

Before long, the delicious aroma of burgers and sausages sizzling over the barbecue began wafting into the air, tempting people over to the farmyard where trestle tables had been set out with plates, cutlery, side dishes and condiments. Cans of drinks were kept cool in a couple of tin baths filled with ice cubes. Heading over to help his dad on the barbecue, Finn stopped in his tracks as he spotted Romy standing alongside his mum and Elizabeth Fairfax – Jimby and Kitty's mother. Romy was scooping coleslaw and potato salad onto plates, smiling and chatting away in her usual friendly manner. He was glad and not a little relieved that what had happened the other day hadn't affected how she behaved with his mum.

He'd been rehearsing what to say to her, hoping to catch her alone after the rounders match, but Jimby, Ollie and Pip had landed beside him again, and he'd been drawn into the conversation they were having about the new prize-winning Cheviot tup Molly's dad had bought from the mart over at Middleton-le-Moors. Frustratingly, the match had finished by the time Finn had managed to pull himself away. But now, seeing her here, looking so relaxed and happy, it galvanised his resolve to clear the air with her. 'Seize the moment, Finn. It's time to man up about your feelings,' he said to himself sotto voce.

With his paper plate piled high with food, he headed over to the field on the other side of the yard where a rustic seating area had been created using rectangular bales of hay. Sounds of the countryside filled the air, the low thrum of a tractor over at Tinkel Top Farm, Bill Campion's dairy herd baying over at Camplin Hall Farm as they moseyed their way along to the milking parlour. The moors acted as a backdrop, with the thatched rooftops of Lytell Stangdale in the distance. It made for a stunning sight, with the plush green fields butting-up to the more rugged moorland, not to mention the ancient ramparts of Danskelfe Castle further along Danskelfe Rigg. His gaze loitered on Holly Tree Cottage on the opposite side of the dale. It was a sight that warmed his heart, particularly when he knew Romy was staying there, even before these new and unexpected feelings had landed with a thud inside him. Glancing around, he spotted her sitting beside Ella, burger in hand, laughing and nodding at something her friend was saying.

Finn noted there was a space beside her, so plucking up every ounce of courage he could muster, he headed over to her, trying to keep his body language casual, and hoping that no one would be alerted to the turmoil currently raging inside him. He wasn't going to broach the subject with her straight away, his plan was simply to strike up a conversation with her, then ask if he could talk to her in private. He hoped with all his heart she was going to be friendly towards him because either way, he was going to get this off his chest. Despite his internal bravado, the thought had his stomach churning. *Oh, blimey!*

'Now then, Romes, all right if I park my bum here?' Finn asked, doing all he could to sound breezy and casual despite his galloping pulse.

She turned her face to him, shielding her eyes with her hand. 'Oh, hiya, Finn. Yeah, course, no probs.' She smiled broadly, sending a wave of relief washing over him. He noticed she'd caught the sun; her usual sprinkling of freckles had increased and her nose and cheeks were rosy. Strands of wavy hair had come loose from her plait, some curling around her face.

'Hiya, Finn.' Ella leant forward and smiled. 'Great barbecue, by the way. You and your parents have done an awesome job.'

'Thanks, I'll pass that on to them. My mum's been panicking about not doing enough food for everyone, but there seems to be plenty.'

'Tell me about it, my mum and dad were just the same when we hosted the barbecue at our farm the other year.' Ella giggled along with Romy. 'But there was definitely plenty; felt like we were eating pasta salad for days afterwards. And you're right, there's loads here.'

Before Finn had a chance to say anything else, they were surrounded by a group of their friends from Middleton-le-Moors Young Farmers', all eagerly talking about their next joint venture which was a Halloween disco at a farm just outside of the market town.

Dusk was closing in and Finn still hadn't found a suitable

opportunity to speak to Romy. He was gripped by frustration and disappointment in equal measure, though part of him did wonder if he was subconsciously avoiding it, fear of bringing the situation to a head holding him back. He cast his gaze around the dale, basking in the gentle, golden glow he so loved at this time of day. Lights from the cottages and farmhouses in the valley were appearing, and the birds were gradually heading off to roost. Just a few straggler Young Farmers remained. Sensing someone standing beside him he turned and was startled to see Romy. She looked up at him and they exchanged a smile. Finn was suddenly conscious of his thoughts grouping together, putting themselves in order, nerves making his pulse up its speed. This was the moment he'd been waiting for all day and he didn't want to blow it.

They stood together, not speaking as they looked out over the moors, the smell of the barbecue still lingering in the air. Finn's stomach was turning over as he gathered up every ounce of courage he possessed. He cleared his throat, his heart pounding so hard he felt sure she must be able to hear it. 'Romes...' Feeling oddly detached from his voice, he cleared his throat again. 'Romes, I... um...' *Oh, for crying out loud, Finn, spit it out!* He drew in a fortifying breath, aware of her turning to face him. 'Romes, first off, I just want you to know I'm sorry for grabbing your sketchbook. I didn't know it was going to upset you, and I'm really sorry it did.'

Romy shook her head. 'Finn, it should be me who's saying sorry for flouncing off the way I did. I—'

'It's okay, you don't need to apologise. Anyroad, there's something else... I need to tell you something and I want you to promise that once you hear it, if you don't like it... I mean, our friendship is... Well, what I'm trying to say is that I don't ever want to lose your friendship, it means too much.'

'But you won't, Finn,' she said softly. 'And I'm sorry if me going off in a daft huff made you think that.'

He heaved another sigh, looking down at her pretty face, her big green eyes flecked with gold gazing up at him so earnestly. He was sure his insides had turned to mush. 'The thing is, and I'm making a right muck-up of telling you, I... er... I've started to think of you in a bit of a different way – as in, more than a friendship sort of way, if that makes sense?' *Talk about a cackhanded way of telling a lass you fancy her!*

A loaded silence stretched out between them. Regret started to creep over his initial feeling of relief at getting his secret off his chest. If he thought his stomach had been churning before, it was doing massive somersaults and backflips now. He'd only gone and made a complete turkey of himself and had very probably lost his best friend in the process. He took a step back, dragging his hand around the back of his neck. *What have you done, you idiot?* Oh God, why did he have to go and open his big mouth? He needed to backtrack, and fast. 'Listen, Romes, just ignore what—'

'Finn, shh.' Romy pressed her finger to his lips. Then, taking his hand in hers she led him to the side of the barn where they were out of view of the farmhouse.

'What's up?' He looked down at her, his eyes searching hers. She looked so beautiful in the soft light. His gaze fell to her full lips, the urge to kiss them almost too much to bear. He reached out, tentatively cupping her face as his heart thudded, half expecting her to run off again. Instead, she stood on her tiptoes, wrapped her arms around his neck and kissed him.

What felt like a million fireworks exploded inside him as his brain played catch-up with what was happening. His mind started swirling, thoughts of how soft and warm her lips felt, how good it was to feel her in his arms at last tumbling into the mix as his emotions went into overdrive. He was completely lost in the moment, never wanting their kiss to end when Romy pulled away, leaving his body tingling for her.

They stood in silence for a moment, eyes locked on one another, breathless.

Romy was the first to speak. 'Thing is, Finn, I've been feeling the same way about you.' She shyly tucked a stray strand of hair behind her ear. 'Kind of crept up on me. I guess it's why I was sketching you the other day; cringe as it sounds. I felt embarrassed at you seeing it, thought you'd think it was weird or something.'

'Weird is the last thing I thought.' He gazed down at her, the evening light soft on her face, her eyes sparkling. He pulled her close; how was it possible to feel this happy? He gave in to the urge to kiss her again, thrilled to find his eagerness matched in her. He'd kissed other girls before but, wow, they'd never made him feel like this.

Their moment was shattered by the sound of Finn's dad calling him from the farmyard. They pulled apart quickly. 'Ey up, best not get caught snogging by the parents.' Finn pushed her hair off her face. 'Mind you, my two had actually guessed we fancied each other, you know?'

'Really? I thought I was being pretty good at keeping it to myself, and I never had the foggiest that you were feeling the same way. I wonder if anyone else has picked up on it? Ella hasn't mentioned anything.'

'No one's said owt to me either,' he said, his heart still soaring.

'Can't even begin to imagine how weird it's going to be 'fessing up that I fancy my best mate,' said Romy.

'Yep, it's going to be an odd 'un all right. Mind, I reckon we're not the only best mates who fancy each another. Joss and Ella?' He hitched a knowing eyebrow at her.

A smile spread across Romy's face. 'Ah, so you've spotted it too, then? I'd kind of suspected, but didn't know if I was heading off down the wrong track 'cos they've known each other for so long.'

'Hard to miss it, especially the way Joss gazes at her with his puppy dog eyes. Maybe when they find out about us, it might make them do something about their own feelings.'

'Here's hoping; they go well together.'

'True.' Finn nodded.

'Anyroad, we'd best go, your dad's looking for you and we don't want him to think we're up to no good.' She landed a playful punch to his bicep. 'And where did these things suddenly spring from?

Last time I looked you had the build of a stick of celery.' She gave his arm a squeeze.

'A stick of celery?' he said, amused. 'I can honestly say, I've never heard anyone be compared to a stick of celery before, and I reckon it's not a compliment.'

Romy was laughing too. 'It was the first stick-like thing that popped into my head. I s'pose a string bean would've made more sense. What I was trying to say was it's not long since you were a bit on the puny side.'

'Still not a compliment,' he said, shaking his head as Tommy's voice, calling Finn's name, rang out in the fading light.

SIXTEEN

Romy

Romy could have danced with happiness! Her worst fears hadn't just been allayed, they'd been sent well and truly packing. Not only had she hung onto her best friend, but their relationship had blossomed into something she'd hardly dared think possible – she didn't want to spoil the moment by worrying what would happen if things didn't work out; the way she was feeling right now, she couldn't ever imagine having to face that. Nobody had been more surprised than her when Finn had stood beside her and poured his heart out, telling her how he felt. She almost had to pinch herself at the way the situation had changed in a mere matter of days.

After she'd stomped off home, Romy had cursed herself for giving into the yearning to draw him that had taken over that day, unable to resist taking advantage of the perfect excuse to focus so intently on his handsome face. She'd been rumbled. She'd felt sure he'd think of her as some kind of loony stalker, and it was all her own doing. She'd been mortified, hardly able to sleep for torturing herself, her face burning with embarrassment every time it had popped into her mind, which had been practically every waking second.

But the following day, she'd given herself a good talking to. She reasoned that she was the only one who knew of her true feelings; she hadn't shared them with anyone, not even her good pal Ella, so why would Finn have the slightest clue about them? He knew she liked to draw. Granted, the sketches and paintings he'd seen so far had mostly been of the moors, moorland creatures and farm animals, not to mention the odd caricature, but Romy took comfort from the fact that she was sure she'd mentioned to him that she'd sketched her family before. This reasoning had helped assuage her dread of showing her face at Castlegate Farm for the barbecue, which she told herself she should do if only for Finn's parents' sake. The last thing she wanted was for Jill and Tommy to think she was upset with them. And she didn't want the awkwardness to continue with Finn. His friendship meant too much to her, and the thought of not seeing him again had triggered an agonising, physical ache in her heart. She'd go to the barbecue, help out as she'd promised she would, and act as if nothing had happened. Simple as that.

And now, after *those* kisses, she couldn't put into words how ecstatic she was that she'd done just that!

SEVENTEEN

Finn

As expected, Finn's parents hadn't been at all surprised when their son shared the news that he and Romy were an item. 'Well, it's taken you both long enough to get your bloomin' act together,' Tommy had said, laughing. 'I can't think of a more suited pair.'

Jill had beamed. 'And it's good that you were friends first, just like your dad and me.'

From what Romy had told Finn, it would seem her dad had been just as enthusiastic, but then again, he'd made no secret of the fact that he was fond of Finn.

'My dad said he couldn't think of a better lad for me to go out with, and he's known for being a really good judge of character, so you must be all right,' Romy had said jokingly, nudging Finn with her elbow, making him break out into a wide smile. Hearing that her dad held him in such high regard meant the world to Finn, and the feeling was mutual; he was fond of Vernon too.

It came as no surprise to the couple that Dulcie's response was cooler. 'She reckons if things don't work out, we won't be able to go back to just being friends,' Romy said. 'But don't take any notice, you know what Mum's like, she always takes the doom and gloom point of view. Says it's not good to live with your head in the clouds or see the world through rose-tinted glasses. I told her whatever happened, we'd always be friends.'

'Oh right.' Finn hadn't expected Dulcie to be so blunt about it and throw cold water over her daughter's happiness.

Romy had evidently sensed what was going through his mind. She'd slipped her arms around him and brushed her lips against his. 'Just ignore her, she's forgotten what it's like to be young. I don't think she knows how she sounds sometimes. And I think she might even be a bit jealous; she's always complaining about my dad putting his work before her.'

But Finn hadn't been able to ignore Dulcie's words, they'd sent unease curling around inside him. It had been something that had lurked at the furthest corners of his mind but he hadn't wanted to face it. Having someone else vocalise it, even if it was Dulcie who was known for her pessimism, added weight to his concern. Romy may be his girlfriend now, but he still thought of her as his best friend, still wanted to share his thoughts and dreams and secrets with her. It would be unbearable if things didn't work out. And though he was only seventeen, whenever he pictured his future, Romy was there. He'd hoped their relationship would progress like his parents' had, that they'd be together forever. Losing her friend-ship wasn't an option, he'd decided. He'd do all he could to keep it.

He'd been pulled away from pondering any further when Romy went on to share Tristan's reaction to hearing that they'd moved on from being just "friends" to boyfriend and girlfriend. 'Honest, it was so funny. He scrunched up his face and just said, "*Weird*".' Romy had collapsed into a fit of the giggles with Finn joining her as he pictured her brother's expression. He didn't know Tris all that well, since her brother kept himself to himself and never got involved in any of the Young Farmers' social activi-ties. He'd always given Finn the faint impression he looked down his nose at them, not that he'd shared this with Romy. Dougie had voiced his opinions more bluntly to his brother, describing Tristan as a stuck-up prat who should take his superior attitude and shove it where the sun don't shine. Finn couldn't help but agree.

It had been five months since the Young Farmers' barbecue at Castlegate Farm. The time had whizzed by in a blur. Finn and Romy had grown closer with each passing week, grasping every opportunity to be together. Rather than feeling weird – as Tristan had put it – starting off as friends seemed to have galvanised their relationship. They already knew each other well; there were no unexpected personality traits to take them by surprise and cause their romance to falter. They'd even talked about Romy moving to Lytell Stangdale full-time after she'd finished at college, which they agreed would be the perfect place for her to start her career as an artist, having so much inspiration on the doorstep.

It wasn't long before Finn had found he'd fallen more deeply in love with Romy than he'd ever thought possible. Even at such a young age, he had a feeling in his gut that told him he'd found his soulmate.

And, despite the initial surprise, their group of friends had soon grown used to Finn and Romy's new relationship status, regularly commenting on how well they went together and wondering how they hadn't spotted it sooner. 'Oh my God, you two look so cute together!' Ella had said after Romy told her. It had been on the tip of Romy's tongue to suggest that she'd sensed something bubbling under the surface with her friend and Joss Campion but thought better of it for the moment, not wanting to make things awkward between the two friends if she was wide of the mark.

Finn had been dreading the end of the summer holidays when Romy and her family would return to Rickelthorpe, though he'd taken some consolation in the knowledge that they would be back for their weekend visits.

When September arrived, it would seem absence most definitely did make the heart grow fonder and Fridays couldn't come round quickly enough for Finn. He'd wait until the farm's landline would ring, usually just before seven p.m., with Romy calling to say she'd arrived at Holly Tree Cottage – though they both had mobile phones, the signal was patchy and unreliable in their part of the North Yorkshire Moors. Then, with anticipation coursing through his veins, he'd jump into the Land Rover and race over to the village to meet her. While the evenings were still pleasant and daylight allowed, they'd go for a walk, heading out over Great Stangdale Rigg where the air was particularly clear and fresh. They'd chat about what had gone on in their week and more recently, their plans for the future, their conversations punctuated by heady kisses.

As autumn, and eventually winter, drew in, and darkness ruled out walking to the rigg, Finn would scoop her up and take her back to the farm. Much as Romy's parents were fond of him and he of them, her mother's strict and slightly disapproving nature hung heavy in the air of Holly Tree Cottage which, Finn thought, might have added to the reason Romy had become eager to escape rather than for them to hang around there for long. In the little time he'd spent with the family it had often crossed his mind that her parents were an odd match, which was the complete opposite to his own parents who'd just always seemed so comfortable and happy together. Whereas Romy's dad, Vernon, was jolly and upbeat and never without a smile – traits Romy had inherited from him – Dulcie had become more pinch-lipped and serious, her face rarely troubled by a smile. Her frostiness appeared to have increased over the last few months if the atmosphere she created was anything to go by.

'I don't know what the heck's bothering my mum at the minute but she seems preoccupied, keeps biting my poor dad's head off which isn't like her. She's been going on about how he cares more about his business than he does her and that he hardly spends any time with her, that when he's here, he's always working. I even overheard her telling him it's causing them to drift apart,' Romy had said as Finn drove her back to Castlegate Farm one Friday evening, the lights from the Land Rover picking out the way along the dark country lanes, frost sparkling on the ungritted roads.

'Well, just try to enjoy yourself tonight. People say all sorts when they're angry,' Finn had said.

The following week, something reached Finn's ears that had shocked him to the core, and made him realise what it was that had been bothering Dulcie Stainthorpe.

A rumour had started circulating, and if he'd been asked to guess the identity of those involved, never in a million years would he have got it right. The knowledge had made him feel sick and he would have given anything to unhear it.

Once the details had sunk in, he'd been torn between feeling he should mention something to Romy, and not wanting to be the bearer of news that would cause her distress. He'd tried to put himself in her position, wondering how he would feel if she delivered a piece of unpalatable gossip about his parents. Or, on the other hand, how he'd feel if she'd kept it to herself, arguing that it was just a rumour and nothing concrete. He'd sought advice from his parents, who'd also heard the rumblings. Between them they'd come to the conclusion that Romy would probably be more hurt if she found out he'd kept it from her and, difficult as it would be, that it would probably be best for him to tell her. Much as Finn had felt it was the right thing to do, the prospect had kept him awake at night, his stomach twisting and churning into the early hours. It didn't help that it was the week before Christmas and the family would be arriving for their usual fortnight stay over the festive period.

And now that day had arrived.

The timing couldn't have been worse.

Though Finn and his parents had agreed it was only fair that Romy be given the chance to prepare herself in case things blew up over Christmas, knowing the right time to deliver such awful news wasn't easy. And it didn't help that the young couple were due to join their friends for the usual pre-Christmas get-together in the back room at the Sunne that evening. The landlord let them hang out and listen to music there on the condition they bought crisps and drinks, which was something they were only too happy to do. Romy had mentioned in their phone call earlier in the week how much she'd been looking forward to it and the excitement in her voice had been tangible. Tonight wasn't the time for dropping bombshells, so he decided to speak to her about what he'd heard the following day. He felt inexorably relieved of the day's grace it allowed him. He just hoped his assumption that no one in their circle of friends would say anything before then would be proved right.

Finn and Romy had been sitting at a table in the back room of the Sunne with Ella and Joss since they'd first arrived, Christmas pop songs blaring out from the portable CD player. The festive decorations that trimmed the shabby room had seen better days. The tinsel festooned from the beams was bald in places and appeared to have come out in sympathy with the artificial Christmas tree that stood at a lopsided angle, its branches bent and sparse. The fairy lights draped around it didn't work and a broken star sat wonkily on the top branch, which just about summed-up the spirit of the pub. But the young revellers expected nothing better from Hacky Harold; they were just grateful for the effort and that he let them have the use of the room every weekend.

With the CD coming to an end, Ella and Joss went over to change the disc. Romy set her glass of Coke down on the table and leant more closely into Finn, who put his arm around her. 'I've been talking to Dad about potentially moving to the cottage full-time after college is finished. I mean, I know it's quite a long way off, but I thought it'd give him plenty of time to get used to the idea.'

'Oh aye, what did he have to say?'

'He was surprised, but when he'd had a chance to think about it, he said it sounded like a good idea, especially since I've sold some of my watercolours of the moors for a decent price and have even got some commissions out of it. Haven't mentioned it to Mum yet. Dad thought I should wait for the right moment; said he'd tackle her with me, moral support and all that.'

Finn's stomach clenched at Romy's mention of her mother but he forced a smile and tried to inject a cheerful note into his voice. 'Wow! That's great, Romes, I mean about your dad being on board with you moving here.'

'I know, I'm really chuffed.'

'And did he give you any idea of how he thought your mum would take it?' He couldn't imagine Dulcie giving her approval at the best of times, never mind if what he'd heard recently was true.

Romy pulled a face. 'No, he didn't. She's been so prickly recently, none of us dare speak to her. Even Tris is being wary, said she's got a face like a slapped backside. And you know how unlike him it is to criticise her. Said she'd bitten his head off the other day when he asked...'

Finn gulped, Romy's words fading as his focus slipped away, wondering if the whispers had filtered through to Dulcie, contributing to her mood. He told himself she was probably still oblivious, reasoning if she knew, she probably would've stayed well clear of the village. But then again, doing that would raise other questions, encourage people to draw conclusions that may not necessarily be right. He rubbed his brow with his fingertips. Ughh! He wished he didn't have this taking up so much of his headspace, especially not tonight.

'What do you think?' Romy's question snapped him back into the moment. He turned to see her looking up at him, a troubled expression clouding her pretty features.

'Sorry, Romes, I was lost in my thoughts for a minute there.'

'You're not kidding. You still like the idea of me moving to the cottage, don't you?'

He reached for her hand, pressing it to his lips. 'Course I do. You know I can't wait. I miss you when you're away, the week seems to drag 'til Friday. I was just thinking how cool it'll be having you here all the time.'

Finn was relieved to see her frown lift and her smile return. 'Yeah, I can't wait either. Hopefully Dad will make Mum see what a good idea it'd be, plus it'd get me out of her hair, which I'm sure she'd be happy about.'

Just then, Ella and Joss returned to the table and for the next forty-five minutes the four of them watched with great amusement as Joss's older brother attempted to chat up the new girl who'd recently moved to Rigg End Farm in the dale.

'Looks like that's another lass our Rich can add to his extensive list of those he's bored to tears,' Joss said, snorting a laugh. 'She keeps looking around for a way to escape.'

'Aye, I have to say, she's not looking too thrilled,' said Finn.

Their attention was snatched away from the couple by Tris bursting through the door, his face white as a sheet, his chest heaving. He hurriedly scanned the room before rushing over to them. 'Romy, you need to get home now,' he said, his words coming out in a rush.

Romy stared at her brother for several long moments as panic reared in Finn's stomach. He had a gut-wrenching feeling he knew what this was about, though it flitted across his mind that Tris's reaction seemed a little over the top. And why did Romy need to be dragged into it in such a dramatic way? If anything, such behaviour would only serve to fan the flames of the rumours.

'Why? I'm not ready to go yet. Don't tell me Mum's still in a bad mood and has decided she's going to make everyone as miserable as her this Christmas. She's had a face like thunder since we got here; I was glad to get out of her way.'

'It's nothing to do with Mum! It's Dad. Will you just come on,' Tristan said urgently, his breathing ragged. 'I'll tell you on the way back to the cottage, but we need to leave now.'

'Is everything okay, Tris?' asked Finn, noting the distress in Tristan's eyes. Surely this wasn't the result of him finding out about his mother?

Tris shook his head, his voice faltering. 'You've got to make Romy listen, Finn. It's urgent. My dad's—'

'Why? What's the matter with Dad? Where's Mum? Why has she sent you to come and get me?'

Tristan dragged a hand down his face. 'For crying out loud, Romy! Why do you always have to be like this? Always questioning things. Only doing what you want to do, constantly pushing back. It's exhausting and you need to listen, okay? For once in your life can you just do as someone asks you?'

'All right, keep your hair on.' Romy threw her brother an angry look. 'I just don't get all the cloak and dagger stuff, it's totally over the top.'

'I don't want to tell you here, okay?' A tear plopped onto his cheek. 'We need to leave. Now.' He reached for her arm, attempting to pull her to her feet.

A sense of doom fell over Finn like a brooding shadow.

'Why? Tell me what?' She shrugged her arm free. 'For God's sake, Tris, just tell me what's going on. I'm not moving until you do.'

'We need to go back to Rickelthorpe. Now! I'll tell you why outside, but please, come on!'

Tris's frustration hung in the air, creeping over the friends and snuffing out the celebratory atmosphere. Ella caught Finn's eye and pulled a face that suggested she'd heard the gossip about Dulcie, too.

'Romes, I think you should maybe listen to Tris,' Ella said softly. 'You can always come back here afterwards, we're not going anywhere.'

'I agree, and it would be better coming from your mum,' said Finn. He had a bad feeling about this; something told him there must be more to the rumours than he'd originally thought.

'Why do I get the feeling you know something I don't?' She eyed Finn warily, making his insides twist. He struggled to meet her gaze. 'Have you been keeping something from me?' She glanced over at Ella.

'I was going to mention—'

'What? How come you know when we've just heard?' Tristan said sharply, cutting Finn off.

'This is too much. Heard what?' Romy pushed her hands into her hair, frustrated. Finn could feel her shaking beside him.

'Come on, Romes, I think we should talk about this outside.' He got to his feet and reached for her coat, helping her on with it, all the while wondering how she was going to take the news.

They followed Tris as he rushed outside where a thick frost had the village in its grip. Hurrying to catch him up, Romy grabbed her brother's arm, bringing them both to a halt as she almost lost her footing. 'I'm not going any further until you tell me what's going on. I'm not having Mum take her bad mood out on me, dragging me back just so she can spread her misery.'

Under the light of the streetlamp, Tristan's distress was even more apparent, his face wet with tears. He threw his head back frustratedly as a sob wracked his body. 'Please, Romy, stop this!' His words came out in a cloud of mist. 'We need to get back to Rickelthorpe tonight. Why don't you get how urgent this is? We don't have much time. Dad's in hospital, in intensive care. He collapsed. It's his heart. We need to go.'

Romy gasped, her hands flying to her mouth. 'No!' Tears started spilling from her eyes. 'No! No! No! I don't believe it! You're wrong! It's someone else! It's not Dad, it can't be Dad!'

Shock rammed into Finn, rendering him unable to speak. This wasn't what he'd expected to hear and it took a few moments to sink in. He glanced over at Romy, her stunned expression making his heart twist. 'I'm so sorry, Romes.' He instinctively went to wrap his arms around her, but she stepped away from him, shaking her head.

'Is he going to be okay?' she asked, her body shaking, her eyes wide with shock. The dim lighting did nothing to hide how the colour had drained from her face. 'Tell me, Tris! Is Dad going to be okay?' she shouted.

Finn had never felt so helpless.

'I don't know, it's too early to say,' Tris said. 'But we need to get back to the cottage now, no more wasting time. Mum wants us to go back to Rickelthorpe so we can be near him. Come on.'

'How are you getting there?' Finn asked. He knew Dulcie didn't drive; wouldn't be fit to anyway, nor Tristan for that matter.

'It's sorted,' Tris said, reverting to the cool tone he usually reserved for Finn. 'Mum just wants Romy back so we can set off as soon as possible, especially with the weather about to get worse.' He turned to walk away.

'Course.' Finn nodded, myriad thoughts rushing through his mind. Romy had mentioned how her father had taken a call to do with his work just before she'd headed out that night. She'd said he'd looked uncharacteristically concerned, but that he'd told her he was just miffed that he'd been troubled with a problem so close to Christmas. She'd joked it was probably more to do with her mum being in a grouchy mood and that he'd just been trying to cover for her. But in Finn's mind none of this added up and now he didn't know what to think.

'You know where I am if you need me, Romy,' he called after her, but she didn't turn around and his words fell unanswered onto the ground around him.

As he watched her rush along the icy trod, trying to catch up with her brother, he had no idea that it would be the last time he'd set eyes on her for twenty-one years.

EIGHTEEN

PRESENT DAY – THE SUNNE INNE

Finn

Finn wasn't sure how long he'd been standing there, staring at Romy Stainthorpe, his mouth opening and closing like some sort of comedy goldfish, as those last six heady months he'd spent with Romy twenty-one years ago hurtled through his mind. He blinked, gradually becoming aware of Jimby's voice breaking through his muddled thoughts. 'Now then, Finn lad,' said the blacksmith in his familiar jovial tone. 'It's grand you came. I can guarantee you won't regret it.'

'And Ted seems to be enjoying himself already.' Ollie nodded towards the Labrador who was sitting beside Romy.

Pulled back into the moment, Finn looked over at his friends, then to Ted, who he noted was wearing his familiar hapless smile, but his brain was still too fuddled to form any sort of coherent reply. 'Um, er... yeah.' He moved his gaze back to Romy, his heart lifting when she smiled at him. It made him think of the sun coming out on a cloudy day, just as it used to all those years ago. He smiled back, happiness unexpectedly creeping over him, the clouds in his mind clearing. He felt suddenly glad he'd accepted Jimby's offer of the spare ticket, and that he'd bothered to get changed into something half decent and not the jumper and jeans that had seen better days he usually opted for whenever he ventured off the farm and into society.

'You remember Romy Stainthorpe, don't you?' asked Jimby.

'Course he does, Jimby,' Kitty said softly, throwing Finn an apologetic glance.

Finn could swear he detected a mischievous glint in Jimby's eye. 'Yeah, I do. Not seen her for a while though.' He gave Kitty an uncertain smile.

''Ere, let me get you a pint of that beer I was telling you about the other day, Old Micklewick Magic,' Jimby said, oblivious to the fact he'd just plonked his size tens into a delicate situation. 'It's right grand stuff.'

'Thanks, Jimby, that's kind, but I'll have to try it another time; I've come in the Landie so I'm just on the shandy tonight. Jonty was on with it when Ted did his disappearing act.' He shot Ted a faux stern look and the Labrador responded with a quick swish of his tail. Finn couldn't help but smile. 'I'll just go and grab it. Everyone else okay for a drink?' he asked, his gaze sweeping the table while his heart danced a happy jig as he caught Romy's eye. Maybe tonight wasn't going to be so bad after all.

Returning as quickly as he could, Finn set his glass down on the table in front of the empty seat which, he noted, was conveniently opposite Romy, his mind swirling with a million questions as he unbuttoned his jacket and slid it over the back of the chair. Sitting down, he allowed his gaze to linger on her for a moment. The beautiful girl of his memories, with the cute button nose and striking green eyes, had blossomed into a stunning young woman. She was a year younger than him, so that would make her thirty-seven. Her hair was still the glossy chestnut waves of his memories – if not a little tamer – though it seemed to have taken on a golden hue in the soft lighting of the pub. And she still exuded that joyful air that used to draw people to her, made her feel good to be around. He wondered what she'd been doing in the years that had passed since he'd last seen her. Had they been kind to her? He hoped so, especially after the tragedy surrounding her father. Her eyes met his and she smiled, her cheeks flushing, which set a flutter away in his stomach.

He took a sip of his shandy as he marshalled his thoughts. Ted, who was now sitting on the floor beside him, pushed his head into his lap. Finn reached down with his free hand, absently rubbing the Labrador's ears. 'So, how've you been?' he asked Romy, aware that the others at the table were doing their best not to listen.

'Good, yeah. How about you?'

Years' worth of questions stretched out between them. It was as if the lid of an old box had creaked open, the memories that had lain dormant within, slipping out and dusting themselves off, mingling with the long-forgotten feelings they'd disturbed.

How have *I* been? How the heck did he answer that after the last eighteen months he'd had? Where did he start without it sounding all doom and gloom? Never mind how he'd felt when Romy had left so abruptly without a word of explanation all those years ago. She'd even ignored his calls. Ghosted him, he believed was the fashionable word for it these days. Finn had first heard the term when Britt had told him she didn't have the luxury of "ghosting" him since their boys still tied them together. '*Ouch!*' he'd said to himself at the time. He rubbed his hand over his chin; he didn't want to think about his ex right now, he wanted to hear about Romy, the girl he'd loved with a passion he hadn't thought himself capable of – nor felt since – and who'd just disappeared without a backwards glance, leaving his heart in tatters. What he'd learnt later had gone some way to helping him understand, but at the time, he'd been utterly baffled by her complete break of contact. Seeing her again tonight had resurrected the numerous questions he'd harboured for so long, but he was conscious of not wanting to start off on a negative note. Nor did he want to launch into a splurge of what had happened with his marriage, the hurt he felt at how rarely he saw his sons; he didn't want to risk it coming out in a bitter, angry vomit. Inflicting something like that on her, after all these years, was hardly likely to create a good impression, which was something he found he was keen to do. Added to the mix, there was also the fact that he suddenly felt inordinately overjoyed to see her and the feeling was growing with surprising speed, lifting his spirits along with it.

'It's been a bit of a trying eighteen months but things are getting better.' He gave a smile, hoping she wouldn't push him to elaborate right now, especially since he had so many questions of his own – not being a fan of social media, he didn't have any of the usual accounts that might have helped him track her down, so he really was genuinely in the dark about her. He was desperate to know what she'd been doing with her life over the last twenty-one years, that she'd been okay. All he knew was that she *looked* well, but other than that, he hardly knew where to start. Was she married? Did she have kids? 'So, how come you're back in Lytell Stangdale? Whereabouts are you staying? Have you come with anyone else?' He found himself hoping she hadn't come with a partner. 'Sorry for all the questions.' He pulled an apologetic face before reaching for his glass. He hadn't even got started yet.

'It's okay, we've got a lot of catching up to do.' She gave an uncertain laugh and drew in a deep breath. 'You're not going to believe this, but I'm staying at Holly Tree Cottage. I've booked it for two weeks over the festive break.'

He paused, his glass halfway to his mouth. 'Holly... Holly Tree Cottage, as in the one your parents used to own? Where you used to spend the summer?'

She nodded, laughing at his surprise. 'Yep, the very one.'

'Wow. That must feel kind of weird.'

'Not as much as you'd expect. Obviously, the décor's changed a lot since we had it, and all the scrappy, dilapidated furniture's gone, but I was really pleased to find it's still got its lovely, cosy atmosphere like it did when it belonged to my parents. I know it's going to sound daft, but it actually feels like I've never been away; all the memories are still there.'

He nodded, wondering what sort of memories she was referring to; from her expression, he guessed they were happy ones and that thought gladdened him, especially after what had happened; he found he wanted her to feel happy. At the time, he hadn't known what had caused her family to pack up and leave so suddenly, a "For Sale" sign appearing at the gate of the cottage straight after Christmas, but the news had slowly filtered through; it hadn't just been to do with the rumours he'd heard about her mother. It would have been a hard time for Romy, especially with how close she'd been to her father.

He stole a look sideways at the others to see they were all now engrossed in a conversation about Jimby's wayward cockerel, Reg, and his latest misdemeanours chasing the new postman around the village, the obnoxious bird clinging to the postie's mailbag and squawking vociferously. He briefly wondered what Romy would make of the cantankerous Leghorn Jimby seemed so fond of despite the grief it caused him.

'So, has paying the village a visit been on your mind for a while?' He wondered as to the reason behind her return. He desperately wanted to ask if she'd thought much about him over the years, as he had her, but pride, and not wanting to sound pushy, meant he held back. Nor did he want to put her on the spot.

'No, not at all. It all happened quite by chance, and at a time when I was keen to get away from everything.' He listened as she told him how she'd spotted it advertised in a magazine.

'I've had a bit of a year too. It's going to sound daft, but seeing the cottage there, looking back at me felt like a sign, that fate was somehow talking to me, guiding me back here.' She gave an embarrassed giggle. 'So I went ahead and booked it straight away.'

'Doesn't sound daft at all. It sounds like a sign to me, too,' Finn said softly. 'And I'm glad you did.'

'Yeah, so am I.' Their eyes met and they shared a smile.

Their conversation was interrupted by Jonty ringing the shiny brass bell above the bar, accompanied by the sound of a guitar tuning up. 'Can I have your attention please, folks?' he said in his plummy tones. 'First of all, I'd like to thank you all for coming this evening. As you're aware, tonight's buffet has been arranged to raise funds to help with the running of the community minibus. Continuing in the spirit of things, Bea and I have decided that, since it's for such a wonderful cause, we're going to add tonight's profits from the bar to the pot too.' He paused, waiting for the small round of applause his words had generated to peter out. 'And now, you'll all no doubt be pleased to hear that Gabe is poised and waiting to give our ears a treat for the next half hour. After which the buffet will be open for those of you who have tickets.'

Finn leant over the table to Romy. 'I'm guessing you got the other ticket that was "going spare",' he said with a chuckle. It crossed his mind that Jimby and his sister had very likely been working in cahoots to get them together once they found out Romy was back.

'I did.' She laughed too.

'So, without further ado,' said Jonty, 'I give you the one and only Gabe Dublin and his band.'

A cheer accompanied by enthusiastic applause rang around the pub, punctuated by whistles and thumping of tables.

'Thanks, everyone, you're always so kind,' Gabe said in his soft Southern Irish accent once the cheers had settled. He was wearing his usual garb of ripped jeans and slogan T-shirt. 'I'm gonna start with the Christmas song I wrote a few years back. So, if you know it, please join in, especially with the chorus. I'm a little rusty since I gave up performing professionally, so please forgive any bum notes.' He flashed a grin from beneath his floppy fringe. 'And, before we get going, I'd like to thank my best buddy Sim and his little sister Fleur for being my band tonight. Cheers, guys, you're the best.' In the next moment, the pub was filled with the sound of Gabe's distinctive indie/rock music. His rich, smoky voice, with a hint of his Dublin accent, was complemented perfectly by Sim's rousing beat on the bodhran and Fleur's lively fiddle playing. The Sunne's clientele didn't hold back, clapping, tapping their feet and singing along with great gusto as Gabe and his band spent the next thirty minutes blasting out their lively renditions of Christmas songs, adding their own twist to familiar contemporary festive tunes.

'Oh my days, that was *amazing*!' said Romy, her eyes shining as she clapped her hands enthusiastically.

'Yeah, Gabe's awesome,' Finn said, smiling at her, their eyes locking. 'He moved to the village a while back. He's close to Lady Carolyn Hammondely who's Sim's missus, and used to hide out at Danskelfe Castle with them, 'til he bought the Manor House and moved in there. He's very quiet, down to earth and not at all starry, fits in well round here.'

'That's good to hear.' Romy nodded.

The bell above the bar rang out once more. The group of friends paused their chatter and turned to face Jonty. 'Huge thanks to Gabe, Sim and Fleur for that amazing performance. What a wonderful start to the evening.' Yet more cheers and clapping broke out, Jonty waiting until it had subsided before he continued. 'Bea has just informed me that the dining room is now open, so those of you with tickets are welcome to make your way there whenever you're ready. Our new barmaid, Lydia, is waiting at the door, and she'll give you a plate in exchange for your ticket. You'll see the buffet's set out on the table at the back of the room and I'm very happy to confirm, in my capacity as chief of quality control, that Bea and Lucas have excelled themselves and the food is absolutely scrumptious. We'll be continuing our singalong afterwards, so tuck in, folks, and enjoy.'

Finn felt suddenly hungry; his stomach growled, reminding him he hadn't eaten since midday and even then, he hadn't had much. He'd lost his appetite since his last call with Britt. And he'd left his mum's casserole in the Aga, expecting not to stay long enough to eat at the Sunne. Experience of the range oven told him it wouldn't come to any harm there and it would no doubt enrich the flavours.

'Fancy getting a bite to eat?' he asked Romy, as the others at the table started making their way over to the dining room.

'Definitely, especially after what I've been hearing about the landlady's cooking. Plus, I'm starving. I could eat a scabby horse...'

'...between two mattresses,' they said in unison, before bursting out laughing. It used to be a favourite saying of Romy's all those years ago, with them joking about her claims that she was constantly hungry. She'd used it with such regularity that it had almost become her catchphrase. Their eyes locked, an unspoken moment passing between them.

'What about Ted? Will he be okay here?' Romy asked, breaking the spell. On hearing his name, the Labrador shuffled over to her and she smoothed her hand over his velvety ears.

'Hmm. Might be best if we wait for the queue to die down. Then I'll hook his lead under the table leg, ask Jimby to keep an eye on him while we're gone.'

'Sounds like a good plan,' she said.

Finn was finding it hard to take his eyes off Romy. It still felt surreal seeing her sitting here in the pub, actually having a conversation with her, and yet something about it felt so comfortable.

When just the two of them were left at the table, her smile fell and a troubled expression made her brows draw together. 'Finn, I just want to say how sorry I am about... about ignoring your calls and texts, and not getting in touch with you after that night. I feel I have to say it before it eats me up inside. You didn't deserve that, me disappearing without giving you an explanation, especially after what happened with my dad.'

Seeing her discomfort tugged at his heart. 'Hey, it's okay, I understand. It can't have been easy for you.' He resisted the temptation to say she could have got in touch at any time afterwards.

'It's not okay, not okay at all. It's just... well, a lot had happened, and everything with my dad, and... well, it was a really difficult time. And I thought you knew more than you did. But if you'll let me, I'd like to explain it all to you – obviously not right now – but it's really important that you know. I felt terrible doing what I did but... well, everything was such a mess... and the longer I left it, the harder it was to call. Seeing you again has brought it all back to the surface. Is there any way you could find time to meet up so we can have a chat, just the two of us? If your wife or partner wouldn't mind, that is.'

His eyes fell to his glass and he swallowed. 'I don't have a wife, or partner, or girlfriend for that matter. I'm divorced, so it's just Ted and me up at Castlegate Farm now; my parents live in a converted barn on the farm, they moved out so me and Britt – my then wife – could have the farmhouse.' He glanced up, pushing a smile onto his face. The last thing he wanted was Romy feeling sorry for him, that he was seeking her pity or sympathy.

'I'm sorry to hear your marriage didn't work out,' she said, giving a sympathetic smile.

'Don't be, it was a long time coming, I can see that now.'

'Same here. I'm divorced, too, and single.'

Well, this was a turn up for the books. Finn felt a thin shaft of light pierce through the dense cloud of darkness that had hung over him and dampened his spirits for so long. As he studied her face, taking in the expression in her eyes, a feeling of warmth started slowly spreading through him. It was as if a thaw had set in, melting the ice that had surrounded his heart for the last eighteen months. He'd kept it packed away, his defence mechanism, saving it from further hurt.

Suddenly things didn't seem so bad.

NINETEEN

Romy

The food had been delicious. Romy had particularly enjoyed the miniature Christmas-dinner pies. They'd been jam-packed with plump pieces of succulent turkey and complemented by just the right amount of winter vegetables and herbs, oozing with a rich gravy and encased in the most mouthwatering buttery pastry. She'd been amazed to find they had genuinely tasted like a Christmas dinner! And she'd enjoyed them so much she'd treated herself to two. They went perfectly with the pigs in blankets and homemade cranberry sauce which were on offer amongst an array of other mouthwatering bitesize treats. To finish there was a huge cheese board piled high with a variety of cheeses and biscuits – the cheese flavoured with spiced apple sounded particularly tasty – draped with plump grapes, while pots of sticky homemade Sunne Inne chutney sat alongside. For those with a sweet tooth, there was a choice of mini trifles, sprinkled with sparkling praline, or clementine cheesecake topped with crushed brandysnap and served with Christmas pudding ice cream. Everything was done with flair and packed a punch of flavour.

While they were tucking into their food, Finn and Romy had

been in conversation with Kitty and the rest of the group, catching up on local happenings, the chatter lively and animated. It had felt good to be able to slot back in so easily.

Soon Romy found the conversation had shrunk to just herself and Finn, the others talking amongst themselves. Something told her it had been deliberate, to allow them to catch up. Ted looked on patiently in the hope of a stray morsel coming his way; his expression made her smile. The awkwardness of earlier had slipped away between Romy and Finn, and she couldn't remember the last time she'd felt so relaxed in someone else's company. The conversation between them flowed with such ease, it was as if the years since they'd last been in one another's company had shrunk away to nothing.

'So, how are your mum and dad?' she asked, the glow from the fire shining in her eyes. She felt a squeeze of guilt in her chest at the reminder of how she'd repaid the kindness they'd shown her by blanking them from her life.

'They're doing fine, thanks. My dad's been grumbling about having a dodgy knee, but other than that he's doing all right. And my mum's always busy what with all the clubs and meetings they have going on in the village. And she still looks after the hens.'

Romy smiled, a fond memory of feeding the hens and collecting eggs at Castlegate Farm filling her mind. 'Ah, that's good to hear.'

'How about your family? How're they doing?' he asked. The discomfort that briefly flickered in his eyes didn't escape her.

'My mum's just the same, still despairs of me and my decisions.' She laughed, making light of it, though in truth it hurt at times. 'Tris is still the golden boy in her eyes; she followed him when he moved down to Oxford. He's an accountant, like our dad, has his own firm, is very successful...' She paused, wondering how much Finn thought, like everyone else, how it was an odd choice of career after what had happened with their father, but his expression was inscrutable. 'As for Tally, she's just got married. She's settled in Australia now after travelling back and forth for years, works as a yoga instructor. She and her husband, who's an Aussie, have a beachside restaurant – very successful by all accounts. She's totally embraced the lifestyle, even has an Australian twang to her accent.'

Finn smiled. 'Wow. They seem to have their lives sorted.'

'Yep, there's just me who is, to quote my mother, "floating aimlessly around with no goal in my life or plans for my future".' She held back from saying her relationship with her mum had never properly recovered after the revelations of that evening all those years ago.

'I'm sure that's not the case, and I'm sure she doesn't mean it.'

Romy gave a shrug. She'd long-since given up letting her mother's negative opinions bother her, especially after she'd taken Russ's side in the divorce. 'Part of the reason I came here is to see if I can recalibrate; get my life back on track.'

'Well, if you ask me, you came to the right place; if anywhere can do that, it's Lytell Stangdale.'

'I reckon you're right,' she said.

'So, did you follow your dreams and become an artist?' he asked.

She drew in a breath and was just about to answer when Jonty called for last orders, ringing the bell above the bar.

'Anyone fancy a last drink?' Jimby asked, smiling round at the group of friends.

Finn looked at his watch. Romy could see he was torn; he'd need to be up early for the farm the following morning. In truth she was feeling tired; she'd hardly slept the night before, her mind had been too wired, anticipating her return to the village, plus she'd had enough wine. But then again, she had enjoyed the unexpected pleasure of being in Finn's company after all these years.

'I think I've had my quota of shandy, thanks, Jimby, I'd best be heading off,' said Finn.

Though she'd expected him to decline Jimby's offer, it didn't stop his words from triggering a wave of disappointment rushing through Romy. 'Yeah, I'm whacked, I think I'll head back to the cottage,' she said, taking Finn's cue.

'Fair do.' Jimby flashed a knowing smile. 'Been good to see you both.'

The others all agreed enthusiastically. 'Don't forget everyone's welcome to join in with the carols round the Christmas tree on Christmas Eve,' said Kitty.

'And, not that I want to put the dampeners on the evening, but don't forget to keep the doors to your outbuildings secured. I heard another quad bike was nicked over at Beckinthwaite last night,' said Ollie.

'Aye, I'd heard about that. Seems like we're having a bad spate of it,' said Finn.

With a flurry of goodbyes, Finn and Romy left the pub, a waggy-tailed Ted in tow.

Outside, though the cold air caught in Romy's throat, she was thrilled to find it was snowing, silent flakes tumbling from the sky illuminated in the glow of the streetlights. A couple of inches of snow had settled on the village since she'd set off for the pub, muffling the sound of a four-wheel drive as it went by leaving a trail of tyre tracks in its wake. The hoot of a tawny owl as it echoed around the cottages made Ted's ears twitch, but his attention was taken by a black cat that slinked silently across the road then leapt effortlessly onto a snow-topped garden wall before disappearing into the darkness.

She pulled her hat further down over her head and gave a shiver, glancing up at Finn. Her heart fluttered to see him looking down at her.

'It's been really good to see you tonight, Romy. My parents won't believe it when I tell them.'

'It's been good to see you, too.' She wasn't ready for her evening with Finn to come to an end. 'Don't suppose you fancy a cuppa back at the cottage, do you?' A snowflake landed on the tip of his nose and without thinking, she reached up and brushed it away. He caught her eye, electricity sparking between them.

'Sorry.' She dropped her gaze, feeling her cheeks grow warm. *What was that all about?*

'Don't be,' he said softly, making her knees go a little wobbly. 'And yes, come to think of it I usually have a cup of tea at this time of night; it'd be good to join you for one.'

'Great, let's make tracks then.' A thrill ran through her as they headed off, their feet crunching over the fresh snow.

She was glad of the blast of warmth that hit them once she opened the door of Holly Tree Cottage, kicking the snow from her boots before stepping over the threshold. Though it was only a short walk from the pub, her feet were numb with the cold and the contrasting temperatures made her nose and cheeks tingle.

Finn followed her through to the kitchen, along with Ted. 'Oh, wow! This is amazing!' He looked around in awe, the Labrador sniffing the floor with great interest.

'I know, it's stunning, isn't it?' She laughed at Finn's reaction. 'Here, let me take your coat. I'll hang it up in the utility room; there's a radiator just below the coat pegs which'll have it warm and dry by the time you come to leave. Whoever designed the kitchen and where to locate the radiators did a brilliant job; they planned everything really well actually. Wait 'til you see the living room and bathroom, they could be straight from a magazine photo shoot.'

'That I can believe if the hallway and this room's anything to go by. And at the risk of this is sounding odd, the place somehow manages to feel familiar even though it looks so different. I know that doesn't make sense, but I can't think of another way of putting it.'

'It doesn't sound odd at all; it's exactly how I felt when I first arrived.' Romy filled the kettle at the Belfast sink before setting it down on the Aga. 'Don't suppose you know who owns it, do you?'

'Nope, 'fraid not.' Finn shook his head. 'It's been a holiday cottage for ages, though I'm aware it last changed hands a couple of years ago. Wouldn't know the owner if I saw them, though, and I don't have a clue what they're called. All I do know is that it's nobody local.'

Ted finished his sniffing and went to sit beside Finn, nudging his hand for an ear ruffle.

'I'm not sure if it's common knowledge so I'd appreciate it if you'd keep it to yourself, but it's actually going on the market in the New Year. The owner's moving abroad and wants to sell it.'

'I didn't know that. Shame to have done all this work on it, but I dare say it'll go for a pretty penny and they'll get their money back. Property round here is selling like hot cakes right now, so it won't hang around for long. Not tempted, are you?'

'That would be quite the turn up, wouldn't it?' They both laughed at that, but despite Finn's light hearted question, Romy had found the temptation to at least consider it growing stronger by the hour! She reminded herself to keep her impulsive nature in check and not give it any further consideration until her fortnight in the village was up.

Taking their mugs of tea into the living room, Romy flicked the table lamps on, the soft light lending a warm glow to the room. She threw a log onto the embers in the base of the wood burner and in an instant flames were dancing behind the glass. Ted didn't waste a moment, and flopped down onto the rug in front of it with a 'harrumph'.

'Are you sure Ted's welcome in here?' Finn asked, sitting down on one of the armchairs and looking around at the pristine room.

'Don't worry, he is. I can distinctly recall the details on the holiday cottage website mentioning that one dog was welcome, so Ted can fill the role of that one pooch, which I have to say he's doing rather finely at the moment.' Romy popped her mug down on a coaster on the coffee table and settled herself in the armchair opposite Finn. 'And I don't know about you, but I wouldn't like to be the one to break it to him that he has to move.'

They both looked on as Ted stretched languorously before closing his eyes with a loud, contented sigh.

'Yeah, good point. I don't think he'd take it well.' Finn gave a throaty chuckle.

Romy adjusted the squishy cushion behind her back and relaxed into the generous proportions of the armchair. 'It's been a great night. I honestly didn't know what to expect when I first arrived in the village. I didn't think I'd be spending this evening at the Sunne – or for it to have been given such an amazing makeover, Bea and Jonty have done an awesome job. And I certainly didn't expect to hear Gabe Dublin sing live! He seems so down to earth and friendly.' She refrained from saying she hadn't expected to run into Finn so quickly, never mind prepare herself for it.

'Yeah, Gabe's a good bloke, he's not starry at all; you'd never guess he was famous. His girlfriend's Ollie's daughter, Anoushka. She was the girl with the long, blonde hair, runs a dance studio just outside of Danskelfe.'

Finn's words triggered a memory. 'Was it Anoushka's mum who walked out on her when she was a baby?' She had a vague memory of the local outrage it had caused and how the villagers had rallied, offering Ollie their support.

'It was; Ollie brought her up on his own, with the help of his parents, of course. Did a good job by all accounts, she's a nice lass, well-liked. And I don't know if you'll remember that Kitty was married to some hot-shot barrister? Him and his mother used to look down their nose at everyone. Kitty ended up divorcing him and getting married to Ollie – they were childhood sweethearts, albeit briefly.'

'Sounds like she's been through a lot. I'd heard that her and Jimby's parents had been killed in a car accident.' That information had filtered through the Fairfax family grapevine.

'Mm. Poor lass had it tough for a few years, but she's happy now. Has two kids from her first marriage and a daughter with Ollie. She and Vi have a successful business making wedding dresses.'

'And am I right in thinking that Jimby and Vi used to have a bit of a thing when they were younger?' She reached for her mug and took a sip of tea.

'Aye, they did.' He nodded, smiling. 'They finally got together a few years ago when Vi moved back to the village. They're married with a little girl.' His smile dropped. 'But I don't know if you heard about what happened to Molly's husband?'

Romy shook her head. Her only memory was that Molly had fallen pregnant with twins when she was a teenager and that she and Pip had married as a result. From what Romy could remember, they'd seemed happy and well suited. 'No, why? Did they divorce?'

'No, Pip died in a quadbike accident on the moors. Moll and the lads were devastated, as you can imagine. Little Emmie was only a toddler when it happened.'

Romy pressed her hand to her mouth as she absorbed Finn's words. 'Oh my goodness, poor Molly and her family, that's awful.'

'But then Camm came along and made her smile again; he's a decent bloke too. The twins – Tom and Ben – took a while to warm to him, but they think he's great now and little Emmie adores him, and, from what I can gather, the feeling's mutual. It's Camm who's got the contract for ploughing the roads round here, he does a good job.'

'Blimey, seems like a lot's happened since I was last here.'

'Aye, and we've only just skimmed the surface. You know what village life's like, it's owt but quiet.' Finn gave her a knowing look.

'You're not wrong there. Something always seemed to have gone on during the week while we were in Rickelthorpe. I s'pose my family added to that after we left.'

Finn looked thoughtful for a moment. 'So can I ask what happened after you left that night? Though no pressure, I'll totally understand if you'd rather not talk about it, or would rather save it for another time.'

His question made her heart stutter, and her mouth felt suddenly dry. 'Like I mentioned in the pub, I want more than anything to tell you, Finn. In fact, since I first saw the cottage in the magazine, the need to tell you has grown stronger every day. I'd hoped to see you when I got here, hoped you'd want to hear it, and hoped you'd be able to forgive me for freezing you out.' She inhaled deeply, releasing the breath slowly through her mouth. 'I'll apologise in advance if I cry while I'm telling you, it's still hard to get my head around most of what happened that night and the weeks that followed.'

'You don't need to apologise for that, Romes.'

The kindness in his voice almost undid her before she'd even got started.

Romy took a moment to steady herself, though she struggled to stop the hammering in her heart. Fixing her gaze on the mug she was nursing in her hands, she went on to describe how the landline in the hallway had been ringing off its hook when they'd first walked through the door at Holly Tree Cottage that dreadful Friday night before Christmas. It only added to Dulcie's already sour mood.

It turned out the call was from Judith, Vernon's secretary. She'd been trying to reach him since he'd left the Stainthorpe & Clayborne offices earlier than usual in a bid to avoid the pre-Christmas mass exodus, and had set off for Lytell Stangdale with his family just after four p.m. that day.

At the time, Vernon had told his family the reason for the phone call was owing to an oversight and that his signature was urgently required on a document before the festive break. He'd told them that no one had been able to get hold of his partner Roger Clayborne to sign on his behalf, which meant Vernon had no choice but to dash back to the office, much to Dulcie's annoyance.

Romy learnt later that what her father had told them couldn't have been further from the truth and the real reason was about to shock her family to its very core.

TWENTY

Romy

During the brief phone call to Vernon that Friday evening all those years ago, Judith had been in a distressed state, telling him that several police officers had arrived unexpectedly at Stainthorpe & Clayborne's offices just as she was putting her coat on to leave. They'd quizzed Vernon's secretary about his whereabouts and began rummaging through his desk and filing cabinets, removing files, filling boxes with paperwork. His partner, Roger Clayborne had looked on with interest, but the smirk he was wearing hadn't gone unnoticed by Judith. The police informed her that someone had contacted them with accusations of the embezzlement of clients' money at the company, with the finger being very firmly pointed at her boss. To make matters worse, Judith had been outraged when she'd overheard Clayborne telling one of police officers how he'd had his suspicions about Vernon for some time and had even confronted his business partner a couple of weeks earlier.

'Of course, he flatly denied all knowledge of everything, just as you'd expect,' Clayborne had said. 'But I didn't have concrete proof at the time, so couldn't do anything about it. I'd planned to investigate over the festive break while he was out of the way. Unfortunate as it is, I'm grateful a client has come forward and we can start putting things right now we know where to begin.'

Judith had expressed her outrage, declaring Vernon to be nothing like the version of the person Clayborne had portrayed him to be. 'He's an honourable man. Why else do you think he's headed straight back here? I don't believe for one second he's guilty of what Mr Clayborne is accusing him of!'

But the police had still insisted that they needed to interview her boss. They'd also told her not to leave town as they'd be calling on her for a chat, too.

Vernon Stainthorpe's funeral had been a quiet affair at the local crematorium, with no public announcements appearing in the local press and very few mourners in attendance, which was how Dulcie had wanted it. She'd been unable to bear the shame of being thought of as the wife of a criminal and have people stare at her.

It was after the service that Judith and Romy had found the opportunity to speak – Judith had always had a soft spot for Vernon's daughter. His secretary had recounted what had happened at the office and how Vernon had been devastated to think the man who'd once been his closest friend would speak so ill of him. Vernon had even doubted Judith's words, thinking she must have heard wrong with her being in such an understandably distressed state. By the time he'd arrived at the office later that evening only Judith remained, so he'd called Roger Clayborne, putting him on speaker phone in the hope that Judith would hear his friend clarify the situation and clear up any misunderstanding. But Vernon had been further shocked to find his business partner's tone hostile. He'd demanded that Clayborne retract his words, admit they were shameful lies, and call the police, tell them they were making a mistake, that whoever it was who'd contacted them had no grounds for such wildly ridiculous accusations. He further requested that Clayborne stress to the police, that the firm had an exemplary reputation, one they'd built up with their sound business ethics over many years. But instead,

Clayborne had been scornful and mocking, telling Romy's father his career was over.

'Tut, tut, Vernon. It would seem you've been found with your sticky little mitts in the cookie jar,' he'd said, adding with relish, 'Oh, and you might as well know that while you've been foolishly working all hours, focussing your attention on your needy clients, you've been neglecting your rather wonderful wife. But don't worry, I was more than happy to step into those highly-polished shoes of yours; Dulcie and I have enjoyed what you might call a delightfully illicit affair for the last ten years. And, if that information makes you suspicious about the identity of Tally's father, then – in for a penny, in for a pound – you might as well know, it's not you.'

Romy had listened to Judith, stunned.

'I'm so sorry to have to tell you all this, Romy, especially at such a terribly sad time.' Judith had taken a fresh tissue from her bag and dabbed at the tears that were pouring down her cheeks. 'But I think it's only right someone in your family knows what Clayborne is really like. I can't tell your mother for obvious reasons, nor Tristan for that matter; he'd only go running straight to her and she'd dismiss it. And poor little Tally's only eight, bless her, so she's too young, as are you really.'

'I'm glad you've told me, Judith. I think we should tell the police, don't you?' Anger and outrage were forcing their way through the numb feeling that had gripped Romy since the day her father died.

Judith's tears were pushed out of the way by a determined expression Romy had never seen on her father's secretary before. 'Oh, don't worry, lovey. I intend to, but not until the time's right. I've got something planned.'

Romy took a moment, feeling the weight of Finn's gaze as Judith's words echoed around her head. She hadn't expected reliving such an awful time in her life to trigger such a physical ache in her heart after so many years. She thought she'd come to terms with her grief, that the passage of time had dulled it slightly.

But it had been a long time since she'd talked about it to anyone so she supposed it was bound to resurrect the sorrow she'd felt at that time.

She swallowed down the lump in her throat and blinked back the tears that threatened, determined to continue and tell Finn everything now so she didn't have to relive it again.

'So my lovely, hard-working, honest dad was faced with being at the centre of a massive scandal in his professional life and on top of that he'd also just discovered his marriage had been a sham, with his wife and best friend making a mockery of him for years. I can't imagine how he must've felt having so much stress piled on top of him all at once.' Her voice wavered, but she remained determined to plough on. 'The police must've had a tip-off that he was at the office – no doubt Clayborne was responsible for that – and they turned up to arrest him, which was when Judith said he collapsed. Hearing it all had been too much and he suffered a massive heart attack.' Thoughts of her dad's last moments caused the dam to burst and before she could stop them, tears were streaming down her cheeks.

Finn went to speak but she shook her head, she just wanted to get the words out. 'He was rushed to hospital but had passed away by the time we got there. It still kills me that I never got to say goodbye to him, that he died alone. And, hard as it sounds, part of me will never forgive my mum for her role in it.' She covered her face with her hands as she fought to control her emotions.

'Oh, Romes, I'm so sorry. I'd heard a few things, but what you've just told me is beyond awful. I wish I'd been there for you.'

'How were you to know?' she said through her sobs.

In the next moment, Finn appeared beside her, crouching down, the smell of his mossy cologne and something distinctly "Finn", causing a stir in her memory; it was indescribably soothing. He tucked a stray lock of hair behind her ear and rested a box of tissues in her lap. Ted joined them a moment later. Sensing her sorrow, he pushed his glossy head into her hand, whimpering. She took the hint, stroking the Labrador absently.

'It's why we never came back. Mum said the shame of what Dad was accused of was too much to bear so she put the cottage on the market straight away. Though I don't doubt it had something to do with the gossip about her affair with Clayborne, which I believe she ended soon after. And she said he was lying about Tally being his, reckoned he was just trying to goad Dad. In fairness, Tally's the double of Dad, so I believe her.'

'Does Tris know about it; the affair and what was said about Tally, I mean?'

Romy sniffed. 'Yeah, I told him, but he didn't want to discuss it, said he didn't believe it, that Clayborne was just twisting the knife. Tris went in on himself like he always did when he was upset, buried his head in the sand and concentrated on his studies. I suppose we all grieve in different ways. Mum focused all her attention on Tally – we've never told Tall what Clayborne had said; couldn't see the point of causing her any further distress or confusion. From that day on, Mum has refused to talk about Dad, says it's too difficult for her. Tris is the same and Tally barely remembers him.'

'That must've been a heavy weight for you to carry, Romes. And it sounds like you didn't have much support.' He took her hand, smoothing his thumb over her knuckles.

She heaved a sigh, taking comfort from his touch. 'I had Judith; she was amazing, we supported each other. I was devastated when she was diagnosed with dementia and ended up in a care home, poor thing. I visited her 'til she passed away last year. Can't tell you how much I miss her.' Over the years, Romy had grown close to her dad's former secretary, thinking of her as a link to her father.

'I'm sorry to hear that. Sounds like she was an amazing woman and a bit of an ally for you.'

'She was, my dad thought highly of her, he couldn't understand why Clayborne didn't have a nice word to say about her.'

'She probably saw him for the worm he was.'

'Oh, she did that all right. Judith was so convinced my dad was innocent she started to do a bit of investigating on her own – it was the thing she mentioned she had planned. Dad always said she had a keen eye for detail and he was right. She managed to discover that it was Clayborne who'd been embezzling clients' money, but sneakily making it look like it was my father.' She felt a pulse of anger at the reminder. 'Judith's nephew was in the police force and she literally nagged and nagged him until he looked at what she'd found. Luckily, she'd kept duplicates of everything. And she worked through it all methodically, mapping every sneaky little detail Clayborne had used to syphon off clients' money, which she said had been extremely elaborate. He'd set up bogus accounts, transferring money into them, moving it around here, there and everywhere before finally depositing it into his own bank account. He'd even set up something bogus in Tally's name, can you believe?'

'What? That's low.'

'I know. But he couldn't wriggle out of any of it since the evidence proved it all led irrefutably back to him. The upshot being he was charged with embezzlement and ended up being given a three-year prison sentence. Annoyingly, he didn't serve the full term owing to some ridiculous sentencing rules. Though, last I heard he was back inside after being found guilty of swindling a great long list of elderly people out of their life savings and this time got a much heftier sentence. Hopefully he'll rot in there.'

'He sounds like a nasty piece of work.'

'He's the worst.'

'But thank goodness for Judith.'

'You've no idea how many times I've thought that,' said Romy. 'And what's worse is that it was recently in the news that Clayborne's son was found guilty of something similar where he lives down south. So father and son are both languishing in prison for their nasty little crimes.'

'Proof indeed that the apple never falls far from the tree.'

Romy nodded. 'The worst thing in all of this is that my dad passed away thinking people would regard him as being dishonourable, not to mention how hurt he'd have been after what Clayborne had told him about Tally.' Fresh tears started to fall and she soon found herself enveloped in a pair of strong, comforting arms. She rested her head against Finn's shoulder and let herself melt into him, soaking up the reassuring warmth of his embrace.

'Romes, don't cry,' he said, smoothing his hand over her hair.

Eager not to miss out, Ted pushed his head under his dad's arm and pressed a cold, wet nose to Romy's cheek. In the background, the thud of his waggy tail hitting the coffee table could be heard. She couldn't help but laugh.

Finn sat back, his eyes roving her face. 'You okay?'

'Mm-hm.' She gave him a watery smile. 'Sorry about that. I knew I'd get upset but I didn't realise talking about it again would hit me so hard.' She assumed it was because it was Finn she was talking to, tapping into the close bond they'd once shared, though she'd taken some comfort from the knowledge that Finn knew her dad was a decent, respectable man and that he wouldn't doubt his innocence for a moment.

Finn slipped onto the sofa beside her chair, resting his hands in his lap while Romy ruffled Ted's ears, willing her mind and her heart to settle.

'I'm not sure if this is going to help at all, so please stop me if you find it upsetting.'

Romy's hand stilled on Ted's head, her gaze moving to Finn who was suddenly looking awkward. 'Okay,' she said slowly, her chest tightening. What could he possibly have to say that she might find upsetting?

'I know when Tris came to the pub to get you that night, you got the impression I already knew about your dad, but I can say with all honesty, I didn't know a thing about it at the time.'

'Yeah, I know that now. I'd guessed you knew something, though I wasn't certain what. But I was in shock and couldn't process my thoughts that night, still struggled for months afterwards, too.'

'That's completely understandable, Romes.' He gave her a sympathetic smile. 'So, the week before that last Friday night you were in Lytell Stangdale, something had got back to me about your mum.'

'Okay.' Romy's shoulders heaved with a sigh. *Here we go.*

'Apparently, the source was that dreadful old gossip who used to live in the village down Church Street, Andrea McKenna – remember her?'

'Ughh! How could I forget. She was always spreading her spite around to anyone who'd listen, and what she didn't know as fact she'd make up if it made her gossip juicier. I'm guessing with you saying she *used* to live in the village that she's not here anymore?'

'She's the one, and you guessed right, she left, must be a good fifteen years ago now. Ended up falling out with pretty much everyone in the village. No one was sorry to see her go. Anyway, getting back to that night, she was telling folk she'd been to see a play in Rickelthorpe where some relation of hers lived, and while she was there, she reckoned she and this relative had seen your mum in a compromising position with another man. Turns out it was Clayborne.'

Romy rested her hand on her chest. 'Oh my God!' *A compromising position?* It was bad enough her mum had cheated on her dad but to hear she'd been seen doing it and been the subject of such sordid gossip added insult to injury. Her blood curdled at the thought as respect for her mother plummeted to new depths.

'Sorry, Romes.' Finn shuffled uncomfortably on the sofa.

'There's no need for you to apologise. S'just the thought of my mother being so indiscreet, and people like that hideous McKenna woman gossiping about what she was doing behind my poor dad's back that's got to me.'

'I understand.' Finn scratched his head, discomfort writ large across his face. 'Anyroad, much as I hated the prospect of spreading her poison, I knew I had to tell you before the gossip reached your family. I'd planned to speak to you about it as soon as possible but 'cos you'd been looking forward to the do at the Sunne on that Friday, I didn't want to spoil it for you, so I was going to leave telling you to first thing on the Saturday. I was absolutely dreading it, mind, but I didn't want you to get ambushed by anyone.'

'Thanks, Finn, that was kind.' She dredged up a smile.

'Turned out I was too late, though.'

'I hope you haven't been beating yourself up about that.'

'It was hard not to for a good while after.' He rubbed his hand across his chin. 'Kept telling myself if I'd warned you sooner, you wouldn't have had so much land on you all at once.'

'It wasn't your fault. And let's not forget the role my mother played in all of this. I found out later that the reason she'd been in such a bad mood at the time was because someone had approached Clayborne and told him they knew all about his relationship with her and were trying to blackmail him – could've been that McKenna woman or her relative, I suppose. And to make matters worse, when I confronted her about her sordid little affair, she told me it was because she was lonely. That my dad was always too busy to show her any affection, that he thought more about his clients than he did her, unlike Clayborne who apparently lavished attention on her. Hearing it made me sick to my stomach and I lost any respect I had for her for a long time.'

'I'm sorry you've been through all that, Romes.'

She huffed out a sigh. Her mind was reeling, tension gripping her shoulders at the reminder of that terrible time. 'But, thankfully, it's all in the past now. I've tried to focus on the future.'

'That's always the best plan.' Finn gave her a sympathetic smile.

She felt tiredness wash over her, but she was determined to update Finn with everything, determined to get it out of the way.

'I'm ashamed to say I went off the rails a bit after Dad's funeral. I couldn't speak to anyone and I was so full of anger and grief all mixed up together, I was a nightmare for my mum. We'd always clashed a bit with our personalities being so different, but after that night things were a million times worse. A month later after the most blazing row we'd ever had, I ended up packing my bags and leaving home. Didn't tell anyone, just got on the train to York, then down to London. Flew out to Spain, moved around quite a bit; Portugal, France, Greece; worked in bars, slept on sofas or in grotty bedsits.' She gave a shudder at the thought of some of the grimy places she'd stayed not to mention the seedy characters she'd had to fend off. 'Couldn't face painting or drawing, couldn't imagine ever wanting to pick up a paintbrush again. I lived like that for a few years before gradually heading back to Rickelthorpe. I enrolled on a felt-making course with a view to setting up a business making my own stuff from felt, which is what I did. The only person I'd kept in touch with through that time was Judith and we grew close when I came back. I still barely saw my family though. I eventually met Russ – he's the man I ended up getting married to, he's from Rickelthorpe, too. He was quite a bit older than me, he was actually closer in age to what my dad would've been. I guess a psychologist would say I was looking for a father figure and they'd probably be right.' She smiled wanly. Looking back to that time, Romy recalled craving the need to be cared for and Russ had filled that role for a while. Their marriage had lasted for five years, until Belinda came along and it started falling apart.

'Sounds like a tough time for you.'

'What's that saying? What doesn't kill you makes you stronger? I think I just needed to work my way through everything. And you've no idea how many times I wanted to call you over the years. I was desperate to tell you how sorry I was for being angry with you and for turning my back on you. I held back because I knew I wouldn't have been able to bear it if you told me you didn't want to know, though I understand it's no less than I deserve.'

'You need to stop being so hard on yourself. Do you honestly think I'd have said something like that?'

She gave a small shrug. 'My mind was skewed, I wasn't thinking straight. Grief had twisted it. Luckily, I found an amazing counsellor who gave me the tools I needed to get my head sorted and I haven't looked back.'

'I'm pleased to hear that, Romes.'

Romy sat back, a sense of relief rising inside her. Finally getting to speak to Finn and explain everything to him felt like a physical weight had been lifted from her shoulders. And though reliving such a heartbreaking time of her life had been exhausting, she could feel happiness creeping back in, joining the relief and nudging the sadness that lingered out of the way.

'Right then.' She clapped her hands on her knees, making Ted, who'd been resting his head on her feet, jump up with a start. 'Oh, sorry, fella, didn't mean to startle you.' She gave him a quick tickle under the chin. 'What I was going to say was that's more than enough about me, your ears must be ringing with all the talking I've done tonight. Can I interest you in a top-up of your tea while you fill me in on what you've been up to – if it's not too late, that is?' She was conscious of the time, and that Finn would probably want to head back home, but she didn't want him to think she wasn't interested to hear what the last twenty-one years had dealt him. Her eyes went to the clock at the same moment he checked his watch.

'Hmm, much as I'd love to stay, it's almost midnight and I should really be getting back.' He pulled a regretful face.

'Course, I understand.' The level of disappointment that landed in Romy's chest took her by surprise. She guessed she must've scared him off with talking about herself for so long. She couldn't blame him; it had been heavy stuff and not the sort of thing you wanted to listen to on a Friday night. Romy was beginning to regret launching in with so much detail all at once.

'I don't suppose you'd fancy popping up to the farm tomorrow, would you? My mum and dad'll be there, I know they'd be over the moon to see you,' he said, a hopeful gleam in his eyes. 'You could stay for Sunday dinner, my mum always does one at the farmhouse; we could maybe go for a walk afterwards if the snow isn't too bad. I can fill you in on what's happened since I last saw you then.'

Romy's face brightened and a smile started to spread across her face. 'I'd love to, and I'd be over the moon to see them, too.'

'Great!' Finn's smile matched hers. 'How about I pick you up in the Landie at about twelve-thirty? Oh, and I should warn you, my mum hasn't changed, she'll expect you to eat as many Yorkshire puddings as she puts in front of you.'

'There'll be no complaints from me on that score, I used to love your mum's Yorkshire puds.'

After exchanging mobile numbers, they walked through to the kitchen, Romy reaching into the utility room for Finn's coat. 'See, I was right, it's completely dry, and warmed through as an added bonus.'

Opening the front door revealed that there'd been no let up with the snow while they'd been chatting over the last hour-and-a-half, with the covering looking a good few inches deeper. And from the way everywhere was sparkling, not to mention how bitterly cold it was, the temperature had plunged further.

'Are you sure you won't mind heading back over here tomorrow?' she asked.

'It'll be fine, don't worry. I'll be in the Landie and I daresay Camm will have been up and down the roads a couple of times with the plough by lunch time so the roads'll be clear.'

'Okay.' She was inordinately glad to hear that.

'So,' they said in unison before each giving an awkward laugh.

'It's been lovely to see you, Romes.' Finn held her gaze, his eyes soft, as snowflakes floated around him.

Her heart lifted and a wave of joy rushed through her. 'It's been lovely to see you too, Finn.'

'Until tomorrow...' He bent and kissed her cheek, his stubble brushing against her skin and making her stomach somersault.

'Yeah, until tomorrow. Drive carefully on your way back to the farm.'

'Three flashing lights?' he asked, making her laugh. In their younger days, whenever he'd dropped her off at the cottage and the weather had been inclement, he'd let her know he'd got home safely by switching his bedroom light on and off three times in quick succession.

'Or you could always just send a text; whichever's easier.' She grinned, the cold air nipping at her skin.

He kissed her cheek again, pulling back in an instant. 'Oops! Sorry, I've already done that!'

'It's okay.' She looked up at him, giggling, trying to ignore the fact her knees were practically knocking and it had nothing to do with the cold.

'Right then, where's that wayward Labrador of mine?'

She watched as he whistled for Ted, who was sniffing around the garden, and the two of them made their way down the path. Finn gave another wave as he closed the gate and headed off to his Land Rover that was parked near the pub, whistling as he went.

Closing the door behind her, Romy's hand went to where Finn's lips had brushed her skin – twice! She hadn't expected that seeing him again would stir such strong feelings inside her, but one thing was for certain, she knew she couldn't wait until she saw him again.

Fifteen minutes later, she was sitting in her old bedroom in the dark, looking out across the dale. She smiled as a light over at Castlegate Farm flashed on and off three times. Jumping up from the bed, she dashed over to the light switch, and did the same.

In the next moment her phone pinged with a text, finished with a slew of laughing face emojis.

> I already know you're home, Romes!!! Fx

She giggled, firing off a quick reply, thinking better of adding a heart emoji and including a laughing face instead.

> I know! Couldn't resist though! Rxx

'Home...' Romy read his text once more. She rather liked the idea of Holly Tree Cottage being home.

TWENTY-ONE

Finn

'Are you sure you mean Romy Stainthorpe? That little lass whose mother is related to the Fairfaxes? Her parents used to have Holly Tree Cottage?' Tommy Tindall pushed his flat cap back and scratched his head. He'd just joined Finn and Jill in the kitchen at Castlegate Farm. '*Our* Romy?'

Finn and his mum exchanged an amused look and laughed.

'Yes, Dad, I mean *our* Romy.' Boy, did it feel good to say that, he thought, smiling to himself as he set the mats and coasters out on the table.

'What other Romy d'you think he means? We only know one, you daft thing.' Jill chuckled as she basted the large joint of beef that was surrounded by golden roast potatoes, the mouthwatering aroma filling the room.

'I was just checking, it's been a while since the lass was last here,' Tommy said, peering over his wife's shoulder. 'By, that looks grand.'

'It'll be nice to have her sitting at the dinner table again. I'll do some extra Yorkshire puds, I remember how she used to enjoy them,' said Jill.

Ted, who was watching proceedings from his bed, threw his head back, closed his amber eyes and sniffed the air appreciatively, making Finn smile. It tickled him how much character the Labrador had.

Finn turned back to his parents. 'You're not wrong, she did love her Yorkshire puds. Anyroad, she's looking forward to seeing you both.'

'Ah, bless her. And how did she seem?' his mum asked, sliding the roasting dish back into the Aga, her cheeks rosy from the heat of the stove. 'Poor lass went through a lot when she left. Much as it's a shame, I can't say I blame her for waiting this long to come back.'

'She seemed good.' Finn didn't want to stir up trouble by saying it was her mother who'd forbidden the family from returning; he knew his parents had never been too fond of Dulcie Stainthorpe and he wasn't keen to hear a rant about her. 'I'll fill you both in on everything later; Romy said she was okay with me telling you. But you're right, she has been through a lot, and has had a divorce to contend with on top of everything else. I don't know the details of that, so no quizzing her, you two, okay?' He'd hardly been able to sleep as his mind had turned over everything she'd told him. At sixteen, she'd been young to experience the tragedy of losing her father, never mind finding out about her mother's affair with the man who'd essentially sent him to his grave. He didn't know how she'd got through it all and come out of the other side so well.

'Our Finn, what d'you take us for?' His mum jabbed her hands on her hips. 'We know she's had a rotten time. Your dad and me are just looking forward to seeing her, that's all. We know full well we need to be sensitive to her feelings.'

'Aye, course we do,' said Tommy. 'Felt like we'd lost a member of the family when she left and we have no intentions of scaring her off. That lass you married is no comparison. We always thought it'd be Romy you'd take down the aisle, not some gold-digging—'

'Dad,' Finn said softly, shooting him a warning look as he

reached into the cutlery draw and scooped out a handful of knives and forks.

'Speaking of Britt, have you heard much from her?' Jill said, segueing a little too easily into the topic for Finn's comfort. 'Are the lads still coming for Boxing Day or has she changed her mind about that as well?'

Finn heaved a sigh. He intended to make this Christmas as peaceful as possible for the sake of his sons. He hated being caught in the middle of the animosity between his parents and his ex-wife, though in fairness, Britt did little to help herself where they were concerned. If either of them answered the landline at the farm when she called, she'd hang-up abruptly. And he knew they got upset on his and the lads' behalf when she chopped and changed the days Kyle and Toby could visit, giving flimsy excuses. But experience had told him not to be difficult with his ex, he didn't want to run the risk of her putting more obstacles in the way of their visits, especially with them being so few and far between now.

'As far as I know, the plans are still the same. She's dropping them off at ten o'clock on Boxing Day morning and they're staying for a couple of days.' His heart lifted at the thought of seeing his sons again. It had been months since their last visit and chatting with them via a computer screen was hardly the same.

'Champion,' said Tommy, beaming. 'It'll be good to hear their enthusiastic voices around the place again.'

'Aye, it will,' said Finn.

'Ooh, I can't wait. I'll bet they haven't half grown,' said his mum, sifting flour into a bowl for the Yorkshire puddings. 'I've tidied round their rooms and put some brushed-cotton bedding on for them so they'll be nice and toasty and I've put their new pyjamas under their pillows. Oh, and I've got their Christmas stockings ready from your dad and me. We'll make it just like another Christmas Day for them.'

'That we will, lass,' said Tommy.

The clock on the dresser chimed quarter past twelve, startling

Finn. 'Ey up, is that the time? I'd best head over to Lytell Stangdale. I told Romy I'd pick her up at half past.'

'Best not be late, you don't want her to think you've changed your mind,' his dad said, chuckling.

Finn didn't want her thinking that for a second. He added a knife and fork to the last setting and headed to the utility room, pushed his feet into his wellies and shrugged on his padded waxed jacket, a thrill thrumming through him. The lighter mood triggered by seeing Romy had lingered. 'I'll set out spoons for pudding when I get back. Won't be long.'

'Don't worry, your dad'll do it. Mind, drive carefully, son,' his mum said as he headed through the door, Ted shooting past him.

Outside was bitterly cold and an icy wind whispered around the yard Finn had cleared of snow and gritted that morning. He climbed into the Land Rover, put the key in the ignition and turned the vents on full blast, freezing air blowing at him in an instant. Experience told him the vehicle would have only just warmed through by the time he pulled up outside Holly Tree Cottage. Having said that, he wouldn't swap his Landie for the world. It was reliable and tough, and always got him safely from A to B.

With Ted on the passenger seat beside him, Finn headed down the snow-covered track from the farm, gazing at the winter wonderland spread out before him. It had snowed through the night and great drifts had banked up against the dry stone walls. It never ceased to amaze him how the moors and farmland had the power to look breathtaking whatever the season, from the rich, jewel colours of autumn to the vibrant greens of spring and the stark, sparkling beauty of winter. The fields, reminiscent of thick white blankets, were peppered with the footprints of the wildlife that roamed the moors, rabbits scampering around, game birds scratching about for food. He braked carefully as he reached the end of the lane and turned onto the road that led to Lytell Stangdale, noting it was clear and the snow had been pushed back into the verges. Camm must've been out with the plough and judging by the salt scattered across the road's surface, the gritter will have followed soon after. He noted with a hint of disappointment that the blue skies of the morning were gradually being replaced by clouds that were creeping in from Arkleby way, a threatening air about them. He'd hoped to head out for a walk with Romy after they'd eaten, retrace their steps from when they were younger and had loved exploring the moors.

Before long, he found himself pulling up outside Holly Tree Cottage, his heart thudding with anticipation. 'Here we are, fella,' he said to Ted.

'Oh wow! It's the same Landie you had when you were younger! I recognise the number plate,' Romy said as she climbed into the passenger seat alongside Ted, giving the Labrador a quick fuss. Holding the door open for her, Finn noted she was wrapped up well against the cold and had a pair of sturdy-looking wellies on her feet.

'Aye, she's been a faithful little beauty.' Finn patted the bodywork affectionately. 'She's never let me down yet.' The vintage Land Rover had been a seventeenth birthday present from his parents and he'd loved it from the moment he first got behind the wheel. In his spare time he enjoyed tinkering about with it, never more so than this last year.

'I'm so excited to be travelling in her again. How about you, Ted? It looks as if you enjoy being up front here.' She smoothed her hand over his silky head.

Ted responded with a spot of vigorous tail wagging, his tongue lolling from the side of his mouth. Finn laughed before shutting the heavy passenger door and heading round to the driver's side.

'Oh my days! I'd forgotten how everywhere looks so stunning here when it's been snowing!' Romy swept her gaze around the panoramic windscreen as they rumbled along the Danskelfe road. 'And there's Danskelfe Castle! I'd forgotten what an imposing sight that was too, like it's silently watching over everything. Everywhere looks so beautiful! I can't believe I've stayed away for so long.' She looked over at Finn, the pair of them exchanging wide smiles. It gladdened his heart that Romy still felt the same way about this little part of the North Yorkshire Moors as she had all those years ago.

Ted started dancing from paw to paw as they pulled into the yard back at the farm. Before they had the chance to climb out of the Land Rover the door of the house was flung open and Finn's parents appeared, wearing matching smiles.

'Jill! Tommy!' Romy said, her voice faltering. She jumped down and rushed over to Finn's mum, throwing herself into Jill's outstretched arms. 'Oh, Jill, it's so good to see you.'

'Romy lovey, it's good to see you too.' Jill's voice wobbled. She stroked Romy's hair as the younger woman sobbed hot, heartfelt tears on her shoulder.

Finn felt a tug in his heart, watching as Romy's emotions were released in a whoosh.

'Oh my goodness. I'm so sorry, I don't know what came over me, I really didn't mean to cry. If it's any consolation, they're happy tears.' Romy wiped her eyes with the sleeves of her coat. 'I'm just over the moon to see you both.' Her voice wavered again and tears started tumbling once more.

'And we're over the moon to see you, too, sweetheart.' Jill dabbed her eyes with the edge of her pinny.

'Aye, that we are, lass. Come 'ere.' Beaming broadly, Tommy pulled her into a hug, almost knocking his flat cap off in the process. 'By, it isn't 'alf grand to have you back, flower. Jill and me thought we must've heard wrong when our Finn said he'd bumped into you.'

Finn looked on smiling as Ted danced around them. He still couldn't believe that Romy Stainthorpe was back and it gladdened him to see his parents welcome her so warmly.

'Come on, let's get you inside, you'll be absolutely nithered if you stay out here much longer,' said Jill, as fresh snowflakes started to float down from the sky.

'Ah, I have so many wonderful memories of this kitchen,' Romy said, gazing around the room after she and Finn had kicked off their wellies in the porch. 'It was always so homely and filled with the delicious aroma of baking or roast dinners and Yorkshire puddings; it's good to see nothing's changed there.' The four of them laughed; Romy was fondly remembered in the Tindall family for her liking of Jill's Yorkshire puddings and her capacity to devour even more of them than Finn. 'And I love the new colour scheme and the Christmas decorations, too, they're gorgeous.'

'Aye, it's had a few colour changes over the years, but I think this French grey is my favourite,' said Jill.

Finn was relieved his mum didn't go on to say anything about the changes that had taken place when Britt lived there. Many of them hadn't gone down well with his parents particularly when the kitchen table that had been in the family for generations, their much-loved dresser and the stick-back chairs had to go into storage during Britt's reign – they'd since been reinstated – though they'd stood their ground and given a firm no when she'd wanted to have the Aga removed. 'I don't care what her majesty wants, that's staying put,' Jill had said firmly. Finn had regularly found himself in a tricky position with his mum and Britt. And, much as he could see both sides as far as the kitchen was concerned and he appreciated how his now ex-wife would want to put her own stamp on the place, he had to agree with his parents about the Aga. Castlegate Farm without its trusty range belting out heat was unthinkable!

Like the kitchen at Holly Tree Cottage, the one at Castlegate Farm was brimming with character, boasting a heavily beamed ceiling, though here they were higher than the head-skimming ones at the cottage. York flags covered the floor, worn smooth with age, and there were two large sash windows that allowed light to flood in. Though the colour of the walls and soft furnishings had changed, the furniture was exactly the same as it was when Romy had last visited. A huge pine dresser sat against one wall, still playing host to the floral tea service Jill collected – and added to every birthday, Christmas and wedding anniversary. Alongside it was a jug filled with pens while Christmas cards were slotted in any available space. The same long, battered table still occupied the centre of the room, bearing the scars of years' of family meals and homework, when school books had been scattered across it. The old armchair had been re-covered and the cushions replaced, as had those on the two wooden chairs, but the kitchen units were the same, though they'd been painstakingly sanded down and repainted by Jill when Britt had left. The furniture had been moved back in then, too, along with Jill's treasured tea service since there was no room for it at the barn conversion.

'Here, let me take your coat, lovey,' said Jill. 'And make yourself at home.'

'Aye, and I'll pour you a cup of tea,' said Tommy. 'It should be mashed to perfection by now.' He grinned over at her. Tommy was known in the family for his liking for mugs of strong builder's tea.

'Thank you.' Romy unwound her scarf, handing it to Jill while she unbuttoned her coat. It crossed Finn's mind how instantly at home she seemed.

'Oh my goodness, that was seriously delicious. Thank you, Jill,' Romy said, an empty plate before her. 'I reckon the last time I had a Sunday dinner as good as that was the last time I was here.'

'It's a pleasure, lovey, I'm glad you enjoyed it. There's apple crumble with ginger ice cream or custard for afters.' Jill, who was sitting beside Romy, beamed happily, catching her son's eye.

Finn smiled back at her. His mum was always pleased when her meals were devoured with enthusiasm. She was a simple cook, but the meals she created were always hearty and packed with flavour. He wasn't going to give any headspace to how picky Britt used to be about his mum's cooking and how she'd refuse her homemade desserts, saying they were "old fashioned" and "full of stodge".

'I can highly recommend the crumble,' he said, looking at Romy. 'And Mum made the ice cream herself with her nifty new ice cream maker.'

'Aye, me too. I'll be having both ice cream and custard,' said Tommy, stretching his arms above his head.

'Ooh, I can remember how yummy your crumbles were, Jill,' Romy said. 'You used to make the most delicious gooseberry one with the goosegogs Finn and me had collected from the bushes over in the garth. And your summer puddings were *amazing*. It's making my mouth water just thinking about them! And please tell me you still bake those scrumptious oaty biscuits that were all gooey with golden syrup? I used to *love* those.'

The Tindalls laughed fondly at her enthusiastic foodie reminiscences.

'I'm very pleased to say, she does, though not as often as I would like,' said Tommy.

Finn was struggling to take his eyes off Romy. Her cheeks were rosy from the warmth of the kitchen and her green eyes were shining. Something inside him stirred.

Jill put her arm around their guest, pulling her close and planting a kiss on her cheek. 'You always were a little ray of sunshine. And I'll tell you what, flower, we haven't half missed having you round this table.'

'Aye, too right we have. Should've been you living here instead of that—'

'Tommy!' Jill pinned her husband with a warning stare. 'Anyroad, it's just lovely you're here now.' She gave Romy's shoulder a squeeze before getting to her feet and reaching for the empty plates.

'Sorry, love.' Tommy looked suitably chastised as he stood to help clear the table. 'Anyroad, it's grand to see you can still polish off a decent amount of my good lady wife's Yorkie puds.'

Romy giggled. 'I'd forgotten just how delicious they were. My only regret is that I don't have room for any more.' She sat back in her seat and patted her stomach.

'How about we head out for a walk and have the crumble when we get back? Maybe walk our dinner off and make a bit of space for it? Wouldn't spoil if we did that, would it, Mum?'

Ted leapt to his feet at hearing "walk". He'd been watching them tucking into their Sunday dinner, drool dangling from the corners of his mouth as he shivered with anticipation. There was always a slice of roast beef in his food bowl at the end of the afternoon and it tortured him until he'd devoured it.

'Course it wouldn't, son. I'll just move it to the warming oven, should keep it nice in there.'

'What about the washing up? We can't leave your mum and dad to do it all. How about you and me get stuck in like we used to, then we can go for a leg stretch?' Romy asked.

'No need, flower,' said Jill. 'There's one of those fancy new-fangled dishwashers tucked away behind that cupboard over there. Tommy and me can stack it in no time. You two should head out while there's still plenty of light.'

'Oh, okay.' Romy switched her gaze from Jill to Finn. 'And you're sure I'm not keeping you from your work here?'

Finn shook his head. 'We try to have a bit of an easier day on a Sunday.' From the corner of his eye he noticed his parents exchanging glances. It had been a while since Finn had done anything but work since Britt and the lads had left. They knew he couldn't sit still in case his brooding thoughts caught up with him and sent his mood spiralling downwards, which had been the case since his marriage had fallen apart.

'And I'm happy to bob out and check on the sheep,' Tommy said, smiling. You should make the most of the sun while you can. The forecast for next week is a stinker.'

Finn chose not to dwell on the heavy snowfall that had been predicted and the potential impact it could have on the visit from his sons; he'd worry about that when the time arose. Camm had already told him he'd do all he could to keep the roads clear which had offered a degree of reassurance. Finn had told his parents he'd dig his way to them if he had to.

Romy glanced over to the window to see the snow had stopped and the yard was now filled with winter sunshine. 'If you're sure you don't mind?' she said, turning back to the three of them.

'Of course we're sure, come on.' Finn grabbed Ted's lead and, on cue, the Labrador raced across the room, his claws skittering over the flagstone floor to the porch, his enthusiasm making everyone laugh.

'Someone's keen,' Romy said through her giggles.

He's not the only one. Finn couldn't wait to get Romy to himself again. His feelings may have been numbed over the last year but he was certain he hadn't imagined the chemistry that had danced between them over the dinner table. He'd seen that sparkle in her eyes before. It may have been a long time ago, but it was having the same effect on him now as it had then. He wondered if she'd noticed it too. And if she had, how did she feel about it?

TWENTY-TWO

Romy

Romy couldn't remember the last time she'd felt so utterly carefree and content. The few hours she'd had back in the fold of the Tindall family had buoyed her mood no end, not to mention the sparks she'd felt crackling between her and Finn. She didn't know what it was about him, but there was something indefinable that made it feel so good to be around him. It was like déjà vu. Though she reminded herself that she hadn't been back five minutes, and it was way too early to let her feelings get carried away with themselves. All the same, she wondered if his parents had noticed the frisson that had been dancing between her and their son over the dinner table, the lingering gazes as they'd reminisced – she was sure she hadn't imagined it. At least, she hoped she hadn't.

As for the guilt she'd felt at severing all contact with Finn and his parents, that had been assuaged by their warm welcome, much to her relief, and she'd been delighted to find they'd been genuinely pleased to see her, as she was them. It had been wonderful to sit around the kitchen table with the Tindall family once more, recounting tales of her and Finn's time in the Young Farmers' Club, laughing at the anecdotes Tommy told in his familiar dry manner. She'd almost choked on her roast potato she'd been laughing so hard as he'd recounted the time Finn's jeans had fallen down in the middle of a tug of war at a Young Farmers' rally in Beckinthwaite. Finn had been undeterred and had carried on pulling at the rope with all his might, his jeans around his ankles, until the Danskelfe branch was declared the victor.

'I reckon the sight of our Finn's skinny, chicken legs frightened the life out of the opposition, and they gave up just so he could pull his trousers back up and get 'em covered up. Good tactics, lad.' He'd given Finn an exaggerated wink and had them all howling with laughter.

Romy had witnessed the tug of war, but the way Tommy had described it was priceless. She'd forgotten how hilarious he could be and she'd laughed so hard over the meal her ribs had hurt by the end of it. It was as if the years she'd spent away had shrunk to nothing. Her dad used to describe the Tindalls as being "the salt of the earth" and today she understood exactly what he'd meant. They were magnanimous and generous spirited, something she was thankful for. She wouldn't have blamed them if they'd been cool with her after how shabbily she'd treated their son, but they'd welcomed her with open arms, full of empathy for what she'd been through herself. It felt good to be back, and she regretted staying away for so long.

And now, out in the crisp, fresh air, with the moors looking so breathtakingly beautiful and Finn walking along beside her, Romy was aware of those long-forgotten emotions she'd had for him coming back to life. She didn't know how it was possible, she'd only been back a day. All she knew was that something about it felt so right.

She stole a look at him, her heart lifting at his handsome profile. His strong, well-defined jaw had lost the layer of puppy fat that had softened it all those years ago. It was the perfect complement to his straight nose. She felt a pang of affection at how his hair still stood on end just as it used to when he was younger. The unexpected urge to run her fingers through it was so strong she had to consciously stop herself; she wasn't sure how well it would go down after all this time.

Finn glanced across at her and she felt her cheeks grow warm at being caught studying his face so closely. She returned his smile and switched her attention to Ted who was having a whale of a time charging about, kicking up lumps of snow, and wearing an expression of pure joy.

'I think it might be best if we just follow the track through the farm as far as we're able to. Dad and me cleared it up to the furthest field where the sheep are this morning and it looks like we haven't had too much more snow since then, so it should be okay.'

'Good plan.' Romy paused, her blushes fading. She sucked in a lungful of chilly air as she gazed out at the view. Her eyes landed on Lytell Stangdale in the distance, smoke snaking from the squat chimney stacks of the cottages there. It made for a cosy sight. 'How could anyone not want to live here?' she said with a sigh.

'You'd be surprised,' Finn said, stopping beside her. 'Can't imagine living anywhere else, myself.'

The hint of sadness in his voice made her turn to face him. Feeling bold, she said, 'I'm guessing you're referring to your ex?' She gave a sympathetic smile. He hadn't shared what had happened with his marriage but then again, since she'd taken up most of last night talking about herself, the poor bloke hadn't had the opportunity.

'Aye, she seemed happy enough at first, but once the lads went to school, she found being married to a farmer and living out in the sticks wasn't for her. Said the pace of life was too slow and all folk could talk about was tups, heifers and tractors; reckoned it was "mind-numbingly boring".' He chuckled at that. 'Mind, at times, she might've had a point, especially when a few of us got together in the Sunne. I reckon the conversation might not have been too thrilling for her. Molly still pulls us up about it – does it in a jokey way, but we're in no doubt she means it – or at least she did when I was a regular.' He smiled at that and Romy found herself smiling back.

From the way he'd spoken about his sons, she knew that though he was making light of his split with Britt, the lack of involvement in their lives hurt him deeply. Even at the tender age of seventeen, he'd never made a secret of his desire to be a dad; he used to talk about how he wanted at least four children – two boys and two girls – and she knew it was a future he'd planned with her at his side. She'd been enraptured by the idea too, dreaming of the pair of them with their noisy little family living happily at Castlegate Farm.

She stuffed her hands in her pockets and stifled a sigh; now wasn't the time for wishing she could turn the clock back, undo some of those ill-founded decisions she'd made in haste. And besides, it was Finn's turn to talk; she needed to give him her undivided attention, just as he'd done with her the previous night.

'So what happened with you and Britt? I want to hear everything that's happened in your life since I was last here – if you're okay to talk about it, that is,' she said softly. 'But I wouldn't blame you if you think I don't deserve to know.'

'Don't say that; 'course you deserve to know, Romes.'

He blew out a long breath that billowed into a cloud in front of his face, then turned and started heading down the track again, pristine white fields stretching out either side. Romy followed his lead, their wellies sinking into the snow, while Ted gambolled along in front of them. 'I suppose the writing was on the wall right from the start, if I'm honest. I met Britt on a night out over in Middleton-le-Moors. It was a mate's stag do – Will Smith from Danskelfe, you might remember him – and a few of us had hired a minibus to get us there and back, doing the usual you know, bit of a pub crawl, finishing off at the Indian restaurant that was there at the time, the imaginatively named Middleton-le-Moors Tandoori – I dare say you remember it.'

'How could I forget? Their butter chicken was out of this world.' Romy caught his eye and gave him a cheeky smile, sharing a memory of how they occasionally used to get a takeaway as a Saturday night treat.

'Ah, well, I beg to differ, I reckon their lamb pasanda had the edge, if I'm honest.' He smiled back, his eyes crinkling in a way that made her insides flutter.

'Ah, then I reckon we'll have to agree to disagree,' she said, nudging him with her elbow and making him chuckle. 'Anyway, sorry I interrupted you.'

'No problem. So, the night was pretty tame, easy-going sort of stuff, boring by some standards, I s'pose. Anyway, Britt was in The Golden Fleece that night when we walked in. Turns out she was on a hen do with some lasses she worked with and wasn't having a great time by all accounts. We got chatting and seemed to hit it off, so I took the plunge, asked for her number and we met up again a week later.'

'So far, so good,' said Romy.

'Hmm. What I hadn't realised was that Britt was on the rebound. A couple of weeks before I met her, she'd split up with her fiancé. She'd been with him for nearly four years and engaged for one of them. Apparently, he'd woken up one morning and decided he didn't want to marry her. Told her he didn't want to marry anyone, and that was that. They called the wedding off. Her sister told me later that she'd been devastated, even more so when she found out he'd started seeing someone new shortly afterwards.'

'Ouch! That can't have been nice for Britt,' said Romy. She had first-hand experience of being dumped for a newer model and it hurt like heck.

She listened as Finn told her that his relationship with Britt had moved quickly and they'd married a year later, with Britt being the driving force. He was keen to point out that he'd been happy to go along with it. 'It felt like a new start. I'd put my life on hold until then.'

Guilt pinched hard in Romy's chest as he told her that after she'd left and he'd accepted that their relationship was over, that she wasn't coming back, it had taken him a while before he'd felt confident enough to dip his toe in the dating pool again. She'd been surprised to hear that he hadn't dated many girls between her and

Britt; not only was he good-looking, tall and muscular but he had a good sense of humour too. She used to see how the girls eyed him appreciatively, flirted around him, though she recalled how he'd always been oblivious to it, unlike his brother, Dougie, who seemed to have a different girlfriend every week.

'What "relationships" I had fizzled out before they'd even got started. And I take full responsibility for that.' He swallowed audibly. 'I'm going to be honest here and say the reason was because no one was you, Romy. Anyone else was second best and who would want to be that? Things seemed different with Britt, but if I'm honest, though I did genuinely love her, it wasn't the same all-encompassing love I had for you, And I know we were kids, but I've never felt the same way about anyone the way I felt for you. There were never any sparks.' He puffed out a sigh. 'There, I've said it.'

Romy's heart stilled; much as she was desperate to look at him, she was too scared to see the feelings etched across his face, she knew it would undo her. It was bad enough that her legs felt ready to buckle at any moment.

'I don't want you to think I'm being full-on telling you all this when you've just come back but—'

'It doesn't feel like that at all.' She rested her hand on his arm, forcing her gaze to meet his. 'It's only right we're honest with each other, Finn. We'd been close for so many years. I'd much rather we were open right from the start. Get the air cleared.' She smiled up at him. 'It was the same for me, I never found that depth of love with anyone else either. In the end, I gave up looking for it.'

He returned her smile, his eyes, full of questions, lingering on her face.

'Anyway, sorry, I interrupted you again.' Much as Romy knew they needed to talk about this some more and address the feelings they both shared, Finn still needed to tell her about his marriage and she didn't want to hijack the conversation. After all, they had plenty of time now; she was in Lytell Stangdale for two weeks.

'S'okay.' He smiled again. 'It wasn't just me whose heart wasn't in the marriage, I don't think Britt ever got over her ex, but we just seemed to plough on, go through the motions, and I realise as I'm telling you this how awful it makes us sound; that we clearly didn't take our marriage seriously.'

'It actually feels scarily familiar, if I'm honest.' She gave a shiver, suddenly aware of how bitterly cold it had become.

TWENTY-THREE

Finn

It felt good to talk to Romy, just like it used to. Finn had kept his feelings to himself and hadn't want to burden his parents with all his sadness and sense of failure over his divorce, especially with how devastated they'd been when Kyle and Toby had moved out. But talking to Romy felt cathartic. She'd always been a good listener, never judging, knowing the right words to say and when to say them, making him laugh when the moment needed lifting.

As they walked, he told her how his mum and Britt had clashed when Britt had moved in at Castlegate Farm. His new wife had been more than a little tactless with her opinions and wishes for the farmhouse, seemingly oblivious to how hurtful her blunt comments could be. Britt had not only wanted to redecorate – which he and his parents had expected and completely understood – but she'd swept in with plans to gut the place or, "drag it kicking and screaming into the twenty-first century," as she'd announced. As well as having the Aga removed, these plans had included ripping out the original stone fireplaces in the kitchen and living room, both of which were over two-hundred years old, replacing them with modern alternatives. She'd also wanted to concrete over the original flagstones in the kitchen and fit vinyl flooring, declaring it would be easier to maintain. Tommy and Jill had been outraged by these suggestions, saying such drastic changes would impact on the character and history of their beloved farmhouse. Finn had to agree; he'd been as shocked as they had by Britt's ideas. It hadn't gone down well with her when her new in-laws had told her in no uncertain terms that, while they had no objections to her redecorating, there was no way any fireplaces were going to be removed, nor flags permanently damaged by concrete. However, Tommy and Jill had been mindful that their refusal would no doubt create a stressful time in their son's marriage, so they'd agreed to the installation of an extra cooker in the form of a new electric oven with a Calor gas hob which could be used for cooking on instead of the Aga. They'd hoped it would soften the blow, saying Britt could have the oven of her choice and they'd foot the bill. It had come as no surprise when she'd chosen a top of the range model with a price tag to match.

Much as Finn had been able to see both sides of the argument, he'd felt uncomfortable being in the middle, caught in the crossfire. Britt's and his taste in décor was different to that of his parents, so he'd agreed with her that the rooms would benefit from a refresh in that respect. But the drastic changes his wife had suggested were too brutal and insensitive to the lovely old farmhouse, so he'd been able to fully understand his parents' outrage and hurt. And it wasn't as if he and Britt owned the property and were free to do what they wanted with it; it was in the farm trust his parents had set up. On top of that, they were living there rent-free, with just the utility bills to pay.

'Sounds fair to say it wasn't the best start to married life with so much animosity bubbling away between your new wife and your parents,' Romy said. 'Can't have been easy for any of you.'

He gave a wry laugh. 'You're not wrong there. But it wasn't all stress and doom and gloom. We did have some happy times together, especially when the lads arrived.' Images of his sons as newborns filled his mind, raising a smile. 'They seemed to bring us closer together for a while. And in fairness to Britt she doted on them when they were little.' He pushed down the wave of regret that was rising in his chest and drew in a long breath, the cold air filling his lungs. 'I'm so lucky to have the lads in my life.'

'And they're lucky to have you in theirs, I'll bet you're an awesome dad.' Romy smiled up at him. 'Kyle and Toby have been something really positive to come out of your marriage; it was something you needed to go through in order to have them.'

'Aye, and I'd go through it all again if I had to.' Though he wasn't so sure Britt would agree that he was an awesome dad.

They were distracted as a small squadron of brightly coloured crested birds flitted by in a blur, landing on a nearby hawthorn hedge, the red berries vivid against the stark white of the snow. In a moment, the colourful birds' high-pitched trilling filled the air as they set to work, stripping the hedge of its fruit.

Romy gasped. 'Oh, they're so pretty!'

'They're waxwings. I've heard there's higher numbers overwintering in the UK this year.' He watched as she whipped out her phone, and snapped away at them. 'Useless piece of information here, they fly over from Scandinavia for the winter and a large influx is known as an "irruption", believe it or not. Happens when there's not enough food for the number of birds, apparently.'

'Check out Mr Wildlife Expert over there.'

Finn couldn't help but laugh. 'I should probably 'fess up that I saw it on a farming programme a couple of weeks ago.'

'Well,' she said, putting her phone away, 'you learn something new every day. And I'm already getting some ideas of how to use waxwings in a piece of needle felting, they're such gorgeous little birds.'

He gazed down at her, losing himself in her green eyes with the gold flecks that he remembered so well. Her cheeks and nose were glowing red from the cold. She smiled, drawing his eyes to her full lips, the very ones he'd kissed so many times before. He longed to do it again right now, wondering if they'd feel the same.

His thoughts were unceremoniously disturbed by snow flying

towards them. 'What the...?' He scrunched his face up as icy clumps landed on his cheeks.

'Arghh!' Romy shielded her face with her hand, laughing. 'What's happening?'

They both risked a look, to see Ted with his back to them, digging frantically in the hedgerow and sending snow hurtling in their direction.

'Ted! Stop!' Finn said through his laughter.

The Labrador ceased his digging in an instant and bounded towards them, his haste impeded by the deep snow that had drifted to the side of the track. He stopped in front of Finn and gazed up at him as if to say, 'Yes, Dad? What's up?'

Finn's heart squeezed with affection at his hapless pooch and he couldn't help but smile at the snow covering Ted's face and dangling from his whiskers. Romy was shaking with laughter beside him, her giggles infectious.

'Snow brings out his excitable side, or maybe that should be it *increases* his excitable side, not that it takes much,' said Finn.

'That right, Ted?' She bent to tickle Ted under the chin which had his tail wagging so hard his whole body wiggled.

They watched as he took off, giddily leaping backwards and forwards before circling around them, ears flapping, tongue lolling. That done, he pushed his face into the snow, reappearing a second later, sneezing and spluttering.

'Oh, Ted, you're hilarious.' Romy threw her head back and roared with laughter which only added to the Labrador's excitement.

Before they knew what was happening, Ted hurtled towards them and leapt into the air, catching Romy with his solid body and knocking her off her feet. She lay flat on her back in the snow, arms outstretched, laughing hard until the high-spirited Labrador pushed a whiskery face into hers and made her shriek.

Finn could barely speak for laughing. 'Ted! Stop!' But his words fell on deaf ears as Ted continued with his mischief, the stillness of the dale echoing with the sound of Finn and Romy's laughter.

Finn reached for the Labrador's collar and pulled him back which took a couple of attempts, then quickly bent down, offering Romy his hand. As he went to pull her up, Ted, who evidently thought this was all part of the game, leapt at his dad and knocked him off balance too. Before Finn knew what was happening he found himself lying on top of Romy, his face inches away from hers, the steam of their breath merging into one.

'Oh!' she said, those green eyes he'd been thinking of before Ted's untimely interruption, looking into his and sending his pulse racing.

In that moment, their laughing ceased and electricity crackled between them, Ted's antics forgotten. All Finn could think of was how much he wanted to kiss Romy. And from the way she was looking back at him, he was pretty sure she was thinking the same thing too. His mind hurtled back to twenty-one years ago and the last time he'd seen her looking at him that way. It was the evening of the Young Farmers' barbecue, when they'd shared their first kiss. That precious memory and the look in her eyes offered him hope. He cupped her cheek with his hand, watching her reaction closely. Snowflakes started falling but he was too lost in the moment to notice. He moved tentatively closer, his gaze never leaving hers. Her lips parted as Finn's spirits soared, only to be brought crashing down by the unwelcome smell of dog breath as Ted pushed his whiskery face between them, swiping a warm, wet tongue across his cheek. 'For crying out loud, you little shi—' He felt Ted's tongue slurp across his face again.

Romy started to giggle and Finn pushed himself up. The moment hadn't just gone, it had been well and truly shattered; he knew when to admit defeat.

Ted gave a bark as he looked on, apparently pleased with himself.

After he'd helped Romy to her feet, Finn brushed the snow off his jacket, eyeing Ted with faux irritation. Much as it would have been so easy to be cross with him, the look on the Labrador's face melted his heart and he couldn't help but laugh. 'Remind me to do something about that breath of yours, fella. I don't know what you've been eating but it just about melted my eyeballs.'

Ted responded with another wag of his tail, sending yet more snow flying.

'Hmm. Much as I find you adorable, Ted, I'm afraid I have to agree.' Romy laughed, wiping Ted's slobber off her face.

Finn was suddenly aware of the cold biting harder and noticed Romy shivering, no doubt exacerbated by the pair of them ending up in a heap in the snow. 'Looking at the sky, I reckon we'd best head back before the snow starts getting heavy.' He was trying not to think too much about their "almost" moment, telling himself it was probably for the best it hadn't happened. *She's only been here for one day, what's the rush?*

Romy glanced upwards, her teeth chattering, the occasional snowflake drifting down. The blue sky of earlier had been smothered by a dense blanket of clouds that hung low over Danskelfe Dale and the surrounding area. They were tinged with purple which usually signalled heavy snow wasn't far away. She rubbed her gloved hands together and nodded. 'I reckon you're right.'

Finn whistled for Ted, whose excitement had finally subsided, and the three of them set off for Castlegate Farm. Finn set the pace, putting his best foot forward in the hope walking quickly – or as quickly as was possible in the snow – would generate a bit of warmth in Romy and that they'd get home before the snow got too bad.

On the way back, Romy gave Finn a potted history of her marriage to Russ. As she spoke, Finn noticed that what she'd said earlier about looking for a father figure seemed to ring true. He got the impression she'd been a lost soul, just looking for someone to love her and for her to love back. He'd found himself longing to wrap his arms around her and hold her close. Instead, he'd listened as Romy went on to explain how she and her husband had simply rubbed along together, neither of them being driven by any great passion for the other. He hadn't told her until after they were married that he didn't want any more children – he had two daughters from his first marriage with whom Romy had got on well.

'It made me realise we should've talked about it before we got married, but it simply hadn't occurred to me then. I just foolishly jumped in without thinking about it, or very much else, actually. One of his daughters, Leesa, told me that he was looking for a wife who could look after him in his old age!' And though she'd said it jokingly, it had set alarm bells ringing.

'You're kidding me?' Finn said, aghast.

'I'm not.'

'Did you confront him about it?'

'I did, and he told me it wasn't the *only* reason he'd married me, that he *did* love me, but then he went on to say that marrying someone younger than him meant he wouldn't be a burden to his daughters when he got old. I should've realised before that; he had a big thing about getting older, went on about it all the time, and it didn't help that he was a bit of a hypochondriac and every time he got so much as a sniff, he thought he was at death's door. Unfortunately, it got worse during the last couple of years of our marriage.'

'I hope you don't mind me saying, but isn't making sure you've got a carer in your old age a weird reason to get married?'

'No weirder than someone doing it because they were looking for a father figure, I suppose. Though I have to say, my reasons were subconscious. The first time I gave it any thought was when Russ pointed it out to me after I'd mentioned what Leesa had said about his reason for marrying me. I couldn't really argue when I thought about it. Still didn't stop it hurting or coming as a shock when he told me we were over.'

'Divorce is never easy whichever side of it you're on,' Finn said ruefully. 'Were you married long?'

'Five years. And, at the risk of sounding cold and heartless, though it was hard, it wasn't the worst emotional pain I've felt in my life. Losing my dad the way we did, and the aftermath, that was, well... you know?'

'I do, Romes.' Impulsively, he threw his arm around her and gave her a squeeze, taking comfort in the fact she didn't pull away. And, unless he was mistaken, he could swear she was leaning into him. 'But you're on the right side of it all now. Ready to make a new life for yourself.'

'You're right, and that's exactly what I intend to do.' Finn was glad to see her face brighten. He reluctantly let his arm drop.

'So, have you made any plans for your stay here?'

'I haven't really. I didn't know what to expect so I thought I'd play it by ear. I'll check my online shop, see if anything needs sending off. I brought all my equipment to make some new stock if the mood took me. Other than that, I was hoping to go for lots of walks, catch up with folk – if anyone wanted to meet me – that kind of thing. I definitely want to get in touch with Ella.'

'She'll be chuffed to bits to know you're back.'

'I hope so.'

'And what about Christmas Day?'

'Christmas Day? Hmm, well, I'll be at Holly Tree Cottage. I'm going to pay a visit to the village shop in the morning and stock up on some tasty stuff for a Christmas dinner. And on the Big Day, I intend to slob out in front of the telly, have a long soak in the bath. *Bliss!* Oh, and I'm hoping to catch up on my reading – my TBR pile is so high it's in danger of toppling over, even though a load of the books are actually on my Kindle.' She chuckled at that.

Finn stopped in his tracks, Romy coming to a halt beside him. 'You're seriously telling me you're going to be on your own for Christmas Day?' Saying it out loud made it seem worse, if that was possible. The Romy he remembered was a sociable, bubbly person who liked to be around people, being on her own on such a special day felt wrong.

'I am and it's fine. I've brought a fluffy onesie and fully intend to stay in it all day, as well as do some serious damage to the huge box of chocolates I treated myself to from The Chocolate Cherub in Middleton-le-Moors when I stopped off yesterday.' A snowflake landed on the tip of her nose and she puffed it away, smiling up at him.

'I know I can speak on behalf of my parents when I say you'd be very welcome to join us up at the farm on Christmas Day. Oh, and feel free to bring your onesie.' His eyes twinkled at her; he noted from the roses in her cheeks that their faster walking pace had gone some way to warming her up a little. It reminded him they needed to keep moving, especially now the snow was falling more heavily.

'But what about Kyle and Toby, won't they be with you for the day?'

'No, they'll be with their mum; I've got them for a couple of days after Christmas.' He started walking again, Romy in step beside him. He could almost hear the thoughts turning over in her mind.

'The last thing I want is to be a nuisance or intrude on your family's day.'

He gave her a "Really?' look. 'Romes, you've seen how chuffed my mum and dad are that you're back. Honestly, they'll be over the moon if you join us. And so will I.' They exchanged a smile, Finn willing her to say yes.

'In that case, I'd love to, but on the condition you run it by your mum and dad first. I don't want them to get a shock if I rock up unannounced on Christmas morning. *Tada!*' she said, making jazz hands.

'Fair enough, but I reckon they'd still be happy to see you if you rocked up unannounced.'

She linked his arm. 'Tell you what, can we get a bit of a speed-wobble on? The rest of me might have warmed up but my feet are absolutely nithered and I can't feel my toes anymore.'

'Course, come on.' He hugged her arm close to him as they strode on, Ted jumping around and snapping at the snowflakes, his enthusiasm apparently unwavering.

By the time they arrived back at the farmhouse, the snow was falling thick and fast and they were covered in a generous dusting.

'Brr! It's *so* cold out there!' said Romy as they kicked off their wellies in the porch. 'And it's not just my feet that are like blocks of ice, my fingers are literally numb, I can't even undo the buttons on my coat.'

Finn chuckled. 'Here, let me help.'

'Thanks.' She glanced up at him. 'And I'm aware of a red glow in front of my face which I'm guessing is my nose.'

He chuckled again. 'It is a little rosy, but I promise to keep all Rudolph jokes to a minimum.'

'I'd appreciate that.' She giggled, which was a sound Finn was growing to love all over again.

'There, done,' he said, once he'd finished the final button.

Hanging up their coats, they pushed open the door to the kitchen, Romy releasing an appreciative sigh as the warmth from the Aga wrapped itself around them.

After a quick rub down with an old towel, Ted shot over to his bed, checking his food bowl en route just in case the food fairies had been and left him a treat or two. He wasn't disappointed, and devoured the bits of beef he found there with his usual enthusiasm, making Romy chuckle. 'Did you get a chance to taste that, Ted?'

Ted's tail gave a quick swish.

'Ted reckons taste is highly overrated, don't you, fella?' Finn smiled over at the Labrador. 'He eats like there's competition for whatever's in his bowl. Hasn't dawned on him yet he's the only dog here.'

'I know the feeling, I've been told I wolf my grub down in exactly the same way,' said Romy.

'No comment.' Finn grinned at her.

'Hey, cheeky!' She nudged him with her arm.

'Cuppa?' asked Jill, kettle in hand, looking pleased to see them back.

'Sounds good,' said Finn. 'You happy to stay for one, Romes?'

'Only if you think it's okay, weatherwise, I mean. I don't want to delay getting back and you having to risk being out on the roads if they're likely to be dangerous later on. Then, again,' she said, looking thoughtful, 'I could always walk back.'

'You'll do no such thing, lovey!' said Jill. 'I heard Camm go by in the plough not half an hour ago. And our Finn wouldn't think of letting you walk home in this weather, you'd be soaked through and chilled to the bone by the time you got to Lytell Stangdale, and it'd be dark too.'

As Jill went over to the sink to fill the kettle, the porch door flew open and in walked Tommy, his flat cap topped with a layer of snow, his already ruddy cheeks almost purple with the cold. Ted trotted over to greet him.

'By, it isn't half raw out there now,' Tommy said, blowing into his hands that were glove free before reaching down and giving Ted a quick pat. 'Now then, lad.'

'Wellies, love!' said Jill, rolling her eyes and shaking her head in her usual affectionate way.

The four of them were sitting around the table, drinking tea as Finn told his parents about the waxwings he and Romy had seen.

'Aye, they're bonny birds,' said Tommy, dunking an oaty biscuit into his mug and cursing mildly when it crumbled before it reached his mouth.

'Nice one, Dad.' Finn grinned.

'You're very welcome to stay for your evening meal, lovey,' Jill said to Romy. 'It's only soup and some homemade bread but there's plenty to go round. I'll be putting it on to warm in about an hour. Or if you'd prefer, I could put some in a tub for you to heat up back at Holly Tree Cottage.'

'Thanks, Jill, that's really kind but I think I'd best be heading back once I've finished my tea.'

The question prompted Finn to bring up Romy's invitation to join them for Christmas dinner.

'We'd love to have you, sweetheart,' Jill said, clapping her hands together, a wide smile reaching all the way up to her eyes.

'Tommy and me had actually been discussing it while you were out.'

'Aye, we were, and we can't think of owt better, lass.' Tommy looked up from scooping up the soggy lump of biscuit and beamed at her. 'This table's too big for just the three of us. And besides, it wouldn't be right, you spending the day on your tod over at the cottage; it'll be grand having you with us.'

It was exactly the sort of response Finn had expected from his parents. And from the way Romy was smiling, he could tell she was thrilled by their enthusiastic reaction.

'Thank you. But you've got to let me contribute in some way; is there anything I can bring?' she asked.

'Just yourself, flower, nowt else. You should see the state of the pantry, the shelves are bulging, we're stocked up with everything we need.' Tommy's smile was now as wide as his wife's.

'Having you with us will make it extra special, lovey,' said Jill.

'Told you they'd be chuffed about it,' said Finn.

'Thank you, that's so kind.'

If he wasn't mistaken, Finn thought Romy looked a little choked up; her eyes were glistening and he was sure her bottom lip wobbled.

'Right then, time for one last top up.' Jill scooped up the teapot and was refilling Romy's mug when the sound of a mobile phone rang out into the room.

'Ey up, who could that be on a Sunday?' said Tommy, making to push himself up.

'It's our Finn's phone, love.' Jill glanced out at the snow before shooting her son a loaded look.

Finn's heart sank; from her tone, she was clearly thinking the same as him: it was Britt, cancelling the lads' visit on account of the weather. He knew she'd be keeping as close an eye on the forecast as him. He felt torn about answering it, not wanting to appear rude to Romy but also desperate to put himself out of his misery knowing it would torment him until he knew. And if it was Britt, she always complained if he didn't pick up straight away. 'I'll call back later,' he said, making a quick decision; he was prepared to suffer her displeasure on this occasion.

'Please don't on my account.' Romy looked at him.

'It might be Britt, I'd at least check, son,' said Tommy.

Finn strode over to the dresser and scooped up his phone. His shoulders tensed as he saw his ex's number glaring back at him requesting a FaceTime call. He had a horrible sinking feeling she was going to confirm his fears and cancel their sons' visit to the farm.

TWENTY-FOUR

Finn

Finn accepted the call and was thrilled when he was greeted by the sight of his two sons beaming out at him. His heart soared. 'Hey there, lads.'

'Hi, Dad,' they said in unison, both waving enthusiastically.

'This is a nice surprise! How are you both? How was your flight? And are you excited to see the snow?' He laughed, beyond delighted to see their cheeky faces. A cheery chorus of yeses followed.

'We had some tumbulents on the flight, Dad,' said Toby. From the way he was bouncing up and down Finn could see his youngest son was excited to share this piece of news.

'He means turbulence,' said Kyle, adopting a grown-up tone.

'That's what I said, Kyle.'

'No, you didn't, Tobes.'

'Boys.' Britt's gently reproving voice filtered through from the background.

'Anyway, it was *so* cool! Mum's coffee splashed *everywhere* and my candy fell on the floor.' Though Toby's eyes were wide with excitement, they were tinged with tiredness which Finn attributed to the remnants of jet lag. He'd also notice that a hint of an American twang had crept in with both lads – not to mention Toby's use of the word "candy" instead of "sweets" – which, to Finn's ear, made for a slightly incongruous mix with their North Yorkshire accent.

'Are you looking forward to coming over to the farm?' he asked, unable to stop smiling. He wished he could reach in and hug them to him.

'Yeah,' they both said brightly, Toby punching the air and dancing in his seat. He'd always been the most expressive of his sons, with Kyle being the more reserved; more like Finn. Kyle had also inherited his dad's sticky-up hair and bright-blue eyes, where Toby bore a strong resemblance to Britt with her blonde hair and grey eyes.

Their rush of enthusiasm came as a welcome relief. On the last few video calls, he'd noticed Kyle had seemed subdued. Finn had started to worry his eldest son was drifting away from him, that he'd lost interest in talking to his father now his life was filled with bigger and brighter things, and that the farm had lost its appeal, was something he'd moved on from and would rather forget. The thought had saddened Finn. Of the two of them, Kyle had been the one who'd loved being out on the farm with his dad and grandad, seemingly taking pleasure in telling them how he was going to be the next generation of Tindalls to take over at Castlegate Farm. Under the guidance of Finn and Tommy, he'd even started his own small flock of Cheviots and had been eager to learn how to improve it. Much as his younger brother enjoyed being outdoors and helping, Toby's interest waned quickly and he'd slip back inside to play on his games consoles.

After a brief catch-up, Finn heard Britt telling the boys it was her turn to speak, and before he had a chance to prepare himself, his ex-wife's face appeared on the screen.

'Hello, Finn.' She gave him a tight smile, instantly snuffing out the joy he'd felt at speaking to Kyle and Toby. He noticed she looked tanned, her blonde hair extra glossy and she was smartly dressed as if she was getting ready to go out. There was no escaping it, she'd always been an attractive woman

'Hi, Britt. How's things? You look well. Good flight?' He could've kicked himself as soon as the last question had slipped out of his mouth; Toby had already mentioned the turbulence. *You really don't help yourself, do you?* On the few times Finn and Britt had been abroad together and experienced a bumpy flight, she'd been on the verge of hysteria, gripping the armrests for dear life. Her fear had been real and he'd done all he could to reassure her at the time.

She gave a barely-discernible roll of her eyes. 'Turbulence aside, I suppose it wasn't too bad; bit long.'

'Yeah, I can imagine.' For the sake of his sons, he forced an upbeat tone into his voice and, praying she hadn't changed her mind, asked, 'So, are we still on track for Boxing Day?'

He couldn't help but smile as Kyle and Toby's excited cries of, 'Yes!' rang out in the background. 'We can't wait, Dad,' said a voice he recognised as Kyle's. It made his heart sing with happiness.

'Provided the weather doesn't get so bad we can't get through, of course,' Britt said coolly, bringing him back down to earth. She flicked her shiny blonde hair over her shoulder, her long, scarlet nails catching Finn's eye, along with her huge diamond engagement ring that glittered under the light.

'Of course, their safety is paramount. All I'll say is that Camm's aware of their visit and is doing all he can to keep the roads as clear as possible. He's even been ploughing the road up to the farm which he doesn't have to do. It's a straight run up at the minute.'

'Fair enough. But make sure you keep me up to date with the weather. It's snowing quite heavily here in Middleton-le-Moors right now. I don't want to have to venture out and end up hitting dangerous driving conditions.' Her tone was as frosty as the weather outside.

'I can assure you, Britt, there's no way I want you tackling the roads with the lads if there's the slightest chance the conditions could be dangerous. But if you're at all worried, I can come and get them in the Landie.'

She snorted scornfully at that. 'That won't be necessary. Felix has hired a Jeep Wrangler. I'm sure that'll be safe and it'll be way more comfortable that your old Land Rover, not to mention warmer.'

Finn ignored the slight to his beloved Landie and had opened his mouth to speak when he felt a hand on his shoulder.

'We're just going into the living room with Romy,' Jill said in a loud stage whisper. 'Then you can carry on your chat in private, lovey. Wouldn't mind saying a quick hello to the lads before you end the call though.' She gave him a smile, gently squeezing his shoulder.

'Oh, right. Okay.' He flashed her a quick smile back, his gaze sliding to Romy who'd got to her feet, mug in hand.

'Did I just hear your mother mention the name Romy?' Britt said in a sharp whisper.

He turned back to his phone to see his ex-wife looking more than a little put out. 'Er, yes, she did.' Did he really have to tell her who called at their house?

'And I assume this is the Romy who used to be your little girlfriend?'

He felt a prickle of annoyance running up is spine. 'Romy used to be my girlfriend, yes.' He kept his voice low, too; he assumed she didn't want their sons to hear this part of the conversation.

'She's the one who ran off and didn't bother to get in touch, isn't she? The one who dumped you?'

This was a perfect reminder of what he didn't miss about Britt. He released a sigh, determined to keep calm and not rise to the bait. 'She'd had a tough time, but anyway, she's back for the festive break and she called up to see us all.' Finn didn't feel an ounce of guilt at his small white lie. And, anyway, Britt had a nerve; she'd essentially dumped him and run off herself!

'How kind of her.' Britt pushed her mouth into a disapproving pout, the one Finn had been on the receiving end of more times than he cared to remember.

When he didn't react, she said. 'I just want to make something perfectly clear before Boxing Day.'

'Fire away, Britt,' he said patiently.

'I'll have to insist that this prodigal Romy isn't around when *my* sons are staying with you at the farm. This year has involved a lot of major upheavals for them and I'm so proud of how well they've adjusted. They're just getting settled and the last thing they need right now is to be confused by you and a new lady friend who, for all we know, might do another runner before the festive season's over.' Though she was whispering, her words lost none of their impact.

Anger seared through Finn. *The nerve of the woman!* She appeared to have forgotten that she was the one who'd ripped the lads from their home and taken them to live with another man and, not content with that, then went and whisked them away to a different country! He clenched his jaw, taking a moment, gathering his thoughts and counting to ten, waiting for the heat to dissipate from his rage; there was no way he was going to let this escalate into a row, especially with Kyle and Toby within earshot, not to mention potentially Romy.

'I'm very proud of *our* sons too. They've done amazingly well after all they've been through and the last thing I would ever want is to cause them any distress or upset. Just as they're your priority, they're mine too. However, Romy is not just a friend of mine, she's also a friend of my parents and I can't, nor do I want to, dictate who they invite here, especially since they own the farmhouse. In fact, I'd like nothing better than for the lads to meet the girl who was my best friend for the bulk of my childhood, let them put a face to the name of the person they've heard me tell them stories about. But, having said that, we haven't discussed plans for her to visit on any other day but Christmas Day.' He resisted the temptation to say, 'yet'. Not only did he want to avoid annoying Britt any further, but he also didn't know what Romy's plans were beyond the big day. He wasn't going to assume that she'd accept every invitation they extended to her, especially with her having family in the village.

'Well, as long as you've taken my views on board,' Britt said, her face pinched.

'As always,' said Finn.

Their conversation continued coolly, with him asking after her other plans while she was back in the UK to which she gave perfunctory replies. As per Jill's request, it ended with Kyle and Toby having a quick catch-up with their grandparents, before which Britt had agreed to keep their arrangements for Boxing Day in place, albeit reluctantly, reminding him again of the proviso regarding the weather.

He slid his phone back onto the dresser, the usual uneasy mix of feelings swirling inside him after one of their calls: happiness at speaking to his sons, and tension caused by his interaction with Britt. He hoped Kyle and Toby hadn't picked up on any negativity, especially with it being Christmas. He was keen for them to have happy memories of their festive visit to North Yorkshire and the farm.

'Sorry about that call earlier.' Finn stole a look over at Romy in the passenger seat of the Land Rover, the wipers swiping snow from the windscreen. Darkness had descended and her face was masked by shadows.

'Hey, no worries. They sound adorable, full of fun – not that I heard much at all,' she added quickly.

He knew she was being considerate to his feelings by trying to imply she hadn't heard what Britt had said about her. It was very much like the Romy he used to know.

'Yeah, they are adorable; full of mischief, especially Toby.'

'You told them about me?'

He hadn't expected the surprise in her voice. 'Course I did! Did you honestly think I wouldn't tell them about my best mate and the things we got up to – before we were, erm, an item, of course.'

That made her giggle. 'I should hope you didn't tell *anyone* about what we got up to after then!'

They were both laughing when they became aware of the headlights of a vehicle behind them. From the dazzling brightness that filled the Land Rover, they appeared to be on full beam and had started flashing on and off, the driver sounding the horn impatiently.

'What the heck's his problem? These are hardly conditions to be belting along,' Finn said, squinting as he checked his rear view mirror.

'He's a getting a bit close for comfort.' Romy turned to look behind her.

The vehicle made as if it was going to overtake which was impossible, the road being made narrow by the snow that had been pushed into the sides by the plough.

'He's gonna clip us if he's not careful,' Finn said, a frown line appearing between his brows.

With the driver not letting up, Finn was forced to pull in as far as he was able, the vehicle finally overtaking, skidding and sliding all over the place.

'Flaming lunatic!' Finn shouted.

'You see if you can remember the first half of the number plate and I'll try to memorise the second half.' Romy's words came out in a rush.

'Good plan, it's not one I recognise. I only hope whoever was driving hasn't been up to no good and that's why they're in such a hurry.' Finn went to pull out, the Land Rover's wheels taking a moment to gain purchase in the deep snow. 'With the recent spate of thefts of farm vehicles and outbuildings being broken into round here, I'll give Jimby a call when I get back, just in case. He helps with the local social media pages, might be an idea if he gives it a mention in a post.'

Living "out in the sticks" as she called it, was something else

Britt had found unsettling, especially after a spate of dog thefts their part of the moors had been troubled with a couple of years earlier on the run-up to Christmas. She'd told Finn she couldn't sleep for worrying about criminals creeping around the farm, wondering if they were going to break into the farmhouse. She'd cited it as another reason for taking the boys to live in Middleton-le-Moors and a house that boasted a state-of-the-art security system. It was something else he found he was unable to compete with.

'Sounds like the local community pulls together even more than when I was last here,' said Romy.

'I reckon it does, especially since the Village Committee was set up a few years ago. Jimby's the driving force behind it; he's good at roping folk in. Mind, knowing what he's like, you might find yourself getting dragged into things for the couple of weeks you're here.'

'That I can believe.' Romy looked across at him and smiled.

TWENTY-FIVE

Romy

When Romy had returned to Holly Tree Cottage the previous evening, the first thing she'd done after watching for the three light flashes from Finn's old bedroom over at Castlegate Farm, was to light the stove in the living room. That done, she'd checked her website and Etsy shop, where she'd been pleased to see a manageable amount of orders had come in, all of which would be easy to pack. In the spirit of being organised, she'd cracked on straight away, wrapping the items and parcelling them up in readiness for dropping off at the local Post Office first thing.

It was while she was sorting through the box of stock she'd brought with her that Romy had spotted the needle-felt picture she'd been working on before she left for her trip to Lytell Stangdale. She'd brought it to the cottage with the intention of working on it in the evening during her stay there. It was a scene of the moors she'd created from memory. The heather was in full bloom, its soft purple hues a contrast to the dark tones of the dry stone walls and the shades of green that represented patches of farmland and verdant hedgerows. The blue sky was trimmed with the occasional fluffy white cloud. Extra interest and texture had been created by the addition of handstitched butterflies and bumble-bees, and all that remained to be done was a little bit of stitching on the faces of the sheep, subtle flecks of gold in the sun and a few more French knots in mixed shades of purple adding to the heather. As Romy had studied it, an idea had started to grow and she'd tried to visualise how the piece would look if she added a further element. Would it make it too cluttered? she'd wondered. Would it affect the balance of the design? The more she'd tried to picture it, the more she became convinced that, with the odd tweak here and there, her new idea would work rather well. It had sent a thrill zinging through her and she'd set to, making the changes straight away, Christmas carols playing softly in the background.

As she'd stitched and snipped and teased-out the felt, she'd found herself thinking how quickly she felt settled, not only in the cottage, but in Lytell Stangdale too. It was a feeling she hadn't enjoyed for more years than she cared to remember. She'd mulled over the events of the day, and how much she'd enjoyed spending time with Finn and his family again. It really was as if she'd never been away. Granted, Jill and Tommy looked older – didn't they all! – with flecks of grey in their hair, extra lines around the eyes. Tommy in particular looked more craggy-faced than he had the last time she'd seen him, which was no doubt owing to him working outside in all weathers. But beneath that, they were still the same warm-hearted, generous-spirited people she remembered. The welcome they'd given her was adding weight to the prospect of a permanent return to Lytell Stangdale.

Ella Welford had slipped into her thoughts, triggering a tug in her heart at yet another person she'd turned her back on. She hoped her friend would be as forgiving and as happy to see her as the Tindalls had been. Once she'd posted off her orders, Romy promised herself she'd make contact with Ella, see if she'd be willing to meet up.

It wasn't all that had occupied her mind that night, though. Despite her best efforts, Romy had found her thoughts leading her back to one thing or, rather, one person: Britt. She wondered what

Finn had told his ex-wife to trigger such a reaction to her presence at Castlegate Farm. Romy hadn't been able to shake the uncomfortable feeling there was trouble brewing there, though she had no idea what form it would take. She'd ended up telling herself not to be so daft, that Britt was just thinking about making Kyle and Toby's visit as carefree as possible without the added complication of having to explain an unfamiliar female presence, which was completely understandable. She was sure she'd be the same if she was in Britt's shoes.

The little Post Office, which was situated in the main street that ran through the village, had barely changed since Romy's last visit more than twenty years ago, though the lady behind the counter didn't fire any sparks of recognition; it had evidently changed hands since then. Making small talk with the post mistress, Romy duly sent off the orders that had come in over the weekend. That done, she headed back out onto the street and picked her way carefully along the trod in the direction of the village shop. Though it had been cleared and a sprinkling of rock salt thrown over the flagstones, she was mindful of the icy patches where the sun was yet to reach.

She gave a happy sigh, glad to be outside on such a perfect winter's morning. She cast her gaze around her. The picture-perfect village sat under a pale winter sun that was making the snow-covered cottages and their respective gardens sparkle enchantingly. Bells rang out from the nearby church, the sound muted by the snow, while birds twittered in the frost-covered branches of the trees. Further down the road, Romy's eyes landed on the huge Christmas tree on the green. It exuded a majestic air, its bushy boughs trimmed with yet more snow. Beside it were a cluster of snowmen made by the local children which brought back happy memories of snowman-building with Finn, Ella and Joss when she was younger.

Her attention was taken by the low rumble of a farm vehicle

and she looked up to see a large tractor heading towards her, a snowplough fixed to its front. She noticed the attachment was raised off the ground and guessed it was because the road in the village was clear of snow. The tractor slowed beside her and she was pleasantly surprised to see Camm behind the wheel. He opened the cab window. 'Now then, Romy, how's things?' he asked, a friendly smile on his face, dark curls escaping his woolly hat.

'Hiya, Camm. Things are good, thanks.' She returned his smile. 'How about you? Oh, and thanks for keeping the roads so clear. It's a far cry from when I used to visit as a child. I can recall the village regularly used to get cut off in winter. One year we actually missed the start of school after the Christmas holidays 'cos we couldn't get back to Rickelthorpe. As you can imagine, my brother and me were gutted about that!'

'Now, that I can believe.' Camm gave a hearty laugh, dark eyes crinkling at the corners. 'I've just come from Castlegate leading up to the farm and yon side of Danskelfe Castle, so all the roads that way are clear, as is the one leading onto the road to Middleton. I know Finn's concerned about the lads getting across from there later this week so I'm trying to keep on top of the ploughing.'

She nodded. 'Yeah, I think his ex isn't keen to drive if the snow gets too bad – not that I blame her; I wouldn't be either.' She was eager to make sure Camm didn't think she was trying to draw him into a negative conversation about Britt.

'Aye, it's best to avoid driving in snowy conditions if you can, especially the sort we get out here. We're due another covering tonight but I'll keep an eye on things. Ploughing the roads is one thing, but it helps if the gritter does its bit too.'

'Wintry weather still seems to be a bit of a challenge out here, then.'

'You're not wrong there.' Camm nodded. 'Anyroad, it's been nice to see you again, Romy, but I'd best be off. Moll and me will no doubt see you at the Sunne this week.'

'Yeah, I'd like that. See you, Camm.'

He closed the window, raised his hand in a wave and drove off. She was glad to get moving again, with the cold biting at any exposed skin and penetrating through the soles of her boots.

The door to the village shop opened with a cheerful jangle, just as it had done the last time Romy stepped inside all those years ago. She was instantly greeted by the delicious aroma of freshly baked scones that she guessed had wafted through from the attached teashop. It crossed her mind that it was a great marketing ploy. Her stomach growled; there was nothing she liked better than a warm buttered scone with lashings of jam, topped with a naughty dollop of clotted cream. Mmmhmm! She'd have to pay the tearoom a visit before she left.

She glanced around the shop to see an array of well-stocked shelves set out in a fashionably rustic style, utilising reclaimed wood, hessian and chunky baskets. Fresh fruit and vegetables sat alongside all the usual items you'd expect to find in a small shop, as well as a decent selection of artisanal produce that was arranged appealingly on a table display in the centre. Romy's interest had been piqued before she'd even set foot in the store, with the chalkboard on the wall outside advertising a range of frozen "hearty, homemade" ready meals. She wasn't the biggest fan of putting her cooking skills to use so was hopeful there'd be something that would appeal to her tastebuds. She'd noticed the fridge at the cottage had a small freezer compartment which was currently playing host to a lonely tray of ice cubes, and she was sure there'd be enough room for a few meals for one. *Meals for one* – she didn't want to dwell on how sad that sounded. Another thought crossed her mind; she could always double up the quantities and ask Finn to join her. The prospect of them sharing a meal together sounded way more appealing and put an extra spring in her step.

As she reached for one of the wicker shopping baskets that were stacked by the door, Romy noted there was a handful of customers involved in a friendly conversation with a smiley-faced young woman at the counter. She recalled how the village shop had always been a hub of chatter, where local news was exchanged and caught up with – gossip, too, which her family had no doubt fuelled at one time.

Slipping a tub of hot chocolate powder into her basket, she was making her way over to the large freezer when the door opened, admitting a chilly blast of air. She turned to see a woman with a thick auburn locks escaping a conifer-green felt hat. Romy was struck by the beautiful wool coat she was wearing in a deep shade of aubergine and a scarf in contrasting shades. She made for a cheerful sight. An older woman tripped in beside her, declaring how cold it was outside. The two of them caught Romy's eye, each giving her a warm smile, and bidding her a friendly hello. Romy had to do a double-take when she spotted a familiar bag slung over the younger woman's shoulder. It was one she'd made about a year ago. It was a rich sea-green and she'd embroidered it with complementary autumnal shades, trimming it with a selection of shiny beads. She'd been so pleased with it, she'd even considered keeping it for herself until she realised how low her stock had become thanks to her mind being occupied by her failed marriage and subsequent divorce. It had been one of the first bags she'd made in that style and, if her memory served her correctly, she'd sold it from her stall at a craft fair in Rickelthorpe. It wasn't often she spotted one of her own creations out in the wild, as she called it, and since the two women had kind faces she couldn't resist approaching them.

'I hope you don't mind, but I just wanted to say how much I love your coat, and also, your bag is one I made; I think the two go really well together.'

'Oh, wow! Thank you.' The younger woman's smile widened, along with her hazel eyes. 'You made this?' She patted the bag.

'I did. I've made a few more since that one, all different. They're one of my best sellers.'

'Oh, gosh! I'm not surprised. I love mine, it's one of my very favourite things. It was a Christmas present last year and I use it all the time. I think it's great how you can dress it up or down; it's so versatile.'

Romy's face lit up. 'Ah, that's good to hear, I'm really pleased you're getting lots of use out of it. I'm Romy, by the way.'

'Pleased to meet you, Romy. I'm Livvie and this is my stepmum Rhoda, who very kindly bought me the bag.'

'Hello there, Romy,' said Rhoda, smiling warmly. 'I remember you from the Christmas market at Rickelthorpe.'

Romy was instantly taken with their friendliness. It also crossed her mind that their accents were ever-so-slightly different to that of the moorland locals; it wasn't quite as broad. She didn't remember either of them from her earlier time in the village, which suggested they were probably newcomers.

'Ah,' she said, so you bought the bag from my stall there?'

'I did, lovey. You had so many beautiful things, I ended up buying quite a few Christmas presents from you.'

Romy laughed. 'Yes, I remember now, you did buy quite a lot.' It suddenly struck her, their accent sounded very similar to her own, but before she had time to dwell on it, Rhoda spoke again.

'Livvie and I are originally from Rickelthorpe and I'd popped back to join my friends for our yearly Christmas catch-up. We were having a mooch around the market and spotted your beautiful stall. In fact, I think between us, we pretty much wiped out all of your stock in one fell swoop.' Rhoda chuckled.

Romy's stomach clenched and she struggled to keep the smile on her face. Much as Livvie and Rhoda seemed absolutely lovely, she found the knowledge that they were from her home town and would no doubt be all too aware of her family history, bothered her. The realisation suddenly took the shine off her stay in Lytell Stangdale. How unfair would it be if rumours and gossip followed her here? She'd made peace with what had happened all those years ago, and much as she'd been surrounded by the memory back in Rickelthorpe, she hadn't realised how much it had subconsciously been bothering her until she'd come to Lytell Stangdale. Her attitude back in her hometown had been to hold her head up high, her father and her family had done nothing wrong. But until the police investigation had discovered the identity of the real culprit, the gossip had been cruel and relentless. And though he'd been exonerated and Clayborne proven guilty, Romy still didn't like to be unnecessarily reminded of what had brought about her dad's demise.

'I was very grateful; I got to pack up and go home early.' Romy forced a laugh, hoping neither of them would sense a change in her demeanour; she didn't want to appear rude, especially when they were being so friendly.

'So what brings you to Lytell Stangdale?' asked Rhoda. 'Is there a craft fair we don't know about somewhere local? I'm sure I could always be tempted to buy some more of your beautiful hand-made Christmas decorations. Those little felt Christmas trees I bought last year are so sweet! When I got home, I actually regretted not buying more.'

'And don't forget the little mice and hares with festive outfits,' said Livvie, pressing a hand to her chest. 'They're adorable.'

'Oh, thank you. I'm thrilled you like them.' Romy's mind was suddenly cluttered with thoughts.

'Sorry, lovey, we got that carried away, we didn't give you a chance to answer our question.' Rhoda rested her hand on Romy's arm.

'No worries at all. I'm actually holidaying here for a couple of weeks.'

'How lovely. Whereabouts are you staying, if you don't mind me asking?' said Livvie.

'Holly Tree Cottage.' Romy held back from telling them it had once belonged to her family.

'Oh, that's a beautiful property,' said Rhoda. 'I'm sure you'll have a lovely stay there.'

'It underwent an expensive refurbishment project not that long ago, and whenever we walk by we crane our necks to see in, don't we?' Livvie stretched her neck and pulled a jokey face as if to demonstrate. 'Not that we're nosy or anything.'

'Hmm. I suppose we might have shown it a healthy interest.' Rhoda feigned a guilty smile. 'So are you and your family spending Christmas here?'

Romy paused a moment, not keen to lie. 'I'm here on my own, though I'm spending Christmas Day itself with friends.'

'Oh, okay.' Rhoda exchanged a look with her stepdaughter, clearly feeling uncomfortable at the prospect of putting her foot in it.

'I've been wanting to pop back for a while – I used to visit the village years ago.' Romy hoped that would help assuage Rhoda's discomfort. Despite the connection to Rickelthorpe, Romy couldn't help but like these two women, they were warm and friendly, just the sort of people she was drawn to, and she didn't want either of them to feel uncomfortable on her account.

'Tell you what,' said Livvie, 'and please feel free to say no. But Rhoda and I were going to pop into the tearoom for some tea and cake before we grab what we need from the shop; we've got an hour free of children while Zander, my husband, babysits – I'd feel guilty leaving him any longer since it's his afternoon off and he's offered to look after our little brood while Rhoda and I escape. They're all under the age of four, our youngest is just a couple of months old.'

'Oh, wow!' Romy's mind boggled at the thought of managing a "brood" of young children.

'Nothing much fazes Zander, he'll be fine,' said Rhoda, taking in Romy's expression.

'True,' said Livvie. 'Anyway, you're very welcome to join us, if you'd like to.'

'You most certainly are,' said Rhoda. 'Livvie and I can take advantage of the opportunity to find out how to get our hands on more of your delightful Christmas decorations.'

Romy considered it for a moment, their invitation tapping into her sociable nature and not wanting to appear rude, but she was unable to push aside her worries that they were from her hometown and that it wouldn't be long before they joined the dots and realised who she was. Plus, she was keen to call on Ella and didn't want to push that back.

'That sounds really lovely, but I've got a piece of work I need to finish, so I'm afraid I'm going to have to decline. Thank you for the invitation though.'

'Not to worry, I dare say we'll bump into you again while you're here, lovey,' said Rhoda.

Livvie leant into Romy conspiratorially. 'I don't need much of an excuse to escape to the teashop. We'll give you a knock the next time we have a sneaky visit planned, if you fancy? The scones are not to be missed.'

'And the chocolate brownie cake is pretty special too.' Rhoda gave Romy's arm a pat as she walked by.

Romy watched the two women make their way to the teashop entrance, mixed feelings churning up her insides.

With her basket filled to the brim and digging into her fingers, Romy headed to the counter where the three customers were still chatting to the woman she assumed was the shop's owner. She was sure she recognised the customer with the chin-length, brunette bob as Molly's mum, Annie Harrison, and the other she was convinced was a lady everyone used to know as Little Mary. The taller of the three, who had fuchsia-pink hair hanging below her cowboy hat, turned to her and gave a gap-toothed smiled. She was wrapped up in a colourful patchwork coat with clashing scarf, and made for a striking image. Romy would definitely have remembered if she'd seen her before!

'Ee, what are we like? Standing here, gabbing away while you're struggling with that heavy basket, pet,' said the colourful lady, who must be getting on for six-feet tall. 'Haway, give us it here, bonny lass.'

She had a jaunty, friendly accent that Romy thought sounded Geordie. Before she had a chance to reply, the basket was whipped out of her hands and deposited on the counter.

'There you go, flower.' The lady who'd come to her aid treated her to another wide smile.

'Goodness, Mary lovey, don't go doing yourself a mischief. That basket looks heavy,' said the lady whose voice confirmed Romy's suspicions: she was Molly's mum.

'Thank you, that's very kind; it was heavy. I hope you didn't hurt yourself.' Romy had been tempted by several of the ready meals she'd spotted in the freezer, throwing them in the basket without a thought to the weight.

'Don't you go worrying about me, I'm happy to help, flower,' the colourful lady said.

Romy was about to introduce herself to Annie and Little Mary, hoping they'd remember her, when she noticed Molly's mum observing her closely. She opened her mouth to speak but Annie got there first.

'It's Romy, isn't it? she asked. 'Romy Stainthorpe; your family used to have Holly Tree Cottage.'

Romy beamed at her. 'Yes, that's right. I thought it was you, Annie. It's lovely to see you again, and you too, Little Mary.'

'You're never little Romy Stainthorpe?' Little Mary's mouth fell open as her eyes grew wide.

'I am.' Romy chuckled. To her, the petite, bird-like Little Mary had barely changed a scrap, the only apparent difference being the neat curls peering out from under her woolly hat seemed to have grown a shade or two whiter.

'Oh, lovey, it isn't half good to see you. Our Molly mentioned you were back. How've you been keeping? We were sorry to hear about your dad, by the way.' Annie gave Romy a sympathetic smile.

'Oh, flower, it is grand to see you, and Annie's right, we were sorry to hear about your dad passing away. He was a lovely, lovely man.' Little Mary took Romy's hand, patting it gently, her eyes full of sympathy.

Romy felt her throat tighten. Would it ever stop hurting when people offered their condolences?

She swallowed and pushed up a smile. 'Thank you. It wasn't

an easy time, but we got through it.' She was relieved when the inevitable questions that followed, asking after her mum and siblings, were over and done with. Not that she was ungrateful for people's concern or kind words, but she dreaded the old feelings that were always resurrected.

'Well, I for one am chuffed to bits you're back, lovey. You always used to look so at home here; you fitted in just right. It wasn't the same when you'd gone, not seeing your bonny little face in the village and that lovely smile of yours,' said Little Mary.

'That's so kind, I missed everyone too; it feels really good to be back.'

'Aye, I reckon there's one person in particular who's very happy to see you here again.' Annie quirked an insinuating eyebrow.

'Ah, very true. Young Finn Tindall will be over the moon.' Little Mary's eyes twinkled. She still had hold of Romy's hand and gave it another pat.

'Young Finn Tindall, eh? I'm guessing there's a bit of a story there.' The colourful lady let out a cackle and gave Romy a nudge. 'You'll have to share it when you've got a minute, pet. I do love hearing a romantic tale, especially if it's one where the romance gets rekindled.'

'Well, I saw him yesterday and I can honestly say, he looked the happiest I've seen him in a *very* long time. He was whistling away to himself, happy as Larry.' A knowing smile danced over Annie's lips.

'That right, eh? I reckon you're quids in there.' The brightly dressed lady winked at Romy.

Uh-oh, here we go! Catching the eye of the woman behind the counter, Romy gave her a smile and said, 'I'm so sorry about this, I appear to have barged into your conversation. In case you hadn't guessed my name's Romy, and my family had a holiday cottage in the village more than twenty years ago. This is my first visit back since then.' Laughing, she held out her hand.

'Pleased to meet you, Romy, and there's no need to apologise. I'm Lucy. I run the shop with my husband, Freddie.' She took

Romy's proffered hand and shook it. 'Bet you didn't expect to be given such a grilling when you called in for your groceries.'

Romy laughed again. 'Pleased to meet you too, Lucy. Your shop's amazing by the way. And, to be honest, I kind of expected the questions, but in fairness, it's lovely to catch up with everyone, and I really don't mind.'

'And I'm Mary, pet.' The colourful lady wrapped an arm around Romy and squeezed her tightly. 'Mind, with there being that many Marys in this village, I tend to be known as Big Mary, for obvious reasons. I'm hardly what you'd call delicate and dainty, unlike this lovely lady here.' She gave a throaty laugh, towering over Little Mary who was standing beside her and barely scraped five-feet tall if she was lucky.

'Pleased to meet you too, Mary.' It crossed Romy's mind that it wasn't just Big Mary's height that lent itself to her nickname. She reckoned her personality was also a contributing feature; the village would definitely be a brighter place with her presence.

After Romy had explained where she was staying, which generated lots of "oohs" and "ahhs" from Annie and Little Mary, Lucy started totting up her shopping as Romy popped her groceries into the bags she'd brought with her.

'Don't be a stranger, lovey,' Annie said as Romy went to leave. 'You're welcome to pop up for a cuppa anytime. Jack and me live in a barn conversion at Withrin Hill now; we let our Molly and her family have the farmhouse, but we're easy enough to find.'

'Thanks, Annie.' It sounded like a similar set-up to the one at Castlegate Farm.

'And there's always a lot going on at the Sunne, my husband Gerald and me would love to see you there.' Big Mary treated Romy to another wide smile.

'Ooh, and don't forget the carols around the Christmas Tree on Christmas Eve. Starts at six o'clock prompt,' said Little Mary. 'It's always a wonderful event. I think Aggie might be joining us this time.'

'Who?' The name wasn't familiar to Romy.

Big Mary gave a loud hoot of laughter. 'Who indeed!'

Annie rolled her eyes theatrically. 'Ughh! Don't ask!'

'Uh-oh,' said Lucy, catching Romy's eye.

'Hang on a minute, let me get this right,' said Annie. 'She's our Molly's deceased husband's grandmother – never gets any easier saying that! She moved here a few years ago and she's caused nowt but trouble since, tormenting the vicar with her mucky text messages. Once accused him of being a strippagram. It's a wonder the poor man hasn't fled the village because of her.'

'Wow!' said Romy.

'Aggie's got bad arthritis in her fingers, bless her, and she struggles with that reproductive whatdyermacallit text thingy,' said Little Mary by way of explanation.

'*Predictive* text, Mary, not reproductive,' said Annie, though she didn't look convinced by Little Mary's excuse. 'And the old goat needs blessing, I'll give you that. She has our Molly running round in circles, putting things right and smoothing over all the trouble she causes. As for poor Rev Nev, she persecutes him, and don't get me onto those books she reads.'

'Little Mary and Granny Aggie have an exclusive book club; s'just the two of them. They read books of the racy variety, if you know what I mean.' Big Mary gave Romy a theatrical wink.

'I think you'll find that's a massive exaggeration, thank you very much, Mary.' Little Mary's cheeks had flushed pink.

'I think you'll find it's not, pet,' said Big Mary in her sing-song voice. 'I've seen with my own eyes the sort of reading material you borrow from the library bus. Filthy's the word.'

'It's not our fault we happen to pick up the odd book with a few spicy scenes, but I can assure you, we skip over those pages,' Little Mary said defensively.

'Aye, if you say so, flower,' said Big Mary, flashing Romy a mischievous, gappy smile.

'On that happy note, I think I'll bid you goodbye,' said Romy, giggling. 'It's been lovely to see you all.'

'Are you sure you can manage those bags?' asked Lucy. 'If you don't mind waiting, Freddie could drop them off for you, he's doing home deliveries this afternoon.'

'I'll be fine, but thanks for the offer. I'll definitely remember for next time.' Romy called goodbye again as Annie opened the shop door for her.

Outside, the cold air took her breath away. She readjusted her bags, in a bid to distribute the weight more evenly, then started making her way carefully along the trod, glad she didn't have far to go; the handles were already digging into her fingers. She'd got to the Post Office when she became aware of someone calling her.

'Romy! Romy! Wait up!'

She turned to see a young woman waving at her from a little further down the road. She was wearing a snuggly padded jacket and a woolly pompom hat, a thick plait snaking over her shoulder. It took Romy a couple of moments before she realised it was her old friend, Ella Welford.

'Ella!' she exclaimed, her heart lifting. With a huge smile on her face, she watched as Ella waited for a pickup and quad bike to go by then rushed over the road to Romy as quickly as the icy conditions would allow.

'Oh, my God! I thought it was you.' Ella's cheeks and nose were pink from the cold, but her wide smile told Romy her friend was overjoyed to see her.

Romy's heart soared. 'Ells!' She set her shopping down and threw her arms around her friend, squeezing her tight, tears stinging her eyes. 'It's so good to see you!'

'It's good to see you, too!' Ella said happily. 'I'd heard a whisper you were back. How've you been? I've got so many questions.' She released her friend and took a step back, her eyes roving over Romy's face. 'You've hardly changed at all.'

'And neither have you.' They both laughed heartily at that.

Romy blinked back her tears. 'I was going to come looking for you after I'd got that lot back.' She nodded to the bags of shopping. 'I just popped into the village shop for a few things and came out with all this stuff.'

'Here, let me help. You looked like a packhorse when I first spotted you.' Ella bent to scoop up one of the bags. 'I gather you're staying at Holly Tree Cottage.'

Romy picked up the other. 'I am; hard to believe, isn't it? I can tell you all about it when we get there, if you've got time?' Bumping into her friend after so many years didn't feel anywhere near as strange as Romy had been expecting. Just as it had with Finn, it felt surprisingly comfortable.

''Course I've got time! I was all set to come and find you!' Ella grinned at her.

'In that case, what are we waiting for?' Romy asked.

The two friends wandered along the trod, chatting away as if they'd last seen one another yesterday.

Back at Holly Tree Cottage, they dumped the bags on the worktop in the kitchen. Romy popped the ready meals straight into the freezer compartment of the fridge while Ella gazed around the room admiringly.

'Wow! This is seriously gorgeous! Someone's got good taste and deep pockets. Mind, it still has the same feel it used to when your parents owned it.'

'That's what I thought too.'

'Did it feel weird coming back here?'

'A bit, but the overwhelming feeling was that it was the right thing to do. I felt settled straightaway.'

'Aww, that's so good to hear.' Ella turned to Romy. 'Jeez, Romes, we've got so much to catch up on. I didn't half miss you when you left.'

Ella's words triggered a twist of guilt in Romy's chest. 'I missed you too, and you're so right, we have loads of catching up to do. Have you got time for a cuppa?' she asked. 'Maybe we could make a start now.' As well as catching up on everything, Romy was keen to run something past her friend.

''Course! As I said before, I was going to call on you. I just need to pop and check in on Joss's dad, make sure he's okay, see if he needs anything. Pete's living in the village now and Joss and me are up at the farm. He's been laid low with a heavy cold and I've got a casserole in the Landie to drop off for him. See you in about twenty minutes?'

'Perfect. Say hi to Pete from me.' She wondered if Joss's father was still as crabby and dour as he used to be.

'Will do.'

Romy was relieved to have the interlude, it would give her the opportunity to get her thoughts straight. Her head was in a whirl, particularly after the conversation in the village shop. Just when she thought she'd do one thing, something happened to make her doubt herself. Which was why she'd be interested to hear Ella's take on things.

TWENTY-SIX

Romy

As Romy unpacked the shopping and put it away, her mind was busily turning over how good it had felt to see Ella after so many years – glad and relieved that her friend's greeting had been warm – along with the other thoughts that had occupied her mind since she'd first arrived in Lytell Stangdale. Well, if she was really honest with herself, since she'd first seen the cottage in the pages of the magazine in the salon that day. Nowhere had properly felt like home since her dad had passed away and that feeling had only intensified after her split with Russ and her divorce had been finalised. But suddenly, the unsettled feeling that had thrummed away in the background for all those years had finally ceased.

Romy had sensed something was different when she'd first woken yesterday morning, but as she lay there, snuggled up under the luxurious goose down duvet, she'd struggled to pinpoint what it could be. All she knew was that she'd just enjoyed the best sleep she'd had for as long as she could remember. Though, at the time, she'd attributed this new sensation to the benefits of a restful night, she couldn't shake the feeling that there was more to it than that.

It wasn't until she'd stepped outside into the winter sunshine first thing that morning, still in her pyjamas, mug of tea in hand, with the sense of the village wrapping around her, that she'd been struck by exactly what it was. This was where she belonged. Here, in Lytell Stangdale. She could feel it in her gut. Being back here had silenced the background feeling of unease that had held her in its grip for so long. It didn't matter that she'd only been here a few days, Romy knew it was unequivocally where she was meant to be. Granted, she'd been dreaming about it since she'd first seen the photo of the cottage, but at the back of her mind a little voice had kept telling her it was just a dream and she'd have to go back to reality once her fortnight's break was up. But now, when she thought about it, there were so many reasons for her to make a permanent return. A great big one being that the cottage was going to go on the market soon. If that wasn't a sign, then what was?

Despite all of that, Romy couldn't argue that she'd been going back and forth with the idea, though hadn't given it proper, serious thought until now. But her excitement had been building as she'd walked to the shop that morning, absorbing the atmosphere of the village that looked so pretty as it awaited the arrival of Christmas. She knew without a doubt she could make her home here, just as she'd planned to do once she'd left college all those years ago. She could easily continue her business from the cottage; the extension would be the perfect space for her workroom.

It wasn't until her conversation with Livvie and Rhoda when she'd learnt of their shared hometown, that her dreams had been given a thorough shaking, setting an unwelcome seed of doubt in her mind.

By the time she returned, Ella had been gone closer to forty-five minutes rather than the twenty she'd estimated.

'Sorry I'm late, Romes.' She was out of puff as she pulled off her wellies at the door, frosty air clinging to her clothes. 'Pete needed a few bits and bobs from the shop, then I made him a cup of tea and popped some washing in for him.'

'That's okay, I'm not in any rush. Is he all right?'

'Aye, he seems a bit brighter today.'

'That's good to hear.'

'I told him I'd seen you and he said to say hello,' said Ella.

Aww, that's kind of him.' Romy smiled. Do you still have time for a cuppa?' 'I'll understand if you need to get back.'

''Course, I have time; I'm desperate to hear what you've been up to since you left.'

'And I'm desperate to hear all about you and Joss!'

'Fair point.' Ella chuckled.

Romy paused, kettle in hand. 'Actually, how about a hot chocolate rather than a cuppa?'

'You really need to ask? Thought you said I hadn't changed.'

'Marshmallows and all the trimmings?'

'Duh?' The two women burst out laughing at Ella's use of the expression that had been a favourite of theirs as teenagers when anyone asked an obvious question.

'Right then, Ells, while I'm making the hot chocs, why don't you park your bum on one of those chairs and tell me what you've been up to since I was last here.'

Ella plonked herself down and blew out a breath, flicking her plait over her shoulder. 'Okay, before I start, I should warn you, there's quite a lot to tell.'

'I'm all ears, especially the bit where you and Joss finally admitted you fancied one another! We could all see it, by the way. Couldn't believe that you two were so oblivious.'

'Er, isn't that a case of the pot calling the kettle...?' Ella said jokingly.

'Yeah, good point.'

Romy listened as her friend told her how she'd had her own business as a local dog walker until she and Joss had got together three years ago. Like Romy, Joss had returned to the village after a lengthy absence. His reason for leaving had been a heated row with his father, from which there'd apparently been no return. Joss had left Camplin Hall Farm in a blaze of anger and recrimination, going to live with his aunt and uncle at Skeller Rigg Farm in Helderthorpe. He'd only returned when his brother, Rich, had called to say their father had collapsed and been rushed to hospital. With their mother having passed away when they were younger, and Rich having washed his hands of the farm, there was no one else to help run the place and look after the livestock. Against his better judgement, Joss had returned to Lytell Stangdale and unexpectedly found himself settling back in. 'And I can't tell you how glad I am he did,' said Ella, nursing her mug of hot chocolate. Like Finn and Romy, Ella and Joss had been best friends when they were younger, ignoring the spark of attraction that had caught them both unawares when they were sixteen, the summer after Romy had left. It was on Joss's return that those feelings had gradually been rekindled with the two of them falling in love. They finally took over the running of Camplin Hall Farm where Ella set up her luxury home-from-home dog kennels. Since then, both her business and her relationship with Joss had been going from strength to strength. 'Honestly, Romes, much as I resisted it at first, getting together with Joss is the best thing that's ever happened to me. I've never felt this happy before, and he says he feels the same.' Ella lifted her mug to her mouth, peering over it at Romy. 'Puts me in mind of another couple.'

Romy fixed her friend with a faux stern look.

'Just sayin'…' Ella set her mug down and flashed Romy a cheesy grin. 'Don't tell me you've forgotten how quickly news travels round here. Just 'cos Joss and me couldn't make it to the pub the other night, doesn't mean to say we haven't heard about the sparks flying between you and Finn Tindall. It's the best news we've had round here for ages.'

'Oh.' Ella's reminder of how quickly gossip flew around the village made Romy's heart leap. It was the very thing that had put doubts in her mind.

'Yes, "oh",' said Ella. 'Anyroad, you've had my update, now it's your turn. I'm eager to hear what you've been doing with yourself. I was really sorry about your dad, by the way. He was a lovely man, and if you'd rather not go over what happened right now, I'll understand.'

Romy took a moment, putting her thoughts in order. 'I hardly know where to start, I kind of feel like I've been hit by a bit of a whirlwind since I arrived here if I'm honest.'

'Am I right in thinking a certain tall, dark and handsome farmer features in there somewhere?'

Romy nodded. 'I had no idea it was so obvious.'

''Fraid so; you've been rumbled, like I said, the fireworks between the pair of you could be seen from Arkleby.'

'Ah.' Romy had thought she'd been the only one to sense it, well, maybe Finn too. She was quiet for a moment.

'Sorry if I've put you off your stride. I won't speak until you've finished telling me what's on your mind, promise.' Ella made a zipping motion, running her fingers across her mouth.

Romy flopped back in the dining chair and her words slowly began pouring out, the years since the two friends had last confided in one another seemingly shrinking away. She described how happy she'd felt at spotting the cottage in the magazine and the impulse that had urged her to book a break there. How, though she'd been nervous about coming back to her former family holiday home, it was if it had welcomed her with open arms, making her feel at ease as soon as she'd walked through the door. She went on to speak of the unexpected resurrection of her feelings for Finn that had been pushing their way through, saying she was sure he felt the same. The thought of their moment in the snow looming in her mind, and what might have happened if Ted hadn't intervened in such an untimely manner. 'We seem to have reconnected straight away, kind of like I have with you, Ells. It's totally unexpected, but I'm so happy it's been this way.'

'It's hard to explain, isn't it? Though I totally get where you're coming from, it was the same with Joss and me when he came back after being away for so long. And as far as it goes with you, feels like you've only been away five minutes and everything's just sort of slotted together, like we've picked up where we left off. And I have to say, it's great having one of my old besties back.'

Romy smiled, glad Ella felt the same, that she understood. 'It feels so good to be here again, which is why I've been considering a permanent move back. I've got my divorce settlement from the sale of our house – it was a wreck when we bought it and we did it up ourselves, making a really good profit when we sold it – and there's a lump sum my dad had put into a couple of trusts for me. The amount together should be enough for a pretty decent deposit on a new home, meaning any mortgage should be manageable.'

Ella sat up straight in her chair. 'Really? Oh, Romes, it would be so good to have you properly back.'

'It would?'

''Course it bloomin' would! I've missed you! And I didn't realise just how much until now.'

Romy's face broke out into a wide smile and Ella's followed suit. Her friend had voiced exactly how Romy felt about coming back to the village and catching up with the people she used to be close to.

'So would you be looking to settle here in the village?'

'Well, funny you should say that, but I've been reliably informed the owner's putting this place up for sale in the New Year.'

'You're kidding me?' Ella's eyes widened.

'I'm not.' Romy couldn't help but giggle at her friend's reaction.

'This gorgeous place is going to be up for sale?'

'Apparently so.'

'Well, if that isn't telling you something, Romes, I don't know what is! And if I were you, and you're serious about it, then I'd act quickly, get in before it actually goes on the market. Property round here's been getting snapped up super-fast at the moment, you don't want to miss out.'

'Hmm, yeah.'

'"Hmm, yeah"? What kind of answer's that?'

'It's just...'

'S'just what?' A frown replaced Ella's smile.

'I suppose, I'm trying to hold back from being my usual impulsive self and am trying to think things through carefully before I wade in headfirst like I normally do.'

'Totally understandable, buying a house isn't something anyone should do on a whim – not that I'm saying that's how it would be for you. But why do I get the feeling that's not the full story?'

'Oh, God.' Romy pushed her fingers into her hair as her stomach started to churn. 'So, this morning when I was in the shop, I met a couple of really lovely ladies; Livvie and Rhoda—'

'You're spot-on there, they are lovely. Livvie's married to our local GP, Zander Gillespie – I've lost count of how many kids they've got now – and Rhoda moved here to be closer to them; she helps out quite a bit; loves being a grandma by all accounts.'

'Oh, okay.' Romy took a breath. 'See, the thing is, they come from Rickelthorpe.'

'And that's a problem because...?'

'I suppose it's time to tell you what happened after I left and the reason we never came back.' Romy girded herself, determined not to break down in tears again.

'Okay.' From her friend's expression, Romy could tell news of what had happened to her father had reached her ears.

Drawing in a deep breath, she said, 'Here goes...' She went on to give an abridged version of what had happened with her father and his business partner, keeping it brief in order to keep her emotions in check as much as possible.

Ella's mouth fell open as she listened.

'Oh my God, Romy, what a truly awful experience for you. I'd heard he'd died but didn't know all the details.' She rushed around the table and wrapped her arms around her friend. The gesture made Romy's eyes prickle with tears and she had to struggle to hold them in. 'But I can honestly say, Livvie and Rhoda aren't gossips. They're really decent folk and wouldn't breathe a word to anyone, if they realise who you are, that is, or if they even remembered what happened. And let's not forget, your dad did nothing wrong. He was the innocent party in all of this.'

'I know you're right, it's just the idea of leaving it all behind is part of the appeal of coming here. I know it's a long time after everything, but I liked the thought of a completely fresh start. My divorce from Russ has made me think differently about things. 'Cos he's from Rickelthorpe, he kept reminding me of what had happened with my dad – inadvertently, of course – but it got me down at times, the way he'd drop it into a conversation, and I didn't realise how much until we split up.'

Ella went back to her seat, her eyes never leaving Romy. 'But you *would* be leaving it all behind. And if you're thinking Livvie and Rhoda would judge you on what happened, you can get that thought right out of your head pronto. They're not like that, trust me on this, Romes. And I know for a fact they'd be absolutely gutted if they got so much as a whisper that you didn't move to the place where you feel happiest because of them.'

'You really think so?'

'A million percent.' Ella reached across and took Romy's hand. 'You could always talk to them about it, you know, they're very approachable. Might make you feel better.'

'You tell a convincing story, Ella Welford.' Her friend's words had made Romy feel a little brighter.

'I've only told it as it is, flower. Mind, I'm not gonna lie, like everywhere, there are a couple of notorious gossips in the village, and I can't guarantee that they won't spread a bit of tittle-tattle. But if I were you, I wouldn't give them a second thought, everyone knows what they're like and no one takes any notice of them anyway. This is where you belong, don't let some daft notion or village busybody tell you otherwise. Okay?'

'Okay.' Romy felt her spirits rising. 'And since when did you become such a force to be reckoned with, madam?'

'I'd say that would be since I realised I wanted to be with Joss.' The two friends exchanged happy smiles. 'Oh, and I don't know if you're aware of this, but Livvie actually works for Kitty and Vi at their wedding dress business. You could always have a quiet word with Kitty if it'd help, see if she thinks Livvie's the gossip-spreading sort. Mind, I'm sure she'll tell you exactly the same as me, that you have nothing to worry about on that score.'

'From what you've said, I don't think that would be necessary.'

Romy's mobile phone pinged from the worktop by the biscuit tin, interrupting their chat. Ella glanced at her watch. 'Ey up, have you seen the time? I'd best get back up to the farm. Joss'll be wondering where I've got to.'

'Thanks for listening, Ells, and for your words of wisdom, I really appreciate it.'

'Not so sure about the wisdom bit, but you're welcome, flower.' Ella giggled, pulling Romy into a hug. 'Will you be joining us for the carols round the Christmas tree? Can't beat a good warble you know. Lalalalaaaaa!'

Romy couldn't help but laugh. 'Wouldn't miss it for the world, though remind me to wear earplugs if I'm standing next to you.'

'That's what Joss says, funnily enough.' She grinned. 'And we always pop into the Sunne for a quick snifter afterwards; you're welcome to join us if you fancy.'

'Sounds more tempting by the minute.'

'Great, see you then. Oh, and wrap up, it's usually brass monkey.'

With Ella gone, Romy headed back into the kitchen and picked up her mobile. Her heart leapt when she saw the text was from Finn.

TWENTY-SEVEN

Finn

Finn drained the tea in his mug and rinsed it under the tap. He'd been dithering with the idea of asking Romy if she fancied meeting up that night, but hadn't wanted to come across as pushy. Since she was only going to be in Lytell Stangdale for a fortnight, he felt he needed to grab every opportunity to spend time with her – if she wanted to, of course. He hadn't been able to get their "moment" in the snow out of his mind, wondering what would have happened if Ted hadn't stuck his whiskery nose in their faces, breathing his dog breath all over them. Talk about a passion-killer. Finn was sure he wasn't mistaken; he'd seen that look in her eyes before; she felt the same way he did. He couldn't let it pass; couldn't let her go back to Rickelthorpe without finding out for sure. If those feelings were still there he was determined to act on them. He didn't want to lose her for a second time.

After going back and forth with the idea, he grabbed his phone and fired off a quick text; there was no point wasting any more time overthinking it.

> Hi Romy, was wondering if you fancied meeting up tonight? Maybe we could have a bite to eat together? Will understand if you're too busy. Finn

Ever since he'd pressed "send", he'd been like a cat on hot bricks awaiting her response as well as torturing himself about whether or not he should have added a kiss after his name.

Ten minutes later, his pulse jumped when his phoned pinged. He pulled it out of the back pocket of his jeans, his heart thudding, his face breaking out into a smile to see Romy had replied.

> Hi Finn, sounds lovely! Do you fancy coming here? I picked up some tasty-looking ready meals from the village shop earlier. How does salmon en croute with veggies sound? Rx

In his haste to reply, he was suddenly all fingers and thumbs and had to delete and retype several times. 'Calm your jets, Tindall,' he said, earning himself a curious look from Ted who was curled up in his bed.

> Sounds perfect! What time would you like me to lard? x

Seeing Romy had signed off with a kiss, he didn't think twice about adding one himself this time.

> Any time after 6.30pm's fine with me. "Lard"??? x

Her comment and the slew of laughing face emojis made him chuckle; he really had been all fingers and thumbs.

> Sorry about that! Meant land! See you at 6.30pm. Looking forward to it. No lard will feature at all! Promise! x

Moments later another text arrived from her.

> Phew! That's a relief!!! Forgot to say, Ted's
> welcome too x

'Wow, Tedster, you've only gone and got yourself an invite out tonight, fella. You've clearly made a good impression.'

Hearing his name, Ted shot up and raced over to his dad, his tail wagging with its usual gusto.

> Ted sends his thanks x

A heart-shaped tapback followed.

That afternoon, as he checked on the sheep and dropped off bales of hay, thoughts of Romy filled Finn's mind, along with the Boxing Day visit from Kyle and Toby. But they weren't the only things that dominated his thoughts. Not long after he'd finished texting Romy, he'd had an unexpected video call from Britt. It hadn't gone unnoticed that she was done up to the nines, her hair had been fluffed up and her lips were glossy. She'd evidently taken time with her appearance. Maybe that was how she was on a daily basis these days, he'd mused. Her unusually soft tone had taken him by surprise as had her reason for getting in touch, especially after her frosty demeanour the last time they'd spoken. She'd told him she just wanted to check-in with him while there were no other distractions, see how he'd been doing. 'It's ages since we had a chance to talk, just you and me,' she'd said, treating him to a rare warm smile. Her sudden change in attitude had put Finn's senses on high alert, his suspicions rising to the surface. Her face hadn't softened like that since long before she'd left, and seeing it now only added to his wariness. She had a reason for the call and it wasn't just because she wanted a friendly chat, of that he'd been absolutely certain.

And it hadn't taken long for him to find out.

. . .

'So, how've you been?' Britt asked, giving him what looked annoyingly like a sympathetic smile. It instantly got his hackles up.

'Fine, busy. Looking forward to seeing the lads.'

She nodded. 'Good, good. And have you done anything interesting recently? I don't like the thought of you sitting all alone up at the farm, especially now the nights draw in so early. I assume you still pop to the Sunne every now and then?'

'I was at the Sunne the other night, yeah.' This was seriously weird. She hadn't given two hoots about how he spent his evenings when she left, and he couldn't work out why the sudden interest now.

'Yes, of course you were.' She gave another of her forced smiles.

'You don't have to worry about me going out and leaving the lads with my parents or a babysitter. I'll be spending all my time with them.' It suddenly struck him that she might be looking for a reason not to let them stay with him, hoping that by being friendly, it would make him drop his guard. 'I'm telling you the truth, Britt.'

'Oh, goodness, that's not what I meant at all.' Her shoulders slumped and she tipped her head to one side. 'I just want to know that you're happy, that's all, Finny. Seeing you on the screen the other day filled me with the worst possible guilt.' She pressed her hand to her chest, blinking her eyes as if fighting back tears. 'I feel absolutely terrible for hurting you the way I did. I didn't mean to and I want you to know that I really am very sorry.' Her voice wavered and her bottom lip wobbled.

Finn shuffled awkwardly, confused by this sudden change. Nothing about it seemed genuine, in fact, if this was an awards ceremony, he felt sure she'd win the trophy for best actress. A spike of irritation shot through him. She was playing games and he didn't like it. It was time to change the direction their conversation was taking. 'There's no need to be sorry. We've all moved on. The lads are our priority; as long as they're okay, that's the main thing. We're both in agreement about that.'

Though she looked momentarily taken aback, she recovered quickly. 'Yes, of course. I totally agree. The lads always come first.'

Silence hung in the air for several awkward seconds, but Finn felt bizarrely more at ease with that than the gushing fake concern.

He was the first to speak. 'Right, well, if that's all you were calling about, I suppose I'd better get cracking, I've got the sheep to—'

'Oh, erm, before you go, I was wondering if you plan on seeing any more of that Romy girl, apart from Christmas Day, that is?'

So that's what this is all about. 'Why d'you ask?'

'Oh, I was just wondering, that's all.' Her smile was so sickly sweet it almost set Finn's teeth on edge.

'I dare say I'll run into her in the village.' He thought it best not to tell her about his arrangements for that evening, not that he was obliged to. He didn't have the time nor the inclination to encourage any further questions.

'Okay, so nothing definite then?' Was he mistaken, or did she look relieved?

'Look, Britt, I can't stress enough that when the boys are here, they'll be my priority. I don't want you to go thinking otherwise.' *How many times do I have to tell you?*

She raised her palms. 'Finny, I totally understand. That's not why I was asking, I just wanted to make sure you were happy that's all. With it being the festive period, you've no idea the guilt I've been feeling over leaving you. I just want to be sure you're not going to be lonely, that's all.'

Could she be any more patronising if she tried?

'You can rest assured I won't be lonely. But now, if that's it, I really need to get a move on; it'll be dark before we know it. Bye, Britt.' With that, he ended the call.

'You all right, lad?' his dad had asked as they crossed paths in the yard shortly after Finn's call with Britt, Ted dancing between them. 'You look a million miles away there.'

'Aye, I've just had a weird video call with Britt.'

'Ughh. What's the problem now? Don't tell me she's trying to make excuses about the lads coming to stay.'

'No, nowt like that. More like she was checking to make sure Romy wouldn't be here then.'

'I hope you told her it's none of her bloomin' business who you have in your home.' Tommy never made any secret of his dislike of his ex-daughter-in-law.

'Much as I was tempted, Dad, I held back. Didn't want to antagonise her.' Finn decided against mentioning her change in demeanour knowing his dad would latch onto it. He didn't want her call to take the edge off spending the evening with Romy.

As if sensing the dip in his son's mood, Tommy said, 'Don't know about you, but I aren't half looking forward to tea tonight. I forget what it is your mother said she's going to cook, but it sounded nice.'

That made Finn laugh. His mum regularly joked that Tommy and Ted were kindred spirits and would happily eat anything without tasting a bite of it. 'I'm sure it'll be delicious, Dad.'

'You're welcome to join us at our place, or your mother says she can plate some up for you to have at the big house when you're ready.'

'Actually, Romy's invited me for a meal down at Holly Tree Cottage.'

'Has she now?' Tommy didn't bother to hide his smile. 'And will you be taking your toothbrush, d'you reckon?'

'See you later, Dad.' Finn walked off, shaking his head and laughing. He very much doubted he'd need to take his toothbrush, but he'd got an idea brewing for something else.

'I was only asking in case your mother needed to know about breakfast; she might need to adjust the quantities if you're not going to be joining us.' Tommy followed up with a hearty chuckle.

'Aye, course you were.'

Finn's insides were doing somersaults as he arrived at the doorstep of Holly Tree Cottage. With his hand poised to knock on the door, he paused and looked down at Ted who was gazing back up at him, evidently wondering what they were waiting for. 'I'm expecting big things of you tonight, fella. No chewing, no whining and no smelly dog-farts, okay?'

He hadn't quite finished his sentence when the door flew open and Romy appeared, her eyes filled with laughter. 'Are those instructions for Ted or for me?' she asked with a giggle.

Finn let his hand fall to his side and gave an embarrassed laugh. 'You'll probably be relieved to know they were for this young renegade here.'

'Thank goodness for that! There's no way I'd be able to guarantee not to do any of those things.' She took a step back, smiling. 'Come in.'

'Should I be worried?' Finn asked as he stepped into the hallway, the warmth of the cottage welcome after the sub-zero temperatures of the village.

'I think you'll be okay, for now.' She chuckled, closing the door behind him. Ted didn't wait to be invited and trotted off into the kitchen following the source of the delicious aromas that greeted them.

'Phew!' He bent to kiss her cheek, the scent of her perfume playing havoc with his emotions; she smelt wonderful, her cheek warm and soft against his.

'Ooh, blimey, you feel cold!' she said.

'It's freezing out there; there's going to be a hard frost tonight.' Standing back, he took in her glowing complexion and glossy hair that curled over her shoulders in gentle waves. She was wearing a tunic top and skinny jeans. He wanted to tell her she looked lovely, but held back in case she thought it was too much.

Following her into the kitchen, he held out a small festive gift bag. 'I brought you these; didn't want to come empty handed.' He was struggling to push down the smile that was tugging persistently at the corners of his mouth.

'Oh, there was really no need,' she said, looking surprised as she took it from him.

'I reckon that's exactly what you'll think when you see what it is.' His smile broke free, earning him a baffled look from Romy.

'Okay.'

He watched as she reached inside and lifted out the small paper bag and looked inside. She threw her head back and let out a hoot of laughter. 'Oh, I *love* it! You remembered!'

'Of course I did.' He laughed with her, pleased by her response.

'I had no idea they still made these.'

'Neither did I 'til I popped into the village shop intent on bringing something with me tonight. I spotted these and thought they'd be perfect.'

Whilst scanning the shelves at the shop, his eyes had landed on a jar of the infamously sour boiled sweets that had been hugely popular when Romy and Finn were youngsters. The two of them, along with their friends, used to compete for who could last the longest without pulling a face as the sour tang assaulted their tastebuds.

'Fabulous! Come on, we've got to have one now.' She held the packet out to him. 'Finn Tindall, I challenge you!' she said, adopting the same serious tone she'd used all those years ago.

'Challenge accepted, Romy Stainthorpe.' Finn's tone was equally grave as he took a sour apple sweet. He held it poised between his fingers, waiting for her to begin the count down.

'Right, three, two, one. Go!' They popped the boiled sweets into their mouths, eyes growing wide as their tastebuds objected to the tartness.

Ted ran over, watching them, perplexed.

Finn had never been a boiled sweet fan and he'd forgotten just how much he disliked this particular variety. His mouth was twitching and before he knew it he was scrunching up his nose and squeezing his eyes tight shut. 'Oh, man, this is rank! You win.' He was happy to concede defeat; the sooner he could get the vile thing out of his mouth the better!

Romy punched the air victoriously before quickly grabbing a

square of kitchen roll and offering it to Finn. He didn't waste a moment, spitting out the sour apple straight away. Romy followed suit, her face crumpling. 'Yuk! Bleurgh! Who would even think to make those for kids?'

Despite their ordeal, they were both laughing hard and pulling faces, the disgusting taste apparently not keen to relinquish its grip.

'Oh, jeez, they're even worse than I remembered,' Finn said, still pulling a face. 'Remind me why we ever used to do that.'

'For the fun of it, of course,' Romy said, giggling. 'Which I expect is why you bought them today. And to remind you that I'm still the undefeated sour apple champion, of course.'

'You're welcome to that title.' Finn's cheeks were aching with laughter.

Ted gave a little whimper and rested his paw on Finn's leg.

'Trust me, fella, I think even you would turn your nose up at one of those horrors.'

The Labrador's tail swished back and forth over the flagstone, his expression telling Finn he was unconvinced.

'What a start to the evening,' Romy said. 'I reckon it'll all be downhill from now on, there's no way we can top that.'

Contrary to Romy's prediction, the evening went anything but downhill. They'd sat at the kitchen table, tucking into the salmon en croute – which had been delicious – and al dente jewel-coloured vegetables, as they chatted away, the conversation flowing. Finn told her some more about his sons, pride shining in his eyes, while Romy elaborated on her plans for her business and how she hoped to branch out and start holding classes on felt-making and felt picture-making. 'Much as I love creating things, it's quite solitary, so running classes would be a good way to be around people,' she said.

'You always were a sociable sort, I can see how being on your own wouldn't be ideal for you. And I reckon you'd be a natural teacher, too, with your friendly personality.'

'Thank you.'

'So are you thinking of holding these classes in your home, or would you hire somewhere?' He watched her expression closely, noting she seemed to be giving her answer some consideration. He held his breath, hardly daring to hope her reply would include staying in Lytell Stangdale on a more permanent basis.

'I suppose, ideally, I'd prefer not to hold classes in my home. I'd have to hire a venue if I could find somewhere reasonably priced. I'd want to keep the course fees as cheap as possible while still allowing me to make a profit.'

'Makes sense.' He swirled his alcohol-free beer round his glass, his thoughts gathering pace. 'I don't suppose the news that Lady Caro Hammondely took over the running of Danskelfe Castle travelled as far as Rickelthorpe, did it?'

'It didn't. How's that been going? Last I heard, she used to be a bit of a wild child.'

'She did, but she's calmed down massively since she got married; she's a completely different person. Anyroad, amongst a whole load of other stuff, like music events in the woods on the Danskelfe Estate, opening up part of the castle to the public, hosting weddings, she's overseen the renovation of some old buildings not far from the castle.'

'Sounds like she's been busy.'

'Aye, she has. Seems once she's got one thing sorted, she's onto the next.' He took a glug of his beer before going on to explain how the idea behind the building renovations was to create affordable premises for self-employed locals to rent. He told her how there was already a variety of businesses operating from the units, including a beauticians and a dance studio run by Ollie's daughter, Noushka.

'I'm aware there's a still a couple vacant from the latest round of renovations that have recently been completed. Just thought I'd mention it.'

'Hmm. Sounds interesting.' She pushed her mouth into a pout, clearly giving some thought to what Finn had told her.

Before long, they migrated to the living room armed with mugs of tea. Romy threw a log onto the embers in the stove and seconds later flames were leaping behind the glass. Finn made himself comfortable on the sofa and, instead of taking one of the armchairs, he was pleasantly surprised when Romy plonked herself beside him. Ted collapsed on the rug in front of the log burner, stretching out contentedly as if he'd lived there for years.

Romy's delicate floral perfume wafted gently under Finn's nose and, hard as it was, he fought the urge to put his arm around her and pull her close, uncertain how it would be received. Instead, they fell into easy conversation, reminiscing about the fun they'd had at the Young Farmers' meetings and rallies when they were younger. They hooted with laughter as they recounted the time a barn dance had been organised for them and they'd just about tied themselves up in knots trying to learn the steps. 'If I remember rightly, we didn't take it too seriously, did we?' said Romy.

'We didn't, much to the annoyance of the fella who was shouting out the instructions. He flatly refused to do it again.'

'And d'you remember the time Jimby Fairfax climbed the maypole on the village green and got tangled up in all the ribbons?' Romy said, giggling.

'That sort of thing was so typical of him. His dad had to fetch a ladder and a load of people held onto the bottom, including Ollie, so it wouldn't topple over with the pole being so thin.'

'And then it somehow slipped and he was left dangling above the pond on the end of the ladder with everyone gripping onto it for dear life.'

'And despite all their efforts, he still ended up getting dunked for his trouble. The ducks weren't impressed at all. It was like watching a scene from a comedy. I've no idea how that even happened considering where the pole was in relation to the pond. Mind, knowing Jimby, anything's possible,' said Finn, chuckling.

'Ahh, happy times,' said Romy wistfully.

'Yeah, and good old Jimby hasn't changed a bit. Still doesn't take himself seriously, still accident prone.' Finn absently stretched his arm along the back of the sofa and Romy rested her head on his shoulder as if it was the most natural thing in the world.

The two of them sat in comfortable silence, Finn bringing his arm around her, the cosy atmosphere of the room washing over him. He allowed his head to press gently against hers, inhaling the light floral notes of her shampoo. It took him back to them sitting on his bed in his teenage bedroom as they talked about their plans for the future, the pair of them so full of hope, so sure it was one they'd face together.

'Feel free to tell me to mind my own business, but I wondered if you'd considered moving back here? On a permanent basis, I mean. I only ask after what you said about not feeling settled since your mum sold the cottage.'

'I've thought about it loads. I hadn't even been here half a day when the idea first popped into my head, but I'm trying to think my options through carefully, which, as you know, is something I don't always do.'

He smiled; he knew exactly what she meant. 'And what sort of path have those thoughts taken? Is there an option that's coming out on top, or is there something holding you back?'

'They've been going back and forth between me staying here being a no-brainer and me making a fresh start somewhere totally new, which has its own appeal.'

Disappointment landed with a thud in Finn's chest though he tried not to show it. 'And what's the appeal of starting somewhere new rather than somewhere... um, rather than somewhere you know?' He stopped himself from saying 'somewhere that makes you happy' in case it came across as him trying to push his hopes onto her. After all, she'd only been here a few days, though it didn't feel that way. It wasn't lost on him that his thoughts were completely out of character. Usually, he was careful, measured, took time to think before he spoke or acted, but having Romy back here in Lytell Stangdale had turned all of that on its head. He was already dreading her leaving the village; he knew it was going to hurt.

'At the moment, there's only one thing that has made me think twice about moving here permanently, but after talking it through with Ella earlier today, she pretty much convinced me that it wasn't enough of a reason. But every now and then, I get a moment of doubt which unsettles me. I'd be interested to hear if you think I'm overthinking things and being daft.'

Finn sat quietly, his arm still round Romy, his hand smoothing up and down her arm as she explained the situation with Livvie and Rhoda.

'What do you think?' She sat up and turned to look at him, the concern in her eyes evident.

He hated that something like that was troubling her. 'I agree with Ella, you're worrying unnecessarily. Livvie and Rhoda are really decent people. I've never heard anyone say a bad word about either of them, and I've never heard them described as gossips. If that's what's influencing your decision, I think it's a real shame,' he said truthfully. 'And like Ella said, you get gossips everywhere, and everyone knows what they're like. The decent folk won't take any notice, and there's more of them round here than the spiteful, gossipy variety. I don't think they're enough of a reason to stop you from moving back if that's what your heart's telling you to do.'

'You really think so?'

'I really do.'

'And there's also the matter of me only being back a few days. I mean, don't you think that's a bit quick to be making such a momentous decision? Buying a house is hardly a small thing.'

'Sometimes you just know when something's right. If your gut's telling you it is, then you can't go far wrong. And it's not as if the cottage and Lytell Stangdale are completely new to you.'

'True. And if I'm being honest, the feeling in my gut's been sending strong messages since...'

'Since when?' Finn found it impossible to tear his eyes from hers as a frisson danced between them. He reached up and cupped her face with his hand, the two of them drawing closer together. He felt the now familiar flutter in his stomach that being around

Romy generated. He lowered his eyes to her lips just as a loud thud came from outside. Romy and Finn jumped apart in an instant as Ted leapt to his feet, barking vociferously, his hackles standing up on his back.

'Oh, my God, what was that?' Romy's face had paled, panic chasing away the sultry look in her eyes of mere seconds ago.

Finn got to his feet, Ted still barking frantically. 'I don't know, but whatever it was sounded like it came from behind the cottage. You stay here, Romes, Ted and me will go and investigate. It's probably just the wind blowing summat over, it had picked up when I left the farm earlier.' He didn't want to worry her and say there was a chance it could be the unsavoury characters that had been troubling the area recently.

Finn flicked the outside light on and unlocked the back door, Ted growling and snarling beside him. On a day-to-day-basis the Labrador was described by Finn's mum as being "as soft as washing", something Finn couldn't argue with; no one would ever guess at his protective streak which only came out when necessary.

Ted shot out into the back garden as soon as Finn opened the door, the Labrador continuing his barking and growling. Finn gazed around carefully, the wind whistling through the naked branches of the trees, pinhead-sized flakes of snow making him blink as he checked for recent footprints in the snow or shed doors standing open when they shouldn't be. Finding nothing untoward, he gave one last look around then whistled for Ted, the pair of them heading back indoors. Finn was glad to be out of the cold as he made sure he locked and bolted the door.

'Did you find anything?' Romy asked, her eyebrows drawn together in concern.

'I reckon it was just the wind making a door slam in the garden next door. Like I said, it's whipped up a bit since I arrived.' He was glad to see his reply made her shoulders fall and her concerned expression fade. Ted seemed less wound up too.

'That's a relief.'

Finn couldn't argue with that, but he was gutted that it had interrupted their moment.

'I hate to say it, but have you seen the time?' Romy nodded towards the clock.

Finn's heart sank, the evening had raced by. 'Yeah, I guess I'd better be heading back to the farm.' He hoped he didn't look as disappointed as he sounded, he wouldn't want Romy to mistake it for him being grumpy which Britt often complained of.

At the front door, Romy stood on her tiptoes, reached up and pressed a kiss to his cheek. 'Thanks for coming, Finn, I've had a really lovely evening. We'll have to do it again before I leave.'

Her words, "before I leave" were echoing in his head, sending his emotions into turmoil. He mustered up a smile. 'Thanks for the invitation, it's been lovely,' he said, his gaze lingering on her.

'Thanks for coming – I'd say thanks for the sour apples, but... you know?' She grinned and he couldn't help but laugh at that.

'You're welcome. Hope you enjoy the rest of them.'

'Not so sure *enjoy* is the word I'd use.'

'Good point.'

Ted huffed out a bored sigh.

'Hint taken, Ted,' said Finn. 'Come on, let's get your lead on, lad.'

That done, he looked down at Romy. 'So, I'll see you on Christmas Day.'

'Looking forward to it.' She went to open the door. 'Does that mean you won't be joining everyone for the carol singing around the Christmas tree?'

'Oh, yeah, I'd forgotten about that. Will you be there?'

Romy nodded. 'I will, it sounds great fun. Kitty said she'd give me a knock so I could walk along with her and her brood.'

'In that case, I'll see you round the Christmas tree.' He gave one last smile, resisting the temptation to press another kiss to her cheek and stepped out into the frosty night, snowflakes dancing around him.

TWENTY-EIGHT

CHRISTMAS EVE

Romy

Romy hadn't been ready to go to bed after Finn had left the previous night. Her mind had been too busy, running over the conversations she'd had with him and Ella concerning her idea of a permanent move to Lytell Stangdale. Instead, she gathered her crafting paraphernalia around her and continued her work on the felt moorland picture until her mind and eyes were tired and she could do no more.

Or at least her brain had been tired until her head had hit the pillow. Then it had pinged back to life, and all she could think about was Finn and the burgeoning feelings she had for him. After the time they'd spent together that night, she was in no doubt she was falling for him all over again. Nobody else had ever made her feel the way he did; feel that it was okay just to be herself. Ella had used a term earlier for Romy's return to the village, she'd said everything had just "slotted into place". It had been that way with Finn, too.

She'd woken that morning with one thing singing loud and clear in her mind and excitement pulsing through her veins: she was going to move to Lytell Stangdale. I didn't matter that it was all happening so quickly, it felt unequivocally right; whatever happened with her and Finn, here was where she was meant to be, here was where she belonged. As soon as Boxing Day was over and done with, she was going to speak to Maisie at the holiday cottage company and ask if she could double-check with the current owner of Holly Tree Cottage and make sure that they were still planning to put it on the market. Once she had confirmation of that, Romy was going to tell them she was interested in buying it; with the money that was sitting in her building society account and how her earnings had taken off recently, she was sure she'd be able to afford it. She decided to keep her decision to herself until now, just in case the owner had changed their mind, not that she wanted to contemplate that scenario.

At ten to six that evening, Romy answered a knock at the door to see Kitty on the doorstep, smiling, while Ollie was with Lily and Lottie on the other side of the gate. From the glow of the streetlight, she could see they all looked bundled up well against the cold. She assumed that Kitty's son, Lucas, would be working in the Sunne's kitchen that evening.

'Hi there, Romy, ready for some carol singing?' Kitty asked.

'I so am.' Romy grinned as she pushed her feet into her wellies, the warm air of the cottage sneaking out onto the path.

Earlier that day, she'd joined Kitty and her family at Oak Tree Farm for a lunch of soup and sandwiches and they'd discussed the best time to set off so they wouldn't be hanging around in the cold for too long before the carol singing got underway. While she was there, Romy had picked Kitty and Ollie's brains about the units on the Danskelfe Estate where Noushka had her dance studio. The more Livvie heard, the more she realised that renting one for her own business would be perfect, adding another reason to move to Lytell Stangdale.

As they made their way along the trod in the direction of the snowy village green, the sound of voices and the occasional peal of laughter floated towards them on the clear, frosty air. The village looked enchanting with its festive lights illuminating the way and Christmas trees twinkling from front windows. It sent a thrill through Romy. It had been a while since she'd enjoyed herself on a Christmas Eve.

'There's Jimby and Vi.' Kitty gave them an enthusiastic wave. 'Ah, how sweet does little Pippin look in her snowsuit?' she said, using the nickname Jimby had given his little daughter before she was born owing to Vi's insatiable craving for apples while she was pregnant. Romy looked over in their direction to see a little girl snuggled up in brightly-coloured snowsuit, topped off with a woolly hat with a huge pompom. She was stomping around in the snow by her parents.

'Hi there,' said Vi, when they reached them. She was looking as glamorous as ever in an emerald-green wool coat that flared at the waist, the waves of her aubergine-dyed bob topped with a dark-green beret. Romy wondered how on earth she managed to walk in her high-heeled boots with all the snow and ice that covered the ground.

'Ey up, you lot.' Jimby gave one of his trademark smiles. 'Good to see you're joining us, Romy. Hope you're ready for a good old sing-song.'

'Been looking forward to it.' She beamed back at him.

Before long, they were joined by Molly and Camm who'd brought Molly's young daughter, Emmie, as well as one of her twin sons, Ben, and his girlfriend, Kristy, who lived in converted stables at Withrin Hill Farm.

'Hi there, everyone.' Romy turned to see the angelic face of Ollie's daughter Anoushka, her golden hair spread out over her shoulders, almond eyes shining. She was holding hands with Gabe Dublin who was looking relaxed and happy. Seeing him like this in a village setting, rather than on the television screen, still felt surreal to Romy.

'Hi, folks,' he said in his soft Southern Irish accent before falling into conversation with Ollie.

Romy scanned the ever-increasing sea of faces that had gathered on the green, a buzz of excitement filling the air along with the evocative aroma of pine from the Christmas tree. Amongst them, she spotted Rhoda with a tall, thin man, but there was no sign of Livvie. Lucy from the village shop was standing beside them with a smiley-faced man Romy assumed must be her husband. Her attention was drawn by a familiar cackle of laughter and she followed the sound to see Big Mary dressed in the colourful coat she'd been wearing at the shop the previous day. She was enjoying an entertaining conversation with a man who was sporting a long beard that was dyed a vivid shade of red and was dressed as vibrantly as Big Mary herself. The pair of them made for a larger-than-life sight. Romy felt sure they must be a couple.

Her eyes swept the crowd once more, her heart sinking at the prospect of Finn changing his mind, or being too busy to join them round the Christmas tree. Just as she'd convinced herself he wasn't coming, she heard the muted hum of an engine and the headlights of a vehicle illuminating the road. She watched as an old Land Rover came into view, parking up near the Sunne. It was too far away to read the number plate, but it didn't stop her pulse from cranking up a notch or two. In the next moment, the vehicle's lights were cut and the driver's door opened. Seconds later, Finn stepped out, triggering a rush of joy through Romy.

'Hi,' he said when he reached her.

'Hi,' she said, gazing up at him. From the corner of her eye she caught Jimby nudging Molly who turned to look at them. 'No Ted tonight?' Romy asked.

'I've left him snoring by the Aga in his new fleecy bed he got as an early Christmas present, thought it'd be a bit chilly for his paws standing so long in the snow; he's a lad who likes his luxuries.'

'Can't blame him for that,' Romy said with a chuckle, just as Ella landed beside her, holding hands with a tall, broad-shouldered man who was wearing a broad smile.

'Now then, Romes,' Ella said from the depths of the scarf she'd looped around her neck several times.

'Hi, Ells.' A beat passed before the identity of the man clicked with her.

'Oh, my goodness! Joss! It's great to see you! How're you doing?'

Joss laughed. 'Hi, Romy, s'great to see you too. Ells said you were back– in fact, it's all she's been talking about since she bumped into you.'

'Can't deny it,' said Ella, giggling. 'I'm just chuffed to bits my buddy's back.'

Before they could say anything further, the small brass band on the opposite side of the Christmas tree struck up – new for this year, it was comprised of a handful of local musicians – and the carol singing started with a rousing rendition of *Hark! the Herald Angels Sing.*

Much as she'd been enjoying herself, especially standing in such close proximity to Finn, Romy was glad when the last carol had been sung. Her feet were so cold she'd lost all feeling in them; it was the same with her nose, and her teeth had chattered their way through the last two carols.

'Bloomin' 'eck, I'd forgotten how cold it gets when you're standing in one place for a while. I'm absolutely frozen.' Vi rubbed her leather-gloved hands together briskly. 'Are you okay, little pudding?' she asked her daughter who'd been picked up by Jimby and was snuggling into him, her plump cheeks rosy with the cold.

'Yes.' Pippin nodded vigorously before turning and blowing a loud raspberry into her daddy's neck, making everyone laugh.

'She's a proper daddy's girl, that one,' said Molly.

'She is, and she's inherited his sense of mischief, as you've just witnessed,' Vi said, smiling indulgently at her daughter.

'That's my girl.' Jimby beamed proudly before delivering a load of noisy kisses to Pippin's cheek, making her squeal with delight.

'Right then, that's the Christmas carols done for another year,' said Ollie, clapping his hands together. 'Is everyone heading to the Sunne for a drink and a nibble?'

A chorus of 'yes' rang around their group. Romy looked up at Finn, keen to see his response.

'Are you going?' he asked.

'Sounds very tempting. How about you?' Shivering, she crossed her fingers, hoping he wasn't going to say he had to slope off back to the farm.

He smiled, offering her his arm. 'Come on then, you look frozen, let's get you thawed out. I know just the thing.'

'Steady on there, Finn, this is a family show,' said Jimby, shooting him a cheeky grin as he passed.

'I meant a glass of mulled wine, Jimby!' Finn said, shaking his head and laughing.

Romy was delighted to find the atmosphere in the Sunne was buzzing. Traditional Christmas carols played in the background while the delicious aroma of food sneaked out from the kitchen and permeated the air, mingling with woodsmoke from the fire.

'Jimby and Ollie have grabbed another couple of seats, so you're both welcome to join us at our usual table, if you like,' said Kitty, squeezing Romy's arm as she passed.

Romy glanced up at Finn, hoping it sounded as appealing to him as it did to her, especially since the table was right next to the fireplace.

He looked down at her. 'Talk about pleading puppy-dog eyes, you could give Ted a run for his money. Two seats by the fire it is, then.' He chuckled as he led the way.

With Jimby pulling two tables together, the usual group of friends were joined by a younger crowd, namely Anoushka and Gabe, Ella and Joss and a couple Romy didn't recognise, though they seemed friendly enough.

'Romes, have you met Brogan and Nick, yet?' Ella leant across Joss.

'I haven't, no.' Her eyes met those of the young woman sitting beside Ella and was treated to a friendly smile.

'This is Brogan Hopwood and this is Nick Heuston. They live at Pond Farm just out of the village. Broges is a vet nurse and Nick's one of the local vets. They're based over at the new Danskelfe business units where Noushka has her dance studio.' Ella turned to Brogan and Nick. 'And this is an old bestie of mine from our Young Farmers days, Romy Stainthorpe. Romes is staying at Holly Tree Cottage for the festive season.'

The three were exchanging hellos when a cut-glass voice cut in. 'I hope you don't mind me asking, but did I just hear you say you're staying at Holly Tree Cottage? I'm guessing it's the one in this village, and not the Holly Tree Cottage over in Beckinthwaite?'

Romy looked up to see a tall, slender woman smiling at her. She was wearing a grey cashmere sweater dress flecked with fine silver threads and had an air of sophistication about her. Her pale-blonde hair was fastened in a messy up-do and she had silver earrings dangling from her ears. She was holding a tray of glasses filled with mulled wine, steam rising from them, their cinnamon fragrance infusing the air around the table.

'Yes, it's the one next to Oak Tree Farm. My parents used to own it years ago. Looks a bit different now.' Romy laughed. 'It's *very* stylish but still nice and cosy.'

'Oh, gosh! I do hope you approve of the refurbishment,' the blonde woman said, setting the tray down on the table and squeezing onto the edge of the banquette next to Kitty and opposite Romy and Finn. 'Please help yourselves to a glass, folks. There are some soft drinks following for the littlies.'

'How could I not approve? – not that how it's decorated is any of my business – but I think it's so clever how it's retained the character of the cottage but somehow brought it tastefully up-to-date. I'm sure achieving that won't have been easy.'

The blonde woman beamed, feigning wiping sweat from her brow with her delicate fingertips, a white gold ring, studded with tiny diamonds glittering under the light. 'Oh, Phew! I'm so relieved to hear you say that! My wife and I are responsible for the interior design brief; I do the designing and Saffy does the sourcing. We'd be utterly *devastated* if you hated it, especially with your family connection to it.'

'Not at all! I love it; I wouldn't change a thing, it's a great advert for your company.'

'Oh, that's *so* sweet, thank you, darling, you've made my day. I'm Portia, by the way, the landlord and landlady's daughter, for my sins – or should that be theirs?' She laughed heartily and Romy found herself instantly liking her.

'Pleased to meet you, Portia, I'm Romy.'

'It's fabulous to meet you too, darling.' Portia glanced between Romy and Finn, a knowing smile hitching up the corners of her mouth. 'So how long have you two lovebirds been an item? I had no idea you were back on the dating scene, Finn, though I have to say, you do make a rather delicious couple.'

Romy felt her cheeks flame and was thankful for the dim lighting in the bar, though it didn't stop her from wishing the floor would open up and swallow her in one quick gulp. Finn coughed uncomfortably beside her. It didn't help that his leg was pressed against hers. Up to that point, the contact had made her want to grab his face in her hands and kiss him hard. She was sure if they were alone somewhere private she'd do just that. But now they were pinned under Portia's searching gaze it was a massive distraction and she felt the heat of embarrassment spread through every inch of her.

'We're old friends from when I used to live here,' she said, aware of not just Portia's eyes on her but those of everyone else at their table.

Jimby snorted. '"*Old friends*".' He got a quick elbow in the ribs from Vi for his trouble. It was accompanied by a pointed glare. He rubbed the point of contact and gave his wife a hurt look.

It hadn't gone unnoticed by Portia whose smile grew wider, her perfectly microbladed eyebrows quirking in amusement. 'Old friends, hey? I supposed that explains why you look so... Hmm.'

She tapped her finger against her mouth. 'What's the word? *Right* together.'

'Porsh,' said Brogan, adopting a good-natured chastising tone.

'It's not like you to make mischief, Portia,' Ella said with a hint of sarcasm.

'It's not mischief, I'm just pointing out the obvious, that's all. I daresay I'm not the only one amongst us who can see it.' The interior designer gave a sweet smile before turning to Romy. 'So, getting back to the cottage, it's actually owned by a chap called Quentin who's a good pal of mine and Saffy's. He's moving abroad and was going to keep it as a bolt-hole for when he's back in the UK but, unfortunately, his circumstances have changed and he's going to have to sell it; he's absolutely devastated. He told me he's going to instruct an estate agent in the New Year and get it on the market pronto; poor darling needs a quick sale.'

'I'd heard the owner was thinking of selling it,' said Romy as the information Portia had just imparted started running through her mind.

'Don't suppose you fancy taking it off his hands, do you? It'd be nice and close to our Finn here,' Portia said with a waggle of her eyebrows.

Romy was relieved when attention was taken from her and Finn by Molly asking Portia how the brief was going for the latest collection of lodges on the Danskelfe Estate. While the designer headed over to Molly rather than shout her reply, Romy mouthed a 'thank you' in Molly's direction.

As Romy was taking a tentative sip of the mulled wine, her thoughts whirring with Holly Tree Cottage, a lady with a swishy bob and a pair of glasses perched on top of her head arrived at the table. She was holding two large plates of delicious-looking nibbles which Jimby and Vi quickly relieved her of and placed on the table. Behind her stood a tall, fresh-faced teenager with sandy-blond hair who Romy guessed must be Kitty's son, Lucas. He was holding a further couple of plates, these being filled with festive-themed sweet nibbles.

'Wow! This all looks amazing,' said Jimby. 'Which of these did you make, Lukes?'

'Bea did the savouries and I did the sweet ones.' The trainee chef smiled shyly.

'They look awesome, Lukes,' said Molly.

'Thanks, Auntie Molly.'

'Lucas is already showing all the signs of becoming a very gifted pastry chef,' Bea said in her warm, plummy tones. 'And I can't tell you how good it is to have him in the kitchen, he's like a breath of fresh air, brimming with ideas and enthusiasm. He'll have me out of a job if I'm not careful.' The landlady chuckled.

'Go Lucas!' said Ollie, smiling proudly at his stepson.

'It's 'cos I've got a good teacher, that's why,' Lucas said, beaming at the praise. Kitty reached forward and gave her son's hand a squeeze, smiling up at him.

'I've had a sneaky taste of all of them and I can assure you that the word delicious doesn't cover it,' said Portia. 'Lucas and Mummy make a fabulous team.'

'Thanks, Portia.' Lucas's eyes shone happily.

'Thank you to you and Jonty for all of this, Bea, we're really grateful,' said Vi.

'You're very welcome, darling, it's the least we can do for all your loyal custom. However, I really must love you and leave you, there are more tables to be served so Lucas and I had better crack on. Tuck in, folks, and merry Christmas to you all, have a wonderful day tomorrow.' With that, Bea and her young protégé headed back into the heat and bustle of the kitchen.

As a way of thanking the locals for their custom throughout the year, the Sunne's landlord and landlady laid on free mulled wine and nibbles every Christmas Eve straight after the carol singing. It was a far cry from Hacky Harold's day when all he offered his customers for free was flea bites from the mangy carpet and food poisoning from the rancid pickled eggs that had been stuck to the end of the bar for more years than anyone cared to remember at the time.

Forty-five minutes later, with the drinks and nibbles consumed, Jimby reached for Pippin's snowsuit and pompom hat. 'Right then, I reckon it's time we got these little rascals off home so they can get tucked up in bed before Santa Claus gets here.'

The children didn't need telling twice and jumped up, Pippin giving an excited shriek as she wriggled off Vi's knee. Emmie had her snowsuit on in a flash, so eager was she to make tracks home to Withrin Hill Farm.

'So glad you've come back, Romes.' Ella flung her arms around Romy, squeezing her tight and kissing her firmly on the cheek. 'Don't you dare go disappearing again, okay?'

'I'm glad to be back, Ells.' Romy hugged her friend with equal enthusiasm, feeling a flood of affection for her friend. 'And I won't go disappearing.'

'Promise?' said Ella.

'I promise,' said Romy.

'Are you heading back to the cottage, Romes?' Finn asked when Ella and Joss had left, his blue eyes causing a flutter in her stomach.

She glanced at her watch, feeling torn. She still had a couple of things she needed to finish tonight but at the same time, she was reluctant for her evening with Finn to come to an end. It made no difference knowing she was going to see him the next day, she found herself wanting to spend every spare moment with him.

'Quick one here?' she asked. 'Or are you done with shandy?'

'I'm good for another if you are.' The way he was looking at her made it impossible for her to think straight.

'I could manage a fizzy orange.' She didn't want anything else alcoholic since she needed to keep a clear head for what she'd be working on later.

With all the goodbyes and wishes of merry Christmas out of the way, Romy and Finn were the last of their group of friends left at the table. They spent the next half hour discussing what Portia had said about her friend being keen for a quick sale of Holly Tree Cottage.

'So, following on from our conversation that we didn't get finished last night, are you tempted?' Finn asked.

'I am actually. I've taken on board what you and Ella said about Rhoda and Livvie, and the gossips in the village, and I can see how daft I was to even let that influence me. My dad did nothing wrong, he was a well-respected, decent man and I can walk with my head held high. And trust me, if I hear anyone say anything to the contrary, I'll be sure to put them straight.' She glanced up at Finn to see a huge smile on his face. It made her heart swell with happiness.

'That's great news.' He reached for her hand and wrapped his work-roughened fingers around it, their eyes locking.

Before Romy could reply, Portia appeared beside them. 'Please don't take offence, but I honestly can't think of a couple more desperately in need of this.' She gave them a wide smile as she deposited a large sprig of mistletoe on the table before them. 'You're welcome!' she said, before sashaying off.

Romy clamped her hand over her mouth and started laughing, her face a vibrant shade of red. Finn caught her eye and shook his head.

Arriving at the gate of Holly Tree Cottage – Finn had insisted on walking her back – the pair stopped, Romy tilting her head to look up at him, the glow of the streetlight casting soft shadows over his face. They stood in silence for a moment, their breath merging and curling in the air around them. It was bone-numbingly cold, but Romy didn't care; she didn't want her evening with Finn to end.

He fished about in his pocket for a moment, carefully pulling out the mistletoe, holding it above them. 'It's lost a few berries but I don't think that really matters,' he said, his voice soft.

Romy's heart started thumping as he reached out with his free hand, cupping the back of her head. His eyes darkened and she closed her eyes as his lips met hers, heady emotions exploding in her chest, just as they had with their very first kiss all those years ago. No other man had ever generated such a reaction.

'Ee, Romy pet, sorry to interrupt.' A loud, familiar voice sliced through their moment, bouncing around the village.

Romy's heart stuttered, her eyes pinging open at the same moment as Finn's.

'You've got to be kidding me.' He released a frustrated sigh, resting his forehead against hers.

They both turned to see Big Mary and her husband tentatively picking their way along the trod just past Oak Tree Farm.

'What would Big Mary want with me?' Romy said.

'I reckon you're just about to find out,' Finn said under his breath.

They looked on as the older woman started waving what appeared to be a scarf at them. 'You left this behind, flower. It's a bit too nippy to be without one so we thought we'd better catch you up and get it back to you.'

Finn's eyes dropped to the scarf around Romy's neck. 'But you're wearing one.'

'I know, that one's not mine.'

'Oh.'

The two larger-than-life characters arrived beside Romy and Finn, huffing and puffing from their exertion.

'Portia found it on the banquette where you and your pals were sitting so Gerry and me volunteered to return it to you.' Big Mary didn't appear to notice the scarf Romy was wearing. 'Oh, and this is my hubby, Gerald, he's a local artist.' She turned to her husband. 'This is the young lady I was telling you about earlier.'

'Hi, Gerald.' Romy smiled at him.

'Pleased to meet you, bonny lass,' he said, his lisp and smile revealing he was even more dentally challenged than his wife.

'Teeth, Gerry!' Big Mary gave her husband a nudge. 'He's got a new pair; early Christmas present. He's a right one, mind, I always have to remind him about wearing them.' She rolled her eyes.

'Sorry, pet.' Quick as a flash, Gerald fished around in the

pocket of his garish trousers, pulled out a pair of false teeth and pushed them into his mouth. After a few moments' wrangling with them he said, 'There, thatsh better.' His attempt at a smile revealed a set of dentures that were clearly too big for his mouth, giving him a horse-like appearance.

Romy couldn't contain the laugh that was rising up her and was forced to disguise it as a cough, keen not to hurt Gerald's feelings. She was aware of Finn having the same struggle beside her.

'He got 'em second-hand off the internet – he hates going to the dentist with a passion, so buying them this way saves him the ordeal. Mind, like his last couple of pairs, he hasn't got the fit right just yet,' Big Mary said in her melodic Wearside accent.

'Aye, I need to dig a file out of the shed and give 'em another go.' Gerald gave another horsey smile.

Romy, whose eyes were now glued to him with morbid fascination, frowned as her brain played catch-up with his words, the ill-fitting false teeth making it hard to understand him.

'Fair enough,' said Finn, clearly doing all he could to contain any further laughter.

Just then, the wind whipped up, curling it's icy fingers around them, reminding Romy of the freezing temperatures. 'Mary, it's really kind of you to bring the scarf, but I'm afraid it's not mine.'

'Oh?'

'I think it's Molly's,' she said.

'Yeah, I think it is, too,' said Finn.

'Ee, well, fair enough, I'll give her a call and let her know we've got it. Gerry and me are sorry to have interrupted your snog, kids. Please feel free to lock lips again and carry on.' Big Mary's trademark cackle was joined by an equally loud one from Gerald. 'Merry Christmas, kids.'

'Merry Christmas,' Romy and Finn said together.

They watched in disbelief as the couple made their way slowly back along the trod.

'What the heck was that all about?' said Romy; she wasn't so sure she believed Mary's story about the scarf and wondered if

Portia had sent them along to see if Finn had joined Romy at the cottage.

'It's just Big Mary and Gerald being Big Mary and Gerald,' said Finn, chuckling. 'And maybe with a bit of Portia thrown in.'

'Hmm. Interesting mixture.'

'Aye, isn't it just.'

'And who knew you could buy second-hand false teeth on the internet?' Romy wasn't sure it was true, or if Big Mary and Gerald were pulling her leg.

'I was just going to say makes you wonder who'd buy them, but I guess we already know the answer to that.' The pair looked at one another and burst out laughing.

With the spell of their romantic moment well and truly broken, Romy and Finn reluctantly said their goodbyes. But it hadn't stopped Romy's lips burning from their kiss. It didn't matter that it had been interrupted, nothing could erase that feeling. She doubted she'd get much sleep for thinking about it all night.

TWENTY-NINE

Finn

If anyone had told Finn a week ago that he'd actually enjoy Christmas Day that year, he would've told them they were bonkers. But today, he'd woken feeling happier than he'd felt in a long time. Though it had been hard, he'd accepted as well as he was able that his sons weren't going to be spending the day with him and his parents, but after the tension that had hung over the farmhouse the Christmas before Britt had left, he had to concede that it was probably for the best for all of them. Though both Britt and he had tried their hardest to keep their animosity for one another to themselves, it was inevitable that Kyle and Toby would pick up on it. Kids were sensitive to the smallest of changes and he was determined it was going to be different this year, especially with the lads moving abroad.

On top of that, Romy Stainthorpe had walked back into his life and they'd shared a kiss last night. And it wasn't just any kiss, it was the sort that had sent waves of electricity rippling through every fibre in his body. It may have been cut off in its prime but the touch of Romy's lips against his had generated feelings that had kept him awake all night. He hoped they'd get the chance to pick up where they'd left off at some point during the day – though several points would be better!

And now, with the house filled with the evocative aroma of Christmas dinner, he was on a video call to his sons which filled his heart with joy. Toby was bouncing with his usual enthusiasm, telling him what Father Christmas had brought him, making Finn smile. He noted Kyle seemed quieter which tugged at his heart, though Finn maintained his cheerful tone, hoping it might elicit a few more words from his son. 'Santa's been here for you both too. When I came downstairs this morning, there were a couple of sacks with your names on left in the living room, and there are some presents under the tree, too.' Toby gave a 'woohoo' at that and Finn was glad to see it generated a smile from his oldest boy.

The FaceTime call was going on longer than he'd expected and Finn felt torn; he should have set off for Romy fifteen minutes ago. He was reluctant to pull himself away from his sons, but he'd also been hoping to take advantage of a few moments alone with Romy in the hope they'd be able to indulge in more of their heart-stopping kisses. But his boys came first, and he had no doubts Romy would understand, especially since she'd been so close to her dad. He was relieved when his father dangled the Land Rover keys in front of him, pointing to himself and then in the direction of Lytell Stangdale. Finn nodded and gave him a thumbs up.

Once the lads had finished and run off, Britt appeared on his phone's screen and Finn was surprised to find her in a chatty mood again, with no sign of her usual impatience or irritation. But instead of her new demeanour putting him at ease, or affording him some relief that they were at last on amicable terms, his senses instantly snapped into high alert, suspicion slithering up his spine. He couldn't shake the feeling she was up to something. He only hoped whatever it was, it wouldn't affect their sons' visit the following day.

Britt was in the middle of an over-sentimental reminiscence about their first Christmas as parents, when his father landed back with Romy, instantly souring his ex-wife's mood. Finn couldn't resist the pull Romy's presence had created and stole a look in her direction, giving her a quick wave and a broad smile when she looked up from fussing Ted who'd immediately raced over to her. When he glanced back at the screen Finn saw Britt's expression had darkened. Checking herself, she fixed her smile back on her face and continued with her one-sided conversation, repeating how they'd had so many wonderful Christmases together, until Toby's yells for help with one of his toys became more insistent and they were at last able to end the call.

Sliding his phone onto the dresser Finn turned to face Romy, thrilled to be met with a loaded expression in her eyes. His emotions leapt to attention. They really would have to find time for just the two of them at some point during the course of the afternoon. There was no way he could wait until he dropped her off at the cottage before he got to sample those lips again. It didn't help that they were looking so decidedly plump and tempting right now.

Shaking his wayward thoughts from his mind, he steadied himself and said, 'Sorry I couldn't get over for you, the lads were in a chatty mood and I didn't have the heart to cut them off.'

'Quite right, too, and besides, your dad was an excellent chauffeur,' she said, making Tommy and Jill chuckle.

'Happy to be of service, ma'am.' Tommy doffed his flat cap.

'Oh, my days, it smells so good in here. I made sure I had a small breakfast so I'd have plenty of room for Christmas dinner,' Romy said, before going to hang up her coat in the porch.

'You'll be pleased to know we have Yorkshire puds with our Christmas dinner, though I know some folks don't.' Jill peered into the pan of the gravy she was making.

'Music to my ears.' Romy grinned as she walked back into the kitchen. 'Is there anything I can do to help?'

'Not at all, lovey, everything's under control. You sit yourself down and our Finn'll pour you a cup of tea.'

''Course.' Finn went to get a mug from the cupboard. 'I see you've decided against the fluffy onesie you were telling me about.' He grinned at her, thinking how cute she looked in her black trousers and over-sized Christmas jumper that featured a large snowman and lots of sparkly snowflakes.

'I thought this would be more fitting for the occasion.' Smiling, she flicked her hair over her shoulder and pressed something on her sweater that set the snowman's nose glowing red.

Tommy gave a hearty chuckle

'Good choice,' said Finn.

'Actually, I've got a little something for you.' Romy headed over to the bag she'd left by the door, noting Ted had his nose stuck in it. Before she could stop him, he'd grabbed a parcel wrapped in Christmas paper and started prancing round the kitchen with it in his mouth, looking inordinately pleased with himself.

'Ted! Here!' said Finn, as the Labrador continued his circuit of the room, Finn after him. 'Ted, you little...'

Tommy, Jill and Romy hooted with laughter as Finn lunged for the wayward pooch who leapt out of reach just in time.

'Sorry, Romes, the little toad doesn't seem to want to give it up. I hope it's nothing breakable.'

'It's fine, don't worry.' Romy patted her leg and called gently for Ted. Finn didn't know how she did it, but the Labrador actually listened and trotted over to her, the parcel still in his mouth, his tail wagging.

'Give.' Ted obeyed Romy's command and dropped the stolen goods. 'Good boy!' She smoothed her hand over his head and scooped up the parcel.

'Looks like we've got a Ted whisperer in the house,' Tommy said, dryly.

'Thing is, this present is actually *for* Ted,' said Romy, giggling. 'Though I had expected to give it to him minus the wrapping paper.' She'd popped the chewy stick into her basket, along with some Christmas wrapping paper and sticky tape, when she was at the village shop yesterday morning.

'You need to have a word with Ted about not poking his nose in a lady's handbag. I've heard they have mantraps and all sorts in 'em,' Tommy said, chuckling.

'You'd better believe it, buster.' Jill winked at Romy.

'Is Ted okay to have it now if I remove the wrapping paper?' Romy asked. 'It's a dog chew.'

'Put it this way, I wouldn't like to be the one who tells him he's got to wait for it,' said Finn, taking in the Labrador's pleading looks.

'Fair point.' Romy quickly removed the paper and offered it to Ted who took it gently. 'Good boy,' she said, patting his head before he rushed off to his bed with it clamped between his teeth.

'Jill, I've got this for you and Tommy. It's just a little something to say thank you for welcoming me back so warmly and for putting up with me on Christmas Day.'

'Ah, lovey, there's really no need, Tommy and me are just thrilled to bits you're back.' Jill threw the tea towel she was holding over her shoulder and took the oblong parcel Romy was holding out to her.

Taking a seat at the table, Jill carefully peeled the sticky tape back, pressing her hand to her mouth when she opened out the gift paper to reveal the needle-felt picture Romy had been working on for the last couple of days. 'Oh, Romy, it's absolutely beautiful. Look, Tommy, see, it's our farm.' With a few tweaks, Romy had been able to add a felted version of the Castlegate Farm house along with a few hens scratting around beside the door.

'Wow! Romy, that's stunning,' said Finn, peering over his mum's shoulder. He'd struggled to visualise exactly what Romy meant when she'd told him she made felt pictures, but this went way beyond his expectations.

'By 'eck, lass it's bloomin' beautiful. You haven't half got some talent,' said Tommy.

'You're right, Tommy, it is beautiful.' Jill's eyes brimmed with tears. She went over to Romy and wrapped her arms around her, kissing her firmly on her cheek. 'Thank you for such a thoughtful gift, sweetheart.'

'I'm just glad you like it. I wasn't sure it would work, or if you'd be able to tell it was your farmhouse.' She looked over at Finn, her expression suddenly changing. 'I've got something for you, too.

Mind, don't build your hopes up, it's only something daft.' She handed him a thin, A4 sized festively-wrapped gift. 'There you go.'

'Thanks,' he said. He was puzzled as to why she appeared to be trying not to laugh.

As it felt thin and delicate, he opened it carefully, revealing a piece of cartridge paper. He turned it around and immediately burst out laughing which acted as a cue to Romy who did the same.

'Whatever are you two laughing at?' asked Jill.

Finn turned the paper to his parents causing them to fall about laughing too.

'Tell you what, it isn't half a good likeness,' said Tommy when they'd all finally got their merriment under control.

'Isn't it just,' said Jill. 'Let's have another look.'

Romy had presented Finn with a caricature of himself. Taking inspiration from the gift he'd brought to the cottage the other night, she'd drawn him with a vivid green sour apple sweet in his mouth, his face distorted by a comedic gurn.

'I'll treasure it,' Finn said, chuckling as he took in the details.

'Aye, same with ours,' said Jill. 'Actually, we've got a little something for you, too, lovey.'

Jill and Tommy had bought Romy a gift box of bath products from the beauty salon based at the Danskelfe Estate units, while Finn had picked up a snuggly jumper in a rich shade of burnt orange from the newly refurbished Campion's store over in Middleton-le-Moors. Romy was thrilled with it which pleased him no end. He avoided the temptation to compare how his Christmas gifts had been received by Britt; he'd never managed to get it right, no matter how hard he'd tried.

With Christmas dinner devoured and the dishes cleared away, the four of them sat at the table, poring over a pile of photo albums Jill had dug out of the sideboard in the living room. Finn hadn't realised how many photos there were of him and Romy together, with a generous amount at Young Farmers' events. He was taken by how happy they both looked, particularly so when they moved onto those taken after they'd become an item. It shone out from the photos that they were head-over-heels in love with one another. Finn assumed it must've been obvious to everyone who saw them together at the time. There was even one of them undertaking a sour apple contest, which had them hooting with laughter again.

They'd just opened the last album when they were interrupted by Finn's phone ringing.

'By, someone's popular today,' Tommy said as Finn went over to answer it.

Seeing the number illuminated on the screen made his stomach clench. He had a bad feeling about this.

THIRTY

Finn

'Hello, son, is everything okay?' A sob escaped at the other end and Finn's heart twisted. 'Kyle, what's the matter, buddy?' He fought to keep the alarm from his voice for the sake of his son.

'Dad, can I...' Another sob followed. 'Can I come and st... Can I stay with y–you...?' Another sob. 'P–please?' Kyle's voice was barely above a whisper and Finn was struggling to hear.

'What's happened, Kyle? Where are you? Where's your mum?' Hearing his son so distressed was tearing him up inside. 'Just take a couple of deep breaths and you'll be okay.' He glanced up to see his parents and Romy looking over at him wearing concerned expressions. His mum got to her feet and headed over to him.

'What's the matter?' she asked softly, her eyes filled with worry. 'Is Kyle okay?'

Finn pulled a face that told her he didn't know what was going on.

'Mum and F... Felix had a really big... row. They've been... arguing loads. I hate it. I want... to c–come... home, Dad. P–please let... me.'

Goosebumps prickled over Finn's skin, thoughts hurtling

around his mind. He battled the urge to tell his son to sit tight, that he was on his way. Sucking in a deep breath, he did all he could to calm his emotions, he didn't want to make things worse for Kyle and his brother; it was Christmas, a special time, especially for kids. Even as bad as things had got between him and Britt, they'd agreed not to argue in front of the lads at Christmastime. It hadn't been easy towards the end and he couldn't deny the atmosphere between the pair of them had been on the chilly side. He felt a pang of discomfort at that. But, from what Britt had said, life with Flash Felix was blissful, making Finn wonder what had caused them to have a big row in front of Kyle and Toby. And how was Toby feeling in all of this? He clenched his jaw; he couldn't let Kyle pick up on the emotions that where raging around inside him; he needed to stay calm for the sake of his son.

Something else crept into his mind: did this have anything to do with Britt's sudden change in attitude towards him? He didn't even know where to start thinking about that one. He'd struggled to keep up with her when they were married, never mind now.

'I'm sorry to hear that, son, but I'm sure it'll blow over. Lots of people have arguments around Christmas, it can be quite a stressful time for some folk, you know, trying to make sure everyone's having a nice time. It often has the opposite effect. I'm sure things will calm down.' He spoke with more conviction than he felt, hoping his words soothed Kyle. 'And don't forget you and Tobes'll be here tomorrow, so there's not long to wait. We can have a good chat then, son. Nanny, Gramps and me are really looking forward to seeing you both.'

'No, Dad, I don't want to wait 'til tomorrow! I hate it here! And I hate it in America! I'm not going back, I want to live with you.' Kyle started sobbing again.

Hearing Kyle's heartache was the worst kind of agony. Finn wished he could reach down the phone and wrap his arms around his son. His eyes misted with tears and his throat constricted but he knew he had to stay strong. 'Listen, buddy, we'll have a good chat about this tomorrow, I promise. Okay? Things are never usually as bad as they seem once everyone's calmed down.' God this was hard, the thought that Kyle had been feeling unhappy for all those months in America was killing him. 'Oh, and did I tell you Ted's looking forward to seeing you both too? He's been *very* mischievous, I've got loads of Ted's Tales to share with you and Tobes.' He heard Kyle sniff and give a small laugh down the phone at hearing the name they used for the Labrador's extensive list of impish antics.

'I'm looking forward to seeing him, too. What's he been doing?'

'Ughh! Where do I even start, he's such a rascal? He's been doing loads of stuff, including stealing Christmas presents out of someone's bag, would you believe?'

'What? No way! That's so bad.' Kyle laughed some more, offering Finn a small glimmer of hope that he'd managed to quash his son's tears for the rest of the evening.

'And he's been getting very excitable in the snow, he's so funny to watch, rolling about in it, kicking his legs everywhere, trying to eat it. You name it, the Tedster's done it.'

'I can't wait to see him. There's loads of snow here and it's snowing again.' Kyle's voice had brightened some more. 'Can we go sledging, Dad? And go down to the village and build snowmen like we used to? See our friends? I really want to do that.'

'Course we can, buddy, I know they'll be looking forward to seeing you. It's snowed a bit here this afternoon, too, but Camm's been round the roads all the way to the main one that leads to Middleton, making sure they're nice and clear for tomorrow. If Mum can't get out in her car, I'll come for you in the Landie.'

'Promise.'

'Cross my heart, Kyle.' After hearing his son's distress, wild horses wouldn't keep Finn from getting to Middleton-le-Moors.

'Cool. Oh... I'd better go now, Dad, Mum's calling for me.'

'Okay, son.'

'Please don't tell her I called you.'

'I won't.'

'Promise?'

'I promise, Kyle.'

'Thanks, Dad.'

'No worries. I'll see you tomorrow. Love you, buddy.'

'Love you, too, Dad.'

Finn took a moment once the call had ended. Hearing his son's tears had trampled over the happiness he'd felt only minutes earlier, leaving an agonising ache in his heart. He battled the urge to jump in the Land Rover and drive over to Middleton to see what had been going on, telling himself him turning up would only make things worse. Plus, he'd promised Kyle he wouldn't let Britt know he'd called. He didn't want to break that promise and risk losing his son's trust. From the sound of things, it was the last thing Kyle needed.

'What's happened, lad?' Tommy asked, concern etched on his face.

Finn dragged his fingers through his hair and made his way back over to the table, dropping heavily into his seat. 'I don't know what's going on over in Middleton, but...'

The three of them listened, making sympathetic sounds as he shared what Kyle had told him.

Jill reached across, resting her hand on Finn's arm. 'If it's any consolation, son, experience has told me that nothing on this earth gets to you more than anything to do with your children, whether it's them being upset, ill, angry, or anything else for that matter. We're programmed to keep them happy and safe so we spring into protective mode when we're faced with something that interferes with that. The amount of necks I could've wrung on your and Dougie's behalf over the years, you wouldn't believe.'

Finn was conscious of Romy squirming beside him; he hoped she didn't think his mum included her in that.

Jill continued. 'And what I've also found is that, while you're still focusing on whatever it was that bothered them, your kids have very probably moved on and forgotten all about what it was that had caused them so much grief and left you feeling all torn up and wretched about it.'

'Aye, lad, I can vouch for that,' said Tommy.

'You're a good, caring dad, Finn and it'll be more difficult for you with the lads living away from here and you, more than likely, not getting the full picture. I suggest you try as best as you can not to worry too much about Kyle's phone call. Like you told him, you've got the opportunity to have a good heart-to-heart with him tomorrow, see if you can get to the bottom of what's been going on and why he's so upset.' Jill gave his arm a squeeze before getting to her feet. 'Right then, I don't know about the rest of you, but I'm about ready for that Christmas pudding.'

'Actually, Jill, have you seen the weather?' Romy pointed to the window that gave out onto the yard where snow was falling steadily. 'I think I should probably be heading back to the cottage.'

Finn followed her gaze, his heart sinking. He hoped it would ease up before tomorrow.

In the kitchen of Holly Tree Cottage, Romy stood looking up at Finn, her eyes searching his face. 'You okay?'

'Yeah, I'm fine.' He nodded, placing his hands on the top of her arms. 'I'm sorry about earlier, with the phone calls.'

'There's really no need to apologise, you're a dad, your kids come first. It's how it should be.'

As much as they'd all tried, the atmosphere had lost its lustre after Kyle's phone call, which Romy said she fully understood. Finn had talked her into staying for some Christmas pudding, reassuring her that the roads would be fine thanks to Camm's endeavours to keep them clear, but the laughter was muted, nothing like that of beforehand.

'Aside from everything that's happened, I haven't been able to get you out of my mind since last night.' His eyes searched hers, eager to know it hadn't been a one-off, that she didn't regret their kiss.

'It's been the same for me,' she said. Her smile that followed felt like the sun coming out on a rainy day, lifting his spirits.

'It has?'

'It has, and it helped me reach a decision.'

He held his breath, hardly daring to hope she'd say what he so badly wanted to hear.

Her smile grew wider, lighting up her face. 'I'm going to speak to Portia, tell her I'd like to buy Holly Tree Cottage – as long as the price isn't ridiculous, of course; her friend will need to get it valued, we can go from there.'

Happiness bloomed in his chest. 'That's the best news, Romes. Having you back home it's... I don't know what to say!'

Before he could think any further Romy took his face in her hands and kissed him.

'Who needs mistletoe?' she said, when they finally came up for air.

THIRTY-ONE
BOXING DAY

Romy

Heading out into the village, Romy was surprised to see how much snow had fallen overnight. The trod was completely covered, but the road, at least, was clear. She'd heard the scrape of metal on hard ground as Camm had driven through with the plough just before six-thirty a.m., true to his word and doing all he could to keep the roads clear. Her mind went to Finn and his sons, hoping the roads were equally snow-free at the Middleton-le-Moors end; she knew how devastated he'd be if they couldn't get through, not to mention Kyle.

She'd woken bright and early that morning, determined to set the ball rolling and not waste a moment. Now she'd made up her mind about buying Holly Tree Cottage she wanted to have a good look at her finances and get an idea of what mortgages were on offer. She also wanted to speak to Portia, panic setting in that the interior designer's friend might change his mind, or put it on the market before he'd heard of her interest.

Last night's heady kisses with Finn had left her in no doubt about his feelings of her moving permanently to Lytell Stangdale, despite the fact he'd had his sons at the back of his mind. The power and emotions behind them had confirmed her decision to stay. No one had ever made her feel the way Finn Tindall did, and though it was early days, and they hadn't spoken about the future, she'd found herself tentatively hoping she had one with him.

'Morning, Romy.' The voice made her look up to see Rhoda walking along with the tall gentleman she'd seen her singing carols with on the village green on Christmas Eve. They were with an older lady, and all three were wrapped up well.

'Hi, Rhoda, how're you?'

'I'm well thanks, lovey. Oh, let me introduce you to my friends. This is Len and this is Freda.' She turned to her companions. 'And this is Romy who's spending the festive period in a holiday cottage here in the village.'

The three exchanged hellos.

'Did you have a good day, yesterday?' Rhoda asked.

'I did, thanks. How about all of you?' Romy stole a look at Freda who looked vaguely familiar.

'It was lively, but lovely.' Rhoda laughed. 'Len, Freda and I joined Livvie and Zander and their children up at Dale View Cottage. It was a total joy but we came back exhausted.'

'Aye, we did that,' said Len, laughing. 'My ears are still ringing with the noise.'

It suddenly clicked where Romy recognised the older lady Rhoda referred to as Freda. She used to live a reclusive life on the edge of the moors and had been a little bit grubby by all accounts. Looking at her today, her circumstances had clearly changed for the better. Romy noted she had a sweet smile and kind eyes, a hint of shyness about her.

'Are you doing the same as us and walking off some of yesterday's Christmas dinner?' asked Len.

Romy was just about to reply when a series of ear-splitting squawks sliced off her words before they had the chance to leave her mouth. They turned in the direction of the disturbance to see a large cockerel hurtling down the middle of the road, wings flapping frantically. It appeared to be clutching something in one of its claws.

'Don't tell me that obnoxious flaming bird's causing more grief in this village,' Len said, his top lip curling with contempt.

Before Romy could ask about the bird and the grief it had been causing, Jimby appeared in his wellies, pelting along in hot pursuit. 'Reg, you little shi...' Spotting the group of observers, he tempered his language as he raced by, his feet sliding every which way. 'Reg! Get back here, for crying out loud!'

'Reg?' said Romy, amused.

'Aye, it's the name Jimby gave to his daft bird. It creates nowt but havoc round here,' said Len.

A gentle whirring sound made them turn to see an elderly lady in a mobility scooter. She was whizzing along at an alarming speed, waving her fist in the air. 'Stop! Thief! Get back here with my Bakewell tart, you thieving, scrawny bird or I'll set the vicar on you! He'll give you what for, I'll tell you that for nothing.'

Romy looked on in disbelief, while Rhoda, Freda and Len fell about in a fit of laughter. It was just like a scene from a comedy sketch.

'Oh my days!' said Rhoda, covering her mouth with her hand to contain her giggles. 'Molly said Granny Aggie had taken delivery of a new mobility scooter. Seems she was right to be concerned about it.'

'I had no idea they could go so fast,' said Freda. 'Might have to think about getting one for myself.'

'I'd think very carefully about that if I were you, Freda,' said Len. 'Knowing Granny Aggie, she'd challenge you to a race and heaven knows how that would end.'

'Oof. That doesn't bear thinking about,' said Rhoda.

Romy glanced at the old lady standing beside her, trying to picture the scene Len had just described.

'Aggie wants to be careful, the road's been ploughed but it's been a couple of days since the gritter's been through the village,' said Len. 'It's chance to be like a skating rink.'

They watched, eyes dancing with amusement, as Granny Aggie bore down on Jimby who was now panting heavily.

'Get out of my way, lad!' Granny Aggie shouted as he lost his footing on the icy road, his arms flailing as he struggled to keep himself upright.

Before Jimby could right himself, the elderly lady collided with him, knocking him off his feet and scooping him up, the pair of them yelling at the top of their voices. The mobility scooter spun around several times until it came to an abrupt halt at the side of the road where Jimby tumbled to the ground and landed in a pile of snow.

Howling with laughter, Romy and the others looked on as Jimby got to his feet coughing and spluttering as Granny Aggie delivered a brutal earbashing for hindering her pursuit of the cockerel, while Reg's squawks grew increasingly faint as he hot-footed it further out of the village.

'I wish I was joking when I say that's not your everyday occurrence in this village, but sadly, it is,' Len said, his shoulders shaking with mirth. 'And much as I can't stand the flaming bird, I have to admit, his antics have been quite entertaining over the years.'

After the drama had died down, Romy bid Rhoda, Len and Freda farewell and headed to the pub in the hope of seeing Portia there. She was about to cross the road when she had to stop for a highly-polished four-wheel drive as it cruised steadily along. Behind the wheel was a well-groomed woman pinning Romy with what could only be described as a death stare. Feeling taken aback, Romy stood rooted to the spot. She hoped it wasn't someone who'd moved to the village and had taken an instant dislike to her based simply on appearance. Another, less palatable thought pinged into her mind. What if it was someone who knew about what had happened with her dad but wasn't aware of the full story? *Don't be ridiculous!* Telling herself that wasn't a path worth exploring, that the problem was with the snooty-looking woman in the car who she didn't know from Adam, and not her, Romy crossed the road.

Arriving at the Sunne, she was disappointed to find Portia had gone out for the day. 'She's due back early evening, if you'd like me to pass a message on to her, m'dear,' Jonty said. But Romy declined, preferring to speak to Portia in private. Though she was disappointed to have missed her, she told herself that nothing was likely to happen over the Christmas break anyway.

She toyed with the idea of going for a walk but a quick scan of the sky made her think better of it. A thick wodge of ominous-looking clouds had grouped together, glowering with the impending threat of snow. Thoughts of Finn and his sons sprang into her mind again. She hoped Britt hadn't put the dampeners on the boys' visit and decided she wasn't going to risk the roads. She knew how disappointed Finn would be, not to mention worried about Kyle after yesterday's phone call.

Back at the cottage, she climbed into her new onesie and snuggled up on the sofa, mug of hot chocolate with all the trimmings in hand, intent on watching a movie which was something she hadn't done for ages. Romy hadn't got far into the film when she found her mind kept wandering between Finn and the kisses they'd shared the previous evening and what her mother would have to say about her buying Holly Tree Cottage, which was something Romy had deliberately avoided giving much thought to. She'd never been able to understand why her mother had sold the cottage in the first place. It certainly hadn't been for financial reasons since their father had inherited a large sum from the death of his own parents and had invested the money wisely. Vernon Stainthorpe been keen to ensure his family were well taken care of in that respect. He'd set up savings policies for all three of his children, which came to fruition when they reached the age of twenty-five, and a further one that matured when they were thirty. On top of the various savings accounts he'd held, he'd had the foresight to arrange several life insurance policies ensuring that the mortgage on their generously-proportioned home in Rickelthorpe would be paid off on his death, and his wife would have a large pot of money that meant she'd be able to live comfortably for the rest of her life.

Her mum had spent Christmas Day with Tristan and his

family as she always did, and during their phone call from Oxford the previous day, Romy hadn't actually mentioned what she was doing for the festive period. And neither her mother nor her brother had asked, they'd been too full of their own hectic schedule of festive-themed events. It had been the same with Tally, though in fairness, they'd just communicated via texts, the details from both sides equally brief. Still, none of them had asked if she was going to be on her own at such a special time of year, not that it bothered her. She knew her mother was struggling to forgive her for the divorce, and it hurt that Dulcie still felt compelled to remind Romy using subtle digs that she must have done something to make Russ have an affair. Romy assumed it was more a case of her mother justifying her own extra-marital dalliance with that creep Clayborne, not that Romy ever said anything; she didn't want the hassle. Things had never been easy between mother and daughter since Vernon's death which was something Romy doubted would ever change, and she'd accepted that. Notwithstanding her family's apparent lack of interest in her, it struck her that, until the distressing phone call from Kyle, she couldn't remember spending a happier Christmas Day since her dad had been alive. Her own flesh and blood may struggle to show affection but it had been more than made up for by Finn and his parents. She hadn't realised how much she'd missed being part of a loving, caring family until she'd been wrapped up in the Tindall family's warmth. It had further galvanised her decision to go for the cottage.

Romy became aware she'd completely lost the thread of the film, and a restless feeling had crept over her. She headed through to the conservatory; her fingers were twitching, she needed something to occupy them.

She set up her laptop and clicked on the photo album, scrolling through until she found what she was looking for. She smiled as her gaze alighted on the photo of her father standing at the door of Holly Tree Cottage, he was wearing his Panama hat as the sun shone down on the garden that was in full bloom.

Romy had found the photo at the back of a drawer at her mother's house before she'd sold up and moved to Oxford. She'd slipped it into her pocket, fearful if she told her mother of its existence it might suffer the same fate as all the others. Her father looked so happy, it triggered an ache in her heart. Telling herself today wasn't the day for feeling sad, she inhaled deeply and fixed a smile to her face. Today was a day for making plans and indulging in her creative side. That, she told herself, was what her dad would say.

It had given her great pleasure adding Castlegate Farm to the needle-felt picture she'd given Jill and Tommy, and now Romy was going to do the same for Holly Tree Cottage. And she'd give it extra meaning by including her dad in it. She couldn't wait to get started.

It was dark outside by the time Romy decided it was time to take a break, her mind jumping once more to Finn and his sons. She hoped everything was going smoothly for them all, Jill and Tommy too.

Securing her needle in her work, she checked the time, her mind segueing to the conversation she'd had with Kitty earlier.

Romy had been on her way back from the Sunne when she'd passed Kitty who was heading out of the gate of Oak Tree Farm. They'd had a brief chat and Kitty asked her if she'd like to join them for a bite to eat later that evening.

'It's nothing fancy, just a gammon joint, some bubble and squeak and a few veggies, but you're very welcome to join us. We'll be serving up about six o'clock, if you fancy. No pressure if not.'

Much as she appreciated Kitty's generosity, now Romy thought about it, she quite fancied a quiet night in and trying out another one of the frozen meals she'd picked up at the village shop. Though she was a sociable character, Romy still enjoyed spending time on her own every now and then, especially when her head was swirling with thoughts, as it was right now. She'd had a busy time socialising since she arrived in the village and she hadn't had much time to herself. A night in would do her good, give her a chance to get her thoughts in order and catch her breath.

Her mind made up, she fired off a quick text to Kitty thanking her for her offer but explaining she was going to have a night at the cottage.

Kitty's reply came through ten minutes later, saying she understood and that Romy was welcome to call in any time.

While she had her phone in her hands, Romy decided it wouldn't hurt to send Finn a text too.

Hi Finn, hope you're having an awesome time with Kyle & Toby. Haven't been able to stop thinking about your kisses xxx

She was about to press send but thought better of it, hastily deleting the comment about his kisses in case one of his sons spotted it. She didn't want to be responsible for creating any confusion for them or trouble for him.

Half an hour later, her mobile pinged with a reply.

Hello Romy, having the best time. Britt's here too. She's staying over. Happy families!!

Romy's heart froze. Surely she'd hadn't read that right. Her eyes scanned the text again. There was no kiss and he'd added a heart emoji at the end of the sentence that said Britt was there too. What was he playing at? Myriad emotions bombarded her body. Were he and Britt going to give it another go for the sake of their sons? Finn had been devastated to see Kyle so upset yesterday. He was a decent man, and she knew he'd put his sons' happiness before his own. But getting back with Britt? From what he'd told her, he'd thought it was better for the lads if they weren't together.

She was still trying to make sense of it all when another text landed from Finn. Nausea churned in her stomach, she could hardly believe what she was seeing. Looking back at her was a photograph of Finn and two boys who she guessed were Kyle and Toby. Her eyes went to the woman with them – Romy couldn't help but think she looked vaguely familiar – her head resting on Finn's shoulder. The four of them were wearing Christmas hats and were cuddled up together, big smiles beaming out at her.

Fighting back tears, she pushed her mobile onto the table, her bottom lip quivering. She hadn't seen that one coming. More fool her.

What had she been thinking? She hadn't even been back in the village a week and already she was talking about upping sticks and moving her life there, expecting to pick up with Finn where she'd left off more than two decades ago. Who had she been trying to kid? Did she think her life was like one of those overly sentimental movies where every little problem was fixed at a single click of the fingers, and everyone went on to live happily ever after? She'd made a complete fool of herself. In fact, she couldn't see the point of staying there a moment longer. She might as well pack her bags and head back to Rickelthorpe before she had to face Finn again. There was no way she was going to interfere with him getting his family back together. He deserved to be with his sons; she knew they meant everything to him. And Finn deserved to be happy more than anyone else she knew. Though she couldn't help but think that he could have found a better way of letting her know. But then, maybe he hadn't had the heart to tell her face to face.

A sob escaped her lips. It felt as if her heart had been ripped in two. If ever there was a lesson to teach her that being impulsive and allowing her feelings to run away with themselves was a bad idea, this was it. And she needed to learn from it.

THIRTY-TWO
EARLIER THAT DAY

Finn

Finn heard the car pull into the yard, its tyres swishing through the slush. Ted sat up in his bed, his ears cocked.

'The lads are here, fella.' Joy at seeing his sons propelled Finn to the door. He flung it open wide, the Labrador racing out, prancing about excitedly as Kyle and Toby climbed out of the back seats of the car.

To cries of, 'Dad! Dad!' the two boys raced over to him, throwing their arms around him. Finn held them close, pressing kisses into their hair as Ted nudged them and gave whimpers of delight.

'Oh, lads, it's so good to see you both.' Finn's voice quavered.

The sound of Britt clearing her throat made him look up to see her standing by the large four-wheel drive looking more glamorous than he'd ever seen her. She was wearing a fitted black coat with faux fur collar, claret-coloured leather gloves and black leather high heeled boots that weren't at all practical for walking around a snowy farmyard covered with uneven flagstones. She appeared to be wearing more make-up than he remembered too, her glossy, red lips standing out against her pale skin.

'Hello, Finn. Merry Christmas.' She smiled and made her way over to him, wrapping her arms around his neck and delivering a gloopy kiss to his cheek.

'Hello, Britt.' The warmth of her greeting took him by surprise. She was usually reluctant to get out of the car whenever she dropped the lads off, and she was never keen to hang around. 'How were the roads?'

'I've known them worse, but it was snowing quite heavily coming over the rigg road where it's higher up. Camm's done a good job round here, though it would've been better if the gritter had followed the plough, there are a few lethal icy patches.'

'Aye, it's par for the course round here,' he said. 'I would've happily picked the lads up in the Landie, save you having to tackle the dicey roads.'

'It's fine,' she said, offering another smile.

'Shall I grab their bags?'

'I'll give you a hand, we can bring them in together.'

'Oh, okay.' Finn rubbed his hand over his chin, unable to shake the feeling he was missing something. He'd grown used to dealing with frosty Britt but this friendly, amenable version she'd shown over the last couple of days had totally thrown him. Much as it was easier – not to mention better for their sons – Finn was wary of letting his guard down in case things did a U-turn.

Britt stayed for a cup of tea, watching as Kyle and Toby opened their presents. Finn was relieved to see his parents treating her politely, though he'd expected nothing less despite the hostility she'd displayed to them over the last few years. He knew they'd be thinking of their grandsons, eager for them to enjoy every minute of being back at the farm and not having the edge taken off their time there by even the slightest hint of a bad atmosphere. The only thing his mum had done was to vigorously wipe Britt's sticky lipstick kiss off his cheek, the look in her eyes betraying her true feelings. Finn had struggled not to laugh at that.

He'd watched his sons closely, particularly Kyle who he was relieved to see seemed happier since their phone call the previous evening. Though, Finn noted, there was still a flatness to his son's overall mood. He wondered if Britt had picked up on it. He made the decision not to ask how the lads had settled in the States, not wanting to trigger the reappearance of her prickly side or hear her wax lyrical about how utterly wonderful their life was over there compared to the miserable UK and the backwater that was Lytell Stangdale.

'I'll be back to pick you both up on Friday morning, okay, kids?' Britt said after kissing the boys goodbye. 'And don't forget, you can always call me if you need to talk to me, or you're missing me.'

From the corner of his eye, Finn saw his mum give his dad a loaded look.

Finn stood at the door to the yard with Kyle and Toby, waving Britt off, the boys shooting back inside as soon as her car had turned onto the track.

Back in the kitchen, he wondered if it was just him who noticed the atmosphere was suddenly lighter.

Finn followed his sons and Ted into the living room where a fire roared in the broad inglenook and the television burbled away in the background. He watched with amusement as Kyle and Toby tried to train the Labrador to sit motionless with a dog treat on his nose, waiting for them to give the order for him to eat it. Ted's expression was hilarious, especially when his eyes had crossed while the lads had attempted to balance the treat. Finn had never seen Ted drool so much, or get through so many dog biscuits. Needless to say, all three appeared to be thoroughly enjoying themselves, despite the lack of success on the boys' part.

Their game was interrupted by a knock at the door. Ted reluctantly tore out of the room, giving a cursory bark as he went.

'I'll get it,' called Jill.

Hearing another female voice, Finn wandered through to see Britt standing there, looking distraught, a large overnight bag in her hand, a dusting of fresh snow on her head and shoulders.

'The road to Middleton's blocked. I'm going to have to stay over.'

Finn pushed his fingers into his hair, unable to contain his surprise at seeing his ex-wife back at the farm, not to mention his discomfort. 'What's happened?'

Britt went on to explain that, though it had started to snow as she was driving through Lytell Stangdale, it hadn't been too heavy which meant it had come as a surprise to find the police had closed off the main road that led to Middleton-le-Moors. It was something that happened when conditions got too bad.

'I didn't even consider doubling back and going the long way round as I expect that'll be worse for snow.'

She'd just finished her explanation when Kyle and Toby appeared.

'How come you're back, Mum?' Toby asked, the hint of disappointment making his mum flinch.

Kyle's face dropped. 'You haven't come to take us back have you, Mum?'

'No, lovey. I had to come back 'cos the main road's closed.' She smoothed her hand over his hair, dropping a kiss on top of his head.

'So, does that mean you're staying?' asked Toby, his eyes wide.

'If that's okay with your Dad.'

Finn didn't have to look at his parents to know what they were thinking: Firstly, it really wasn't okay, and secondly, how convenient it was that she'd come prepared with an overnight bag.

'What about Felix?' Kyle asked, a wary look in his eye. 'Won't he be cross if you don't get back?'

'No, he'll be fine.'

'He's not coming here, too, is he?' Kyle's anxious expression clawed at Finn's insides.

'No, he's not.' Finn's jaw tightened.

Britt flicked him a look. 'No, I've told him it's too dangerous, he understands.'

'Good.' Kyle's relief was palpable, the tension draining away from him in an instant. It made Finn more determined to find out what was at the root of the change in his son.

'Where's she expecting to sleep?' Jill asked when Britt and the lads were out of earshot. 'The bed in the spare room hasn't been aired.'

'She'll just have to manage, or I can dig out a sleeping bag, she can bed down on the floor in one of the lads' bedrooms,' said Tommy, a mischievous glint in his eyes. Britt wasn't known for her love of roughing it.

'She can have my bed—'

'What?' His mother cut him off mid-flow. 'I don't think that's a good idea, son, and besides, it'll give the lads the wrong impression. Wouldn't be fair on them. Mind, something tells me her ladyship wouldn't need asking twice, turning up all smarmy smiles and flicking her hair at you. She's up to something, Finn, mark my words. Promise me you'll be careful.' Jill pursed her lips disapprovingly.

'Calm your jets, Mother. I meant Britt could take my bed while I kip on the floor in one of the lads' bedrooms. I'll take Kyle's with it being a bit bigger than Toby's.' That wasn't his only reason, sharing a room with Kyle meant he could seize the opportunity for a heart-to-heart with his sensitive son.

THIRTY-THREE

Finn

With the evening meal out of the way, Kyle and Toby joined their grandparents in the cosiness of the living room to watch a film together. Ted joined them, stretching out in front of the fire, snoring contentedly.

Finn had found himself feeling disappointed that the first day of the lads' stay hadn't gone quite as he'd hoped. He'd had plans to take them sledging so they could join the local kids just as they used to do when they lived at the farm, but Britt's unexpected involvement in their day mean that hadn't happened. She didn't like sledging and there was no way he could have left her with his parents. That thought sent a shiver through him. And now his heart felt heavy at the prospect of her staying overnight with them. He only hoped the snow would ease up sufficiently and the road to Middleton-le-Moors would be passable tomorrow.

His thoughts went to Romy, wondering what sort of day she'd had. The memory of the last time he'd seen her, and the intensity of their kisses filled him with a warm glow.

Britt had nipped upstairs with the large overnight bag she

claimed to have brought "just in case", saying she was going to get changed into something more comfortable. Finn decided to seize the moment and send Romy a quick text. He went to the dresser to find his phone wasn't in its usual spot. He patted the back pocket of his jeans; it wasn't there either. After a quick sweep of the kitchen, he padded to the living room to find it filled with a soporific warmth and his dad snoring gently in his armchair.

'Anyone seen my phone,' he asked softly so as not to disturb his father.

Jill turned, peering over the back of the sofa. 'The last time I saw it was when I was using it to take photos of the lads with you and Britt earlier on. I'm sure I left it on the dresser.'

'I've checked there but there's no sign of it.'

'That's odd, I could've sworn that's where I put it.'

Seeing his mum go to get up, Finn said, 'You stay put, Mum, it'll turn up.'

He headed back into the kitchen to find Britt standing there. She'd changed into an outfit that somehow managed to look expensive but casual at the same time. Her long, blonde hair was now tied back into a high ponytail.

'It's loungewear,' she said, evidently noting his bemused expression.

'Oh, right.'

'Cuppa?' she said.

'Yeah, I'll make it.' He headed over to the kettle. 'I think we need to chat.'

'Okay.' She pulled out a chair at the table and sat down, fiddling with the end of her ponytail while he busied himself making tea.

'There you go.' Finn placed a steaming mug in front of her, before settling himself into the seat opposite. He was putting his thoughts together, working out the best way to broach the subject of Kyle being upset, when Britt spoke.

'You know, I wouldn't mind if you wanted to sleep in our bed tonight – with me, I mean.' She gave a suggestive flick of her eyebrows.

Finn took a moment, not sure he'd heard right. Was she actually flirting with him? 'What?'

Britt laughed. 'Oh, don't be such a prude, Finn! It's not as if we haven't shared a bed before; we've got two lads in there to prove it. And I didn't mean for *that*, though no one could blame us if we were tempted.'

Was she for real? 'For starters, it's not *our* bed anymore and hasn't been for a long time. And I won't be sharing with you, nor will I be *tempted* as you put it.'

Britt's smile fell. 'There's no need to be so cold about it, Finn. I was just joking.'

'Yeah, well, I'm not.'

'Has this got something to do with that Romy girl?' She watched his face intently. 'I spotted her when I was driving through Lytell Stangdale, actually.'

Finn paused a moment, wondering why Britt had been driving through the village when it wasn't en route to the farm. 'It's got nothing to do with Romy and everything to do with the fact that we're divorced, Britt. In case you forgot, you left me for another bloke which, call me old fashioned, doesn't make me feel like jumping back into bed with you as soon as you click your fingers.'

Britt's nostrils flared. 'I'm hardly clicking my fingers.'

'And though I'm not going to pretend it's not inconvenient you staying overnight, I'm glad it's given me the opportunity to find out what's been going on to make Kyle so subdued. He—' Just in time, he managed to stop himself from letting slip about the phone call from their son.

'He what?' she said snappily.

'He doesn't seem very happy, surely you must've noticed.'

He watched Britt's expression change. She hung her head, gnawing on her bottom lip. 'Kyle hasn't settled at school in the States and Felix has been a bit hard on him about it, telling him he's not trying.'

'I can't believe it's just that, though it's bad enough. The lads have been through a lot, they need some understanding and patience.'

'I totally agree.' Britt paused, chewing on her lip some more. Finn was surprised to see tears start running down her cheeks. 'It's not just that, Felix and me aren't getting on so well anymore, the lads have probably picked up on it.'

Kyle's phone call sprang to mind. 'That's a shame, for Kyle and Tobes, I mean.' It rankled that their sons were being exposed to yet more unsettling behaviour. His eyes dropped to her ring finger to see a white line where her engagement ring had been.

Britt's eyes followed his gaze. 'I took it off when I was having my nails done and forgot to put it back on again.'

'Fair enough.' Finn got the feeling she wasn't telling him the truth.

He sat listening while Britt's tea grew cold as she told him how things had changed as soon as they'd got to America, with Felix being out all hours, working and schmoozing with clients. And how he'd been spending a great chunk of his time with a fellow realtor called Paige who was uber glamorous in her designer clothes, minuscule skirts and skyscraper heels. Since they'd returned for their Christmas break, she'd caught Felix on video calls with her numerous times.

'So what are you going to do?'

'I don't know. I mean, he tells me he still loves me and still wants us to get married, so...' She gave a shrug. 'There's a lot to think about. I've got nowhere to stay here if I don't go back. It's too cramped at my parents...' She paused, peering at Finn through damp, sooty lashes. 'I don't suppose—'

'Don't go there, Britt,' Finn said firmly. He knew where she was leading, but much as he'd love nothing better than have the lads live under the same roof as him, there was no way he could ever trust Britt again. And besides, Romy was back in his life and had already taken a huge chunk of his heart, if not all of it. And though he had no idea if a relationship was going to develop between him and Romy, he was prepared to take the risk and give it a chance. And to do so, he needed to make it clear to his ex that she was going to remain exactly that. 'I've moved on, there's no future for us, Britt. You made that decision when you left.'

It clearly wasn't the response Britt had expected. Her expression became thunderous and she did nothing to hide her anger. In moments their exchange had become heated, the bitterness of old resurfacing as they slung hostile words at one another. They may have kept their voices down but their recriminations hadn't lost any heat for it.

Finn pushed his chair back, the feet scraping noisily over the flagstones. 'I'm going to check around the farm.'

'Take your time!'

He stormed over to the porch door and disappeared into the snow-covered farmyard. He was boiling with rage, but at least it meant he didn't feel the bone-numbing wind that whipped around him, hurling icy snowflakes at his face. He was just glad to have removed himself from the conversation with Britt. Anything was better than continuing with that.

But what he didn't know was that while he and Britt had been flinging angry words at one another, Kyle had been lurking in the shadows and had heard every word.

The following morning, Finn woke with a crick in his neck. He stretched, then raised his head, moving it from side to side, hoping to ease the tension in his muscles, last night's conversation with Britt pouring into his mind. He lay back down with a groan and covered his eyes. The prospect of spending another day with her filled him with dread. And if the snow had continued through the night, that's exactly what he'd be doing. But at least the lads were there, which was something.

He pushed himself up on his elbows, peering through the dark in the direction of Kyle's bed to see his son snuggled up in a lump under the duvet. Finn had been disappointed to find Kyle fast asleep by the time he'd got to bed the previous night, but he was hopeful they'd get a chance to chat during the course of the day. He'd make sure they did.

He eased himself out of the sleeping bag and slipped out of the room, ready to start the day, leaving Kyle to catch up on his sleep.

'Finn!'

His mother's voice from across the farmyard where Finn was clearing the snow made him turn. 'What's up.'

'Is Kyle with you?' she shouted over the wind that was hurling itself around the farm.

'No, he was still asleep when I got up. Why?' He was hoping his son might've shown his face to let him know he was up and about, then they could head out with Toby and go sledging. Britt, he decided, would have to entertain herself. He'd already spoken to his parents who'd told him not to change his plans with the boys just because their mother had turned up, saying it wasn't fair on the lads.

'He hasn't had his breakfast and we can't find him. Thought he might have come straight out to help you.'

Instinct kicked in. Something was wrong. Finn rested the shovel against the barn wall and strode over to his mother. 'Have you checked his room?'

'Aye, but he'd put his pillow under his duvet. We assumed he was having a joke, hiding, like, but we've been calling for him and hunting everywhere for ages and there's not a trace of him.'

'Right.' This wasn't like Kyle.

In the kitchen, Britt's pale face told him she shared his concern. 'I can't understand how you didn't notice he wasn't there in bed,' she said in an accusatory tone.

'It was dark when I got up and I didn't put the light on 'cos I didn't want to disturb him. I thought he might still have the tail end of jet lag. Anyroad, how come it's taken you this long to check on him?'

Britt glared at him.

'The lad's bound to be somewhere. Finn and me'll go and check round the outbuildings, he might have gone to see the goats or the hens or summat. Come on, son.' Tommy patted Finn on the shoulder.

'Are you sure he didn't say anything to you, Tobes?' Finn asked.

'No, nothing, honest.' Toby shook his head, his eyes wide with worry. 'Will he be okay?'

'He'll be fine, lovey, we'll find him, don't you fret.' Jill wrapped her arm around her grandson, kissing the top of his head.

'Aye, Nanny's right, we'll find him. Mind, you make sure you stay here, okay, buddy?' Finn ruffled Toby's hair; it felt wrong that he should be so worried after the unsettling couple of years he and his big brother had gone through.

'Yes, Dad. I'll help and have another look around the house. I know all Kyle's favourite hiding places.'

'Good lad,' said Finn. 'You can show Nanny.'

Despite searching the farmhouse from top to bottom and looking in every outbuilding, there was still no sign of Kyle. Britt was becoming hysterical. 'We've got to find him. What if he's wandered off in the snow and fallen into a snowdrift or something? What if he's lying hurt somewhere? You've got to find him! What if he gets hypothermia?'

'Calm yourself down, lass. Let's not head down that route just yet,' said Tommy. 'He can't have got far in this weather, and he's got enough about him not to stray off track. Finn and me'll take the Landie out and check the roads round and about here.'

'I'll ring around, see if anyone's seen him, first, Dad.' Finn went to the dresser for his phone, suddenly remembering he hadn't been able to find it last night. 'Blast! My phone. I don't know where it is.'

'Have you still not found it?' asked Jill.

'No. I hope it hasn't dropped out of my pocket in the snow or summat daft like that.'

'Oh, actually, I remember seeing it in the bedroom last night. You must've left it there. I'll just go and fetch it,' said Britt.

Finn watched Britt disappear out of the room and head upstairs. He was certain he hadn't left it there, but now wasn't the time to give it any further thought.

Britt was back in a flash. 'There you go.' She handed him his phone, apparently reluctant to make eye contact.

'Thanks.' Finn noted the battery was only on four per cent. He quickly plugged it in so it was charging straight away. A niggle at the back of his mind told him he'd only charged it before the lads arrived yesterday, and it hadn't been used that much since.

Not wasting a moment, he worked through his contacts list, calling anyone local on the off chance they might have seen Kyle. He held back from contacting Romy. With Britt being within earshot, he was reluctant to add anything else to her rising stress levels and besides, Romy didn't even know what Kyle looked like so it was pointless asking her if she'd seen him.

'Talking of mobiles, doesn't Kyle have some sort of tracking app on his?' asked Finn, feeling suddenly hopeful. 'Surely we'll be able to find out where he is from that.'

'I'd already thought of that,' Britt said, flatly. 'But he didn't take his phone; it's still in his room.'

Ted looked on from his bed, uncharacteristically quiet and subdued, sensing things weren't right.

Finn's shoulders slumped, his hopes dashed. 'Right, I'd better get calling more numbers.' He dialled Jimby's next, relieved when he picked up quickly.

'Sorry, mate, I'm afraid I haven't seen him at all,' said Jimby, when Finn had explained the situation. 'But I'll get a few folks together so we can start looking for him before darkness sets in. Oh, and just very quickly, have you heard the news?'

'No, what news?'

'The police have arrested four blokes from Leeds way for the break ins round here. They stopped them on the Middleton road yesterday. Apparently they were in a Landie they'd stolen from Titch Ventress and crashed when they realised the bobbies were after them. I heard the road was closed for quite a while. Apparently several vehicles that had been stolen from round here were found at the home of one of the thieves. So at least you don't have to worry about Kyle being out while they're lurking around.'

'Aye, that is good news. And thanks for offering to help look for him.'

'Not at all, I'm sure he'll turn up, try not to worry.'

Finn quickly relayed what Jimby had told him about the Middleton road, thinking it was no doubt why it had been closed when Britt had been heading back. He then hurried over to the utility room where he grabbed a couple of torches which seemed to send Britt into a panic.

'Oh my God, it'll be dark soon. This is a nightmare. We should call the police, report Kyle as a missing person. What if we don't find him? What if they say it's too late for them to start looking for him? We need to let them know!'

Toby started to cry. 'Mum, you're scaring me.'

'Hey, lovey, it's okay. We'll find him, and if I know your brother, he'll be back here as soon as he starts feeling hungry.' Jill rushed over to him, pulling him close, rubbing soothing swirls over his back.

'I don't think the police would do anything just yet, love. They would probably say he hasn't been missing long enough. But try not to worry, we've got plenty of folk looking for him and between us we'll find him,' Tommy said kindly.

'Try not to worry?' Britt rolled her eyes and threw her hands up in the air, walking off in the direction of the stairs. 'What a stupid thing to say!'

'Right, Dad, let's get going.' Finn turned to his mother. 'We'll let you know as soon as we hear anything or find him. In the meantime, if you could ring round your friends or folk I've missed, in case they've spotted him.'

'Aye, 'course, son. Go carefully, both of you.'

Finn had tried to stay calm for Toby's sake and he knew his dad had done the same. It hadn't been easy with so much adrenalin surging through his veins, making his heart pound hard in his chest.

Though they'd both kept it to themselves, he and his dad were all too aware how a person didn't have long if they were stranded out on the moors in weather conditions like these.

With fear and determination pushing him on, he fired up the Land Rover and drove out of the yard.

He had to find his son.

THIRTY-FOUR

Romy

It had taken longer than expected to get her things packed away since she'd had so much of her sewing stuff out on the table in the conservatory. Romy took her time to gather it up and put it back in the right boxes, making sure everything would be easy to get her hands on later. She'd planned on texting Kitty once she'd driven a decent distance away from Lytell Stangdale, telling her she'd had to rush home unexpectedly, and that Kitty was welcome to the frozen ready meals along with the other unused items in the fridge. Romy didn't want to take any reminders of her time at the cottage and the meals would only make her think of the evening she'd shared with Finn. She wanted a clean break; to draw a line very firmly under her brief return to the village.

Her heart was aching and her eyes were still puffy from the tears she'd wept as she'd folded her clothes and put them in her case. She still couldn't believe how stupid she'd been, thinking she could start afresh here, with Finn. Impulsive, her mum would've said. Romy would have to agree with that. Though, she told herself, she hadn't been so impulsive in her decision to leave Lytell Stangdale. Instead of packing everything up last night, in readiness to leave first thing, she'd decided to sleep on it, rather than act in haste. But, frustratingly, she'd found sleep had been elusive and she'd still been lying awake until well into the early hours, thoughts running through her mind on an endless loop. She'd finally drifted off at around four a.m. and had slept through to ten-thirty when she'd been woken by the sound of Camm going by with the plough. It was way later than she'd hoped to be up, the shock propelling her out of bed so she could give her decision some final thought.

She hadn't ventured into the village at all that day, not wanting to risk bumping into Finn and his sons. She wouldn't have been able to bear it if Britt had been with them. That thought had kept her within the bounds of Holly Tree Cottage. The only fresh air she'd had was standing at the kitchen door, nursing a mug of tea in her hands as she'd watched a robin hop about in search of food, the red of its chest a vivid contrast to the snow. Breathing in the crisp air, her gaze had been drawn across the dale to Castlegate Farm, the sight of it causing her heart to constrict, sending her back indoors.

She peered out of the living room window, disappointed to find dusk already creeping across the sky. She had a long drive ahead of her and had hoped to tackle it in daylight hours, especially since it had been snowing on and off all day. It was half past three; if she set off now it would be dark before she'd even left the moors behind. She could kick herself for taking so long to get ready to leave, and it wasn't as if she could head off right now, she still had a final tidy round to do before she loaded her bags and work stuff into her car. The latter task she'd planned to do as quickly as possible, not wanting to risk being seen so very obviously packing up to leave and triggering any unwelcome interest. Her bags and boxes were already lined up in the hallway, except for her suitcase which was still in her bedroom. Part of her wondered if she'd been deliberately dragging her heels, reluctant to leave Lytell Stangdale for one last time.

It wasn't difficult to work out the answer to that one.

Arriving at the decision to set an alarm and leave as early as the roads and weather would allow the following morning, Romy reconciled herself to spending one more night at the cottage. She went round, flicking the table lamps on in the living room and drawing all the curtains around the house. She'd treat herself to a soak in the bath and a read of the new book she'd brought with her, hoping to lose herself in the pages.

After a light evening meal of scrambled eggs on toast, washed down with a large mug of tea, Romy cleared away and settled herself on the sofa in the living room. Thanks to the large traditional-style radiators, the room was warm and toasty, though she hadn't lit the stove, not wanting the extra job of having to clean it out in the morning. She picked up the book and tried to read, but it was no good, she'd read the same few pages over and over again but the words just weren't sinking in. It was all Finn Tindall's fault! No matter what she was doing, he occupied her every thought. *Arghh!*

She reached for the remote control, hoping to find something on the television to entertain her for the next couple of hours. She was about to press the "on" button when she was startled by the slam of a door outside. Her heart jumped and she froze, listening for any further sounds. When none came she crept to the kitchen, her pulse still racing, making sure the bolt was in at the door. Then, turning the kitchen lights off, she pressed down on the switch for the outside light that shone out over the back garden. Holding her breath, she peered through a crack in the curtains, a gasp escaping her mouth.

Though it was snowing, and visibility was reduced, it was still easy to see the snow on the ground had been disturbed, particularly around the door of the shed. Panic ripped through her and her heart started hammering so loud she could almost hear it. She clasped her hand to her mouth, fear rendering her unable to think what she should do next.

She'd finally managed to steady herself sufficiently to grab her phone with a view to calling Kitty and Ollie next door, when another sound caught her attention. She strained her ears, her brows knitting together. She could swear it sounded like someone crying, and from what she could gather, whoever it was seemed very upset.

She paused a moment, marshalling her thoughts, listening harder, trying to make sense of it all.

The sobbing continued. Following her instincts, Romy threw caution to the wind. Somebody out there on this freezing cold night in the middle of winter was feeling sad and there was no way she could ignore them. Without any further thought, she slid the bolt along and opened the door a crack. She gasped and pressed her hand to her chest as her eyes alighted on a small figure huddled on the doorstep, apparently taking shelter beneath the overhanging thatch of the roof.

'Arghh!' She let out a squeal and leapt back as the person got to their feet, icy air rushing at her.

'S-s-sorry. I... didn't... mean... t-to... scare... you.' Snow whirled around the stranger.

Romy's eyes ran over what appeared to be a young boy who, from the way he was shivering, looked frozen to the core. Her heart went out to him in an instant.

'That's okay. Are you lost, or locked out of your house or something?'

'I'm... l–lost.' His teeth were chattering together loudly but from the few words he'd uttered, Romy noticed his accent sounded local with a soft twang of somewhere else.

'You're lost?' she said softly.

The boy nodded.

Romy didn't know what to think other than he needed to get into the warmth right away.

'Would you like to come in out of the cold?' she asked, standing back and holding the door open.

The boy nodded again, his eyes flicking to hers before he stepped inside. Under the light of the kitchen, he looked even colder than she'd expected. Aware that too many questions, or simply the wrong type, could alienate him, Romy was conscious she needed to pick her words carefully. From what she could gather, apart from looking worryingly cold, he looked clean and well-cared for.

'Are you okay in your coat or would you like me to hang it up to dry?' she asked gently.

After a minute's thought, and a brief struggle with the zip – no doubt owing to cold-numbed fingers – he wriggled out of it and handed it to Romy. She took it to hang on the coat pegs above the radiator in the utility room and lay his equally soggy gloves on the radiator itself to dry out. Back in the kitchen, she guided him to the Aga, pulling over a dining chair for him. He flopped down, huddling up against the stove, still shivering. She hoped she was doing the right thing; for all she knew, he could be suffering from hypothermia and should really be checked over by a doctor, but she didn't want to risk scaring him off and send him rushing back out into the icy weather. His jeans looked soaked through and her brain scrabbled about trying to think of something suitable for him to change into. Looking at his face, she guessed he was probably about ten or eleven years old; too young to be hiding in a stranger's garden in freezing conditions. She needed to find out where his family were while treading cautiously at the same time. They'd no doubt be worried sick about him. At least she hoped they were the decent, caring sort who should be concerned for their child's well-being. But he hadn't been hiding out on one of the coldest nights of the year for no reason.

'Can I get you a hot chocolate? I've got some really yummy luxury chocolate powder which is so delicious. I was just about to make myself one.' She hadn't packed the tub away since she'd planned on making herself a mug before she went to bed and now found herself glad of her decision.

The boy nodded enthusiastically, still shivering. 'Yes, please.' The look in his eyes made Romy's heart ache for him. He had such a sweet, open face and she could swear there was something familiar about him.

A thought pinged into her mind. 'Tell you what – and it's

entirely up to you, no pressure at all – but there's a spare pair of pyjamas here; they're blue and white checked brushed cotton and they look really snuggly. They might be a bit big, but you're very welcome to change into them, if you like?' She left out that they were her pyjamas, but they were from a supermarket that sold nightwear for the whole family – including the dog! – so they could easily pass for being from the menswear section.

The boy thought about it for a moment, then nodded. 'I'd like that. I'm still really cold.'

Relief washed over Romy. 'Cool. Give me two ticks and I'll go and dig them out; you can get changed in the spare bedroom.'

She set the jug of milk down, grabbed a binbag and shot off upstairs. Once in her bedroom, she rummaged around in her suitcase, pulling out the pyjamas. Undoing the buttons on the top, in case the boy's fingers were still too cold to manage it, she draped them over the radiator in the spare room, adding a pair of chunky navy-blue thermal socks. While she was there, she dug out the fleece blanket and hot water bottle she'd spotted it in the cupboard the other day, bringing them downstairs with her.

Back in the kitchen she was glad to see the boy still in the seat by the Aga. 'There, sorted. You'll find some clean PJs and chunky socks warming on the radiator in the bedroom that's first on the right at the top of the stairs. If you're up to it, you can pop your wet stuff in the binbag that's up there, too.'

'Thank you.' He gave her a small smile.

Romy watched him trudge out of the room, before slipping the fleece over the rail on the Aga. That done, she filled the kettle then picked up where she'd left off making the hot chocolates.

She was grating chocolate over the marshmallows when her unexpected guest appeared in the doorway. He'd taken a while, which she'd put down to chilly fingers hindering the un-doing and doing-up of buttons and zips. She looked up and smiled. He looked instantly warmer. 'Perfect timing.' She headed to the Aga and lifted the warmed fleece off the rail, quickly wrapping it around the boy's shoulders before pressing the hot water bottle to him. 'If you'd like to sit yourself back down, I'll bring your hot chocolate over.'

'Thank you.' He gave her another watery smile that triggered a flash of recognition, disappearing before she could grab hold of it. 'Smells of chocolate in here.'

'Mmm. It's my absolute favourite smell,' Romy said with a laugh, raising another smile from the boy as she handed him his mug of hot chocolate.

'Thanks. Looks awesome.'

She took a tentative sip from her mug, peering over to him, glad to see he'd stopped shivering. 'Can't have been much fun getting lost in the snow, especially with it being so dark.'

He hung his head and focused his gaze on his drink, taking his time to answer. 'I wasn't really lost.'

'Oh, right.' Romy kept her tone light. 'You were obviously looking for something, which can't have been easy in the snow. Did you find it?'

The boy shook his head.

'That's a shame, maybe I can have a search around for you in the morning when it's light.'

Silence hung in the air, but it was obvious her young guest was wrestling with something.

'I've run away.' He looked up at her, a tear plopping onto his cheek.

The look on his little face didn't just tug at Romy's heartstrings, it positively yanked at them with such force she feared they would snap. She felt a squeeze in her chest and took a moment, trying to find the right words to reply. 'Oh, gosh, it can't have been much fun running away in this weather.'

'Didn't know what else to do.'

Oh, you poor little love.

'I can understand that. And I know it probably doesn't feel like it right now, but I reckon your family will be missing you like mad, not to mention be worried sick. I know I would be if you were my son or brother – actually, I bet you'd be a super-cool brother to have. Mine is the *biggest* pain in the bum at times.' She laughed, rolling her eyes jokingly before taking a glug of her hot chocolate. She needed to find out who his parents were as soon as possible; she hoped they were locals.

'Mine can be sometimes, too, but mostly he's okay.'

'That's good.' Romy noted his tears had abated – for now – and he looked like he was warming through a bit more.

'My brother's older than me and he still thinks it's okay to boss me about. He's called Tristan, but we call him Tris. Well, don't tell anyone but I actually call him Tyrannosaurus Tris when he's being really bossy, not that he knows it,' Romy said conspiratorially. She was pleased to see it raised a small laugh.

'My brother's younger than me but he's the bossy one. He's called Toby, but we call him Tobes, mostly.'

Toby! Oh my days! In an instant it came to her why the boy seemed so familiar. Now she knew, she could see he was the double of his father at that age. He must be Kyle. Romy raised her mug to her face to hide her shock, taking a slow mouthful, the chocolate flavour flooding her mouth. Her eyes went to the worktop where her mobile phone was taunting her next to a tub containing a couple of slices of chocolate cake; Romy had planned on having a slice tonight and taking the other back to Rickelthorpe with her, deeming it too delicious to leave behind. Somehow, she needed to get to her phone and contact Finn without alerting Kyle to what she was doing. She couldn't risk him running off into the snow wearing only pyjamas and a pair of socks.

'Actually, do you like chocolate cake?'

Kyle nodded. 'Yeah, it's my favourite.'

'Mine too. How about a slice to go with your hot chocolate? Let's go for total chocolate overload.'

'Cool.'

Romy rushed over to the cake, surreptitiously sliding her phone into her pocket.

Kyle was tucking into his slice when Romy said, 'I just need to nip to the loo, I'll be two ticks.'

'Okay.' Kyle smiled at her, his cheeks stuffed with cake.

In the bathroom, Romy fished her phone out of her pocket and found Finn's number, hurriedly typing in her message, her pulse racing.

> Kyle's here at the cottage. He's fine. Get here quickly & please don't reply to this text x

She pressed send and waited to make sure the text had been delivered. The wobbly typing bubble appeared almost instantly showing Finn was reading it. She'd asked him not to text back in case it aroused his son's suspicions, but she hoped he wasn't far away.

She flushed the loo to add authenticity to her supposed visit to the bathroom, then headed back downstairs, wondering what could have happened to make Kyle run away, especially since the photo Finn had sent just the other day had shown them all smiling happily at the camera. Even in his message he'd written "happy family".

Back in the kitchen, Kyle had finished his cake, evidence of its consumption in a sticky smear around his mouth. He gave her a small smile 'That was delicious, especially the fudgy top.'

'You can have my piece as well, if you like?' Romy remembered hearing lots of sugar was good for people who'd been exposed to low temperatures.

His eyes lit up. 'Really? Don't you want it?'

'I'd rather you had it.' She beamed at him. He seemed an utterly adorable little boy and it was a shame he was feeling sad at Christmastime.

Kyle was halfway through his chocolate cake when there was an urgent knock at the door, making Romy jump. Kyle's hand holding the cake suspended halfway to his mouth.

'Ah, that'll just be a friend of mine.' She smiled as relief flooded through her.

THIRTY-FIVE

Finn

Finn could have wept with relief when he read Romy's text. It had arrived just as he and his dad were heading out of Lytell Stangdale after scouring the roads around the farm and beyond. He whipped the Land Rover round and drove as fast as conditions would allow, pulling up outside Holly Tree Cottage and racing up the path.

He practically fell inside when Romy opened the door, anguish etched over his face, but she stopped him in his tracks, pressing a finger to her lips and mimed for him and his dad to shush. She spoke quickly and softly.

'I found him sheltering on the kitchen step. Not sure how long he'd been there but he was absolutely nithered and soaked through. Thankfully, he seems okay. He's been eating cake and drinking hot chocolate.'

Finn and Tommy nodded, looking drained as they followed her into the kitchen. Finn wasn't sure how his legs hadn't buckled beneath him.

Seeing his son sitting there, Finn's heart surged with love and a generous dash of relief. 'Oh, Kyle, we've been worried sick.'

'Dad!' The young boy looked stunned, shooting a quick

puzzled look in Romy's direction. He put his plate down and rushed over to Finn, wrapping his arms around his dad's middle where he began sobbing uncontrollably.

'Shh. It's okay, buddy.' Finn got down on his haunches, pulling his son close, smoothing his hair, as he fought back tears of his own. 'Oh, jeez. I'm so glad to have found you. We've been looking everywhere. You didn't take your phone.'

'I'm sorry, Dad,' Kyle said between sobs. 'I didn't mean to worry you, honest. I just didn't know what else to do.'

'At least we know you're safe now, lad.' Tommy squeezed his grandson's shoulder and gave Romy a grateful look. 'I'd best call your mum, let her know we've found you and that she can stop worrying.'

'I don't want to go back, Grampy! Mum and Felix will make me go to America with them and I don't want to! I want to stay here with you and Dad and Nanny. I hate it there and so does Toby.' More tears started tumbling from Kyle's cheeks.

Finn caught Romy's eye and she gave him a small smile. It had registered briefly that he'd passed boxes and bags in the hallway but he'd been too preoccupied with Kyle to give it much thought.

'I promise once we get back to the farm we can talk about it,' Finn said, though he had no idea how they were going to resolve the situation.

'And I thought you said it was a friend who knocked at the door, you told me a lie. I thought you were nice.' Kyle looked accusingly at Romy. 'That's why I ran away in the first place, so I wouldn't have to go back to the house with Mum and Felix, and have to hear all their arguments. You've ruined it!' He started sobbing onto his dad's shoulder

'Hey, no more tears. Romy is my friend, son, she didn't lie. In fact we used to be best friends when I was your age.'

Kyle lifted his head, blinking. 'Really? This is Romy who you've told us about before?'

'Yes, this is her,' said Finn, catching Romy's eye.

'Yep, it's really me.' She smiled. 'And I could tell you some very funny stories about your dad.'

'Really? Like what?'

'Ah, well, I'm afraid that'll have to be for another day, Kyle, there are so many to tell, it would take a long time. I reckon there are people up at the farm who are very keen to see you so it's not fair we keep them waiting.'

With the phone call over with, Tommy came back into the room. 'Your mum's chuffed to bits you're okay, lad. As are Nanny and Toby, they sounded pretty desperate to see you.'

Finn got to his feet and took the binbag Romy was holding out to him.

'Kyle's wet things,' she said.

'Thanks, Romes, and for looking after him. I can't tell you how grateful we are.'

'Hey, it's really no problem. He's a great kid. I'm just glad I opened the door when I did.' She gave him a small smile. 'Hope it works out for you all.'

Confusion flittered across Finn's eyes. 'Oh, right, yeah.' His head was too jumbled to work out why that sounded weird but right now, his priority was to get his lad home and back to his mum. He could give Romy's words further consideration later.

There were some serious conversations to be had up at Castlegate Farm, and the sooner they got started, the better.

Jill and Tommy had made themselves scarce that evening, leaving Finn, Britt and their sons to have an honest heart-to-heart. The four of them had talked for hours. What had been glaringly obvious was that Kyle and Toby had missed Finn desperately, which had made it hard for them to settle in the States. Their luxurious lifestyle offered no compensation for not being with their dad as far as they were concerned and they wanted to come back to the UK. They'd both missed their life on the farm, too, not to mention their friends in the surrounding villages.

Finn had been surprised – and not to mention relieved – that Britt had sat quietly and listened, taking on board what their sons had said. He'd voiced his concerns as softly as he was able yet still managing to get his point across, while Britt admitted she'd been hasty in making some of her decisions. She'd also expressed her sadness at the harsh tone Felix had, at times, taken with Kyle and had been apologetic about the arguments she'd had with him in front of their sons, particularly the ones over the festive period.

Kyle running off the way he had and potentially putting himself at risk had shocked her into taking stock of their situation.

'I can see that moving to the States hasn't been right for you two boys, and I take full responsibility for that. But I have to say, my intentions were good and I thought it would be an adventure for you. I should've realised it could never be that without your dad.'

Finn had been stunned by his ex-wife's honesty.

Britt had gone on to say she'd made the decision that she and the boys wouldn't be returning to America. Kyle and Toby had cheered loudly at that, jumping up and down in their seats. And though Finn had been thrilled to hear it too, a feeling of discomfort squirmed in his stomach. Surely she wasn't going to announce to the boys that she was getting back together with him. That most definitely wasn't an option as far as he was concerned. This news she'd just shared was all well and good but it opened up a whole new list of things that needed to be discussed and given careful consideration.

'I haven't been happy there either, and seeing how it has affected both of you, I think it's only right we should come home permanently,' Britt had said. 'It didn't work, but at least we gave it a try.'

Finn wondered exactly what she'd meant by home and had planned on saving the question 'til the two of them were alone, but Kyle had beaten him to it.

'So what's happening about Felix? Does he know we're not going back to America?'

'I haven't spoken to him about it yet but I will tomorrow. If it's okay with your dad, I think you two should have another couple of days here, while I head back to the holiday cottage in Middleton so Felix and me can get things sorted out.'

'Cool.' Kyle smiled broadly.

'It's not that we don't like America,' said Toby, 'It's really great and the people are really friendly and the food is really awesome, but it isn't home and Dad isn't there. That's all.'

'Or Nanny and Grampy and Ted,' said Kyle, who looked as though he'd had an enormous weight lifted from his shoulders.

When the two boys had finally gone to bed, Britt brought up the possibility of the two of them getting back together. But, much as he was aware the thought of it would make their sons happy, Finn knew the reality would be very different. He and Britt wanted different things. Maybe in the short term she'd be happy living back at the farm, but it wouldn't be long before old arguments and bitterness reared their ugly heads again. And besides, his heart no longer belonged to her, he'd given it wholeheartedly to someone who'd always hung onto a little piece of it. And that someone had looked after his boy and kept him safe and warm until he'd been able to get to him.

Thought of Romy made him start as he recalled the bags and boxes lined up in the hallway at Holly Tree Cottage. His heart leapt. Surely she hadn't been planning on leaving without telling him?

THIRTY-SIX

Romy

A loud knock at the door made Romy jump just as she was about to take a bite out of her toast. She stole a look at the clock that told her it was ten past eight. Who the heck called at this time of a morning, when it was still dark?'

She headed down the hallway in her pyjamas and slippers. It took a few moments of unlocking the door with the keys and sliding the bolts back before she managed to get it open, shocked to see Finn standing there under the soft glow of the streetlight. He was the last person she wanted to see and he appeared to be peering over her shoulder. His timing could not have been worse.

'How's Kyle?' she asked.

'He's good, thanks, doing well. Thank you for all you did.'

'It was nothing; I'm pleased to hear he's okay.'

A pause stretched out, icy air curling around them.

'Romy, can I have a word?'

'I... erm... It's not really a good time, Finn, I—'

'Please, Romes, it's important.' He rested his hands on her shoulders, lowering his head to look into her eyes. The sorrowful expression she saw there sent guilt rushing through her.

'Okay, come in.' She found herself standing back and holding the door open, wondering why she was the one feeling guilty.

In the hallway, Finn glanced down at the bags and boxes before looking back at her askance. 'What's this? I feel like I've missed something. Tell me you're not leaving?'

She couldn't understand how he could stand there and ask that after the text messages he'd sent on Boxing Day.

'I think it's best if I go. I don't want my presence here to cause any trouble for you and Britt.'

'Me and *Britt?* How could you being in the village do that? There is no me and Britt.'

Talk about mixed messages. 'But those texts you sent, the photo of you all looking so happy together on Boxing Day. I thought it was your way of telling me you were getting back with her.'

'What?' Finn scratched his head, a confused expression clouding his features. 'I never sent any texts, or photos for that matter.'

'But they're on my phone.'

'Are you sure they were from my number?'

'I'm positive! I'll show you.'

He followed her down to the kitchen where she picked up her phone, swiped on the screen a couple of times then handed it to him. 'There, you can see with your own eyes.' She wondered how he was going to wriggle his way out of that.

'No way!' He clamped his hand to his forehead. 'This wasn't me. I have no idea... Ughh! Flaming Britt!'

'What?'

Romy listened as he explained how his phone had gone missing on Boxing Day and that it was Britt who'd found it in the bedroom the day after – he stressed how he had no idea of how it had got there since he'd been bunking down on Kyle's bedroom floor. He went on to say how he'd noticed the phone's battery had been run down despite it not being long since he'd charged it, which he assumed was because Britt had been going through his messages and photos as well as sending the texts to Romy. He'd also told her the reason his ex had stayed over was because the Middleton road was closed, which Romy had been unaware of.

Romy was stunned. She'd thought at the time the messages weren't Finn's style but it hadn't entered her head that Britt would do such a thing. 'Wow! She was clearly wanting me to back off.'

'And, judging by the stuff in the hallway, it clearly worked. I can't believe you were going to disappear again without saying goodbye, Romes.' The hurt in his voice made her insides twist.

'I was trying to make it easier for you.' She couldn't meet his gaze.

'Losing you would be anything but easy,' Finn said softly. He heaved a sigh and tilted her chin with his finger. 'Surely you know how I feel about you, Romy, how I've always felt about you. And this might sound mushy, but I'm going to say it anyway. I've never been able to give anyone else my whole heart because when you left, you took a great chunk of it with you. And then when you came back, I kept losing more chunks of it until yesterday, when you took the very last piece. And now you have it all. What I'm trying to say, in my usual clumsy way, is that, Romy Stainthorpe, you've stolen my heart and I don't want it back. It's yours to keep forever. But if you don't want it, then that's it, I'm done with love.'

Romy gazed up into a pair of eyes that were looking down at her with such tenderness. 'It isn't mushy, it's lovely. And I feel exactly the same way about you.'

'I can't tell you what it means to hear you say that.' The relief in his voice was unmistakable.

A thought crossed her mind, casting a shadow over her joy. 'But what about Britt in all of this? Isn't she expecting you to get back together?'

Finn shook his head. 'There is no Britt in anything that involves you and me, please believe me on that score.' He shared the discussion he'd had with his ex-wife after Kyle and Toby had gone to bed. Accepting that there was no chance of a reconciliation, Britt had told him that she'd speak to her parents about staying with them while she found somewhere suitable for her and the boys to live. She'd warned him, not unkindly, that it wouldn't be in the village, but that she was aiming for Middleton-le-Moors, to be near her parents. After that, she was going to speak to Felix and tell him it was over.

'Blimey, that's quite a turnaround from a year ago.'

'Tell me about it. I'm so chuffed the lads are going to be living closer,' Finn said, his eyes shining with happiness.

'I'm over the moon for you.'

'One last thing,' Finn said, smiling. 'Kyle has been telling his little brother all about your killer hot chocolates and how you're the Romy who was my childhood best buddy, and now Tobes is very keen to meet you and hear stories about what I got up to when I was their age.'

Romy grinned. 'Well, I'd very much like to meet him too. They're both very welcome to call in – if it's okay with their mum of course.'

'I reckon after the shock Kyle's given her, she'd give them anything they asked for right now.'

'I can understand that.'

'So, are you planning on leaving all that stuff in the hallway, or can I give you a hand to bring it back in?' he asked, giving a cheeky hitch of his eyebrows.

'I wouldn't mind a hand, if you've got time, that is.' She flashed him an embarrassed smile, giving herself an internal talking to about not being so impetuous in the future. *Famous last words!*

'Actually, there's something I wouldn't mind doing before that,' he said patting the pockets of his jacket.

Romy watched, puzzled as he pulled out what appeared to be a twig.

'I thought it'd still be in there,' he said, looking inordinately pleased with himself.

'What the heck is it?'

'Let me demonstrate.' He stepped closer, dangled the twig above them and lowered his head. Pressing his lips against hers, he kissed her tenderly. Fireworks exploded inside her as her legs buckled, that feeling only Finn Tindall could create taking over. She wanted the moment to go on forever.

When they finally pulled apart, Romy peered up at the twig, dazed. 'Is that the mistletoe Portia gave you?'

'It is.'

'It's only got one berry now.'

'One berry's all it takes.'

'You're a nutter.' She giggled.

'I don't know about you, but I reckon we should put that poor, lonesome berry to good use while we've still got the chance.' He wiggled the branch above her and she slid her arms around his neck.

Smiling happily, she said, 'I reckon you're right.'

EPILOGUE
THE FOLLOWING MARCH

Romy

The last of the boxes had finally been unpacked, leaving just a few things to put away. Romy felt excitement ripple through her. It was hard to believe it was only just over two months ago that she'd first had the conversation with Portia, expressing her interest in buying Holly Tree Cottage. And now, here she was, standing in the living room, a fire dancing merrily in the stove, the purchase all signed, sealed and delivered. As a condition of the sale, Portia's friend, Quentin, had stipulated that the furniture and all the fixtures and fittings were to be included, saying he didn't want the hassle of getting rid of it all. Romy had been more than happy to go along with this since she loved everything in the property and had owned very little of the furniture in the small, terraced house she'd rented on Myrtle Row in Rickelthorpe. What little she'd kept from her former marital home, she was keen to replace.

And now, everything seemed to be falling nicely into place. Her relationship with Finn had been going from strength to strength. She'd spent the last six weeks at the farm living with him, having handed in her notice on Myrtle Row as soon as her offer on the cottage had been accepted. As a consequence, she and Finn had grown even closer. On top of that, she'd signed up for one of the units at the old Danskelfe Business offices and had a waiting list for her felt-making courses. Life couldn't get much sweeter.

'Everything all right?' Finn asked, pulling her out of her thoughts as he walked into the kitchen at Holly Tree Cottage.

'Perfect,' she said, smiling.

Finn

Finn couldn't remember ever feeling so happy. His sons were back living in the UK and not that far away in Middleton-le-Moors and, even better, they'd both got their sparkle back which had been a welcome relief, especially after Kyle had disappeared. Finn never again wanted his sons to feel things were so desperate they had to run away and had stressed to them that if ever there was a problem, they could talk to him and he would listen. Britt seemed happier, too. She had a part-time job on the beauty counter at Campion's of York and was in her element there, especially since the company was funding her through a make-up artist course. Despite their recent hostility, it was good to see her smile again.

As for Finn himself, he still couldn't believe Romy had come back into his life. She was like a ray of sunshine; someone who made him the best version of himself. He'd fallen for her hook, line and sinker – again! – and was revelling in this wonderful second chance they'd been given. He knew, unequivocally, she was *the one*. He'd always known. And if things continued the way they were going, he had plans to celebrate the anniversary of their very first kiss, all those years ago, in a very special way. He couldn't see the point in hanging around and waiting. It gave him happy goosebumps every time he thought about it. And he'd spotted the perfect ring in the little jewellery shop in Middleton-le-Moors. He was going to show Romy she wasn't the only one in their relationship who could be impetuous!

Roll on June!

Huge thanks for choosing to pick up *Christmas at Holly Tree Cottage*. I hope you were hooked on the latest instalment in the Life on the Moors series and getting to know Romy and Finn – and all their moorland friends. If you'd like to join other readers in hearing all about my new releases and bonus content, you can sign up for my newsletter!

www.stormpublishing.co/eliza-j-scott

We won't share your email address, and you can unsubscribe any time.

If you enjoyed this book and could spare a few moments to leave a review, that would be hugely appreciated. It doesn't have to be long, just a few words would do, but for us authors it can make all the difference in encouraging a reader to discover our books for the first time. Thank you so much.

It was a joy to head back to Lytell Stangdale and catch up with all the characters – it's hard to believe there's a two-year gap between since the last instalment of Life on the Moors series. I've no idea where the time went, but I suppose I was rather busy with the Micklewick Bay series. I do hope you enjoyed your visit to my fictional moorland village of Lytell Stangdale and getting to know two new characters, Romy and Finn, not forgetting loveable Labrador, Ted! And I don't know about you, but I can't blame Romy for snapping up Holly Tree Cottage; I'd be just the same. Is there anywhere better than spending the festive period in a cosy cottage in front of a roaring fire, mug of hot chocolate in hand? With all the trimmings, of course!

www.elizajscott.com

facebook.com/elizajscottauthor
x.com/ElizaJScott1
instagram.com/elizajscott
bookbub.com/authors/eliza-j-scott
bsky.app/profile/elizajscott.bsky.social

ACKNOWLEDGEMENTS

So, here's where I get to say thank you to everyone who's helped in one way or another in the process of getting *Christmas at Holly Tree Cottage* ready for publication. And, since this book, as with the other eight in the Life on the Moors series, has been taken on and republished by the fabulous Storm Publishing, I think thanking the team there is a good place to start.

I'm going to begin by saying an enormous thank you to Kate Smith, who is my amazing editor. Kate is warm and friendly, and right from the moment we first started working together, her positivity and enthusiasm has been infectious. On top of that, her edits are always thorough and insightful. Thank you so much Kate!

Next up is the boss, managing director Oliver Rhodes. Huge thanks for setting up Storm, Oliver, and for gathering such a wonderful team together. Thanks are also due to Chris Lucraft, who is Storm's digital operations director and deals with the technical side of things that are way, way beyond me. Thank you for all you've done for my books so far, Chris! Storm's editorial operations director Alexandra Begley also deserves a huge thank you for getting my book into shape for publication day. Thank you also to Storm's lovely new editorial operations assistant Maheen Mehmood for her production support and file formatting – not to mention patience, which I'm sure I must have stretched enormously! Big thanks to Storm's head of marketing, Elke Desanghere, for all her hard work on the marketing side of things and for creating such beautiful social media graphics. And thanks also to publicity manager Anna McKerrow for her delightful social media posts. Rose Cooper needs a mention, too, for the beautiful new cover she designed for *Christmas at Holly Tree Cottage*.

I must also send out a warm thank you to three fabulous people for their input in this book when I self-published it last year. They are: editor Alison Williams – thank you so much, Alison; I learnt a huge amount from you. Berni Stevens for *Christmas at Holly Tree Cottage*'s beautiful first cover, and Rachel Gilbey of Rachel's Random Resources for organising a blog tour for that time. Thank you so much, all of you!

I'd also like to send out a heartfelt thank you to Sarah Kingsnorth and her lovely fellow admins at The Friendly Book Community and to Sue Baker of Riveting Reads and Vintage Vibes over on Facebook for being so kind and supportive of all things bookish. Both book groups are the cosiest, kindest places to be a part of. Thank you for letting me be a part of your community!

In fact, I'd like to send out an enormous thank you to the book community in general, whose kindness and support over social media is heartwarming and humbling. Sending out a special thank you to you all.

There are two fabulous people who I owe a cake-filled thank you, my writing pals Jessica Redland and Sharon Booth. It's been wonderful getting to know you both better over the last couple of years. Thank you for your support and kindness, your friendship means such a lot to me.

Big hugs and thanks go to my fabulous family for all of their never-ending support. I couldn't do this without you guys. Thank you!

My final thanks goes to you, the reader, for choosing my book and taking the trouble to read it. Thank you so much for being a part of this exciting journey with me; I really am most grateful.

Wishing you all a peaceful and merry Christmas and every good wish for the new year.

Much love,
Eliza xxx

www.ingramcontent.com/pod-product-compliance
Lightning Source LLC
Chambersburg PA
CBHW010431170726
48283CB00011B/3160